Praise for *The Bright Unknown*

"A beautifully woven story of a young woman's journey to understanding that the past shapes us but does not define us, and that it is love that gives us the courage to live like we believe it. With prose that is luminous and lyrical, *The Bright Unknown* is a compelling read from the first page to the last."

—SUSAN MEISSNER, BESTSELLING AUTHOR
OF *THE LAST YEAR OF THE WAR*

"Elizabeth Byler Younts writes with heart, a poet's pen, and courage. This I knew when I read *The Solace of Water*. This was reinforced with my reading of her newest offering. Younts has given us a story that is at once powerful and compassionate, revealing and dignified, heartrending and lyrical. Compelling and infused with hope of redemption, *The Bright Unknown* ushers readers on a journey of empathy. I, for one, am grateful to have read it."

—SUSIE FINKBEINER, AUTHOR OF *ALL MANNER OF THINGS*

"With evocative prose and rich detail, Younts draws us into the humanity and hurt of a little-examined chapter in American history. Her poignant details will break open your heart, but with skillful beauty she makes Brighton—and us—whole again in this wonderful story of hope, grace, and love."

—KATHERINE REAY, BESTSELLING AUTHOR OF *DEAR MR.
KNIGHTLEY* AND *THE PRINT~~~~ ~~~~OKSHOP*

"As bold as it is beautiful, a~~~~ ~~~~*Bright
Unknown* is a story that wil~~~~ ~~~~eaders
and not easily let go. With l~~~~ ~~~~unfor-
gettable characters, Younts is ~~~~ ~~~~ark places for the
sake of finding light. I could no~~~~ ~~~~ovel down!"

—HEIDI CHIAVAROLI, AWARD-WINNING AUTHOR
OF *FREEDOM'S RING* AND *THE HIDDEN SIDE*

"I knew Elizabeth Byler Younts was a wonderful writer, but her lyricism, empathy, and psychological understanding of the broken human condition took *The Bright Unknown* to a whole different level."

—Jolina Petersheim, bestselling author
of *How the Light Gets In*

Praise for *The Solace of Water*

"Younts's powerful novel reverberates with love that crosses religious and racial boundaries to find the humanity that connects us all. Highly recommended."

—*Library Journal*, starred review

"Younts has set herself apart with this exquisite story of friendship and redemption . . . I'll be talking about this book for years to come."

—Rachel Hauck, *New York Times* bestselling author

"*The Solace of Water* is a gripping coming-of-age historical fiction story that will stick with readers for some time after the final word is read. Hauntingly beautiful prose is bountiful in this tightly woven tale . . . The characters demonstrate the impact secrets, guilt, and unforgiveness can have on a person in this emotive gem."

—*RT Book Reviews*, 4½ stars, TOP PICK!

"Byler Younts is a marvel with dialect and highly charged emotional scenes. Like a turbulent river, water is ever-present in this story of love, anger, and regeneration."

—*Christian MARKET*

The
Bright
Unknown

Other Books by Elizabeth Byler Younts

The Solace of Water

THE PROMISE OF SUNRISE SERIES

Promise to Return

Promise to Cherish

Promise to Keep

Seasons: A Real Story of an Amish Girl

The
Bright
Unknown

ELIZABETH BYLER YOUNTS

THOMAS NELSON
Since 1798

The Bright Unknown

© 2019 Elizabeth Byler Younts

Published in Nashville, Tennessee, by Thomas Nelson. Thomas Nelson is a registered trademark of HarperCollins Christian Publishing, Inc.

Interior design by Lori Lynch

Thomas Nelson titles may be purchased in bulk for educational, business, fund-raising, or sales promotional use. For information, please email SpecialMarkets@ThomasNelson.com.

ISBN 978-0-7180-7569-9 (e-book)
ISBN 978-0-7180-9927-5 (audio download)

Library of Congress Cataloging-in-Publication Data

Names: Younts, Elizabeth Byler, author.
Title: The bright unknown / Elizabeth Byler Younts.
Description: Nashville, Tennessee : Thomas Nelson, [2019]
Identifiers: LCCN 2019018112 | ISBN 9780718075682 (softcover)
Subjects: | GSAFD: Christian fiction.
Classification: LCC PS3625.O983 B75 2019 | DDC 813/.6--dc23 LC record available at https://lccn.loc.gov/2019018112

Printed in the United States of America

19 20 21 22 23 LSC 5 4 3 2 1

For Joann, my dear grandma-in-love,
and for Kelly, who understands so much

"I am out with lanterns, looking for myself."
EMILY DICKINSON

1990

Gravel Paths

I'm not sure whom I should thank—or blame—for the chance to become an old woman. Though as a young girl, sixty-seven seemed much older than it actually is. My knees creak a little, but I still have blond strands in my white hair.

I have watched the world grow up around me. I was old when I was born, so it seems. Was I ever really young? I've been around long enough to know that *progress* is a relative term. What is progress anyway? A lot of damage has been done in the name of progress, hasn't it? But then I have to think, where would I be without it?

Not here.

There are a few other surprises about making it to 1990. We are still firmly living on planet Earth, the Second Coming hasn't happened, despite predictions, and devices like the cordless phone are at the top of many wish lists for housewives. Another surprise is that housewives aren't so common.

I haven't taken much to technology myself and still use a rotary phone. But I did receive a ten-foot coiled cord as a gift. Recently I heard a girl say the words *old school*, so I guess that's the new way to say what I am. There's something funny about having a new way to say *old-fashioned*.

When you have a childhood like mine, being considered out-of-date is a compliment and means I'm among the living. There were times I never expected to live to be this age. Many women of a certain age would love to move back the hands of time and remember the days of their youth. But I'd rather let them become as dull as my old pots and pans—they carry the nicks and dings from use over the years, but no one remembers how those wounds happened and the flaws don't make them useless.

When I step outside and squint at the June sun, I'm caught off guard by the brightness. The sun and I are old friends, and she greets me with a nod as I walk beneath her veil of heat. The walk to my mailbox that's at the end of a long drive has been part of my daily routine for years. Sometimes I amble down the natural path twice, just for the fresh air, but mostly to remind myself that I can. I don't take freedom for granted. The gravel drive almost didn't make it when we first moved in. My kids wanted us to pave it to make it easier to bike and scooter. But I didn't like the idea of a strip of concrete dividing the green mowed lawn of our yard from the grasses that grew wild and untamed on the other side of the driveway. That path between the feral and the tame is dear to me and too familiar to let go of.

The grit from the stones beneath my soles is a safe reminder of where I come from. Painful memories sometimes rise off other gravel paths—some narrow and dark, and others that weren't there till I made them with my own two feet. My driveway reminds me of the freedom I have to come and go as I please. Things were not always this way.

The mailman waves at me from the other side of the road as he lowers the flag of a neighbor's mailbox. I wave back and don't look before I cross. This road is as isolated as my memories.

I throw a glance inside my aluminum mailbox before I shove my hand inside. The occasional critter sometimes can't resist the small haven in a storm—and we had a doozy last night. The stack of mail looks lonesome, so I wrap my hands around the contents and pull them out. The arthritis in my wrist flares and I wince.

I shut the box, then turn back toward my home. A rubber band wraps a *Reader's Digest* around the small bundle of white envelopes and fluorescent-colored flyers. I flip through the mail to try to force out the throb that remains in my wrist. Electric bill. Water bill. A bright-yellow flyer announcing a new pizza joint in town with a coupon at the bottom for Purdy's Plumbing. The cartoon scissors that indicate to cut along the dotted line have eyes and a smile. I don't resist smiling back.

Underneath the pile is one of those big yellow envelopes. A bulky item inside carries the shape of something too familiar, but I don't want to name it. A chill washes over me. Shouldn't a woman my age be prepared for surprises? The last time this kind of bewitchment caught me unawares I was nothing more than an eighteen-year-old girl—frightened and alone. Learning too much all at once. Trapped inside gray concrete walls. Feeling the loss of my last bit of innocence, which had been tucked somewhere behind my heart but in front of my soul—guiding it, guiding me.

But I didn't lose myself in that Grimms' fairy-tale beginning. My over forty years of marriage made me a survivor of unpredictability. I've crawled through the shadow of death delivering my babies—reluctantly inside the frightful walls of a hospital no less—and became a woman amending her own childhood through motherhood. But this envelope brings me a certain dread that I cannot explain. The contours of the contents. I don't want to open it, even though my entire life has been in anticipation of this.

I consider pushing the package into my apron pocket along with my garden shears and the one cigarette that's waiting to be smoked on my front porch—a habit I started in 1941 and stopped trying to quit in the 1950s. It is only one a day, you see.

But I'm seduced. I turn over the envelope. The name in the corner isn't familiar, but the town in the return address boasts that my nightmares are not dreams but memories after all. The handwriting appears businesslike and feminine.

My gaze travels to the center. It's addressed to someone I shed long ago—so long ago it's almost like that girl never existed. My mother, who'd been a lost soul, gave me the name—sort of. A question mark is scribbled next to the name—the post office doesn't know if it really belongs here. But it is me. This much I know, and I wish it weren't so. After a few deep breaths I pull out my garden shears and slip them through the small opening in the corner with shaking hands. How I do it without cutting myself, I'm not sure.

My suspicions are correct. When I tip the envelope over, a 35mm film cartridge falls into my hands. It's old, almost fifty years old, in fact, and it's warm in my palm. That eighteen-year-old girl named on the envelope cries a little, but she's so far under my concrete skin it doesn't even dampen my insides. I long ago wished I could forget it all, but the voices from my past are stronger than my present. What am I supposed to do now?

The resurgence of guilt, shame, and pain—the bards of my heart—croon at me. I toss the film roll and it lands on the edge of my gravel path between blades of grass.

Who sent it?

Where did it come from?

I look into the envelope and see it's not empty. Before I can bat away my impulses, I pull out the small folded piece of paper. The even and balanced script handwriting reads:

Brighton,
    I have the rest of them if you're interested.
        Kelly Keene

Kelly Keene. I don't know her. Why does she have the film from my dark years? I look back at the ground, and the cartridge stares at me as it lies prostrate there on the gravel and grass. The exhumed voices from within it speak in my ears. They've never been far away. They're always in the shadow or around a corner. A reflection in a darkened window. Their voices bend over my shoulder, their ghostly faces look into my arms full of children and grandchildren, and the memory of their smiles reminds me how far I've come and the strength it took to always take the next step forward.

And yet the whisper of voices also calls to mind a promise I've left unfulfilled. The burden of this guilt nestles next to my soul. Though shrouded in grace, it knows the entwining paths of peace and despair.

For decades I've kept these voices to myself. But this film begins the sacred resurrection of these forgotten souls, and with them comes the unearthing of my past.

These Bright Walls and
the Dark Story They Tell

The flossy gray clouds outside mirrored the blandness inside the walls of my home. The window made me part of both worlds. One I watched and coveted. The other I lived in. Neither was safe.

I flipped through the diary I'd received four years ago on my tenth birthday, and in each entry I noted the dreary weather on the top line. But I didn't need a journal to remember further back than that, since somewhere in the reserves of my mind I was sure I remembered the day I was born—and every rainy birthday since. On that first April morning the storm had pelted the window. The xylophone of sounds was muffled by the press of my ear against my mother's warm breast. I'd imagined all the details of my birth for so long that I was sure they were true, but I would never really know. And my mother would never be able to tell me about those moments because long ago her mind had hidden so well that no amount of searching could bring her back.

A sigh slipped into my throat. I swallowed hard, and the air landed like a rock in my stomach. I breathed my hot breath on the window, then traced a heart. My fingertip made a squeaking sound against the cool glass pane.

I focused past my finger. Not even a single speck of sun lined the edges of the trees in the far horizon across the road and field. A field

I'd never stepped on because it was on the other side of the gates. I was told the grounds where I lived mimicked what neighborhoods looked like. Only I'd never seen a real neighborhood, so maybe that was a lie. The only green grass I'd ever stepped in was the grass that grew on the property of the Riverside Home for the Insane.

I smeared away the heart with angry fingers and lightly tapped the glass, making a dull *clink* sound.

I looked around behind me before opening the window as far as it would go. I grabbed the iron bars and pressed my face into the opening. I stuck out my tongue to catch a few raindrops. The coolness jetted through me.

"Girl," said a voice from behind me. I pulled back and bumped my head on the window frame. "If Nurse Derry catches you doing that . . ."

Nurse Edna Crane—Aunt Eddie, as she insisted on being called—had been in the room right after I was born, slippery and squirmy between my mother's thighs. It was Aunt Eddie who'd fixed in my mind the visions of my birth—the low-hanging clouds and the mist from outside crawling indoors and clinging to the walls like ivy vines curling to catch a glimpse of new life. Me. And to think it was in a place where life usually ended instead of began.

Aunt Eddie walked past me and shut the window. She grunted when she turned the lever at the top, then swore and stuck her finger in her mouth. The latch was fussy, I knew. I'd worked on loosening it off and on for an hour. I'd woken a mite past three when my mother began with her fit, and I couldn't find sleep again after that. When Mother had quieted, though, I'd tiptoed from our room and started in on the window knob. I hadn't broken the rule of not leaving the second floor, but I needed air. The dewy world beyond the window was thick with it. The fresh, rain-soaked whiffs were suffocated in the stale spaces of this place. It was more than simply moist and dank and smelling like rot, more than the decay of daft dreams, more than misery joining the beating of hearts. It was death itself. The scattered remains of us—the barely living—our eyes, ears, hearts, and souls lying like remnants everywhere.

The older nurse squared my shoulders and tried to fix my hospital gown and hair. I knew, however, that I was nowhere pretty enough to be fixed. Weeds bloomed, but that didn't make them flowers.

"Your dress is wet, and how on earth have you already mussed your braid?"

My dress? It was a hospital gown, only Aunt Eddie always called it a dress. The sigh I'd swallowed away earlier whispered at me, begging to be released. I ignored it, and it flitted away.

"Got it caught in the windowsill. There's a nail." I pointed to the window.

"This won't do. When your hair's not done, you look like a dirty blonde at a whorehouse, but when it's all done and pretty—now, you could go to church with that kind of braid." She'd braided my hair before bed, but it was messy when I woke.

I let Aunt Eddie pull my French braid out and tried not to wince as she tucked the strands this way and that way. She combed down my fine flyaway hair and pulled it harder than ever, making slits of my eyes. To please her I smoothed down the gown—a used-to-be-white shift with snaps up the back, though a few had gone missing years ago. Nurse Joann Derry, whom I called Nursey, took it home one day and made it fit my narrow shoulders, since they were made for bony grown women. Their pointy, emaciated shoulders could keep anything up. Nursey did this as often as we were issued new clothing, which was usually once a year.

Last year she had to find me a different gown for a few days while she worked out the stain from my first curse from my issued one. I'd just turned thirteen. The saturated red mark on my gown and bed and the stickiness between my legs hadn't been a shock to me. Before my mother was sterilized—a procedure doctors thought would help her melancholia depression and psychosis—I was always the one to clean her up because Nursey was charged with nearly a hundred other patients and had little help. Nursey had given me Carol's gown; she'd died only the week before and was barely cold in the graveyard out back. Her family hadn't claimed her body. Now she'd just be C. Monroe on a small stone marker. Wearing a dead woman's gown was commonplace around here, but knowing who'd worn it last left me with the heebie-jeebies.

I'd stayed in bed for most of the first day of my curse, and my friend Angel had assumed I was dying when I wouldn't go out for a walk through the orchard and then to the graveyard where we'd memorized every headstone. Nursey gave him an explanation, though I don't know what she said. Later he told me she'd mentioned my burgeoning womanhood and hormones, something we'd learned about when she gave us a few biology lessons.

Nursey had believed my step toward womanhood deserved something special, and when she brought my institutional shift back to me, she surprised me by turning it into a real dress. Her smile lit up when she pointed out something called a Peter Pan collar and the ruffles at the hem. When I put it on I spun around like I did when I was little, before I understood that it wasn't normal for a child to live in an asylum.

I cried when the hospital administrator, Dr. Wolff, refused to let me keep it, claiming he'd already made too many exceptions when it came to me. Nursey said we shouldn't push our luck—whatever that meant. Luck? Me? Luck would be the chance to run away and buy myself as many ruffled dresses as I wanted and wear a different one every day. Maybe fall in love and get married. Maybe even be a mother.

Maybe. Someday.

By now, at age fourteen, I knew that being a resident of the Riverside Home for the Insane was not how everyone else in the world lived. But it had been my life since birth. None of the doctors' diagnoses—*feeble-minded*, *melancholia*, or *deaf mute*—could be used to describe me. I didn't even have a bad temper. All my friends had these labels, and I was familiar with them, but they didn't apply to me. Neither were they used on my best friend, Angel—he was just an albino and didn't see well.

My poor mother was bewitched with voices and demons, and my father never cared enough to rescue either of us—or even visit. He was our only ticket out of this asylum because he was our next of kin. But today, on my fourteenth birthday, the fresh air outside tapped on the windows, taunting me, willing me to make a run for it. But what about my mother? If I left, wouldn't I be as bad as my father? I didn't want to be bad.

"All done." Aunt Eddie patted my shoulders and spun me around to get a good look. My distorted reflection stared back at me through her pooling eyes. I was a plain girl with too big a name. It hung over my identity like the issued hospital gown drooped on my shoulders. But it was the only thing my mother had ever given me.

"Brighton."

Nurse Joann Derry's voice vibrated through the chilled, bleak corners. She came into the small dayroom. "Brighton Friedrich, young lady, where are you?"

"She's here." Edna pushed me past the patients who were filing in after breakfast.

The closer I got to the dayroom door and to the hall that led to the dormitory, the more I could hear Mother in an upswing of a fit. The wails beat my eardrums, and my heart conformed to the rhythm. She needed me. Rain and Mother's fits were like peas and pods that multiplied on my birthday.

Mother's groaning always began around three o'clock in the morning every year. Then, for the next few hours, she would go through the pains of labor and childbirth as if it were happening for the first time. But when she found no baby at the end of it all, she'd mourn this phantom loss. She'd scratch at the concrete walls so severely her fingernails would bleed, and if we didn't restrain her fast enough, she'd lose one or two. After years of pulling out her hair, her roots remained fruitless. If we didn't watch her closely she'd pick at the softest places on her skin—the insides of her elbows, her wrists, her breasts—till they bled. The white coats called it psychosis. She couldn't, or wouldn't, cope. They said they didn't know why, but I wasn't sure I believed them anymore. They'd hurt so many of my friends that I knew not to trust them.

As for my mother, I'd never known her any other way. Besides restraints, my presence was the only thing that helped her. Sterilizing her had not released her from this madness. Her hormones were not responsible.

The doctors depended on a few things to calm her. My presence and touch, even as a baby, was one prescribed method. But if I failed, Nursey had no choice but to camisole or restrain her to her bed or a chair or give her a dose of chloral hydrate. Insulin was the new Holy Grail for fits and mania, putting patients into a coma-like sleep for many hours to days at a time. But the injections agitated her and caused a dangerous irregular heartbeat. There had never been good answers for Mother.

Next door was the Pine View children's ward. The nearby buildings were connected through a basement hall. At Pine View the patients were treated like animals—not so different from my ward. But here, I was safe. Or at least as safe as one could be in an asylum. Joann took care of me like a daughter. After my birth I'd been transferred to the children's ward, but Joann fought for me to be returned to Mother's room, promising to care for me. Nursey had only been eighteen years old then and not in a position to demand much, but the ward doctor, Sidney Woburn, was keen on Nursey and was known to give in to her requests. I would learn more about that when I was older—the wiles of a desperate woman and the web of deceptions.

But today, when I got to Mother's room, I saw several wrapped gifts on the rag rug that Mickey had taught me to make years ago to help my room feel less sterile. How I'd missed Mickey since her unexpected death a few years earlier. Her silvery hair always brushed against her eyelids, and her pink skin looked happier than her reality. On my bed, beyond a small stack of gifts and memories of Mickey, sat a cross-stitched orange cat pillow. Nursey had taught me how to cross-stitch on one of her many off-duty evenings. Those were the hours she would read stories like *Peter Pan* to Angel and me. I would cross-stitch, and Angel would just sit and listen. I named the orange cat Nana and secretly wished it was a dog instead—and that it was real. And that Neverland was real too. A tattered teddy bear Mickey had made from an old brown towel lay limply next to Nana. It was the last gift I got from Mickey.

Today there was also a small cake the kitchen staff must have baked. There was always a shortage of flour and sugar; someone had sacrificed for this cake. It sat on the non-hospital-issued nightstand. That nightstand got stuffed into a medicine closet whenever any official visits were made to see how well things were run. I would get stuffed into a closet, office, or somewhere too—I even had to crawl under a bed once with Nana. I wasn't allowed to be seen. I was used to the lie by now. However, since it was rare we had ward visitors, the farce game of hide-and-seek had not been played for years.

Angel, my best friend, who lived in the children's ward, was sitting on the floor by my bed. His gown looked extra dingy in comparison to his pale skin. His wavy, white-blond hair was mussed and stuck to his forehead. He looked up as we walked in. His smile, even with yellowed teeth, gleamed, and his blue-red eyes looked toward me through what I knew to be blurry vision. I waved at him, and he waved back until my mother's animalistic moan jarred away my attention. Away from Angel and from all the small touches in my room meant to make me feel like a regular girl on her birthday. A regular girl. All I knew of regular girls came from books. But my fictional friends Heidi, Pollyanna, Betsy, Anne, Sarah—none of them had regular lives either. So perhaps there were no regular girls anywhere.

"Helen." Nursey rushed in and patted my mother's shoulder

gently and gestured frantically for me to get closer. She pulled me toward Mother when I was reachable. "Helen, Brighton is here."

"Liebling." Her gravelly voice spoke this German word that I'd heard my whole life, though it had become seldom in these later years. My eyes wandered to the old stack of books under my bed where I used to have a German translation dictionary, hoping for some message from her besides these broken words. But the book had been stolen by a patient and ruined.

Mother's stringy hair, the color of rain clouds and sand, hung like dull curtains around her colorless face. She was not nearly blind like Angel, but still she did not see me. She always stared out into nothing. When I was a child I would sit so that our eyes were level, desperate for her to look at me. Once, her blue gaze lighted on me— though only for a brief moment. In my childishness I thought she might be waking up from this catatonic daze. A soft smile had crept over her stretched, dried lips, but her softness turned into terror and she screamed in my face. I never tried that again.

Today her eyes traveled around but never landed on anything. Mumbled whispers in a fragmented language clouded my thoughts, making it impossible to reason through this annual nightmare. I could only submit to it. Her arms reached out, and when no one handed her a baby, she pulled at her clothing and looked for an infant—me—beneath the single thin blanket. She was wearing no underclothes, which was typical for most patients, and she lifted her gown, searching, before she grabbed at her belly and groaned. Wilted and scarred skin draped on her like poorly fitted clothing. The shell my mother lived in had withered years earlier.

I hated my reality, but hated hers even more. Surely she deserved better than living a life of lunacy. Surely she'd not been the sort of woman who had been so terrible in her right mind that losing it seemed a just punishment. And why had I reaped the consequence of her infirm mind?

As she went through another round of what she believed was

labor, I thought of the tiny and beautiful woman she must have been when she was admitted—already pregnant and uncontrollable and entirely lost. She was just a pebble in the ocean. A raindrop in a storm. I used to ask after my history, but my curiosities were met with short, unembellished answers. Nothing that ever hinted at why my father hadn't returned for me. I knew nothing about this Lost Boy from Neverland, as I had come to think of him.

Joann was up and down the hall, leaving me to deal with my mother. I'd even started helping with baths and cleaning for the last two years—Angel had too. The staff in the children's ward pretended not to notice that Angel was absent most days, since it meant one less patient for them to care for—another allowance Nursey gave me so I could have a friend my own age.

She tried to give me some sort of life, though we had to hide it all from Dr. Wolff. Patients were never supposed to be out of their wards like Angel was, but I also knew that little girls weren't supposed to be born and raised in a madhouse, though it was the only world I'd ever known. So allowances were made—as long as it didn't interfere with Nursey's duties, naturally.

A little later I let Angel open my gifts. Aunt Eddie gave me a new pair of underclothes—two pairs. Angel didn't flinch at the intimacy and handed them to me without shame. We'd shared so much together—too much, according to Nursey—but underclothes weren't much to us, except that we were glad to have them.

The next gift was a chocolate bar from one of the cooks. The smell alone took me out of these walls for a twinkling moment. "Here, take a bite."

"Mmm." Angel took the tiniest of bites and smiled. He always had a shy grin tucked into his mouth. I let my piece melt on my tongue until it wasn't there anymore; the taste filled my senses.

"You have one more gift," Angel's smooth voice reminded me. He held up a yellowed envelope with my mother's name on the front. *Helen Friedrich.* It was from Nursey. "Ready?"

Angel's hands carefully untucked the flap and pulled out a small paper. "What is it?" he asked and held it close in an effort to see the details. He used to have a magnifying glass, but it had been broken to bits when he'd snuck it and a book into his ward. His nurses were ruthless—worse than Miss Minchin. At least Sarah Crewe had never been beaten senseless. Nurse Harmony Mulligan, on the other hand, had no problem administering a beating now and again. That had been months ago now and he had healed up, but he was sad not to be able to read well anymore. He could see well enough in the light, but darkness was nearly impossible for him.

He raised the thick paper to his eyes, but he had turned it the wrong way. The other side revealed eyes that stared back at me. My mother's eyes. I grabbed the old photograph from Angel's hands.

"Mother? It's a picture of my mother." A warm tingle swarmed and buzzed in my belly, but it was chased away by the chill that was always pocketed deep inside. I looked from the image on the paper to the skeletal woman lying flat on the bed. Though she hardly resembled the rounder and healthy-looking woman in the picture, this surprising gift took my breath away. I thought I might even resemble her a little—her high cheekbones and jawline and maybe the soft almost-smile her lips formed.

"Up, up. Time for your birthday picture." Nursey walked in with her camera. She'd done this for years.

"Where did you get this?" I held the photo of my mother as I stood.

"Her file." She held the camera up to her eye.

I looked at the photo again. "I kind of look like her, don't I?"

Exasperated, she lowered the camera. "I have two floors to deal with today, Brighton. Let's go. We can talk about that later." She raised the camera again.

"Can Angel be in this one?" I asked her. She usually said no, but maybe not this time.

"Just you, Bright." She waved Angel away. He continued to smile as he obediently stepped aside.

I stood there, and the feel of the old photograph in my hand made me smile. After I heard the *click* I pulled Angel over. "Please?" I pleaded. My life wasn't much without Angel.

Nursey exhaled and waved him in.

Angel and I stood shoulder to shoulder. I looked up at my friend who was wearing a smile like a warm breeze—and the *click* sounded. Nursey threw me a look of frustration, then stuffed the camera back into her apron pocket and left the room in a flash. What did she do with the photographs? I had never seen any of them.

"Tell me about the photograph." Angel slouched on the bed with me.

I paused, contemplating, trying to take in every detail.

"It's so strange to see her like this. It's almost as if this is a storybook picture and not even real." I paused and shallowed out my gaze to tell him the basics. "She's wearing an ugly, long black dress and she's sitting on a chair. And—"

I pulled the photograph close to my eyes.

"And what?"

"There's a hand on her shoulder, but the photograph has been cut. I can't see who's there."

"Cut? I wonder why."

I ran my finger over the cut edge—it was clean, smooth.

In silence I took in the rest. The older woman in the chair next to her had dull eyes. The serious-looking man gripping the older woman's shoulders like he was trying to keep her still.

I looked so long I memorized it. I traced the length of it with my thumb. The fingernail I'd chewed off earlier mocked me. Nursey would threaten to put rubbing alcohol on it again if she caught a glimpse of it. I tucked it away.

My eyes returned to the hand on my mother's shoulder. The hem of the long sleeve at the wrist was similar to my mother's, and the fingers draped gently over her shoulders were thin and elegant. The hand belonged to a woman—a young woman. Who was she?

1928

An Angel to Watch Over

I looked back at Mickey as I began to run. She was smiling and waving at me. She'd just told me that I shouldn't be gone long. Her soft, warm hug had sent me on my way, out to the graveyard. I liked it back there—it was quiet, except for the birds. The building I lived in was never quiet.

My five-year-old legs were fast. Not long after I first started running out there, Nursey gave up trying to catch me since she and her helpers had so many others to watch. They couldn't catch me anyway.

The friends I lived with didn't even notice me. Mother never noticed either.

And Nursey knew I would come back. I told her not to worry. I did wish Mickey could come with me so she could tell me more stories. But if she or Mother or any of the others tried to run off, Joann would camisole them. I hated that. Nursey said I was different from them. They were a lot older, I supposed, and some of them talked to themselves. But I did that too, some of the time. Sometimes they screamed. But so did I. Some of them told me about visions they had, and they sounded a lot like the dreams I had at night.

Some of them were just like storybook mothers and grannies, though, especially Mickey. Since I didn't have any other children to play with, Nursey picked a few of the women for me to spend time with in my room. She said she'd chosen the best ones. Mostly Mickey and Lorna came. They'd tell me funny stories and read books to me and play games with me. Nursey always made sure that one of them was in my room with me for a few hours every day since I wasn't allowed anywhere else in the building. But outside I could be alone.

I looked back at the patients. Some of them were holding on to the rope that led them to the courtyard and our huge garden where we worked on nice days. Some of them walked on ahead without the rope. No one cared that I wasn't there. I was lucky.

Then I started running again. I liked the way the dry grass brushed my bare feet. The graveyard was the farthest away I'd ever been from the building. After Claudia from room 205 died, I wanted to know what would happen to her body, so Nursey let me watch the gravedigger. Ever since then I liked imagining the people who were buried there. Nursey said it was strange and used the word *morbid*. She wouldn't explain what it meant even after I begged her. But Mickey told me that it meant I was interested in learning about death and dying. It wasn't that I was interested so much as I needed to know where the body went, since Nursey always said they were in heaven and I wanted to know where heaven was. It was the ground.

When I was more than halfway to the graveyard I put my arms out like an airplane and sang the special song my friend Rosina had given me.

"*All things bright and beautiful.*" I sang it as loud as I could, and because I only knew the first four lines, I just repeated them over and over. When I got to the last line I stopped and yelled it as loud as I could in the sky. "*The Lord God made them all.*"

The Lord God was someone Rosina talked to a lot. Nursey did too, just not as nicely.

I ran again and was going so fast that I could feel my heartbeat speeding up. I liked the way that felt. Nursey told me that my heart pumped my blood, and the faster I ran, the faster it pumped. Now when I ran I imagined that every time my heart pumped in and out it was telling me to run like the wind. So I did.

But today someone was near a gravestone in the corner of the yard. I stopped running. It wasn't the big, old gravedigger. It was a small person, like me. But different. Like a pure white person.

An angel?

The word came into my mind as quietly as Nursey's *hush* when I was frightened. But I had to take a minute to remember what the word *angel* meant. I remembered that Joyful, the kitchen lady, had used the word *angel* a while back when she brought up some food. She was a nice lady and always pinched my cheeks, and she gave me a red ball for my birthday a few months ago.

"Better hope a bright and shining angel is watching over her, Miz Joann," she'd said one day. "You keep her close, you hear. If she got to be here, she deserves some protection from all this mess." I remembered how her eyes rolled to the sides and looked extra white against her brown skin.

Later I asked Nursey what an angel was. She told me that children had guardian angels who watched over them and kept them safe. She said that they were beautiful and so bright they would light up the sky. This person standing there was so white—I was sure it was my very own angel.

I walked toward the angel, and when I was close I waved. I could see that the angel was a boy because he was wearing a shirt and pants.

"You're beautiful," I said to the angel.

He was.

He tilted his head like he didn't understand.

The closer I got, the more I could see how bright the angel was. Maybe I was supposed to have been an angel, because my name is Brighton. But I wasn't bright. My skin was peach, and my hair was the same color as the gravy that Joyful served sometimes.

The angel looked at me, but there was something wrong with his eyes. He squinted them like he couldn't see well. I stepped closer. His eyes almost looked purple, but then they looked red and blue too.

"Can you talk?" I asked him.

"Who are you?" His voice was small and quiet.

"I'm Brighton Friedrich. I live in that big building over there." I pointed to it, and his eyes roamed in the right direction, but he squinted real hard. "Don't you see well?"

He shook his head and then looked at the ground. I looked down too. The only color besides his eyes that he had on his whole body was dirt on his feet. I looked back up at him.

"Don't feel ashamed." I felt very grown up using the word *ashamed*. Nursey used it, but usually when she was telling me that I *should* feel ashamed because I'd broken one of her rules. "Maybe angels see better as they get older—you know, so they can guard over children."

He didn't say anything so I kept talking.

"What's your name?"

He shrugged. "I don't think I got one."

"Didn't your mother give you one?"

"Don't have a mother either. Don't think so, anyway."

"No mother?" I gasped. Was it because he was an angel? "Whose room do you sleep in then? I live with Mother in room 201. That means we are on the second floor and the first room."

The angel boy started digging his toe into the dirt. "There was this one woman who used to sing to me a long time ago, but I don't know where she went."

"Maybe she's in heaven." I pointed at the graveyard. "So what do they call you?"

"The albino." He looked toward me.

"I don't think that's a real name. I'm going to call you Angel."

"Okay." He almost smiled.

"Until you are a grown-up angel with wings and can watch over children who need you, I'll watch over you." This was just about the most exciting thing that had ever happened to me.

"Wait till Nursey and Mickey hear about you." I took his hand and started leading him toward our buildings. "And Joyful."

"I know Joyful." He smiled again. "She told me once that she don't know how God made someone so light as me and so dark as her."

"I know who God is," I blurted out and stopped walking.

Angel raised his eyebrows. "You do?"

"Do you know the bright and beautiful song?"

"No. I don't know any songs."

I wrinkled up my face because I didn't know anyone who didn't know any songs.

I sang my song for him. "You're bright *and* beautiful."

"What was your name again?" Angel tilted his head; we were closer now, and I didn't mind how close he had to get to see me. It was nice to have a friend my size.

"Brighton."

"Maybe you're my mother, Brighton?"

"I don't think so. I'm only five. Mothers are usually older." I hated disappointing him. "What were you doing all the way out here?"

We started walking again. "We were outside to get our washing. I hate washing day so I ran away." His rubbed his wrists. "They'll probably strap me down in my bed again."

"They'll restrain you?" I stopped walking again and got real close. Yep. His eyes really were red and blue all at once.

"It makes me cry."

"Nursey would never put me in restraints. But Mother is restrained a lot and everyone else I live with is too—I sneak out of my room sometimes. Nursey said that it helps them calm down, and she lets me pat Mother. Why would you need to calm down?"

He shrugged and let out a big breath.

"Why do you run away? I love baths. Nursey brings the tub right into my room and makes the water nice and warm, and she reads a book to me at bedtime too."

"We just stand in a row next to the building and the aide sprays us. The water is really cold. It's so cold that my elbows and knees get stiff."

He wiggled his arms like a rag doll.

"Naked?" I asked, and he nodded. My heart felt funny—but I

didn't know why. I had heard there were other children who lived near me, but I wasn't allowed to play with them. But this one didn't have a name or a mother or get to take real baths, and I wanted him to be my friend. I would ask Nursey to let him live with me.

When we started walking again I imagined Angel tied down in his bed. My heart started pumping fast and I wasn't even running.

"Brighton?" He took my hand in his.

"Yeah, Angel?"

"What's a book?"

1937

Dry Bed of Grass

*A*ngel was the brightest person I knew. His skin was like the whitest moon hanging in a navy sky. Brighton would've been a good name for *him*. He was left alone at the children's ward door when he was just a tiny shining boy. Nursey said they guessed him to be about three when he was found.

Angel was albino. The only one at Riverside, and he was nothing like most of the other children in his ward. Neither was I. Like the women's ward, the children's ward was categorized in medical terms that I'd learned way too much about when I was young. The majority were children the white coats described as *mentally retarded* or *mongoloid*, but sometimes a blind or deaf child was admitted, or a runaway no one could handle in a real orphanage. Once a child displayed behavior that was deemed *unimprovable* or *imbecilic*, they were brought to Riverside.

Angel did become a guardian over some of the patients. Some of his nurses were kind because he was helpful and didn't give them trouble, but others were as cruel as a stepmother in a Grimms' story.

One afternoon we were in the graveyard and I took Angel's hand and traced his finger over the few dips and curves in an old headstone. For a long time we had tried to figure out what had once been etched on the ancient, cracked headstone. The impressions were so old and worn that unless you looked at the stone closely, it looked blank. We'd decided it was the oldest in the graveyard. It was sunken into the soft earth at an angle and reminded me of one of Mother's crooked teeth.

"It might be a *P*," Angel said and looked at me, his eyes a shade of violet in the afternoon light. The blue in the center of the red blended into an otherworldly color that was now as familiar as my own common blue.

I dropped his hand and slumped back into the dry grass. I tilted my head and squinted my eyes, trying to look real hard at it. Maybe it was a *P*—or maybe it was a number.

"We'll probably never know." I sighed.

He helped me up, and beneath the swirling of the not-quite-white clouds, we played our game. Over the years we'd memorized every etching in the gray stones in the graveyard—always just the first initial and last name. I called out, "H. Cochran," and Angel went searching with his walking stick to keep him from tripping over a gravestone.

"Found it," he yelled a minute later. He started the fictional biography. It was part of our game. "Her name is Hester. She's a mother and bakes apple pies for her children every Sunday." He smiled from the opposite corner. "Your turn."

From where I stood, *E. Ray* and *F. Moscrip* faced me. I closed my eyes and Angel yelled the name.

"B. Bender."

"B. Bender," I whispered and put my hands out to steady my first few steps. I'd have to go down four rows and then over six, and I would be at Bender. I cautiously stepped and winced when I forgot about the small hole in the dirt the exact size of my shoeless foot. I pulled it out and heard Angel snigger.

"I'm here," I called over my shoulder but kept my eyes shut—in case I was wrong. I knew I wasn't, though. I could hear Angel's feet brush through the dry grass between the small grave markers.

"Who is he today?" Angel asked, and I opened my eyes.

We flopped down on the grass, our faces to the sky. The April blue was thin, and the clouds moved faster now than when we'd first slipped through the basement kitchen and out the cellar doors. Both of our hospital uniforms rippled in the breeze. If anyone from the surrounding homes and farms on the outside caught sight of the two of us running through the graveyard, they wouldn't question why we were kept at a madhouse. What would happen if they knew the truth?

Still, we were luckier than most here; Nursey gave us small allowances of freedom. But when Angel turned eighteen he would be removed from the children's ward and put in the men's ward—and everything would change. That time was growing near. What type of plan we would need to keep this from happening, I didn't know.

If he didn't die within the walls of the men's ward, he really would go mad and I'd never see him again.

"Who is B. Bender today?" he repeated as he pulled the dry grass from the ground beside him and let the pieces rain over us.

"His name is Bartholomew. He's a carpenter. He's tall and has thick black hair."

"You always say black hair." He turned, facing me.

"I do not." I elbowed him.

I paused for a moment and looked up. There was a break in the clouds and the sun's rays began to pour over the edge, making the sky glow. I cupped my hand to shield the sun from Angel's sensitive eyes and held it there until the sun moved back behind the clouds.

I was always watching out for him. Only months after I met him in the graveyard, I found him at the bottom of the stairs in his own ward. I'd snuck in through the kitchen in the underground tunnel system, looking for him. He'd been lying at the landing for several hours with a broken leg. He still walked with a subtle limp.

"Okay, Bartholomew Bender was a carpenter, and on his daughter's tenth birthday he built her a dollhouse." I continued my make-believe.

I remembered a picture of a house in a newspaper wrapped around one of my birthday gifts. The caption said something about how it was being turned into a historical museum of sorts. I'd never been in a real house, but I often considered what it would feel like. I'd read fairy tales about houses made of candy and castles with servants. If I wandered through a dark forest and found a house, I wouldn't care what it was made of or how grand it was; I would just be glad I'd found a home. And I'd be glad if there was a glow from the window so that I knew someone was waiting for me.

"The dollhouse was yellow with a white porch. And when he worked—"

"He whistled. His favorite food was pork chops and pancakes with—" Angel added.

"Maple syrup," we finished together and laughed.

Angel and I had never had maple syrup, and no matter how much we tried, we couldn't imagine how it tasted—or how anything that came out of a tree could taste good. We'd never had pancakes either, but those were easier to imagine. We'd learned all about this in the books I read to the two of us. Nursey's work had gotten so busy she didn't read aloud to us anymore. Most of our books had been read so often the spines were broken.

Angel inhaled deeply as if he could smell the warm breath of a coming storm. He relaxed, and we didn't speak for several minutes. Our comfortable silence made me sleepy and content.

"Do you think we'll ever have families?" I didn't look at him, afraid he'd see the desperation in my eyes. "Maybe have a real house and maybe I would make apple pies for my children on Sundays."

"And maybe I could build a dollhouse for my daughter," Angel added. After several slow clouds passed overhead, he sighed. "I hope we get to, but . . ."

I took his hand that lay in the grass near mine and we were quiet together. My eyes roamed over the nearby stone markers and caught sight of one that I often avoided. It said *M. Randall. M* for Mickey. Kind. Warm. She loved me all the way to the end.

"I think my mother was invisible—maybe a ghost or something." His voice was velvety smooth like the skin of a peach.

I turned to look at my friend, confused. Dry, brittle grass poked up between us like little broken fairy towers. Angel rarely talked about where he'd come from.

My vision narrowed like a needle on his eyes, and I could only see the blue in the center. His eyes whispered to me, but the wind picked up and whisked his silent thoughts away. I would only catch his spoken words today.

"Invisible?" I said, trying to match the softness of his tone. I couldn't. My voice was low and throaty.

Angel looked up into the overcast sky and closed his eyes to the brightness. It covered us like a dome, and the trees along the property line began to stir. Lightning flashed, but the low rumble that eventually followed was distant. I turned back to Angel. His cotton-white hair fell on his forehead and over one eye. I pushed it away.

"When my mother left me here, no one saw her come and no one saw her go."

1990

Overexposed

I gently rock the processing tray, waiting for the image to appear. The red light in the dark room and the smell of the developer as I anticipate the photograph all have the best effect on me. The dark room cradled and nurtured me in my midtwenties—as I became my own newly processed and developed person. A new life with images I had some measure of control over. Taking photos is one thing, but seeing them come alive in front of me, like something coming from almost nothing, reminds me of new life instead of death. Something so different from the world I came out of.

And now, even at my age, I still get a thrill when I walk into my dark room and, in the pitch black, crack open the canister and thread the film into the plastic reel and tank. It's a solitary job, and the quiet has become part of me. A different sort of solitary than before.

The developer in the tray ripples lightly on its own now, so I carefully let go. I watch the paper bloom into a photograph. It doesn't take long, which never ceases to amaze me. The gray slowly darkens into real edges until an image arises. Fifty years ago I saw my life through a viewfinder and now, like some sorcery, those fragments lay before me.

But like a passing rain, the image comes and then goes entirely black. I've overexposed and lost the image. I grumble a word to myself that I am glad no one else hears and flip up the light switch. I grab the negative strip again and my magnifier loupe. Am I exposing the right image? With anxiety and reluctance, I bend over and look at my contact sheet, using my loupe. This keeps me at an emotional distance. Seeing these images that I know so well is like being outside of myself. Usually these recurring pictures are held tightly within the confinements of my mind, but now suddenly they're free.

I hold my breath and let my gaze wash over the small image. The loupe magnifies it enough for me to see. The foreground and the subject are in focus, but the background is not. That isn't the one I wanted. I move to the next frame. This is the one. My breath catches, and my eyes squeeze shut.

I reach back and turn off the dark room light again. I flip back on the safe bulb, and the red glow anesthetizes me and I breathe evenly. I pull out another piece of printing paper from the sealed box and put it carefully on the enlarger. Then I return the negative to the enlarger, snap the light switch on, fit it so the image is straight, then check my notes on the exposure. I decrease it by half. It has to work this time.

I'm not in the dark room as often now since I quit teaching at the local art center. But my hands still move deftly—like they lived in this world to cure my own melancholy, slipping from one reality to another. It's hard to leave all you know. The retained scars and damage don't repair on their own. But when your hands can walk you through, eventually your mind and soul follow.

I expose the paper once again, then move it from the enlarger into the developer. I tilt the tub a little back and forth to get the agitation going again. Then I wait. Surely the exposure is close and this will reveal the photo I took when I was a mere girl of sixteen.

The image surfaces on the paper, and after about a minute I carefully pull it out and put it in the stop bath. My heart thuds against my wrinkled-up chest. I feel as young as, well, maybe a fifty-year-old, but my heart is still that teenager who held the viewfinder to her eye and the image in her cast-iron memory.

I put the print in the last tub to fix. The red hue in the room doesn't give me enough light to know if this is going to be a good print, but I can see I'm getting close. Closer than I ever thought I'd be.

I hear the phone ring through the thin walls of my dark room.

It is probably Doc. That's what I call my husband—Doc. He finds it irritating but cute. I started it when he graduated almost forty years ago, and it's rare I use his name anymore. Names are slippery things, aren't they? I've been prone to nicknaming since I was a child. Nursey. Angel. Aunt Eddie. I did it with my own children. Martha Annabelle became Marty-Bell and Lucas John was L.J. before we came home from the hospital. Oh, hospitals, what wonder and awe and disappointment they offer. My Rebekah Joy never had the chance to be nicknamed or to come home. I trap that memory away and focus on the ringing phone.

I shake the names from my rattled brain, and after another quick glance at my newest print I turn on the light and walk out of the room. The light in the rest of the house feels brighter than it really is, and for several moments it's unwelcome. Brightness sometimes has that effect on me after so many years of darkness.

I scold the phone that I'm coming. It doesn't hear me. Only the birds through the open windows hear me. And they don't care.

The ring rattles my beige phone. It shakes the kitchen counter and my nerves.

"Hello," I say when the receiver isn't quite to my ear yet.

"Hi, Mrs. Friedrich?" An unexpected articulate voice cuts through my annoyance.

"Yes? Who is this?"

"My name is Kelly Keene." The articulation has ceased and stuttering has begun. "I-I wanted to see if you received my package?" She has a young-sounding, pleasant voice, but it doesn't keep my leeriness away. "Mrs. Friedrich? Are you there?"

"I received your package, yes," I finally say. "How did you happen to have it? And the others?"

There is silence. Is Kelly Keene as unsure about this conversation as I am?

"I-I'm calling from the *Standard* here in Milton." Her words are stammering yet rushed.

"So you're a reporter," I say flatly. So she isn't after anything but a story, and I am not about to give her anything to talk about. I don't do sideshows. But my heart betrays me still and reminds me that this woman has my film, and for that I plan to make nice. "What's this about?"

"There's a town hall meeting next week, and I was calling to invite you." She pauses. "To personally invite you."

Her emphasis on *you* makes me squint, as if the tiny movement will make me figure out her intentions through the phone cord.

"Ma'am," the voice says. My pause is too long.

"I'm a little confused, Miss Keene. I don't live in Milton, but even if I did, since when does anyone get a personal invitation to a town hall meeting?"

"You're right." She hesitates for a moment, and I open my mouth to give her a piece of my mind for the cryptic package and the invite. What I really want are my film cartridges. They are my belongings. "There's a proposal up for discussion that I think will interest you. I don't want to make you uncomfortable, Mrs. Friedrich, but since you spent so many years at the Riverside Home for the—" She clears her throat and doesn't finish—but I do . . .

Insane.

"I assumed you might have an opinion about it being torn down to be made into a community center," she finishes.

"Please do not call here again, Miss Keene."

"Wait." I can hear her even though my hand hovers over the cradle of the phone. I put the receiver back to my ear.

"No one else knows." The young woman's voice is urgent and almost nervous. "I haven't spoken to anyone about you—about the photos or about your real name. I was asked to help catalog the items in the buildings. Mostly we found old suitcases and medical files. But then I came across the film . . . and a few other things."

She pauses as if she's trying to find the words. But I know there's nothing more intriguing and mysterious than undeveloped film. I am hard-pressed to see the wrong in what she's doing.

"I see," I respond. "Have you developed the other cartridges?"

"No—of course not," she says quickly. "I didn't think it was my place."

Okay, so I am dealing with a saint. Admirable. Maybe. I'm still unimpressed by anyone holding my cartridges hostage. But I want them more than I've wanted anything in a long time.

"Not much of a reporter, are you?" I gave up using tact a long time ago.

"Well, I'm not *really* a reporter. I answer phones." Her laughter is a little too honest. She's nervous, so I get direct with her.

"What do you want, Miss Keene?"

"I wanted to get your film to you."

"And why don't you just mail the rest?"

"I'd like to meet in person. And I think you might have an interest in what's happening with the buildings. Maybe you'd like to see them again—before they're gone."

I am not sure if she is intentionally trying to elicit guilt or if there is some hidden motive, but regardless, learning that the buildings are being torn down without a word from those of us who lived in them—my hand goes to my chest.

I tell her I'll think about it and then we say goodbye. And I will think about it. Though I can't see myself doing anything but requesting the film canisters from her, developing them myself, and adding them to my collection—a collection that may forever be in a secret album almost as hidden as my mental vault of memories. My mind takes a snapshot of what it would look like to have my pictures and life plastered all over the local papers—out there for everyone to see and read about. I don't know where to put that in the boiling cauldron of my brain.

I imagine my children learning more about me in a newspaper than I have told them. They know the general timeline of my life, but not the specifics. Not the dark parts. They don't know much about my mother, and what they do know might compare more to the somewhat innocuous Mrs. Clause, when really she was more like Rochester's wife. Only my closest friends, who are few, know these same facts. I suppose because I am well-adjusted, digging for more details never seemed necessary to them. Since most church and PTA ladies are happy with the veneer of our lives and not the underbelly, I've let them see the easy-to-understand parts of my life. But the truth is that many of the decisions I've made—like getting married, having children, getting an education—have been because I wanted to confront and outbrave what was expected of me. And I think I did that.

I hope my former photography students never have the same motivation for taking photos as I did all those years ago. I am not sure that the idea of snapping an image means the same thing to them as it did to me. To capture a moment in time that otherwise would be lost and muted was no small thing in the gray, dull world of my youth. I didn't take pictures to remember all the good things that happened in my life. To put them in an album. To share with others so they could participate in my reminiscing. I took pictures to document the evil that had been done. The moments in time no one wanted to live and that no one should've lived in or died in.

But to share them? They are too private. Too identifying. Too sacred.

1932

All Dust and Ashes

*M*ickey's gravestone was at the end of the row. A row I knew well.

A. Robinson.

E. Ward.

Then came *M. Randall*. Mickey Randall. My Mickey. The one who had taught me to jump rope, to read, and to be very quiet when any visitors were in the ward and I wasn't to be seen. The one who had given up her spot in Mother's room for me. One of the first to rock me to sleep. She'd been one of the many women who had been brought to the hospital because she was too sad to get out of bed and care for her own children. No one had ever come back for her. By the time I was born, she was over fifty and had spent over twenty years in the hospital. She was a fixture on the ward.

She was like me, though. Forgotten and left behind by someone outside of the walls.

"Ashes to ashes, dust to dust. Rest in peace, my friend," Lorna from down the hall said. Her gown rippled in the sunny breeze, and I could see the form of her skinny legs.

"What does that mean?" I choked out. "Dust and ashes?"

My ears were hot and felt like what red looks like. They rang a little, so I focused on Lorna's mouth, which was moving—but why couldn't I hear what she was saying? I looked from Lorna's old, gray-hued face to my hand that was being squeezed by Nursey's. My

34

nine-year-old hand looked so little in her red-chapped hand. My eyes traveled up from our hands, up her arm, to her white-cuffed sleeve, and then to her face. She looked at me, and I realized I couldn't hear her either.

My lungs inhaled and inhaled and inhaled. But I couldn't get enough air. My gaze rested on the turned dark soil in front of me. Mickey was under all that dirt.

She was in heaven now.

Nursey had told me that the morning before. I asked why, because I didn't understand what she meant. Rosina had explained to me that the graveyard was not heaven. So why would Nursey say that Mickey was in heaven? Then she told me things about souls and spirits and bodies and death. I didn't like it.

My chest ached. And I remembered that this was how Mickey died. She had an ache in her chest that was so bad that she couldn't breathe anymore.

I pounded my chest and felt all of my body full of sadness and gray stir up like a pot of Joyful's watery stew. My skin felt stretched under the strain of keeping all the ache inside. It needed to get out of me somehow.

But how? Would it eventually seep out of me—out of all my open spaces—or would it crack my skin open and give me those stretchy scars like Mother had on her belly?

Angel stood in my view now—between my eyes and M. Randall. He didn't need to say anything for me to hear him. He was crying and then my face was wet too and there was a lot of screaming and scratching and hair pulling—all things I did to myself.

Everything hurt if I quit and then Angel—who had grown much taller than me—wrapped himself so tight around me I couldn't move my arms. He pulled me down to the ground and wrapped his legs around me too.

At first I struggled, and Nursey tried to pull him off. I felt restrained, like I'd seen Nursey do to Mother. But when my skin wasn't tingling or ready to burst anymore, I realized the good Angel was doing. He was helping me—saving me—from exploding into all the dust and ashes Lorna talked about.

"Brighty." Nursey's voice finally cut through all my noise. "Slow down and breathe."

She said it like she thought I could just do it. But I couldn't. It wasn't as easy as all that.

"All things bright and beautiful," Angel began, quoting the song I'd learned long ago. It calmed me. By the time he was on his third go-around, I was able to breathe out the words with him as I was tucked away inside the arms of my guardian angel. Nothing could hurt me now.

1933

Misunderstood Brighton

I hadn't been outside in weeks. My view of the outdoors was masked by the cardboard and newspaper Nursey had put over my bedroom window to try to keep out the icy drafts. The hospital was always cold in the winter—colder than cold. The ice crystals formed in pretty designs on the inside of the windows, but it also made us all shiver at night. The outside light made the inside bearable, and without it all I had were these four walls. This left no space for the stench to seep out, so we breathed the air of what smelled like the dying remains of once free and joyful lives. At least the winter had a heavenly appearance, with its fluffy and white dreams cast everywhere. But also like heaven, it was out of reach to me.

I was ten now, so I knew the graveyard wasn't heaven. When people died, their bodies went under the ground but their souls went to this magical place called heaven. That's where people sang and floated around with the angels. Rosina said the streets were gold and the gate was made of pearls. It sounded as fanciful as Wonderland, but instead of the Queen of Hearts, God lived there. I asked her once to tell me what rabbit hole I needed to fall through to find it, and she said, "Only through death, *chica*," and then she crossed herself. It made me wonder why we cried when somebody died and they got to go to heaven. Shouldn't we cry because we have to stay?

At least when it was this cold, mean old Dr. Wolff would allow the staff to provide old sweaters and bathrobes to the patients who wouldn't peel them off right away or destroy them—or pee on and soil them. Mine, as usual, was oversize, but it was warm. I still wasn't allowed out of my room much, but Nursey made sure that Angel could visit often—his nurses had to agree too. He would run through the basement tunnels, stop by the kitchen to pilfer a few bites of food, then come to my room. Mother was usually sitting in the dayroom or in some therapy, like the rest of the patients. So we had the room to ourselves. We didn't have anyone who taught us anymore. We just learned on our own now. And played games and made up stories, like what we would be when we grew up and what sort of house we'd live in someday. Our days were slower and slower when it was wintertime.

"Nursey's going to be upset if you keep pulling at that cardboard." Angel followed rules better than I did. "You ruined the first one and remember how cold you were until it was replaced."

I sighed and slumped down on my bed. He was right, as usual. He hunched over a book with his magnifying glass so he could read. He'd changed so much since we'd first met. He was so tall now, and his voice had plunged like a raindrop. It made him sound much older and smarter—like he actually knew what he was talking about.

Maybe he did.

"Remember when Betsy played in the snow?" I said and jumped on my cot, making it creak like Lorna's knees, upsetting his reading. When we read *Understood Betsy* recently I felt I'd found a friend. Betsy had had a strange upbringing too—not as strange as mine—but she eventually had a family. Maybe I would too.

"Nursey promised us we could on the first snowfall," he said.

"Do you think she'll actually tell us when it snows, though?" Nursey was more like a mom than Mother in a lot of ways, but I started to wonder about some of the things she told me, like that I couldn't leave this dirty hospital unless someone came to get me even when I was all grown up because of something called *laws*. Surely when I was older I could just leave. Angel too. Why would we have to stay?

"It's only November and I can see out my windows."

He put his fat science book down on our stack of schoolbooks.

Besides science there were a few novels and poetry books, math, and a dull McGuffey Reader.

"I don't know why any of this matters if what Nursey says is true and we'll never be allowed to leave." This frightened me and made me feel like my body was full of tears and like I wanted to scream. Like all the sadness and meanness inside of me were wrapped together.

When Mickey died last year I'd had my first real fit. That's when things changed. I hated living at Riverside, and someday I would leave—no matter what Nursey said. I looked at Mother's empty bed and imagined leaving her behind. Or maybe she'd be in heaven by then. *H. Friedrich* would mark her spot. I took a deep breath.

Things were different for Angel and me too after he'd wrapped himself around me like a camisole jacket and held me as tightly as he could. It felt safe.

Angel pushed our books to the back of the wall under the bed in the heavy silence my comment had created. He was around thirteen now, and while we'd seemed the same age for a few years, we didn't anymore. He wasn't scared like he had been when we met, and he smiled all the time now. But there was something in his eyes that was less playful somehow.

I understood it, really, but I stuffed it far down to my toes—otherwise I was sure Mother's sort of sadness would creep in through my skin and be my sadness too. I loved Mother, but I didn't want to be like her.

Angel slid himself out from under the bed and smoothed down his summer cloud hair. It fell on his even whiter forehead and to his nearly invisible eyelashes. He tilted his head to look at me, and I knew he wasn't sure why schooling mattered either.

But he gave me a smirk, then sat with me with his arm around my shoulders.

"If Nursey says schooling matters—even in here—then it does. Even with the laws, I think she'll get us out of here someday. She'll figure something out," he said. "I think."

I didn't say anything. I was only ten, yes, but I wasn't sure I believed him. I did have fantasies of my father rescuing me, even though he'd never visited or written me. I didn't even know his name or what he was like. What would it be like to be with him instead of Mother? I didn't like to think on that too long, because she needed me. I was glad that every night I could see her thin form and know there had been a time when we were one. Maybe she knew me then.

"When we're adults, she'll help us get out, and Dr. Woburn does almost anything she asks." His hope kept him talking and smiling. "Surely he'll help if she asks."

"I've seen them kiss." My face wrinkled up.

"They've been kissing for a while. You're only now noticing it?" He lay back on the bed, so I did too, and we stared up at the ceiling.

"Do you think we'll get married someday?"

"To each other?" He sat up and his eyebrows reached his hairline.

"Gross." I slapped him and he fell back down next to me.

We were quiet for a moment.

"I think *they're* going to get married," I said.

A few hours later, Nursey breezed in after her shift. She sent Angel back, brought me my tray of disgusting dinner, and then I did what I did every night: I complained about eating alone. She reminded me that it wasn't healthy for me to eat in the ward cafeteria. "Remember when I had to pry a patient's hands off of you."

But that didn't stop me from remembering that everything had changed since Mickey's funeral when I'd had a fit. She was afraid I was becoming like them. Like the incurables.

It wasn't quite my bedtime when she tucked me in as tightly as a thin blanket could tuck. She sat on the edge of my bed, and her eyes were so big and blue, and I felt five years old again. It reminded me of how I used to tell her almost daily that I wished she was my mother. It wasn't because I didn't love my actual mother but because I knew if Nursey was my mother she wouldn't have to leave me every night and I would have a real home.

"Can you be my mother?" I asked her again, even though I felt guilty because I was old enough to know the answer.

"Brighton," she started.

"Never mind." I turned over and faced the wall.

The door creaked open—I didn't have to look to know it was Aunt Eddie bringing Mother. Nursey got up and put Mother to bed, turned off the light, and returned to me.

"You know I love you like you were my own." She rubbed my back.

"Why can't you take me home?" I turned to face her. "I know about adoption. I read the entire *A* encyclopedia."

"It's not that easy. And besides, I'm not married. A woman like me can't just adopt a little girl. And you're not an orphan."

I looked over at Mother. She was staring straight up at the ceiling. That wouldn't last all night, but it would for a few hours. She'd had surgery a few months ago that was supposed to help calm her. It was called sterilization. I knew it meant she wouldn't bleed anymore and could never have another child.

The surgery didn't change anything, though.

"I wish I was like other girls and lived in a real house with a real father and mother." This wasn't new.

I returned my gaze to Nursey. Her eyes were shiny.

"Don't marry Dr. Woburn."

"What?"

"You'll leave me if you do." My lungs squeezed tight.

"I won't ever leave you."

She said it like she meant it, but she didn't say she wouldn't marry him. My hand banged my chest, trying to force my breathing to calm.

"I won't marry him. I'll never leave you." Even though she whipped those words out of her mouth like a syringe of insulin to calm a patient, her eyes left mine. And her quiet was darker than the room.

Then Mother did what she rarely did anymore and began to hum. She was looking in our direction and even though she was just staring off into nothing, I knew she was humming for me. It reminded me of a lullaby, and the melody warmed the cold air as my breathing met the slow and even tempo. This mother of mine understood me better than anyone understood her.

House of Lies

On the front of the Willow Knob building there hung a small balcony. A Juliet balcony. It was really just there for looks—a facade—and nothing like the one the real Juliet stood on, lighted with hope and romance. The house itself boasted a lie to any traveler on the road whose gaze fell upon the beautiful architecture. No one could ever imagine how the inside of the building didn't match the outside. But it was all lies. A houseful.

The balcony was between tall, white-shuttered windows that were supposed to remain unopened. But when the day waned and the sinking sun stretched its pink fingers along the floor of the otherwise gray hall, it summoned me to come and open those windows.

If Nursey caught me, she would do more than scold me. She'd refuse privileges, like limiting my visits to the dayroom to talk to the patients. Or disallowing Angel to come for a few days. If any of the other nurses or aides found me on the balcony, I would be threatened with solitary. Nursey wouldn't let it happen, of course—but I would be punished nonetheless.

But right now Nursey's shift was finishing and Nurse Wilma's was starting. She didn't care much for me and would not forgive my infringing on rules. But I heard at supper that she was in the hydrotherapy instead of my hall. So I slipped out of the dining room—a small freedom Nursey allowed now that I was sixteen. The veil between my world and a patient's was becoming thinner. And the more my independence grew, the more the routine of the life of a patient set in.

And, like any patient, I was not supposed to leave the dining hall early or be on the balcony.

The staff was afraid someone would fall, but the only way I could fall was if I jumped. But why would I want to jump, unless I wanted to die? In order to die I had to live, and I hadn't lived yet. But my thoughts did run in constant circles as I imagined how I might find a way out. Nursey didn't bring up a future outside of this building. I knew better than to believe that I had some magical father to rescue me or that Nursey would marry and then adopt me.

It was up to me—and Angel—to figure a way out. To find out how to get around the laws and rules and locked doors.

For now, though, rules didn't keep me from following the bright path from the setting sun that cascaded down the hall. I wiggled my toes that were bathed in that light and followed the trail like a fairy path that led me to the balcony. Everyone else was finishing their meal—a meager serving of sliced potatoes and a watery tomato gravy. We were so overcrowded that I wouldn't be missed right away as patients were dismissed to their rooms.

I pressed my right shoulder into the warped frame to open the tricky window. It rattled, and I looked around. I heard the shuffling of feet coming toward the cross section of halls. The patients' dismissal came quicker than I'd anticipated. With deft hands I pulled the window up far enough for me to slip through and then closed it, leaving an unnoticeable crack at the bottom that only fit my fingers so I could draw up the window when I was ready to come back in. I peeked my eyes around the edge of the window and watched.

"Daggum taters again." Flo's ancient voice eroded the air as she walked through the hall. At eighty-two she was the oldest on the ward. She was as together as anyone I knew and had only been admitted because her husband took up with a *floozy*—that's how she put it—and she'd tried to hurt him. She was as small as a person could be and she was always complaining about the food. "Soft enough to chew, though." I could faintly hear Flo smack her lips around her few remaining teeth.

Carmen's loud voice agreed. She was about three times the size of any other patient. She ate whatever tiny Flo didn't. While Flo fairly tiptoed, Carmen's gait was more of a waddle. I loved them both.

My mother padded along next, her eyes in my direction. She'd seen me even though her eyes hadn't met mine. Her thinning gray hair hung down like a curtain over the sides of her face. I brought my finger to my lips. Why I did this, I didn't know. Mother's words were like tattered rags tossed about a room, and they were always in German. Mother was an immigrant.

The photograph Nursey had given me on my fourteenth birthday flashed across my memory. Nursey had said little more than that it was in Mother's personal belongings and that the people in the photograph were my grandparents. I kept the picture close, in the soft space between the pillow and pillowcase, and pored over it every few days. In the two years I'd had it, it had aged a decade from all of my handling. But when I'd asked about the hand on Mother's shoulder, Nursey always said she didn't know.

Mother stood and stared as the other patients walked around her. When the aide came—another new one who would probably only last a few weeks—and took her arm to push her along, she pulled away. I winced when he grabbed her again. Her feet tripped as she resisted. Her face grimaced.

"*Nein,*" Mother yelled. *No.* I knew this German word well. "*Nein.*"

I turned away. I didn't want to watch. I watched every day. I watched when she pulled her hair out from the roots and wiped off her bloody fingertips on the walls. I couldn't do anything to stop her. The time I'd tried I'd ended up with the heel of her hand against my temple. I was six.

Every time they strapped her arms down on her iron bed frame, I could do nothing but watch. When she woke in the dead of twilight with her demons dancing between our beds and a curdling scream that could terrify the ghosts in the graveyard—I could only watch. Only watch.

Though I turned away this time, I could still see her in my mind and hear her in my ears. I would always see and hear her, even when I was as old as Flo. Would I still be here then, in this place of concrete and disappointment?

I sank down and pulled my knees up to my chest. The flowering weeping willow's boughs reached for me in the summery breath. It called out to me. *Come to me. Let my delicate white tears fall over you.* I extended my hand, even though I knew the branches were too far away to let their beauty cry over me. When the wind flowed again, delicate white petals fluttered through the air and landed next to me. I gathered several in my hand and rubbed a silky pair together. I repositioned to cross-legged and put the petals in the trough my gown made, making it almost pretty. I fingered the petals' satiny texture and watched the willow stir in the wind and the veil of dusk that was slipping away to night. The low-hanging moon was tiny and insignificant, a reflection of me. It was almost invisible in the outlying hills. The blue hills became a jagged black, the outline etched against a burst of orange.

I wished the beauty could wash my memory and make me as bright as my name. These were the moments that kept my own mind in one place. Reciting the bright and beautiful song didn't help anymore, because there was little that was bright or beautiful about my life.

A voice spoke behind me—close to the window, above my head. I stilled but leaned my ear toward the window.

"Marry me, Joann." I recognized the voice as Dr. Sid Woburn's. He'd been the women's ward doctor for most of my life. He was half handsome. He'd been injured in the war and had a deep scar that ran the length of his forehead. He looked stern and unyielding, though I had to admit he was gentler than Dr. Wolff and many of the aides.

He and Nursey had been sweet on each other for years. How many times had he asked her this question?

I'd overheard a great number of private conversations between them in my sixteen years. The older I got, the more important and serious these conversations became. Sometimes I heard the two discussing sex. My entire body warmed hearing their intimate words. I never intentionally listened in, but their conversations intrigued me. And this time I couldn't get away.

I risked a peek and saw him press in for a kiss.

"Bank's closed." Her hand went to his chest. "You know my answer isn't going to change, Sid." Her sigh was so big I felt its weight. "I'm committed to her, and if we married . . ."

"She's almost grown—actually, she is grown. You've kept her safe and given her so much—even an education." He paused. His voice was soft and tender. "You've taught her how to cope with her life here. What more can you do?"

"It's not enough." A scuff of feet sounded and I squeezed my eyes shut, hoping it didn't mean they'd caught sight of me. "She doesn't deserve to be here."

"Come on, Joann." He hit the window frame. "Why are we talking about this again? She's sixteen, and you've given up your life for her."

Nursey was crying. "But I feel so guilty."

"Listen, you can't make up for her life here—or be responsible for her future. Eventually she's going to have to stand on her own two feet. You did what you thought was best."

"So I should be more like your sister? Feel no remorse for giving up Angel for a life of luxury?" she scoffed. "That's what you want, isn't it?"

Angel? His mother is Dr. Woburn's sister?

"We both know it was Howard's doing. And my mother's. Cynthia didn't know better."

"You could've explained things." Her voice rose an octave. "She was just plain selfish."

47

"She'd have lost everything if she hadn't given him up—that's not Cynthia. And you know that no one says no to Howard."

"Oh yes, the good doctor. Dr. Howard Long." The words were doled out as though they tasted like ward food. "First do no harm, right?"

The quiet was even heavier than the conversation.

"I didn't pull you aside to upset you. I need to talk to you about something else." His tone had changed. It wasn't thin, edgy, and stiff anymore; it was soft and thick. "He's going to be transferred."

"Who?"

"Angel."

I didn't know how to take in everything I was hearing. Cynthia, Dr. Woburn's sister, was Angel's mother? And he was being transferred?

"Oh, Sid, you can't." She spoke almost as loudly as my heart was pounding.

"He's nineteen, and we need space in the juvenile ward. He's slotted to move to Orchard Row in the next few days." The resignation in his voice was a restraint around my throat.

"No." Nursey's voice dripped with venom.

He wanted to take Angel away? Orchard Row was so full that it seemed that the walls swelled with men. Over the years I'd learned all about the other wards. Like the women, the men had two wards, each sex having one designated for the most violent patients—many were convicts. However, in Orchard Row, the nonviolent ward was only a bit less dangerous. Packed tightly, so many men would never be safe. Their yard was fenced—not open like ours. We had looked through the wooden slats as children. Eventually we were run off by an oversize colored aide yelling at us, but we'd kept watch from a distance through our childhood and knew it was a place where nightmares were born.

"Orchard Row is the most overcrowded of all the wards. You know that. And it's too dangerous for him. Are you trying to get rid of him? Is Howard behind this?"

I was paralyzed. I wanted to punch something. I wanted to yell in agreement with Nursey. But I just sat there.

This was a death sentence.

When I heard a thud against the window above me, I peeked. Joann's back was flattened against it as Dr. Woburn's hands wrapped around her forearms. If either of them looked down, they would see my shoulder. I held my breath.

"Get rid of him? The boy is my nephew. I'm not that cruel." He let go of her and ran a hand through his hair. "Come on, Joann, he is years older than anyone in his ward. He's not a child anymore—"

"It's not his fault that most of the children don't live to be as old as he is. You know as well as I do that patients rarely age out of the children's ward—they die there. But he has a chance right now, and we both know it's because of Brighton. He's everything to her. He'd be dead if it wasn't for her. She's kept him safe. He can read anything I give him with a magnifying glass—he's so smart. Give them more time."

"More time for what? They don't have a future, Jo. No one is coming for them, and neither of them can legally leave on their own. We can't change those laws." Whispers like yells heated the air. "It's admirable that you've given them an education, but you've educated them for nothing."

My eyes fell shut. I pulled up my knees and wrapped my arms around myself. *For nothing.* All of this life was for nothing. I was nothing.

"I had to give her something. She deserves more than this. They both do." Her voice broke. "I was sure the laws would've changed by now. They are both mentally capable of leaving."

"The law says it's for their next of kin to decide. Angel's parents will never take him home and Brighton's father is a criminal and—well, he's— Besides, I don't know if they could survive out there. Imagine that. They don't know anything about the real world. Keeping them here is a kindness."

"Shh," Nursey whispered. "Someone's coming."

During a long pause I realized that the sun had relented and gone to bed and I was still out here. The moon had risen and enlarged, and the glittering stars were just beginning their twinkle. I didn't know how such beauty could exist in the moment I was most lost in my life. Was it taunting me? Or was there some hidden message within it?

I knew I needed to get back to my room before Nurse Wilma noticed I was missing. Maybe she already had. But I didn't want to leave this hiding spot. I wanted to hear more so I could form a plan to keep Angel out of the men's ward. But I felt paralyzed.

"Listen, quickly, before someone finds us here. All of this is going to happen fast because the juvenile ward is being audited and we have to have everything shipshape—files and treatment plans. The state wants to make sure we're not spending too much money."

Audits weren't common, but they did happen now and again. I had been hidden on more than one occasion because of them.

"Just change his age." Nursey's voice was insistent.

"I'm done doing all that," Dr. Woburn half yelled. "This isn't the same as hiding Brighton. I could have my license revoked and never practice again if I keep hiding files or concealing patients or covering up for deaths. And Howard is part of the audit. He needs to transfer some children from his hospital here—they're more overcrowded than we are."

"Is that what this is really all about? You're worried that your brother-in-law will see Angel?"

"It's not about Howard. It's about the auditor. Dr. Wolff won't discuss letting Angel stay. He has to be treated like every other patient."

"But he's not."

"Joann—"

"Listen, let's just take them both out. We can help them get jobs and—"

"Joann, stop. We'd both be fired and we'd never work in the medical industry again. There have been too many cover-ups over the years that would surface. What happened with Mickey alone would be enough to ruin my reputation. I'm not going to lose my—everything—over a few mistakes with patients." Dr. Woburn sounded angry now. "But the secrets end here. No more deceptions. He's being transferred."

The silence was like liniment, slathering a layer of numbness over me. His actions had killed Mickey? Flashes of her smile and husky voice surfaced. The warmth of her lap and the sadness in her eyes.

"When Angel was brought here, his grandfather was a ward doctor and his uncle was a resident doctor," Joann spat back. "All these lies. I won't stand by this."

"You've told plenty of lies. Don't become self-righteous now. We both have a lot to lose, so you have a choice. Do you want Brighton to know all you've covered up? Do you want to lose her?"

"Fine, move him," Nursey barked.

I heard someone approaching and the voice of an aide. And then they were gone and I was alone. All the weeds they'd just sown in my garden sprouted and the air was crowded with them.

I stared at the night sky bursting with sparkling constellations. The summer I was eight Mickey taught me all about them. The Crux was my favorite because it was small and hard to find and only showed up for a short period. The presence of the little cross of stars comforted me. It reminded me of me. Small and, unless the stargazer knew exactly what to look for, easily overlooked.

Somehow I was able to slip back to my room unnoticed. Whether it was luck or the God Rosina prayed to, I wasn't sure. All that mattered was that I wasn't caught. But as I curled up in bed, I couldn't sleep. The confessions and private words replayed in my mind over and over again. As soon as I'd almost fall asleep, I'd startle awake. I'd seen plenty of seizures over the years—would the sanding of my heart and senses cause the shuddering to start? Would this be how my own life of insanity began?

Patients often made up entire fictional worlds to lose themselves within. How nice it would be to lose myself in some wonderland. If

I had to be trapped in the back acres of my mind, a false world would not be worse than my reality. But would it free me of all this confusion and disgust and the burden of being a prisoner? No.

All I could think of was that I had to rescue Angel before he became just another patient like Mickey. He was all that mattered now.

1939

Bright-Yellow Canary

A tremor of anxiety woke me the next morning. Angel. He was all I could think about. I couldn't let go of what I'd heard. As much as I loved Nursey, I'd do whatever it took—even if that meant losing her. The air in my lungs was so heavy.

I pulled myself up to sit on the edge of my bed, my thin blanket rumpled around me, my clammy skin and breathlessness catching me off guard. I'd never started a morning like this.

I tried to settle my mind on my surroundings. The voices of the patients moving toward breakfast. The shining morning sun outside. Mother having kept her gown on—uncommon and good.

She was still. And dressed. And so quiet. My breathing improved by a degree.

Nursey rushed in. I turned my back toward her to make my bed. I didn't know what to do or what to say to her. I focused on my breathing as I smoothed and tucked the thin sheet.

"You're not ready for breakfast yet. And you haven't taken your mother to the toilet. If she doesn't go soon, she's going to soil the bed. What's going on with you? You know we depend on you," Nursey scolded but didn't wait for an answer. "Also, there's lice on the ward. Nitpick your mother right after breakfast or we'll have to shave her head again."

A nearly annual occurrence.

I didn't respond. I couldn't even look at her, afraid of what my face would say.

"Bright?" Nursey asked again with more than a sliver of annoyance in her voice. "Brighton."

"What?" I spun to look at her.

Nursey's hands were on her hips. Her bright-red lips were pulled into a straight line. Behind her blue eyes hid secrets about me. I turned away and folded up my threadbare green blanket and put it on the bed.

"I know how to take care of Mother. Don't harp."

After taking a moment to narrow her eyes, she left. I led Mother to the toilet, washed her face, then set her gown to rights. I tried to ignore the demons egging on my anger, but I couldn't stop thinking about Angel's fate. I sat Mother on the bed and pulled a brush through her hair, which was more pieces and patches these days.

She began to hum. It was an older tune from long ago.

I turned her to look at me, and she didn't resist. I often tried to find where she'd gone inside her eyes. Her eyes roamed above to the cracked plaster ceiling and then to the peeling wallpaper. Then her head tilted to look at me—not just toward me. She stopped humming and took a long breath and pursed her lips.

I squinted my eyes at her as if it would help me decipher her better. My ears and soul knew her every groaning; it was her language. But something was different just now. She was trying to say something. Even as I went from standing to sitting, her gaze followed my movements. Her eyes held mine.

I didn't—couldn't—say a word or even breathe for fear of interrupting whatever was happening. The stirring of her mind? A memory? A real word about to be spoken for me?

"M-m-ma—" she stuttered, holding the open sound like a long note. Not guttural. Not wild. Not base. She was trying to speak to me. "Mm-ma-mar—"

"The canary whistles. The mine is safe." Lorna's giggly voice roamed from down the hall into my room. Nursey called her schizophrenic, but I called her my friend. The repetition of words made me turn toward the door. She poked her freshly shaven head inside.

Her facial features appeared too big for her chiseled, gaunt frame. "The canary whistles. The mine is safe." Then she ran off, repeating her words.

She only spoke in riddles now and always with a wide-eyed and clown-like smile.

The canary whistles. The mine is safe.

I didn't know what she meant. Probably nothing. Only then did I realize that Lorna had pulled my attention away from Mother. I snapped my head around and was flooded with disappointment. Mother's blank and distant expression had been restored, and she'd flown back to her faraway place, humming an off-tune melody.

I waved my hand in front of her. "Mother? What were you saying?"

My pleas, silent and spoken, were so numerous over the years they'd become like another organ inside of me. My heart. My stomach. My bowels. My pleas.

I grabbed her shoulders and shook—and not very gently.

"What are you doing?" Nursey unleashed my grip.

"She was trying to talk to me." I yanked away from Nursey and kept my eyes on Mother. I lunged back and my fingers clasped her bony shoulders, but she remained a rag doll. "Mother, what were you saying? Please." My eyes electrified with coming tears.

Nursey pulled me away again.

"What are you going to do if I don't stop? Move me to another ward? Like Angel?" I said it with all the venom I could muster, but as soon as I did, I knew simply blurting out what I'd learned was not wise. Her grip remained, and I didn't pull away.

There was no injection so poisonous as the revealing of deceptions. Her eyes widened and her cheeks paled and grayed like the walls. Even her made-up lips looked pale. A deep swallow traveled down her throat. She loosened her grip and kept her hand on my arm, as though she couldn't entirely let go.

"You don't know what you're talking about." Her words were spoken with the weight of a feather.

"I do so. I know about Angel and Cynthia and Dr. Woburn. I heard everything."

Her breathing grew labored. Was she going to faint? But now that I'd started I couldn't stop.

"Stop the transfer or I'm going to tell everyone everything I know. He killed Mickey," I said through my teeth. I'd never spoken like this to Nursey, or to anyone.

Her face went blurry in my vision and a surge of panic rushed from my stomach to my ears. I needed to say these things to her, but my breath and words were all mixed together. My hand went to my chest as if it would help my breathing.

"You can't think that I would ever let anyone hurt Angel. And Mickey was an accident."

"He covered it up," I said between gasping breaths. "I'll tell anyone who will listen."

Without warning, she tightened her grip and began dragging me down the hall. I'd observed this, of course, numerous times. How she'd break up fights or deal with someone refusing treatment. But never me. She'd spanked me once and then immediately apologized for doing it and never laid a rough finger on me again.

"Nursey, stop," I yelled, and I pulled as hard as I could. "Stop. You're hurting me."

She stopped walking suddenly and my feet fumbled, making an effort to remain upright. "You do not blackmail me or Sid," she said in a low, faltering voice that sounded like it shook more from anger than worry.

My strength and breath were returning by measures.

"He'll die if he goes to that ward. You said that yourself. If you don't stop them from taking him, I'll blab it all. The aides aren't loyal to you. I'll tell them to tell the newspapers." I knew enough about newspapers spilling big stories because we always had old ones on the ward to read but mostly to sop up filth when no one was around to clean.

I got my feet under me and was within a few inches of her face, though I was a half foot shorter. I tried to keep my voice steady to counter my mounting fear.

"You don't make the rules, young lady. I do." She pulled me into the dayroom and into an empty restraint chair.

I knew what was coming. I'd witnessed it so many times in my life. Before I could even try to get away, Nursey put my wrists into the restraints. Cracked, scratchy leather straps. Then she told Nurse Wilma to shave off my hair. My hair. My hair was what Nursey always said separated me from the patients. No one else had time to grow theirs long like mine because it was shorn off almost yearly because of lice. Mine wasn't, though.

How often had Nursey said that I was *her* girl. That I was her long-haired, precious little girl. That I wasn't a patient. But that was no more.

I tried to shake free from her grip as she buckled my wrists in, but this place—this prison with its weapons and hold over all its patients—I couldn't get free of it. I always wondered why patients stopped struggling so quickly. Why didn't they fight harder? But now I knew why. The restraints were so tight it hurt worse to resist. My skin twisted against the clutch of the old leather and metal, but I kept pulling. I growled and tried to bite at Nurse Wilma when she came at me with scissors to first cut off my nearly waist-length hair. My arms wouldn't budge, but my ankles hadn't been secured yet. I kicked Nursey in the shins before she pulled my legs tightly into the straps.

"I don't have lice," I screamed. "Nursey, don't do this. Don't let him kill Angel like he did Mickey."

I repeated my words over and over, sounding crazier than Lorna. Maybe I was. Maybe Nursey had been wrong about me and I was no different from them. Right then I didn't feel any different.

This was the moment I went from being cared for and protected to being a patient along with my mother and so many others. Silky strands trailed down my arms and my head chilled. My hair was gone so fast—and so was the life I thought Nursey had created for me. Would this be an annual occurrence for me from now on?

Dirty clouds of hair littered the space around my feet. And none of it was a part of me anymore.

I didn't know when I stopped struggling, but at some point I did. I didn't feel the razor run across my scalp; I only felt the closeness of Nurse Wilma's hot and soft body that smelled of night-shift sweat. The stench made my stomach jerk and sputter, but there was nothing inside to come up.

Lorna was still chanting about the yellow canary and that the mine was safe. But I knew she was wrong. The mine wasn't safe, and we were all going to die here. Panic filled me while the restraints squeezed my arms and legs. The room was full of other patients, but none of them could help me. Then Mother walked into the room and stood near the chair. Even though her eyes didn't seem to see me, she must have sensed something was happening to me. She rarely came out of the room on her own.

My breathing heightened and I started to scream. Nurse Joann, that's who she was to me now, told me to stop, but when I wouldn't she cupped her hands over my mouth and the back of my neck with such steadfastness I couldn't even try to bite. All I could do was listen to all the other voices and sounds in the room. But no one could hear me.

1939

Deliver Us from Evil

*N*urse Joann pushed me into solitary confinement before my hair had even been swept from the floor. *Solitary confinement.* I repeated the phrase over and over again in my mind and occasionally whispered it, letting it mingle in the damp air around me. This had never happened before.

As a little girl I'd danced and twirled and recited poetry for the nurses and patients at Joann's request, to show off. I wasn't a *patient.* I was their doll to dress up and play with. I was everyone's daughter in one way or another.

But what Nurse Joann had done changed everything.

My face had memorized the press of her hand over my mouth. I had been made silent. Would I ever be unmuted? Would anyone ever know that I was living here, in this place? And what about all the others?

I had been sitting on the cot for hours since a porridge for breakfast had been brought. The cot's itchy blanket was in a ball behind me. The toilet in the corner was small and filled with weeks-old filth that made the tiny room smell of waste. The brick exterior wall was cold and moist to the touch.

I'd resisted every inch of Nurse Joann's pull toward the two solitary rooms. I'd hit, kicked, and scratched. But it made no difference. She even had to release another patient just to stuff me inside.

Not long after, poor Rosina was put in the other. She was praying

59

now as she had been for hours—quoting the Lord's Prayer in Spanish. She'd taught it to me years ago, telling me that I needed some religion. The words came back to me and I said them with her. Together in our separate rooms. Joann told us to stop. So I yelled louder. Until I got to *"Y líbranos del mal."* I didn't move on from that line but repeated it over and over. Louder and louder.

"But deliver us from evil," I began to yell in English to make sure she understood.

I didn't know the context of this prayer. But what it had to do with this place, I knew. Maybe Nurse Joann was evil. Dr. Woburn too. If he was willing to put Angel in the men's ward because of an audit, he was evil. If he had a hand in the death of patients, he was evil. Angel would die in that ward. I had to tell someone what I had learned. I didn't care if that meant Joann would lose her job too and leave me. All I cared about was Angel.

"Y líbranos del mal," I continued to yell. "But deliver us from evil." I yelled those words until my throat hurt.

"Stop saying that," Nurse Joann repeated as loudly and as often as I said Rosina's sacred words.

Once Rosina was released, the words were only whispers, and the small square window in the door showed only the open and empty room opposite me. I had no companion. I was alone. I hated being alone.

Joann silently delivered a small lunch on my second day. She placed it on the cot next to me.

"Are you ready to be rational?" she asked. I answered by flipping over the tray full of food. Refusing to eat was what patients did. And I was a patient now.

The late-afternoon sun filled the broken glass and barred window. It was set high in the brick wall. It was small but big enough that if I could get up to it I would be able to see across the lawn toward the children's ward. It had taken all my angry-patient strength to push the iron bed frame under the window. Maybe I could see Angel.

Maybe if he knew I was in solitary he could convince Joann to let me out. But how would he know? Maybe I would never see him again. Maybe I would be bald for the rest of my life. And cold. And unloved. And worse—unheard.

My toes curled around the damp, cool bed rail. Since I wasn't tall I had to stretch, and when I could finally see out the small window, I nearly let out a hoot and holler. But my feet tired quickly, so I had to take breaks from watching and waiting for any sign of Angel.

I memorized every part of my view of the children's ward. There were bars on the windows, but in the glow of the sun they were nearly invisible, making the building look almost approachable. It was a smaller building and had peaks over the windows that reminded me of houses from storybooks. But I knew better. I knew that the inside front door had claw marks from the children who had tried to escape.

Footsteps sounded in the hall. Someone was coming. Maybe Joann had changed her mind. Maybe she would let me out now. Maybe she would tell me that she'd saved Angel. Maybe I would tell her that I would not reveal her secrets.

But that was a lie. I would tell anyone if it meant that I could save Angel.

I hopped off of the bed rail and stepped to the square window in the door. The hole in the thick door was large enough for my arm to fit through—I'd tested it out as I'd seen other women do on many occasions. But now I peered through it and saw Wilma. She told me to go away, and I stuck my tongue out at her like I'd done since I was three.

But it was the woman behind her that caught my attention. Our eyes met, hers dark brown and mine blue. She was small and sad. Her hair was a disarray of deep chestnut curls. I'd never seen curly hair like that. The palms of my hands went to my scalp. I slapped it, and the sound was so strange I did it a second time. But my eyes never left the new patient.

We got new patients all the time, and every patient started in a solitary room—usually for two full days, longer if they were aggressive. This was a new girl. Who had sent her here? Had the doctors told her family that she'd get better in here? Had anyone told them that this was a place to die more than live? The soul first and then, many years later, the empty body. I'd seen it too many times. I could feel my own soul fluttering, desperate to leave my shell, to leave me behind and go on to somewhere better.

Would this new young woman die here? Even though I didn't know her, I didn't want her to. I could see that she was close to my age. This was unusual. She looked away from me and cried as Wilma unlocked the solitary door. The hospital gown fit on her body better than on many patients. That wouldn't last long. She would lose her healthy weight fast.

After Wilma's footsteps faded away, the girl began screaming and weeping and calling for her mother. I put my ear in the small opening in the door. This grief was something new to me. Usually the women cried incessantly for days and spoke to the spirit of a baby who had died or pleaded with their husband. Often tears would turn to anger and anger into more treatments, more pain, more madness, and always more loss.

But her calling and crying for her mother with such deep sorrow was unexpected.

"Psst. Hey, hey," I said in a loud whisper. "It's all right."

She continued to weep with a mournful sound that I'd never heard before. Sad, not mad.

"Hey, lady. Don't cry, please." I tried to say it sweetly. I wanted to help her. I wished I knew her name. "I'm Brighton. Please don't cry. We can talk—if you want."

The weeping slowly quieted, and I thought she may have fallen asleep.

"We can talk through the little window in the door. Are you there?"

It was another long minute before there was movement through her square peephole. I could see one of her eyes. We stared at one another without a word for so long it seemed like we'd aged.

"What's your name?" I finally asked.

She didn't say anything. All I could hear was the constant din of the hall leading to the dayroom. Maybe she didn't hear me.

"I'm Brighton. I live in room 201 with my mother." Maybe just introducing myself would help.

"Your mother?" I could see part of her face through the doorway cutout now.

I nodded. "Yes. My mother."

"You were brought here together?"

"Sort of." I almost had to laugh. "She was pregnant with me when she was brought here."

She didn't respond right away. I could hear Lorna yelling at the top of her lungs about not letting the bedbugs bite. Was it that late already? I turned to look out the window. It was black. I rushed over and stepped up on the bed rail to look out. All I could see was the glow from a few children's ward windows. I would watch again tomorrow.

I returned to the door.

"So you were born here?" she asked.

"Yes."

"You grew up here?" Her voice rose up at the end. "How old are you?"

"I've always lived here. I'm sixteen."

"You don't sound—" She paused, and I knew why.

"I don't sound insane—mad—crazy?" I suggested and couldn't help but smile a little.

"Yeah," she responded. "Isn't that why everyone's here?" She paused. "That's why I was told I was here."

I shrugged, even though she couldn't see it. Maybe? I didn't know anymore. There was so much jumbled up in my mind, and the line between clear-mindedness and lunacy didn't seem as obvious as it used to be.

"What is lunacy anyway?" I questioned. Many women had just been considered mere inconveniences to their families, though others had such erratic behavior it would have been dangerous not to get help for them. If the doctors didn't know what to do except to tie them down, how would a husband or parent know what to do? But if they came with sickness at any level in their minds, the longer they stayed, the worse it got. This wasn't where people were cured; it was just another type of prison.

"Right. Lunacy," she said like she was thinking of far-off things.

"What's your name?" I asked.

"Grace. Grace Douglass."

"Did your husband leave you here? Did your baby die? Or did you try to hurt yourself or someone else? Do you only cry and not eat?" All the reasons I'd heard flew out of my mouth. "That's why most of the women are here."

"You ask a lot of questions." Her voice was so friendly my heart started to swell. Would this Grace Douglass be my friend?

"My husband didn't leave me here." As she spoke each word her voice sobered. There was a long pause. "My parents did. And I don't have a baby—but my parents are afraid it might happen."

"Oh." I knew what she meant. "So that's why you're here?"

The pause continued so long I almost repeated my question.

"There's more. Mother says I'm too ambitious and Father thinks I'm fanatical about things like photography and travel. And I love the wrong kind of boy. That doctor said it was moral insanity." The sadness in her voice formed a bridge between us.

I leaned my forehead against the door. I didn't know what she meant about loving the wrong kind of boy. How many kinds were there? Mentally disturbed was the most common diagnosis, but I was very familiar with the term *moral insanity*, though I didn't understand that in her case. She was the youngest I'd seen admitted for it.

There were plenty of patients on my floor I was sure would not survive well outside these walls—not that they were doing any more than surviving here. My mother was one. Lorna too, though she hadn't always been as bad as she was now. The ones who needed help with the basics of life or who would hurt themselves or others if given the chance were the ones who could use help from a doctor—but this hospital offered only nightmares. In the dictionary *asylum* meant an offer of protection. There was no protection here.

Sisters Rosina and Carmen weren't insane; they just couldn't speak English when admitted. After their parents died they'd become homeless. Their howling in grief and begging for food were a nuisance to the neighborhood, and without anyone to claim responsibility, they were sent here.

Too many stories. Too much sadness. My shoulders slumped under the weight of it all. My chest heaved. I focused my breathing to be regular and steady. I wanted to keep talking.

"How old are you?" I finally asked.

"Eighteen."

We talked until Wilma yelled at us to sleep. But before that Grace had told me what it was like to go to school. About a woman named Agatha Christie who wrote detective novels. About her camera in her bag that was taken from her when she arrived. She told me about circuses, traveling to England, and kissing boys. All through the small square window. When she talked about those things, her voice shone as bright as the moon and I felt more alive than ever.

I fell asleep with all the images she'd gifted me. They swirled, raced, and spun in my head until it became a real world deep within me. The prettiest, brightest world I'd ever known. Why had Joann never given me these images? What fantastic things Grace had seen. What a life she'd led. And now she was here with me.

The last thing she said before we both retreated to our cots was what I had begun thinking of constantly.

"Do you think we could escape—if my parents don't come back for me?"

That would mean being without Mother. Escaping had been on

the fringes of my mind since I'd received the photograph from Joann on my fourteenth birthday. What Joann probably thought would satisfy some curiosities spurred on a desire in me to leave. Before that, the idea of leaving didn't seem real. My maternal attachment to Joann had filled so much of me. But not anymore. Things were changing. And now I had Grace.

The light was bright through the window in the wall when I woke the next morning. I squinted. I heard a door slam and yelling filtered through the broken glass of my solitary window. I jumped up and stood on the bed rail again. There was Angel.

"Angel!" I yelled through the bars and broken panes. His eyes roamed, looking for me, and I knew he would not be able to see so far away. But he would know it was me. "Angel, up here. I'm in solitary."

The door flew open and hit the wall behind it. Joann stood silhouetted in the hall light, her nursing cap casting a bullhorn-like shadow on the wall.

"Brighton, stop."

I looked at her and then back outside again. Angel was being escorted away, but he was still looking for me. And I was all too sure about where he was being taken. Madness and desperation boiled in me. My hands grabbed at the bars and I pulled myself up higher. I screamed and yelled, and when the broken glass cut me, I didn't care.

As he was being taken away with a man on each side of him, I continued to call for him.

"Get down from there." Joann was pulling me down. My feet couldn't find the bed rail, so my tumble was painful and hard against the concrete floor. I groaned for a moment but got up as quickly as I could, my shoulder and hip aching.

"Leave me alone." I moved to a corner and had my fingernails splayed like claws. The way we looked at each other reminded me of the time Joann—Nursey then—taught me about bulls and how these men would master them with a red cape. Which one of us was the bull? Which one of us was the master?

Then I heard a car motor. I stepped back onto the bed rail before Joann could grab me, kicking her in her middle. She swore and doubled over. A black car with silver edges had driven up. I watched as a man in a suit and a white doctor's coat exited the car with Dr. Woburn. Was that Angel's father? Several other men were with them, each with white coats and clipboards.

"Brighton," Grace's voice called from her room. "What's happening? Are you okay?"

She kept asking, but I was looking in the direction Angel had walked. I couldn't see him. He was lost in the fog that hung in the air. Suddenly I felt a sting. My body involuntarily flinched, and I turned toward Joann just in time to see her pull a syringe from my thigh.

Insulin.

She'd just injected me.

Would I ever see Angel again?

And what about Grace?

What about me?

Rosina's God, deliver us from evil.

Black, White, and Bright

The black-and-white photograph of Joann Derry doesn't look newly developed. The white frame isn't yellowed or curled at the edges, but the film is so old the developing and printing have set off the varied shades of black in a yellowed glaze. Some details have been eliminated, but nothing my memory can't conjure. I carefully pin the new print on the drying line along with a dozen others that have turned out. Not all the images I took have been printable. I was a budding photographer then, with a lot to learn.

I try not to study the photos as memories—not just yet—but only as a photographer. While photos only take minutes to process, my insides will take longer. But thoughts sneak in and I remember taking this photo. It's an entirely different world, but I remember it like I am that girl right now, holding that late-thirties-model Kodak camera. In it, Nurse Joann is closing the back of my mother's hospital gown. Joann's exhaustion is evident—the sag of her jawline, the hunch of her shoulders, the deflation of her spirit. My breath catches in my chest, and as hard as I try, I can't look away. The image holds me captive. This is what I didn't want right now. I just wanted to have the prints, not relive the madness.

But the photo has become a siren and I am not turning away.

Mother's stringy hair cascades down her back, and my stomach shudders at the pointy narrow shoulders. Mother is suddenly so real to me I am expecting her to turn around, point her bony finger at me, and remind me that this was all my fault. Everything that happened the year after this photo was taken was all my fault. Maybe instead of Mother turning it'll be Joann and she'll inject me with insulin again. After a minute of staring I realize I'm rubbing my thigh and I stop. The burden of forgiveness is heavy.

She had loved me. She'd taught me to tie my shoes, to read—and when I asked her about sex, she told me. Now, as a mother myself, I realize what it meant for Joann to do these things and be this person to me. She gave me everything during those long, bleak years, had given up so much, but she had also taken much from me. She'd kept secrets—secrets that revealed the darkest pieces of my life. She is why I am Nell and why I've been Nell for so long. I don't want to be anyone else.

An hour or so later the phone rings again. I rush out of the dark room a second time and grab the receiver. The balm of my husband's voice settles in the old wounds newly opened. He tells me about the child psychology conference and that California feels like another country.

"You'll never guess what I am doing today." I haven't used our small home dark room in years. I tell him about the film canister and the phone call from Kelly Keene. I tell him I have no idea what I'm supposed to do.

I know he's nodding his head. He often does this when on the phone with the parents of his patients.

"I don't know what to do. You know how I feel about that place and . . ." *Who I really am.* I can't finish my sentence, not even with him, even though he knows all my secrets. Some of the things surprised him, but he doesn't shock easily. "It's just been so long and I thought I was past all of this."

"What do you want to do?" He's using his doctor voice. I know Doc isn't going to tell me what to do, though. He never does. He lets me talk and think until I decide for myself.

"I want my—" A cuss word taunts me as it sits in the pocket of my cheek, but then I think better of it. I swallow it back. "I want my film cartridges, of course."

"But what do you really want?"

"Don't use your doctor voice with me." I don't say it angrily but more as a reminder. Sometimes he doesn't know he's doing it.

"Nell." His voice rests against my tense insides and softens me. "I can come home. I can be on a plane by morning."

Would this help? Or is this something I have to figure out by myself?

"No," I sigh. "Grace and I made a promise to each other about those pictures."

"You haven't talked about her in a long time." I hear the smile in his voice. "So you're going to go meet this Kelly woman and maybe— go back?"

The pause after this question could last for years as far as I am concerned. And because my husband doesn't rush anything, he waits until I am ready to speak.

"I think I have to." I realize then that I'm holding the latest photo I exposed and processed. Angel's face is staring up at me, and my breath hitches.

The idea of dragging all of that out again with another person— this stranger, Kelly Keene—makes my stomach want to rid itself of everything I've eaten today. All of it is going to end up in the trash can if I don't get control over this. There will be too much to trudge through. Our children know just enough, but they would never consider for a moment that my first eighteen years nearly shredded anything good out of me—because I never let it seep into my mothering. Oh, how I worked and worked to be the mother I wished I'd had. But in every filled milk glass and tuck-in with a kiss I knew my own buried faraway mother would've wanted to be that mother also. It made me stronger to think of her and know that there was a reason I did what I did.

"Are you still there?"

I blink and shake my head. My mouth is open, but nothing comes out for several long moments.

"I'm here." I sense the surge of strength fighting against the shock of everything Kelly Keene is bringing to my life.

"You are who you are because of those years. I've never wanted to change you, even if that meant taking it all away." He always knows how to talk to me. "If you need to do this, I'll support you, but be careful."

I'm nodding without saying a word. My eyes burn, but I won't close them. I don't want to squeeze any of the tears out.

"I can come home. This conference will happen again next year," he offers again.

"No. It's okay." I inhale so deeply I think my lungs might pop like an overfilled balloon. "I know you should be there, and I'm a big girl." I chuckle and exhale all at once, and look back down at that bright boy who saved my life over and over so many years ago.

Only after I assure him that I'll be careful does he tell me he'll call me tonight and that he loves me, and then we hang up. I return to the dark room, but before I hang the Angel picture on the wire with a metal clip, I eye it a bit more. My building is in the background. The back door is held open with a small rock so we can get back in. Angel stands in the foreground. It's a little blurry, but when I bring the picture close, I can smell the dried grass and fresh breeze and hear the choir of birds that sang to us about our future.

That boy was more than simply the subject in the photograph—he was my everything in those dark years.

"Angel," I whisper to myself. I lift my hand and touch the image of the skinny boy in white standing there with his wide, innocent smile and eyes that played between red and blue. He didn't know what was coming yet, and it breaks my heart again.

I need to see it all again. To remember it and to be close to it once more before it's all gone. Buried dust and ashes. I am not ready to let go yet. But I am ready to find those buried souls and love them and remind anyone who will listen that the invisible still exist.

1939

Heaven Backward

Ylíbranos del mal." I turned to yell it at Joann. While I still had control over my body, I kept repeating the line of prayer. I understood now why Rosina did it. Why she couldn't stop once she got started.

"Deliver us from evil."

I reverted to English to make sure Joann knew what I was saying. I wanted her to know what I believed about her. Evil. This place was evil. The walls were a hell made out of brick and mortar. But instead of heat from the hellfire, there was a constant chill and dampness in the air.

The sting from my feet slapping against the cold floor radiated up to my thighs and hips. Then everything started happening in slow motion. I pulled my arm away from her grip. Her pretty and perfect fingernails scratched against my skin. My own were bitten and torn. Claw-like nails were a weapon against out-of-control patients.

Joann began to blur.

Her words, "Sorry, my love," were drawn out and felt like dandelion fuzz in my ears.

I took a wobbly step away from her. One step back and into the corner of the small room. She had her hands out to me, splayed, and her mouth was moving, but I could feel the insulin rush through me now. Her voice didn't sound like her. A voice somewhere repeated my name. Whose voice was it? I looked around for it.

I looked back at Joann's face—it went from two to four back to one. She really had lied to me my whole life—but now I knew the truth. We weren't the same, she and I, like she'd always said we were. She'd told me for as long as I could remember that she and I weren't like the patients. That we had our minds and they didn't. That we could learn and be rational and they couldn't. There were too many truths and lies braided tightly in these thoughts.

She wore her white nurse's cap on top of her light-blond styled hair. The magazines I'd stolen described the hairdo as *coiffed*, *sleek*, *sweeping*, and I could see all of those words in the beauty of Joann's hair. My hand moved in slow motion up to my scalp, and the stubble rubbed against my palm. I was a patient. But Joann, with a face that looked like the magazine ladies, was not.

Her white uniform fit her well, and I looked down at my gown. Long. Loose. Soiled. Old. Likely had been worn previously by a now-dead patient. It wasn't even mine. It was just the one that had been handed to me the last time the laundry came through. This one hung well below my knees, down to my calves, and had room enough for two or three of me.

She had freedom.

I had nothing.

"Can you hear me, Bright?" Joann's words started cutting through the insulin. "I'm so sorry. I'm so sorry."

I wrinkled up my brow. My mouth frowned. I could feel it now.

"I hate you," I whispered.

The twitch in her face indicated surprise. I was surprised myself. I didn't like the way the words tasted in my mouth, but they were true in that moment. And then I fell, and no one caught me.

I gave in to the insulin and my mind lingered only on how my muscles went from tense to relaxed and how good it would feel to sleep.

But it was the kind of sleep where voices could be heard. Joann apologized over and over, telling me she didn't know why she'd done it. She was afraid and exasperated and didn't know why I wouldn't just stay the little girl who trusted her.

That little girl was gone.

She may as well have been dead.

I heard Mother too. Was I in my room? She wailed and thrashed and made all the familiar sounds. And a few times her sounds seemed to try to form my name. I was alone for so long, left in the dark, and I didn't know where everyone had gone. So far away. How long this went on, I wasn't sure, but slowly there was a fold of light in the corner of my mind and Mother was there. I think I said *Mother* but my mouth didn't move, so I must have only thought the precious word. But the woman in the fold of light didn't look like Mother. Similar but different. She was warm and glowing and whole. She smiled at me, and the glimmer in her eye was so different from how she usually looked at me.

"Mother?" I asked.

She just smiled and waved and twinkled at me. She wasn't wearing a hospital gown; instead, she was in clothes I'd see in Joann's catalogs. Her rounder, soft features invited me to come closer, but when I couldn't, I realized I was in restraints. I was camisoled. I struggled and screamed, but something was in and around my mouth. With every muscle I tried to push, pull, and stretch, but nothing worked. Heat and dampness formed in the crevices. There was no release.

Did this last for minutes or months? My mind and body were equally taxed. I wanted to leave my body. I pleaded with my soul to fly away and leave the rest of me behind. But my soul had wrapped around me, holding me together like glue, while the camisole ripped me apart. But slowly I gave in. I stopped struggling. I let go.

Joann's voice and Mother's humming returned then.

"Brighton," Joann said with a spark of urgency. "Wake up, my darling."

Darling? She wasn't allowed to call me that anymore, just like I'd never call her Nursey again.

My mouth was dry and something was still in it. I tried to speak. A mouthpiece. Was I really at risk of swallowing my tongue? Had

I had a seizure? It was removed as if Joann heard my silent request. My tongue felt large and thick, and when I felt the vibration in my throat, I was relieved that I could still make a sound.

"Brighton, open your eyes," Joann commanded as nurses did when trying to wake patients from an insulin stupor. "Open your eyes."

My eyelids fluttered. The light was so bright I winced. Was this what Angel experience when in the sunlight? I tried to shield my eyes with my hand, but the camisole held me down. Panic rose in me when I realized that it hadn't just been in my subconscious but that I was actually restrained. I pulled harder and could hear Joann telling me to calm down so she could unbuckle the camisole but making me promise to stay under control. I nodded my head. I didn't think I'd have the strength to fight anyway.

She sat me up, and my body felt loose and free of any bones or muscles inside. Joann deftly unstrapped the camisole, and my ears were cued to another voice. It was far away, but I had to remember why it was familiar.

"Grace," I said. Then coughed. My throat and mouth so dry. But I had to try again. "Grace."

"Who?" Joann asked, confused. She tried to keep me in the bed as she pulled away the camisole and placed it by my feet. I pushed her away, but my arms were like the Jell-O Joyful served, and my legs were strapped to the bed rails.

"My legs," I said. Joann let go of my arms and loosened my legs. I swung them over the side of the bed, only to fall as soon as I tried to stand.

"My legs," I repeated. They were numb and growing tingly. I wiggled my toes and then my ankles while Joann tried to explain that it was just my circulation.

"You have to forgive me, Brighton," she pleaded, hanging all over me. "That shot wasn't meant for you. You know I always keep one with me, just in case. You were out of control. I didn't know what else to do."

She continued, and I let her talk without responding. I wasn't considering whether or not I could forgive her; all I knew was that I needed to get to Grace. I needed to help Angel.

"Forgive me, Brighton," Joann said on her knees, her head bowed on the bed next to me.

I contemplated little on her request as my legs gained strength.

"Where's Angel?" My voice chilled the room further.

She shook her head as black streaks from her makeup made pathways down her perfect creamy skin.

"We can talk about him, but you have to forgive me. Please forgive me." She reached for me again, and because I had nowhere else to go, I stood on the small cot, my legs nearly buckling.

Which was harder—the tile beneath her knees or the very tissues of my heart? Forgiveness was something so dearly connected to forgetting, and I wasn't sure the former could happen without the latter. It was like asking the broken window to repair itself. Everything she was saying, the way she was desperate to touch me, all the tears she was shedding made my soul and stomach wind up together. My hunger was only satisfied feasting on my hurt and anger toward Joann. Maybe it would change someday, but maybe not.

"Where is Angel? What have they done to him?"

She didn't answer but kept crying.

"Answer me," I growled at her. I had learned that from a patient long ago—to use my voice like that. That woman was dead now.

"Brighton, you don't act this way. This isn't you." Joann tried to wipe the wetness from her face, but it only smeared the blackness across her no-longer-perfect cheeks. "Come down and let's talk."

"How am I acting?"

Joann blinked and looked away from me.

"Am I acting insane? Tell me, Nurse *Joann*."

I emphasized her name. This wasn't the same woman who had mothered me over the last sixteen years. That woman never would've injected me with insulin. This was not the woman who had read *Aesop's Fables* and *Little Women* to me. Oh, to be a character in those stories and not be me. Not be Brighton. Not be shorn. Not be brittle-souled and lost.

Then I heard a voice coming from Mother's cot and looked at her, and the sight of blood pulled me toward her on my weak and wobbling legs. Her arms were bleeding. This was what she did to herself when she was agitated.

"Mother, what happened?" I asked and moved to sit next to her on the bed.

"I know," Nurse Joann said behind me. I ignored her and grabbed the damp cloth that had been draped over the footrail of her bed, already stained with blood.

I carefully turned Mother over and welcomed the stare of her blank eyes. The look was familiar—though something did flicker behind her eyes when she saw my shorn head. Like she noticed the change. I forced my grimace to a smile. I wanted to put her at ease.

"Mommy." Tears rushed to my eyes when the word spilled from my mouth. When was the last time I'd called her that? "Let me clean you up."

Slurred words escaped her mouth, none of them intelligible. But I knew they were happy sounds. Not the ones she made when she was being dragged to hydrotherapy or forced to swallow powdered water that she knew would sedate her. I knew her sounds, and I knew what she was saying. She was happy to see me. She'd missed me.

I gently wiped her arm where the scratches still bled. She relaxed into my touch. Her free arm rested on my knee, and her fingers thrummed gently against my skin.

"You're so good with her." Nurse Joann's voice broke.

I forced myself to continue my even strokes and not look at Joann. The woman whom I'd seen as a second mother my whole life had betrayed me. The coolness of my scalp was a constant reminder. A shiver fell like water from my head down my back.

"Please don't hate me," Joann whispered. "I didn't mean— I was scared."

I finished with my mother and helped her sit up at the edge of her bed. After I carefully slipped her head through her gown and helped her arms through, I finally turned toward Joann.

"*You* were scared?" I wanted to hiss at her like Lorna. My words started out quiet but grew to fill every space of the room. "How do you think I've felt since I was six and realized that living like this isn't normal?" I gestured around me. "That other children live in homes with a mom and dad and sisters and brothers. They go to school. Eat dinner together around a table. Sit in front of a fireplace and read together. I live in a lunatic asylum with women considered insane and incurable—if they weren't crazy when they came, they are now. None of us can leave. We're all trapped. I'm trapped."

I felt dizzy and squeezed my eyes shut to gain back my balance. I opened my eyes and found Joann wide-eyed with a hand out, as if to calm me.

"I've done the best I could with your circumstances. I haven't taken other jobs—better jobs—because I love you. I've put so much on hold. Even pushed Sid—Dr. Woburn—off, for goodness' sake."

"Dr. Woburn." I shook my head. "He's a murderer, and I'll tell everyone."

"Stop saying that. No one will believe you anyway. I haven't gotten married and I haven't had the family I've dreamed of because I wanted to be with you. As long as you're here—"

I cut her off. "As long as I'm here? Where else can I go? I'm stuck here."

She stopped speaking, her mouth gaping open for several long moments. "I know."

The tremor that went through my heart was like a battle cry from deep inside. I was unprepared to hear her agree that I was trapped. And telling me that she'd given up a future family because of me only compounded my reality. But if she loved me so much to give everything up, then why cut my hair and throw me in solitary?

Why camisole me? Why torture me?

"You don't know what I've kept you from," she continued. "I kept you from the children's ward, insisting that you being near your mother was the best thing for her. That might've been true then, but really it was because *I* fell in love with you. I wanted you for myself. I was a silly eighteen-year-old, barely old enough to be a nurse here. But you—"

She stopped and cleared her throat. The heavy pause wrapped around me as tightly as the camisole had been.

"Look at what you did to me." I pointed to my head. "And then solitary—and—" I pointed at my bed where the camisole and the restraints lay.

"You threatened to ruin us—me and Sid." She spoke in a grave whisper. "We would both lose everything."

"I've already lost everything," I yelled. "Actually, I haven't lost everything. I've never had anything. All I have is the shell of a mother and Angel. And you were ready to let Dr. Woburn take him away from me. Where is he?"

"You know where he is. You didn't give me the chance to fix it. And I haven't left your side since—"

"Was he really taken to Orchard Row?"

Like a dam breaking, tears rushed to my eyes. My throat constricted. My hand went to my chest to steady my breathing. Had she really just said Angel was in the men's ward? My eavesdropping on nurses and aides had taught me that even the non-dangerous men's wing had a weight and height requirement for male nurses and aides. The men could be so violent they had to be handcuffed for basic medical assessments.

"I've been at your side for three days. And there was the audit and—"

"Three days?" I leaned against the wall and finally looked at Joann and took her in. Her hair was in disarray and her cap was askew. Her white uniform was covered in stains. Sweat marks lined her dress under her arms. I'd never seen her look so unkempt.

Suddenly my mind jumped to the new patient.

"Where's Grace? The girl in the other room in solitary."

"The new patient? She's still in solitary." Joann's dismissal of Grace, her lack of concern, stirred my anger.

"Get Grace out," I pleaded. "Why is she still in there? New patients are usually in solitary for only two days."

"She bit Wilma," Joann snapped.

I nearly broke out in a smile. She had spirit, and she wasn't afraid. I liked her even better.

"Get her out, Joann," I insisted. "I still have a lot I can share about Dr. Woburn. Does everyone know Angel's his nephew?"

"Don't," she whispered and shook her head.

I slowly got up from Mother's bed. My legs were gaining strength. Joann followed me like an unwanted shadow.

I held the hall railing and started to walk down the hall like I had bones older than dirt. My feet slid in something wet. I got my bearings again and kept walking. I had to get Grace out of solitary. And I had to figure out how to get Angel out of Orchard Row. If I had to tell every aide and every nurse who passed through here that Dr. Woburn was Angel's uncle, I would. Surely that would uncover other secrets. I wouldn't let this go until Angel was safe and out of Orchard Row. Even if that meant I'd never leave these four walls.

Joann kept following me, and when I turned to look at her, our gazes fixed. I heard a loud motor idling near the building, and I shuffled as fast as I could while still holding on to the hallway rail. Joann followed me into Carmen's room, and we looked through the barred window.

A white bus was parked in front of the children's ward. I watched as twenty-two children exited the bus. The rickety bunch walked in a ruled line, their wrists held by a rope to keep them straight. The front door of the children's building remained shut, and all were ushered around back where they would be bathed. Bathed. Angel had told me all about what it meant to be bathed. None of them could've been older than ten or eleven. Some fought the rope and were immediately chastised by a uniformed attendant who had stepped out of the bus ahead of them.

Now there really wouldn't be any room for Angel.

Farther down the foggy hospital road and then off to the left was the men's ward—Orchard Row. Two two-story buildings connected by a hallway, and they were still overcrowded. Bars on every window—every window broken or completely shattered. Glass littered the ground around the buildings. Angel was in there. Right now. I grabbed my stomach.

"I need Grace," I told Joann as I stared out the window.

I heard her keys jangle as she walked away. The door squealed when it opened, and I shuffled out of Carmen's room and stood in the hall, waiting. Grace rushed out of the room and turned toward me. Even though she'd never seen my whole face, she knew who I was and she ran to me. She held me, and I felt her thick curls against my shaven head. Her touch felt warm and familiar somehow.

Finally, I had a sister.

Doorways

J woke the next morning with a weight in my soul and the feeling I was being watched. I opened my heavy eyelids to see him. Angel. A sheen of light fell over his complexion. Glowy and spirit-like. I looked toward Mother when I heard her moaning in her sleep. Then I looked back at the figment of Angel. He was still there, and his smile twinkled in the morning sunrise. I blinked—was he real or had I moved into the dark unknown of a melancholy mind and would believe now and forever that Angel was present, no matter where he really was?

"Good morning." Angel waved.

I waved and mouthed *Hi*, but no sound came out of my mouth.

Joann breezed in with a medication cart. She looked cleaner than she had the day before.

"You're awake, I see, Sleeping Beauty," she said without much tenderness. She was marking up a clipboard. "Angel, have you told her about your release?"

"You can see him too?" I asked.

"See him?" Joann started pulling Mother into a sitting position. "Angel."

"Brighton, are you feeling all right?" She came over and started to reach her hand out toward me, but I pushed it away. I didn't want her near me.

"Angel, is that actually you?"

The figure of Angel laughed, and while it seemed inappropriate given where we were, it was the best sound I could've heard.

"It is you," I yelled as I jumped out of bed and wrapped my arms around him. He winced and I pulled back. He held my arms and looked down at me with that smile I would never forget.

"Did you think I was a ghost?" He rubbed my arms.

He laughed a bit more, but I saw tears fill his eyes. My empty heart filled up with them.

"You're hurt, aren't you? They hurt you," I said and began pulling at his shirt.

"It doesn't matter." I didn't let him get away with that, and checked him over like any nurse or mother would. His middle looked like a watercolor painting—covered in purple and blue bruises.

"He was in the infirmary within the first twenty-four hours," Joann said as she walked Mother out of the bathroom and then handed her off to an aide who, with several other patients, was heading for breakfast. "Broken ribs."

"I guess they didn't like me." Angel shrugged.

I looked over at the door, but Joann was already gone.

"This is all her fault," I said. "Joann knew this would happen. You're lucky to be alive."

"She's the one who got me released."

"I had to blackmail her," I told him. I'd tell him the whole story later. "You wouldn't have been there if it wasn't for her and Dr. Woburn."

"If it wasn't for them, we'd probably be dead," Angel countered.

I paused long enough to take in the truth that he was safe. For now.

"So she got you *released*." The word surfaced. That was the word that had been used, wasn't it? "So you're leaving?"

I stepped back.

Angel wrapped his arms around me. So gently. So carefully. The kind of delicacy we both needed.

"I'll never leave you." He smoothed a hand over my bald head,

83

and I suddenly felt very naked. I shied away for a moment, but he didn't let me step away. "It'll grow back."

I nodded.

Then Angel told me all the details about how he was released to work with the groundskeeper, Mason. He would be a patient working, not a real employee, but the work was full-time. He would be given a small closet in the basement to sleep in for now. He would be busy. Very busy. But he would be safe from Orchard Row.

There was delivery in this. Had Rosina's God heard my groaning and utterings?

Then I told him everything I'd overheard—it all seemed like years ago. His mouth pulled into the widest grin possible. Why was he smiling? I had told him about all the lies and what I knew about his mother and that Dr. Woburn and Joann had known all of it all along.

"Dr. Woburn is my uncle," he said with awe in his voice.

"He's a liar, Angel. Isn't that more important?"

"Brighton, I have an uncle. I have a mother and a father who are alive." He stood and chuckled and turned in a circle until he faced me again. He held me closely and looked down at me. He'd grown so tall, and I'd stopped growing at least a year ago. The way he looked at me reminded me of the way I'd seen Dr. Woburn look at Joann. His hands were warm and held me gently. There was something new in this moment.

I could almost see all of his thoughts and questions churning in his head. They weren't the ones I'd expected. Where was his anger? Where was the hurt?

"Angel, Joann has been lying to you—to us—about your family our whole lives." I pulled away from him and took a step back.

"I know, but I can't get angry about it. Just knowing something—anything—about where I come from makes me happy. Makes me feel like"—he shrugged—"like I'm someone."

I watched my friend as he laughed and exuded a happiness I

wished I had. His red-blue eyes scanned through the window toward the children's ward—where his father had been the day before.

"Why aren't you angry at them?"

"Are you angry at your mom when she hurts you? Do you hate her because she has turned away from you countless times?"

"That's different."

"But she's hurt you, Brighton. And you still love her."

"Of course." This wasn't the same thing at all.

"I've been wanting to know something—anything—about where I came from for as long as I remember, and now I know a little bit about myself."

But none of them care. I wanted to yell this, but I didn't. But I did speak firmly. "Dr. Woburn is more worried about his job than your life."

"And you are more worried about your life than Nursey's," he returned.

"Don't call her that," I said quietly, but deep down inside I was jealous that the nickname still sounded sweet in his mouth. It was bitter in mine. "And Joann has everything. Why do I need to worry about her?"

He stepped away, and his pale face grew slightly pink.

"She's given up marriage and children for you. She might've made some bad choices, but the choice to love you has kept you alive. That's what Nursey has done."

Our eyes locked for several long moments, and I could tell we weren't going to see things the same. He wasn't wrong, I knew that. But there was still so much wrong that had happened, and I had a feeling that something she'd done, a secret she'd kept, would be the reason I would never get out.

"Angel boy, where are you?" Joyful's voice was as sharp as a sparrow's call and as warm as a hug all at once. She loved Angel and me.

Our stare broke when I heard her voice vibrating through the narrow gray halls.

"I'm here," he said, turning toward the open door, "in Brighton's room."

"I been looking for you for ten minutes, boy. I ain't got time for this," she scolded. The whites of her eyes grew. "Now, come on. I got your uniform ready."

He'd always had this sense of glowing to him because of his albino skin, but the glow I saw now was different. He reached out and squeezed my shoulder. "Be happy for me, Brighton. Maybe I can sneak us some extra food." He lifted his eyebrows in excitement, then he left.

I watched him. From now on he wouldn't look like a patient, he'd look like a worker. I had suggested Joann do something to get him out of the men's ward, but now that it was happening, I was nervous about how this might change us.

The lines had been blurred.

All the patients had jobs. Gardening and harvesting in season, peeling potatoes, sewing gowns for the patients and shrouds for the dead. Cleaning and laundry every day. Those who were capable were given tasks for several hours of the day. But there were plenty of patients who weren't able to do any of these things and who didn't do much more than stand around the dayroom or lie in their beds and move from therapy to therapy. There wasn't much for them to do but exist and survive.

I forced a smile as Angel waved goodbye for the day.

An aide had walked Mother back as far as the door and told me she needed washing. I could smell that she'd soiled herself in the few minutes she'd been away. Mother walked to the bed and sat. I knelt in front of her. She raised up her hand and put it on my cheek, and her eyes searched my face for a moment. Her bald head had transformed her in such a strange way. I didn't want to look at her, but I did. My bald head had transformed me too, only in different ways.

"Mother?" I whispered. "It's me, Brighton."

Her first finger lightly tapped my face a few times. A gentle touch from her was not something I often got. The leftover pieces of my heart tried to right themselves, only to find that too many pieces were missing.

"Mother." The morning's yellow sun cascaded through the broken windows; the rays cast light across my arms and spanned across her face. The image of the sun on her face made me imagine things I had always wished.

I imagined her walking through our little house to my bedroom some sunny morning. There would be a light breeze pushing against my lacy curtains. She'd sit on the edge of my bed and put her hand on my shoulder or my back and rub in circles. She'd gently push my hair back and wake me for school. She'd say my name, Brighton, a few times, like a pretty whispering song made of feathers and clouds. I'd slowly wake up and I'd say, "Good morning, Mother."

When the slap came across my cheek, I was unprepared, having fallen into my own Wonderland. I was back in my reality, and I wanted to run away.

Angel learning a sliver of his own history after living his whole life knowing nothing somehow made me feel less known. Would I ever be known? Would Angel?

Dr. Woburn mentioned my father. A convict. What had become of him? Would I ever have a future outside of this building? Would I get the chance to love someone and get married? No, I would be here for the rest of my life. There would be no husband, no children, no life—unless I escaped.

"Brighton?" Grace stood in the doorway, looking around like she wasn't sure if she was supposed to be here. "I was walking by to go to breakfast."

I barely recognized her. Her mounds of thick dark curls were gone. Her head was as bald as mine.

"Your hair." I breathed the words, unnerved at my shock. I'd relished her normalness, and now she looked like the rest of us.

She smoothed a hand over her scalp, then shrugged her shoulders.

"I guess they were nervous about the lice after all," she said, then turned her gaze toward Mother's bed. "Is that a straightjacket?"

"They call them camisoles here." I gestured toward the restraint lying over the foot of her bed.

"So this is your mother?"

My gaze returned to Mother.

"Yes," I said with a voice laced with disappointment, and my palm touched the place she'd just slapped.

"You look like her."

I looked at my mother. We were both bald and imprisoned. But so was everyone on the ward. We were all the same now.

Grace didn't leave the doorway, almost like she was afraid to approach my mother.

"We need to find a way to escape," I said.

"I don't think I'll be here long enough to worry about that." The truth in that hurt.

"But no one is coming for me." My eyes were fixed on Mother so I didn't have to look at Grace. I didn't want to see how pathetic I looked in the reflection of her eyes.

"Then I'll come for you."

And then there was hope.

1939

Undeveloped

A shift had happened. No longer was I a protected little girl who had been born in a shroud of bad luck. No longer was I given time toward any education and separated from the rest of the patients. Everything had changed. Like a tree drops leaves, like a mower cuts down long grass, like a shot of insulin subdues an anxious mind, there was a before and an after in my life now.

It wasn't that Joann ignored me or cared nothing for me. I disallowed any closeness—though chastised by Angel—and maybe she realized things had changed too. A waxing or waning season, I wasn't sure. But to me she seemed tired and her resilience low. After years of devoting her energy toward me, on top of her regular duties, perhaps now she felt tired of it all. Even me.

Besides the uniform, the contrast between her and the patients grew less and less. Her hair, always neat, was less styled, her lips less red, her cheeks less rosy. Her eyes darker. Her skin more ashen. I saw the signs of someone's soul entangled in melancholy, and I wasn't sure how my own soul was affected by it, but I knew somehow it was.

Was it my withholding of forgiveness, or was her guilt ruining her? It was hard to tell. All I could think about was Grace and Angel, wondering if it was possible to escape, and how. *Escape.* Breathing the word itself seemed preposterous. Grace had no reason to believe she would be left at Riverside long term, and she was sure she would find a way to have me released as soon as she got out. She said if the police knew how we were treated, they wouldn't keep me locked up here. She was sure of this so I believed her.

Angel came to visit when he was able to carve time away from his new duties. And Grace—she was like no one I'd ever met. She was from *out there*. From the real world. Of course, Rosina, Carmen, Lorna, and all the other women from my floor had also come from there, but she was different.

The other ladies had been at Riverside for as long as I had, or longer. The world they'd known had passed away and a new one that sparkled and sang had arrived—or so Grace told us. Grace was also my age, the youngest admitted patient I could remember. And she wasn't plagued with melancholy or paranoia, though she'd been given a diagnosis that said otherwise by doctors, so she could tell me everything I'd ever wanted to know.

Grace was vivacious and filled with stories. The other women had long since lost whoever they might have been before Riverside. When you're treated like a worthless piece of flesh, eventually you believe it. I had seen it happen over and over. The original person disappeared. Someone new was born in their place. It didn't take long before they became unrecognizable.

I knew this was why Joann had made me keep my distance from the rest of the patients for so many years. It had been for my good. Cutting my hair had not been, nor had solitary or the insulin injection.

Joann still pleaded daily for forgiveness. But I only spoke to her to ask for privileges for me, Angel, and Grace. I knew she'd give in to win me back. And I was too hurt to consider the alternative.

I didn't ask for much, but Grace and I wanted her camera back, along with some film. All patients had their belongings taken from them and put in the attic to be returned upon their release. She'd brought her camera, having no idea where she was being taken.

At first Joann said no, citing rules and regulations. But a few days later she handed us half a dozen cartridges with the reminder that I needed to remain silent about the secrets I knew and that neither the camera nor the film could be seen by any doctor. If anyone found out we would end up in solitary or worse. And any photographs we took would be destroyed. We agreed. It wouldn't take many photographs to prove the poor treatment and care we received. Grace would sneak these out and be able to share them to help Angel and me.

It didn't take long before the snap of the camera box began to pull me from my own dark moods. The trapped image of light inside the little box gave me hope of something unknown waiting to be discovered. Grace's Kodak had been a gift from her parents and now it was like a gift to me. I didn't know how it did what it did. And how with a push of my finger I could capture what I saw, images that before could only be captured in my memory.

The only photographs I'd been in were the ones Joann had taken each year on my birthday. And she'd never shown me those. Now here I was on the other side of the camera, with my eye to the view-finder. The camera had quickly become even more to me than it was to Grace. It felt like a part of me, and since one of Grace's roommates was prone to taking things apart, the camera stayed with me.

The camera helped me see things differently. I saw the truth about so much my eyes had merely glanced over before. I saw the dust in the corners, chipped plaster. I traced along the room, and my mother filled the frame. She sat with slumped shoulders and her gaze on the floor. Her hair was spiked in various places, and because she'd pulled out so much of it over the years, it only grew back in patches. I scanned over to Grace. She waved and giggled.

Her hair had also started to grow, and the curls formed like corkscrews against her scalp. My life had changed since the day my hair was cut off and I was stuffed away, out of sight. It was Grace's voice that I'd begun to hear inside my head, speaking to me in a way I'd never known before. Learning about a whole world of things I'd never even heard of before.

Grace taught me about how important light was when taking

photographs. She talked about shadows and framing and how all of it was affected by the light that streamed in. She told me to think about the pictures of starlets in magazines and showed me how to capture the glint in the eye.

Then Grace posed like a fashion model, and we both laughed.

"I'm going to take it." With a gentle press, the button clicked.

"Brighton." Joann walked in and helped my mother stand up. She was going to see a new doctor today who was visiting from New York. He was assessing certain patients regarding a new procedure called a lobotomy. "You know you're not supposed to have the camera out when we have a doctor on the ward."

There was an ache in my heart because she now carried an edge to her voice. I knew that blackmailing her to get my way had been wrong, but I didn't know how I could've done anything differently. I would always do what I could to help Angel and Grace. But that didn't take away the pain held in the cavern between Joann and me.

When Joann walked away with my mother, I pulled at Grace's robe and gestured for her to come with me. "Come on."

"Where?"

"We're going to get a photograph of hydrotherapy."

"You devil." Grace winked as she took my hand, and we tiptoed to the other hall. Photographs of any therapies were, of course, against Joann's rules.

"I can probably get one through the broken window," I whispered to her, pointing at the door.

Grace nodded as she kept an eye out for any nurses or doctors.

I had to go on my tiptoes to see through the window. It was filled with the usual patients. Ghosts of vapor and hope rolled around the room. Eight porcelain tubs were stuffed with patients lulled into complacency, only their heads poking through the bathtub covers. Streams of steam escaped through the broken window above us. Oh, to be steam.

With a snap of my finger I'd captured all the forms of water. Water in the tubs. Steam hanging in the air like curtains. Ice in the water cups the barely present nurses drank while inside. And now the forms of the patients were held hostage in the box in my hand. Doubly captured. Would anyone ever know them and who they were? Who they were to me? Would anyone know me? Did their families remember they'd left them here to decay?

I felt a sense of urgency to pull out the film from inside the camera so I could see it again. To see how the mixture of light had cast upon the thin, dark strip of plastic. It was the light painted upon the dark that created the image; darkness vanished when the light touched it. Was light powerful enough to rule the darkness within our reality? I had slowly stopped believing it. Slowly stopped believing that any plan Grace might have upon leaving Riverside would work. Grace's family was not my next of kin, and there was no guarantee that she'd get out or that she could help my release if she did. All of her assumptions suddenly sounded like a fairy tale.

"I'm never going to see these pictures." When the words left me, the weight of them fell from my thin body.

The moaning of the hydrotherapy patients grew louder—like mourning.

"What do you mean? What about our plan?"

I shook my head slowly in response and stared at the box in my hands. I'd pushed this truth so far back in my mind that I'd forgotten it existed. None of the staff would ever allow these photographs to be printed. Joann would never allow Grace to take the film out of the hospital with her. Why had I fallen for her idea? Joann was only pacifying me. No wonder she'd given in so easily. She knew she would make sure the film was destroyed. The real world would never know how an out-of-control patient could be stuffed inside a solitary room, strapped in a water tub, or secured to her bed, all for the convenience of the staff. It surely wasn't for the healing of the patient. The patients might be left moaning like that for days.

Acknowledging that I would never see the photos I'd taken

suffocated me as badly as the camisole had a few weeks ago. Without the miracle of an escape, I would never see the real world Grace spoke of and no one would ever see the hell I lived in. Like the images in the camera, I would never be known without the door being opened.

Patient

$\mathscr{I}$ stayed in bed the next morning. I couldn't get up. My body wasn't stronger than my mind. All I could think about was spending the rest of my life here—at this home for the mad. I was almost seventeen and knew so little of what eighteen-year-old Grace spoke of—like learning to drive a car or watching a Clark Gable film. She talked about women voting, and I didn't know what that meant and why it mattered. I craved bologna, even though Grace told me it was gross. It was from out there, so I wanted it.

Angel had been my way out of self-pity for most of my life. But it wasn't working anymore. Knowing Angel loved his work and didn't have to sleep in a patient building made him feel different from me now. He was happier than I'd ever known him to be. One day when Dr. Woburn was on the ward, Angel watched and studied his doctor uncle's face as intently as his eyesight allowed. I knew he was looking for resemblances. I refused to see any.

"Brighton." Grace's voice was behind me. "Why weren't you at breakfast?"

I didn't answer.

I stared at the wall. And every brick I placed over my soul, the better I felt. The vacant stare was a balm. I let my mind wander between imagining what my life might've been if I'd had a different mother to pure blankness. My imaginations were as fleeting as Lorna's sensibilities. The barren canvas of my mind was easier to control.

Was this what had happened to so many others who came to Riverside with their wits intact but eventually lost the battle and spent their days staring at walls? Was this what it was like for my mother? Could it be this easy to stop being Brighton and start being a patient? A real patient? To let go of all my hopes?

"Brighton," Grace repeated several more times, shaking my shoulders. "Are you sick?"

I couldn't speak. My mouth was an empty space, and the only words I had left were soundless and littered upon the floor for nurses, carts, and shuffling patients to walk over. I was locked inside myself with the images in the camera box.

"What's wrong with her?" Grace asked whoever had entered the room.

"Brighton?" It was Joann. She came to me, and the cot slumped from her weight. She put her hand on my cool forehead. She whispered to Grace to go.

Grace didn't leave right away. I felt her hand on me for several long moments before she rubbed my leg and then stood up. I heard her feet pad across the floor, and the room felt emptier without her. I hadn't been alone with Joann for weeks. Of course Mother was there, but that was the same as being alone.

In these weeks I'd longed to move a step closer toward Joann. I missed her. But every time I touched my half-inch-long hair, the hurt surfaced, rushing over me like steam rushed out of the hydro room when the door was opened. Then I would let the pain cover me, and I'd dream of the outside world and wake up even further from her.

"Bright, it's me, Nursey." The edges were gone from her voice. So different from the day she'd had my hair cut. It was also no longer the voice that pleaded for my forgiveness. Instead, it was the voice that had grown around me like a vine since my birth. The voice of the person who had always been a mother to me. And she wasn't the eighteen-year-old nurse who had cared for me as a baby anymore. She was a grown-up woman who had set aside her own life for me.

"Where are you?" she asked.

Did I even know? Patients often left their minds and souls lying around while their bodies moved and walked. What far-off places did their minds travel to? I wanted to go there.

I hadn't gone far. My soul was still tucked inside of me. But I was afraid it might fly away at any moment.

Knowing that what I'd seen through that camera box would never matter had changed something within me. The innocent years of growing up alongside Angel with the doting attention of Joann had passed. And now I thought about what Joann's real life was like. Her life outside of this place. With all that she'd given up for me, she'd also kept some things from Angel and me. And then there were all the things she'd done to me.

I began to blame her instead of love her.

I felt as trapped as the images inside the film cartridges.

Joann was not responsible for my being in the hospital, but I saw her as the reason I was still here. My soul hadn't fully captured my reality until Joann had rearranged my whole world with what she'd done.

"Who am I?" My voice had returned.

"Oh, my darling, you're Brighton. The person I love the most." She smoothed her hand over my short hair like she was moving phantom tresses away from my face. My hand gripped the edge of my bed so that I wouldn't push her hand away.

"If you love me so much, then why?" I squeezed my eyes shut.

She cleared her throat, but her hand didn't stop her smoothing caress against my head.

"I was scared. I was so scared of losing you. If you tell anyone what you know and they investigate, we'll be fired. And if we're fired, then Angel will certainly go to the men's ward because there will be no one here to advocate for him. You'd be stuck here without him. You'd be here without *me*. This would be your life."

I turned over like a tornado had rushed over me and my gaze met hers.

"This already is my life." These words flared up like a windstorm of energy. "And you didn't answer my question. Why am I still here? Couldn't there have been another way for me?"

Each syllable held the weight of grief.

"At least we could be together."

"That's not enough." The words were truer than anything I'd ever spoken. I felt a layer of myself peel away like scraped-away skin. What about a future? A real one where I had the chance to be a wife and mother or the sort of woman who lived as vivaciously as I expected Grace had. Or at least have choices. Did I have any hope for that life anymore?

I'd spoken what neither of us wanted to believe. This was my life, yes. But she'd made it sound like it was worth it because she and I could be together. But it wasn't. If I had a choice I'd live anywhere else, even if I'd never see her again. I hadn't known this about myself until now. The kindness and effort given to me from my childhood had anesthetized me to what was real. It had numbed me from the life that was laid out before me. It was as if I was waking from a lifelong coma. I couldn't be enough for Joann, and she couldn't be enough for me.

Joann clenched and unclenched her jaw and diverted her eyes.

"Would you want to live here?" I asked.

"I almost do." She chuckled a little as a tear dripped down her cheek.

I sat up in bed, anger propelling me upright. "No, you don't. You get to go home every day. You get to choose where you live. You get to choose everything you do. You're free." My throat felt full of every patient's voice. "I'm not free. I'm as captured as my snapped photographs. I don't even feel alive."

"There are laws. You're—" Joann paused and stood and turned toward my mother. She sniffed back tears. Or maybe anger. "Legally you're both stuck here until he takes you out."

"My father?" She never brought him up. "Tell me his name."

She shook her head. "It wouldn't matter if I did tell you."

"But he could take me out if you told him about me? My father could come and take me out of here, and I could be his daughter out in the real world? I know how to care for Mother. I could take care of her." This was all I wanted in the whole world of desires. I imagined the moments before Sara Crewe learned her father still lived—would I live in those moments of anticipation for the rest of my life?

She didn't say a word. Instead, she got up and went to my mother, who hadn't had breakfast because I hadn't taken her.

"What was he like? What did he look like? Was he tall?" I sat at the edge of my bed now.

"Brighton, we've been through this." She straightened my mother's gown and held her hands so that she would stop scratching her fuzzy head. "Your mother—your mother was found alone in a condemned apartment. Neighbors heard her fits. Someone finally thought to call the authorities."

This story wasn't familiar.

"So her husband didn't bring her in? Where had he gone?" We looked at one another as if we were both afraid of the answer.

"She had no husband."

"No husband?" I repeated in a whisper. "But I heard you tell Dr. Woburn about him."

My mother had conceived me without having a husband. What sort of woman did that make her? I'd heard the ladies on the ward speak dark, black words of women with loose morals. Had my mom been one of those types?

"Brighton, breathe." Joann came to my side and pushed my head down toward my knees.

I slapped her away. I hadn't even realized I was gasping for air. That night on the balcony they'd called him a convict; they had known something about him.

"But that night on the balcony," I reminded her again, angry now.

"Fine, Brighton. Yes, your father is a convict and was in jail when he should've been taking care of your mother. He could have at least married her and made her an honest woman." The air was peppered with her bitterness. "Is that what you want to know?"

But the practical truth was that I had lost my freedom the moment I was conceived. My mother had been loose and volatile. My father was a criminal. None of that mattered because I was trapped here either way. There was no one to come to my rescue.

But then the thread of an old tune caught my attention. It was one Mother used to hum when I was a child, but hadn't now for many years. My mother, who was sitting on her bed with chasm-deep eyes, was humming. Her voice was more gravelly than in years past, but it was the same tune.

I closed my eyes, and my breaths began to slow and lengthen. In a few minutes I stood and walked over to my mother. I sat next to her and put my head in her lap. Her humming remained calm and strangely steady. A few minutes passed, and then she did something she hadn't done in a long time. She rested her hands on my body, and we were warm together.

Her wordless tune and my life had no voice—we weren't as different as I'd always thought we were.

1940

Where I Come From

I threaded the new film through the camera. We'd been without film for many months. But finally I convinced Joann to give us one more. The other six canisters were neatly tucked into a slit in my mattress. Grace and I made a pact that as soon as one of us was released or we escaped we would develop them and take them to a newspaper.

I imagined a day of escape. When and how we would get away, I wasn't sure.

Though I feared I would never see the photographs, I still imagined the final products. Would Angel's face be entirely washed out because of his paleness, or would you see that he had high cheekbones and a strong jawline? Would it show that he had full lips and not straight lines like Dr. Woburn, his uncle? Would my photos show the clarity of every curl that Grace had as her hair grew back, or would it simply look like a dark mass?

To have the answers to these questions would mean I was free.

A lot had changed since Grace had arrived nearly a year ago. Patients were being added to our ward almost daily, and every room was crowded now. More patients always meant more sickness, and Mother was not doing well. Any illness that came through the ward, she got. She'd had pneumonia several times. She'd gotten shingles. Some type of stomach influenza stuck with her longer than anyone else. She often needed cleaning up and a tender touch. She needed me.

She was like a chain linking me to Riverside, giving me pause whenever I considered a plan of escape. Of course, it was possible that Grace's parents would come for her before we could run away. They were visiting soon. My insides twisted into knots at the possibility. How I wrestled with the sweetness and bitterness of that.

Those thoughts plagued me as I walked my tiny, skin-and-bone mother to another meal. She scooted slowly down the hall, and when she was served her food, she would barely eat. But somehow she was still stronger than seemed possible. It took both Joann and me together to handle her when she became especially agitated.

I tried to take photographs of her when she was still and her version of happy. Those images would be just for me. Of course, she wouldn't pose for me, so often half of her was washed out by the sun's rays from the window in our room, leaving her in the gray. I prayed to Rosina's God that someday these images would come to light. Maybe Grace could sneak them out and take them home. Maybe someday someone would know about our lives here and tell others. Maybe then it wouldn't happen to more people.

A few days later I found myself on the hall floor outside of the stairwell. Grace was on the first floor meeting with her parents. It was all she'd spoken about for weeks. Her father had come to see her six months after she was admitted, and all of our hopes had been dashed when he had walked out unfettered. Grace had pleaded with him to let her go home. She'd even told him about me and how we were treated. But he had been unmoved. Her father did promise he would return in a few months with her mother. Grace was sure the second visit would work.

She wrote to them every week but hadn't received anything except a Christmas card from her younger sister, Hannah, whom she spoke of often. Hannah was my age and had true-blue Scottish red hair. Grace said it was redder than any hair I'd probably ever seen. Grace said Hannah was the only person who loved her.

"But I love you," I told her that day as she gently slid the Christmas card under her pillow. She lay her head down, and I noticed how thin her jaw and neck were. When had she gotten so small? It was like pieces of her had slowly gone missing.

But maybe today would be different. I hated myself for not wanting her to leave. What would I do without her? I still had Angel, but things were different between us. Angel had grown tall and handsome and strong, and he'd begun to watch over me like I'd always done with him. Asking me if I was okay, if I needed more food, if I needed another blanket. What I really needed was a way out.

I heard yelling. It was Grace's voice. There was crying, and the deep voice of a man I didn't recognize was bookended with one I did: Dr. Woburn. They were in the stairwell. I stood and put my ear to the door.

"Please, Gracie," a woman's voice said thickly, layered with emotion. "Your father only wants you to agree."

"I won't," Grace yelled.

"Grace," a calm Dr. Woburn said, "please, come back downstairs. We can talk about this."

I peeked through the long, narrow window on the door. Grace's eyes were as wild as her hair. Her mother was perfect and beautiful. Her eyes and wide, full mouth matched Grace's, but that was the only resemblance. Grace's olive skin and curly hair were so different from her mother's straight black hair and porcelain skin. Her father stood stiffly in a suit. His red and pointy mustache and wavy red hair gave him a fiery appearance that matched the anger in his eyes. His fists were clenched.

"I won't have you disgrace our family with your behavior with that boy and your insistence on what you think you know." He pointed at Grace like his finger could poke a hole through her.

"But I love him and he loves me," Grace yelled. "I don't want to hide who I am anymore."

"Gracie, please, listen to your father," her mother cried. "We just want you home. You'd give up your life for him?"

"I'm not giving up my life for him. I'm trying to live my life being the person God made me, and I can't keep pretending."

Her father scoffed. "Look at you. Your hair is untamed and unkempt. You don't even look like my daughter anymore." Then he turned to his wife. "She's gone completely mad."

"Father, if anyone could understand why I fell in love with a Negro, you could."

Grace had told me that the world of people beyond our doors was as separate as water and dry land. Everyone was segregated by color.

Of course Negroes were treated differently here in the hospital, but the reasons why had never been explained to me. When possible, Negro patients were kept separated from the white patients. They were the last to receive their medicines, food, and treatments. I'd seen this my whole life. The only explanation I ever got from Joann was that the administration preferred the groups to be separated.

"Grace Douglass," Grace's mother scolded. "You will be silent."

The polished older woman's tears were replaced with a stern expression.

"And what will you do to me if I don't *stay silent*, Mother?" Grace yelled back, her wet face shining in the electric lights. "What will you do?"

"Do not speak to your mother like that." Mr. Douglass again pointed a long, refined finger.

"There's nothing more you can do to me." Grace's voice deflated and her arms flopped to her sides. She stood and wept, and when neither parent comforted her, Dr. Woburn pushed past Mr. Douglass and went to her.

"Let's find Nurse Derry and get you calmed down." His sincerity gave me a small measure of affection for him.

"Dr. Woburn," Grace cried into his chest, and his arms slowly went around her shoulders. "I don't want to feel this way anymore."

"That's why you're here, Grace," he said. "We can help you."

She shook her head and pulled away. Slowly she wiped her face with the short sleeves of her hospital gown and shook her head again. "No, you can't help me. You can't make me all white, Dr. Woburn. If you could, then maybe Mother would stay and you could *fix* her too." Her mother gasped, and her father yelled for her to stop. "She doesn't look it, does she? But I do. Don't I? You can see it, can't you?"

She looked up into Dr. Woburn's eyes, and he gently touched her curls. I'd never seen him so gentle.

"I fell in love with a Negro boy, and my parents hate me for it."

Dr. Woburn released a long-buried sigh.

"I think we're done here, Doctor. Grace will remain. She's talking madness." Mr. Douglass's voice shook when he spoke. Then he looked at Grace, like every word was gripped in the vise of his jaws. "I'm sorry for you, Grace. But your outbursts and choice of suitor will ruin us. Completely ruin us. I will not have it. You're acting as mad as your grandmother."

"My *Negro* grandmother?" she yelled at him. "You're race prejudiced, Father, and that means you're against Mother and me. Your wife and your daughter."

Mr. Douglass cleared his throat. He was like a filled syringe waiting to be plunged. He didn't linger and didn't look at Grace again but turned to his wife and with a snap of his head gestured for her to come.

Mrs. Douglass's eyes dripped with longing. She loved her daughter—I could see it. She reached for her from the several steps below Grace.

"Goodbye, Grace," Mrs. Douglass said, then spoke something so quietly I didn't catch it. She carefully walked backward a few steps but kept her eyes trained on her daughter. Then, when she got to the landing, she turned and walked away. She didn't look back.

"My father brought me here before Jonah and I could run away," I heard Grace's muffled voice tell Dr. Woburn. "Everything would be different if he and I had run away a week earlier."

When I looked at Dr. Woburn, I saw, for the first time, the

resemblance between him and Angel. The worry that teased between his brows and caring eyes.

"I don't know what to say." His typical deep and direct voice was lush and velvety.

Then Grace turned and saw me through the window. She looked aged and raw. "At least I have Brighton."

She and I looked at each other. The circumstances that had brought us to the hospital were different, but why we were kept here was the same. We weren't mad or feeble-minded. We didn't belong here. But no one would listen. No one wanted us. No one claimed us. There was nowhere else for us to belong. Any hope of Grace getting out and then her being able to help Angel and me had faded to nothing.

Find the Light

at got your tongue?" Lorna's voice parrots. "Cat got your tongue?" She won't stop. She echoes herself incessantly from down the hall, so I go to find her. She's in the dayroom. It's been so long since I've seen her, and the familiar ache in my soul journeys to my heart, mind, and hand. I wave at her. She waves back and then says it again. "Cat got your tongue?"

"Lorna?" I say. My body feels old, my back is aching, but my laugh and voice are young. I turn to see my reflection in the window, and I'm sixteen-year-old Brighton again. It's been so long since I've seen me too. Lorna suddenly stops repeating her refrain, and I turn back to see that the dayroom has changed into a graveyard. And on the other side of it I see that bright, white light that I wish I could get to but can't. The buzz of an electroconvulsive machine makes me sit up in bed. I'm a mass of sweat and I'm Nell again. And old. My face is wet from sleepy tears, and my heart tries to race and beat itself.

"Calm down, kid," I say aloud. "Doc isn't home to call 911, so you can't have a heart attack."

I stopped feeling silly about talking to myself decades ago. It started when my kids went to school and I was alone in the house again. My kids had been good company, and I made sure they never knew how much I needed their chattering and giggles. The house was so quiet then that it drove me to get a college education to become a teacher.

I never wanted to be like Joann and keep my children hostage from their own lives to make my life better. I wanted to be a good mom and let them grow and have their own unique lives. And they did. They come home for visits, but they live far enough away that it isn't as often as I'd like. They bring home with them those little souls called grandchildren too. It's like all the good in the world was pulled together to make them. Being a grandparent strips away one more layer of pain in my life because I don't want all that burden around them. But I miss them and wish I could see them more.

The only time I was alone when my kids were little was when I was in the bathroom—and sometimes not even then—and I would often think of Mother. She and I were rarely apart. It was hard for me to mother any other way.

Speaking of bathrooms—I have to go. My old bladder is about as small and thin as a tea bag.

Once I'm done I can see that I left the kitchen light on. I hesitate because I know that's where I left those new, old photographs. I can't blame the dreams on them, though. I've had those ever since I left all those gray walls and souls.

I walk into the kitchen and stare at the photos scattered over the kitchen table.

Joann washing Mother on the bed.

Angel in front of Willow Knob.

The hydrotherapy room with women in tubs. Who knows how long they'd been in there.

A few photos are duds—my finger covering up the subject in the shot or poor lighting.

But when I see these faces and the pain in their eyes, or the nothing in their eyes—the swirl and cramp in my stomach won't let me look away.

There is Lorna. The day she'd been put into a camisole and sat on the hall bench all day looking at the floor. A dribble of saliva on her lips had dripped on her lap, creating a wet circle. My young self would've seen this image casted in dark and light and wanted to tell the world of the sadness and mistreatment. But my old self knows if I did that, I would not just be sharing a picture; I'd be putting pieces of myself on display.

And Rosina. Her hand extended out from the solitary room. I knew she was praying behind the door.

Dear Carmen. Cuffed in restraints on her bed. She'd had an outburst that no one wanted to deal with. The restraints remained for several days.

So many women naked in the dayroom. They soiled themselves too often for clothing.

Grace. Looking over her shoulder. Full of life.

Oh Grace.

There she is—my surrogate sister—but where is the grace in these captured moments? And where is the grace for me, watching all of this happen and incapable of changing the outcome? And now they are gone. They'd been held captive in their lives and now again in the film cartridges.

I can still hear them speak in my head. Not just Lorna. All the antics and the praying and the asking for food. And the screaming. The yelling through the solitary-room door. The moaning at night. The shrieks that came when someone was dragged down the hall for electroconvulsive therapy. And, almost worse, the silence when they returned.

Before I know it my arms run against the table and all the photographs go flying. They lie like dead leaves on my laminate floor. But many of them are faceup, and the faces continue to stare at me. Especially Joann's.

To reconcile the good and the bad that is folded up into one person is hard. Who had she been anyway? My nurse? Or a liar and deceiver? Or was she really the one who loved me most like she always told me? Had she been my real mother and Helen my captor?

I move to the floor near the pictures and assume a sitting position

I haven't used since those years long ago when my body could bend and turn better. I grunt a little as I settle. I pick up the pictures one at a time. I have to crawl on all fours to gather several. The stack in my hand is heavy and the voices are loud. Almost all of them lie in that old graveyard in that back quarter of those thousand acres. They'd never be known all the way out there, and someday it'll be forgotten that there was a graveyard there at all. The stones will become dust and the weeds their markers.

1941

Every Key Has a Lock

I pointed the viewfinder at Joann as she handed out medications. Each patient took their small cup of water with the
dissolved powdered medicines in one quick swallow. Joann had never
made me take anything for what was supposed to help depression
or melancholia, but Grace had had to ever since her meeting with
her parents the previous year. That awful row in the stairwell. After
that she was no longer the easygoing, companionable patient. She'd
begun to yell and even hit the staff, especially upon threat of sterilization. Her refusal to eat enough to stay healthy worried me. She was
told her parents were considering sending her to a doctor who did a
special brain surgery that could cure her. It was called a lobotomy,
but I knew almost nothing about it.

Grace had made a poor and unplanned attempt to rush past an
aide who was escorting her near the first-floor door. She'd done this
knowing that if she was successful she'd be leaving me in this prison.
I knew this was evidence that I was losing Grace. She was losing the
battle of her mind. Because of her attempt, now her every action was
scrutinized even more and the possibility of sterilization and brain
surgery was real.

More than half on our ward had been sterilized—my mother had
years ago. Grace and I had not been. Joann told us that Dr. Woburn
made sure I was not on the list for sterilization. But Grace was a more
difficult patient because she had parents who would demand that she
follow a more traditional plan of treatment.

I continued to watch Joann through the camera. We hadn't had film for a few months and Joann refused to buy more. My antics and blackmail opportunities were long wasted. The staff knew I had no film, but I kept watching the life around me through the camera lens. There was a sense of separation it gave me in order to survive.

Joann smiled at me. Things had improved between us. But the life I'd had before Grace was a distant dream. Those years before my hair was shorn and before Joann had broken my trust were not my life anymore.

I tightened the camera's focus on Joann. She had sweat marks beneath her arms and her hands shook as she handed out each little cup. At thirty-six, the aging process had raced ahead in the last few years, but she and Dr. Woburn were still sweet on each other. The doctor had become kinder with age and more present, but Joann was slipping away into somewhere I couldn't reach. An ashen mood and exterior replaced the grit, self-assurance, and beauty she used to have.

The barred windows were behind me and the day was bright. There was enough light not just to see well but to capture the scene. I clicked the shutter. If I had film, would this photograph have shown how the deep creases on her forehead had formed a permanent grimace—much like the old scar of Dr. Woburn's?

Grace walked into the dayroom. She didn't even look over to where I sat on the couch. The shuffle of her feet along the floor was just like the other patients. When had she become a patient instead of Grace?

Grace had been in solitary for three days, and her time in isolation was happening frequently now. In her two years here, she'd become only bones wrapped in skin that was now more ashen than olive. When she got to the head of the medicine line, she put her hand out for the cup from Joann.

I lifted the camera and snapped the pretend photo. I documented this moment in my mind. Perhaps it was the submissiveness that rested alongside such sadness that I was drawn to, proving how there were snatches of time when she'd been broken into obedience. Though she would fight against it other times.

After the first click I kept the camera up to my eye. I watched closely as Grace took her medicine cup and dumped its contents on the tray in front of her. I snapped again. Oh, how I longed to have these moments captured.

Joann looked over at me, and I pulled the camera from my eye. What was Joann asking of me in her gaze? Did she think I could bend Grace back into compliance? While we were as close as sisters could be, she had become angry and distant even with me. She'd ruined an entire cartridge of film because of her temper, intentionally opening the camera box and exposing everything inside. She slammed doors shut. Slammed Joann against walls. She cried a lot.

I let the camera hang on my neck and stood from the putrid couch and went to my friend.

"Can we go for a walk? It'll make her feel better." Of course, nothing but release would make her feel better.

"Brighton," Joann started. "You know the rules. You're not children anymore."

"Send Angel with us," I said. "He's practically an aide now. Besides, where would we even run to? We'll just go to the garden. We could pull some weeds."

This was my best argument because garden work would be starting as soon as it warmed up a bit.

Joann handed out a few more medicine cups before she looked back at me. "All right," she finally said. "But if she gets in trouble, you'll be responsible. I'll ring for Angel to meet you outside."

Once outside, we were shivering, but breathing outside air and sitting in the sun, filled the empty in my corners and spaces. As we sat near the garden, I saw Angel coming toward us. I hadn't seen him in a week. I ran to him and hugged him. His hold on me lingered longer than normal, and I sank into his chest and he buried his face between my neck and shoulder. We sat close together and I felt warmer. Grace just gazed into the distance.

In awkward silence, Angel opened up his coat—with Mason's name on the chest—and pulled out a brown paper package. He unfolded it and handed each of us a bread roll. They were golden brown, and while they weren't very soft, they were better than anything we'd eaten in months. With overcrowding, shortages were at their worst, and I couldn't remember the last time my stomach had been full.

"They're old, but Joyful gave them to me—she baked them for the staff a week ago. She's taking the rest home to her children."

Angel and I ate quickly, but Grace only nibbled. I let the dry, buttery texture linger on my tongue before chewing it. I thought about Joyful taking leftovers home to her family, and I couldn't help but imagine how her children would run to her and tell her how much they missed her. She would hug them and smile at them and give them each a bread roll.

"Brighton." Angel's voice was soft and warm near my ear. "Where are you?"

I smiled and shrugged. I'd been far away for a moment but fought the urge to stay there, fearful that one day I would remain in that distant world.

When I had eaten half of my roll, Grace stood and looked far off, away from the buildings, past the gardens and orchard and everything contained in our world.

"I'm leaving," Grace said and took off. Her bare feet couldn't have felt good against the dried, yellowed grass; but despite her weakness, she ran fast.

Without a word between us, Angel and I stood and chased after her. We wove in and out of the gravestones in the graveyard before we reached the furrows of an ancient garden and then flung ourselves through the trees. We'd never been this far before. I stopped and looked ahead. Angel was only a step behind me, and he too stopped and stood at my side. Grace continued to run through the tall, dead grass, then the trees that grew thicker with weeds and brush and bushes—tangled, unkempt, and dark. This was part of the thousand acres of land that was my whole world, and yet I'd never seen it. I'd never been with Grace when she attempted an escape—if they could be called that. She'd only made it past a few aides and into the stairwell. The audacity of this moment was frightening and thrilling—but it was impossible.

Grace slowed as she pushed her way through the underbrush— and then I couldn't see her anymore. I held my breath and grabbed Angel's arm, pulling him. What if we couldn't find her? What if she actually escaped?

What if that meant that I could too?

But what about my mother? Would she feel my abandonment?

My speed picked up despite the bushes cutting my legs. Angel grunted behind me. None of us were wearing shoes. Grace was in sight again, ahead of me, fighting with thistles that gripped at her hospital gown. She used words Joann had outlawed from my mouth when I tried them out when I was eight.

"I need to get out," she yelled between deep breaths as she pulled her gown free, tearing it. She pushed farther through the thickness and started banging her hands against a metal fence that had appeared almost like a weed. It was tall and impossible to overcome and covered in overgrown weeds and vines. "I need to get out." Her anguish wilted the leaves around her.

She turned to us, her face streaked with tears. With gasping breaths she leaned against the fence. "We need to escape." Her shaky voice was quiet and serious now.

Angel and I looked at each other. In all our years at Riverside we'd never even seen this fence. Was it possible to get through?

Grace hadn't heard from her family since that terrible day in the stairwell. She'd never been the same. But now there was a fire in her eyes, and even though her body sagged like our dingy gowns, there was a renewal in her. She leaned forward and reached for our hands. Angel and I took hers, making a circle.

"Let's escape, please. I can't go on like this. This place is killing me." She looked back and forth between Angel and me. Her arms and legs were scratched and smeared with blood. Her grip was so tight I wouldn't have been able to pull free if I'd wanted to. I knew after thinking about it for too long what we needed to do.

"Let's escape." My voice floated dangerously around in the woods and cut the trees down right in front of me. I put my gaze on Angel to tether me.

"I'm not sure," Angel said.

"We can climb it," Grace suggested.

"There's razor wire on top," he protested.

"Find wire clippers in that shed," Grace threw back.

The back and forth of their words made me dizzy. Then they both looked at me for answers. As if I had them.

"Where would we go?" Angel finally said to Grace. "Besides, I have a job. Responsibilities."

"A job?" Grace spat out. "A job?" Then she got mad. "You're a patient who wears a different uniform, Angel. Do you get paid?"

Angel hesitated, then shook his head no.

"It's not a job. It's slave labor," she yelled.

Angel pulled his hand from hers, and Grace's and mine dropped.

"Where would we go?" Angel asked again, this time more sober. "We don't know anyone out there, unless you think your family is going to take all of us in."

Grace laughed an awful maniacal laugh while she shook her head. "I have friends. They're a little ways away, but it wouldn't be more than a day's walk."

"A day's walk?" Angel repeated, and it was his turn to laugh at her.

"You think that's worse than staying here? Maybe you do belong here, because you're crazy if you think that walking a day would be worse than living out your life here in this loony bin." Her words came out harsh and littered with curse words.

Angel pulled his stare from her, let it land on me for weighty moments, then turned to leave. "I just don't see how it's possible."

Grace yelled so loudly the trees swayed against her force. I turned to look at her. She grabbed a thornbush and yanked at it until her palms were ripped and bleeding.

"Why, why, why is this my life? I can't live like this anymore." The rawness in her throat could be heard in every syllable.

I took a few steps toward Angel. I would never let him get too far away from me. I took his hand. "Wait."

"We need more information before we can escape," I said.

I saw my oldest and dearest friend in denial about his life and my stand-in sister falling apart into a pile of ashes where once a fire had been thriving and growing. And what about me? My mother surely wouldn't want me to live out the rest of my life in this place. Maybe, if I could get out, I could find someone who could help Mother. I knew how to care for her. Maybe I could get a house, find a place for her with me. I would be her next of kin and could take her away from here.

"Information?" Grace asked, breathing heavily.

"We need to get our files." I looked between the eyes of one hopeful friend and one suspicious one. "Angel and I have family out there somewhere and our history is in there. We deserve to know more about ourselves before we run."

"Maybe I could find Jonah."

"I could find my mother."

I didn't know who I had out there, but maybe my files would reveal something. Maybe then we could break through the fence and start a new life.

"They're in there." A windstorm of voices and strong arms of several aides broke our plans and thoughts.

They didn't hurt us on purpose, but expecting a fight they still handled us roughly. Angel pulled his arm away and explained he was needed in the groundskeeping shed. The aides didn't know how to respond, knowing his duties, so they let him go. Grace and I let them take us back because we knew what our next step was now. Finally we knew.

Grace and I were immediately put in solitary. We were across from each other, but Grace didn't stay up and talk with me this time. She retreated to some cavern of the room and left me alone. I slept for much of the time and dreamt of a dad I'd never met. In my wakefulness I prayed to a God I was sure was out there somewhere to help me find something in my files.

The night of the second day my door was opened quietly. I sat up, surprised. Nurses and aides left solitary patients alone at night unless there was a problem, but it wasn't an aide. It was Angel.

He smiled and held up a ring of keys.

1941

Pandora's Call

At first Grace fought us in her disillusionment. It was like she didn't know who we were. But when her eyes sharpened, she stopped her struggling. We had her out a few moments later. With both the solitary doors shut it appeared we were inside and quiet. We tiptoed down the hall toward the back stairwell door. Angel had already made sure the hall was empty. The one benefit of understaffing—no one was around.

We continued to scan the dimly lit hall. We saw no one, and all we could hear were several snoring patients and Carmen's moaning. Her stomach had been hurting for days and she wasn't eating. But Joann didn't know when Dr. Woburn would get to her. There were so many patients, and it could take days.

Angel produced another key and opened the records' office door. We slipped inside and the door clicked behind us. Angel led us between shelves filled with files. We sat together, and Grace began twisting her hands like they were wet cloths being wrung out.

"I came in earlier and found our files. They were alphabetical, so it was easy." Angel was the picture of confidence. His brow unwrinkled and mouth turned up in a smile, his pure white skin a beautiful reminder of the purity I'd always seen in him. He pulled four folders out from the bottom shelf and brought them close to his eyes, reading the name in the corner, then handed us each our files and an extra one for me—Mother's.

I sat for well over a minute looking at the file folder with my name on it. I was afraid. Nervous. Uncertain. Angel and Grace didn't seem to have any hesitations.

"Let's take turns," Grace suggested. "Angel, you go first since you already started."

"Look at this," Angel said and took out a photograph from his file, and as he pulled it close to his face, he leaned toward the small cascade of light. I looked with him. It was of a toddler of maybe three who was purely white. "It's me, right?"

I just nodded, my throat choked to the brim with hope and fear.

His voice was nostalgic and almost wistful. Like he was mining the memory of the photograph. I looked closer and saw a young boy of white sitting—no—nestled in the lap of a beautiful, youthful blond woman.

"I bet that's my mother. Cynthia, right?"

I nodded again. That night two years earlier, when I heard so much on that balcony, now seemed like an eternity ago.

"There's not much here." Still leaning toward the light and squinting, he finally handed me an official-looking document.

"Your mother's name is Cynthia. But her last name and your father's name are blacked out of this paper. See? Looks like your first name was marked over too, except I can see an *L*. Your name starts with an *L*."

He grabbed the document from my hands and desperately tried to see it for himself. He held it up to the light, but after a few moments he sighed and carefully folded it and put it down. He riffled through a few pages of medical records—his checkups and documentation of his poor eyesight. But there wasn't anything else. His smile faltered like a passing breeze, and his gaze returned to the photograph before he put it into his chest pocket.

"It was worth a shot." He sighed and looked over at Grace. "Your turn."

Grace bit her lower lip and slowly opened up her folder. Numerous letters fell out, and Grace pored over them first. Her hospital records fell out of the file toward me. The files listed every outburst, escape attempt, refusal to eat or be medicated, confinement, and more. The words *anorexia nervosa* were listed. I knew this diagnosis well.

"Anything on there about sterilization? I've been threatened, you know." She said the words without emotion as she looked through the letters.

"Yes," I admitted. "It's mentioned that you've been evaluated for it as a possibility."

"More than a dozen here." Grace's whisper rose in pitch as she splayed the letters in her hands. I wasn't sure she'd even heard me.

"From your parents?" I asked.

She shook her head, and a tear dripped down from her face to the papers.

"Mostly my sister. And one from my father. They're all open."

Her hands shook as she carefully pulled out a letter. Her father's name was on the return address. Her eyes scanned the lines, and after a minute she folded it back up. Her face remained blank as she spoke.

"He said that if they deliver any letters to me from my sister or Jonah, he will pull his generous monthly funding." She pinched her lips together. "There are nearly a dozen from my sister. Only one from Jonah."

She looked at the postmark dates and put them in order.

"Go ahead," Angel said to me. "It's your turn to find out who you are."

"Angel, I know who I am." A surge of defensiveness rushed through me. Maybe it was because I was afraid I would learn that there was nothing to know.

Angel tilted his head toward me. "This is what we've been wanting to do ever since Nursey gave you that photograph of your mother on your fourteenth birthday, Bright. Only we never had the guts to do it. And we trusted Joann too much. Go ahead. See what's inside."

I slowly inhaled and opened Mother's folder first. It was thinner than I expected and there was nothing inside except medical findings. No correspondence. No photographs. No old documents with maybe the name of my father on them. There was nothing.

I held my breath as I pushed it aside and opened my own. Several photos slid out. One was of my mother and an older man who appeared to be her father. My grandpa. I analyzed him head to toe, and nothing about him seemed familiar. The next photograph was also of my mother, a little older this time, though with a young man at her side. He had to be my father. He was handsome and had a mustache. He had dark hair. His skin looked smooth, and his eyes were sharp. Like he knew something. They were handsome together, and I guessed Mother to be about my age.

The rest of the photos were ones Joann must have taken of me. One of me getting a bath in a washbasin. One of my mother holding me. I couldn't have been more than a few months old, and my mother was nursing me. She was looking at me. I couldn't see her face; it was curtained by her hair. But the baby—me—in the photo was looking up with a hand raised to my mother's face. So I knew there had been a time when our souls had connected.

I flipped through the annual birthday photos, and when I found the one of Angel and me together I took it, along with the baby photo. No one would ever know.

"Jonah still loves me," Grace whispered. "But he went west to San Francisco to build ships for some war in Europe."

Her voice faded as her eyes continued to scan the letter in her hands. "He wanted a fresh start." She finally released a sigh, then went back to reading her other letters.

I returned to my file and pulled out the medical section. It was small, but I wanted to comb through everything possible while I had the chance. It was Joann's writing, so small it was difficult to read. I glanced through most of it. Nothing more than weights and heights and occasional fevers. Not much of any importance.

"Wait," Angel whispered, putting his hand over mine and Grace's. "I heard something."

I held my breath. Footsteps came down the stairwell at the end of the hall. Angel's hand tightened on mine and our gazes held fast. We were tucked away enough that if someone looked in the office window, they would not see us. A minute later we saw the shadow of an aide dragging a patient toward the therapy room. I couldn't tell who it was.

We waited and listened. We didn't breathe. We heard a few doors open and close and the heavy door to electroconvulsive therapy click shut. Why it was important to administer shock therapy this late at night instead of during their normal day hours, I did not know. But our first concern right now was to get back to our rooms undetected.

"We should go," Angel said and closed his file and carefully put it away. He reached for mine next.

I hesitated.

"I'm not putting mine back," Grace said a little too loudly. Her cut and bandaged hands held her file to her chest.

"Take the letters out of their envelopes and return everything else to the file. We don't need anyone getting suspicious," Angel said. We all knew the nurses were in and out of her file often these days.

She stuffed the folded letters into the back of her underwear.

"If we're caught, we're dead." She eyed us both. "Come on, Bright."

I was still holding my file. I flipped through it and pulled out a sealed yellow envelope before I handed the rest to Angel. I too stuffed the envelope and a few photos I'd grabbed in the back of my underwear.

Angel quickly escorted us with his ring of stolen keys back to solitary. He let Grace back into her room first and then, before closing me inside mine, he held me close.

"We're doing this, right?" he asked.

"Yes. We need to make a plan. Maybe steal those keys again. Maybe find a way through that fence in the back." I shook my head because I really didn't know.

"We'll figure it out."

After Angel left me I got into the dingy cot and pulled out the yellow envelope. It was sealed and blank on the front. I looked over at the high window. The golden moon shone through the bars, and for a brief moment I reveled in its beauty. It didn't matter that I was looking at it through a cracked and ugly window—it didn't keep the moonlight from glowing or keep it from being lovely.

I ran my hands over the envelope. Was this a Pandora's box? If opened would it bring chaos to my world—more than I already had? Pandora had never been able to close it again, and because of that her life was never the same.

Till Death Do Us Part

I didn't open the envelope that night. There wasn't enough light to see what was inside anyway. But even when the sunlight poured into the room the next morning, I still didn't open it. And when Grace and I were both released before breakfast I kept the envelope closely tucked into my thin, worn-out underwear.

We were ushered to the breakfast table, and I watched as Grace tried not to walk stilted because of the letters she'd stuck in her underwear. We sat at the table with Lorna and Rosina and a few ladies I wasn't familiar with. Carmen was in her room, still wailing over her stomach. And Angel was suddenly a few tables over, holding trays of plates to be served by the kitchen staff. It wasn't uncommon for us to see him a few times a week. He peeked over and smiled. I smiled back, and Grace hit my thigh under the table.

"I stole a candle and match from the office last night," she whispered.

"What? I didn't even notice."

"That was not the first time I've stolen something." She winked at me. It was a comfort to see her more like herself this morning. Like the Grace I'd known for the last two years.

"And?"

Her eyes became small pools, and her smile began to shake from emotion. "I used it to read some letters last night. My sister." She sipped the coffee in front of her before making a face. "She is trying to get me out."

Out.

The small word rattled around in my mind like a wild patient in the solitary room. I squeezed my eyes shut for a moment. Would we go from talking about escaping and stealing files to complaining about our rheumatism and growing soft in our middles? If that was the case, my mother would probably be long dead. What if Grace got out and I was left here? Would she even be able to find a way to get me out? And what about Angel? But she'd been here long enough now that being released became less and less expected.

"Is your sister changing your dad's mind?"

"No." She paused and groaned when the bowl of porridge was placed in front of her. "She's trying to trick him into signing papers that he doesn't realize will release me."

Hearing that was a letdown. Tricking and playing games? That was how Hannah thought she could get Grace out? I had only seen her father for a few minutes and knew he wasn't a man who was easily manipulated.

I let her talk until she had no more words. And then I saw Joann down the hall through the open dining room doors.

"We need to talk about—you know." Grace leaned toward me.

Grace talked about hitchhiking, how to earn money on the road by washing dishes, and how we could save enough money to take the train west to California. She went on and on about how we could go to the beach out there and work in the factories that were popping up that her sister wrote her about—something about a war—and how we'd eat steak and drink real coffee every day and on the weekends we'd eat cheesecake and drink lemonade.

There was so much of what she said that made little sense, but what did make sense was that I was losing Grace. Her hold on reality was wrinkling up like an old newspaper that couldn't be ironed out again.

"Lorna"—Grace's eyes were crazed—"did you ever try to escape this hellhole?"

Lorna was in a mood this morning. Quiet and brooding. Her words were few and not entirely in clichés. She whispered under her breath and looked around like she was afraid or suspicious. Oh Lorna. She'd had spells like this for as long as I could remember, but the good stretches had been so good. She looked at Grace and tilted her head, her effort to understand visible all over her face. Her thin, wispy lips came together.

"Dance with the devil." Her whisper back came from both parts of her mind, I was certain. The tilted and the lucid one. "Dance with the devil."

She repeated her phrase and looked around like she was looking for this very devil.

"Don't think about it." Rosina looked up from her bowl of picked-at porridge. But she wasn't looking at Grace; she was looking at me. "There are many ways in, but without someone from the outside, there's only one way out."

I knew she was right.

"Maybe we have to dance with the devil to get out. We're already in hell. He should be easy to find." My words braver than my heart.

Later that day there was a great thunderstorm after lunch. Everything on the property had lost power and we would not be served dinner. The main problem was that the lack of lights made patients difficult to control. It was so dark, I could barely see my hand in front of my face.

Hours into the blackness the emergency lights from the generators finally bloomed. They were dim, and only a smattering of soft light was thrown into the halls. Before Joann had left I had stolen her flashlight when she set it down briefly. It made the rest of her shift incredibly difficult but I didn't care. I wanted the light. I touched my back where the yellow envelope protruded out of my underwear.

Patients were slowly but surely directed or escorted to their rooms. I made sure to help Mother. When I tucked her in, the sharpness of her shoulders pressed against my hands like daggers. She was so thin I was surprised she could still hold herself up in any way. The electro-convulsive therapy had made her sleep deeper, and she seemed to be further away than normal. She didn't even moan much during the night anymore, and there was part of me that actually missed the sound.

I was standing over Mother when a shrill sound from down the hall made me jump. Mother gasped and awoke with wide eyes. It was Carmen. No doctor had made it out to her today as promised.

The shrieking didn't stop. Nurse Wilma yelled from another part of the hall that she was coming. She had her hands full as the only nurse on the ward that night.

I poked my head into the hall, then walked out. My eyes had fully adjusted to the dim lighting, and I could see I wasn't the only one in the hallway. I went across the hall and peeked inside Carmen's room.

Wilma rushed over from another hall, her breathing rapid. When she passed me she left behind a layer of her sweat on my arm.

"She's dying, she's dying," Rosina said as the frantic nurse entered, then she returned to kneel at her sister's bed. She crossed herself. "Jesus, Mary, and Joseph. *Dios te salve, Maria.*" She began to recite what I knew she called the "Hail Mary" prayer. I understood the first few words, but the further she went on in Spanish, the more I lost their meaning. I didn't, however, miss the comfort in her words. Her desperate pleas needed no translation. I became a companion in her prayer.

I hadn't often prayed, but deep within myself I knew exactly what she said. Pleading and begging were a well-understood language. I'd done plenty of that myself, so perhaps I'd prayed more than I realized. Maybe even my first squalling cry as a baby was a type of prayer. Were my words still considered prayers when I wasn't sure anyone was listening? Maybe Rosina's God heard me too.

Rosina's weeping words whispered throughout the darkness. Wilma checked Carmen's vitals, and the dampness in the room crept around me like a second skin. The emergency lights shuddered at a crack of thunder, and another onslaught of rain began pelting the roof. My skin felt clammy, and my toes curled on the cool, moist floor. The layer of stickiness made my stomach churn.

Wilma got a syringe of insulin ready to calm Carmen, and when she tapped the air bubbles, her narrowed eyes almost crossed. As a child, I used to laugh when she did this.

"Wilma, is she going to die?" In the dense air of the room a whisper sounded like a yell and every breath like a gasp for life.

"Go to bed, Brighton," she snarled. "It's probably gas."

"No, no, no." Carmen groaned louder than Rosina's strung-together holy words.

Wilma threatened me again, holding up the insulin syringe as if she'd use it on me. I retreated and returned to my room. Many of the patients had become agitated at the disruption, and the noise all around the hall sounded like the buzzing of bees. Those of us who were well enough were forced to help restrain the difficult ones while Nurse Wilma gave Carmen her attention.

The insulin didn't help Carmen quickly; she didn't settle for a few hours, which was odd. Then the sudden stillness crawled along the halls like spiders. I was covered in sweat—not all my own—and breathing heavily. So were those around me. But the silence was cavernous and growing.

We gathered in the hall near Carmen's room. I leaned against the wall a step away from her door. The beams of light from the few flashlights caught on our shining skin and eyes.

But then came Rosina's cry. Louder than Carmen's had been.

My heart stopped. The tension was tighter than any camisole anyone had ever worn. No one breathed a breath.

Wilma appeared at the doorway of Carmen's room, and Rosina's crying stirred the very molecules in the air.

"I think her appendix burst," Wilma said, her words falling from her mouth between gasps of panic.

Beside me Grace whispered a *no*. I sank to the floor. Memories of Mickey's heart attack years ago resurfaced. Another one lost in this cruel world. And there had been so many others I hadn't known. Bodies in white shrouds carried out so often they were forgotten before they could even become the ghosts that haunted our peeling-plaster-walled rooms.

We were all ordered back to our rooms, and Wilma's own grief made us obey. We left Carmen to her eternal sleep, her dingy gray blanket covering her face. Rosina was at her side, her words trapped by her grief. The entire floor felt like death and shock and sorrow. A death like this happened in the infirmary—not on the ward floor for everyone to witness.

I kept the flashlight with me as I walked to my room. Mother had fallen asleep in her camisole and seemed calm enough now. Given how thin she was, I was amazed at the effort it had taken Grace and me to fit her into the straightjacket a few hours ago. But it was for her safety—though I didn't know when I had come to this conclusion. Why did safety have to come with pain and fear?

Even behind my door I could still hear Rosina crying. How could I possibly sleep with the sorrowful serenade?

I lay corpse-flat on my bed like Carmen would in her casket, but instead of clutching a bunch of flowers in my cold hands, I held a small piece of light. The flashlight moved up and down with my breathing. I flicked it on and then off. On and off. I liked the control, even though the light temporarily blinded me every time it was on.

The ward now was filled with cries, wails, and groans. And the envelope called my name.

I distracted myself for a little while, almost convincing myself to wait another day to read it. I was so tired—but mostly I was afraid.

I turned over and pulled the envelope out from where I'd finally stowed it between the bed frame and the thin mattress. I sat up. I touched every part of the envelope. Then, finally, I carefully peeled back the flap, realizing it had been opened at least once before but so long ago that it had resealed.

There was one sheet of paper inside. I tucked the flashlight under my chin and pulled the paper out. It was folded in two places and appeared to be an official document.

I unfolded it.

Across the top read *Death Certificate*.

Death?

I looked at the name of the person listed as dead.

Female Baby Friedrich.

With the date of my birth.

This was my death certificate.

I, nameless me, was dead.

1941

Waking Up Dead

When I woke the next morning the sun looked different. Mother looked different. The stench down the hall smelled different. Nothing was the same anymore. Knowing that my life had been blotted out of existence broke the small sliver of hope for survival that I'd hidden away in my heart. Every breath I'd breathed was a lie according to that certificate. The greatest of all realities I now lived in was that because of my death, there really was no hope for anyone to come for me.

It made my desire to escape greater and my motivation to plan it impossible. I wanted to hide away and took up my old habit of retreating nightly to the Juliet balcony. Grace's poor behavior kept getting her sent back to solitary, and every time she came out, she looked less like herself. She wasn't lucid long enough to talk about anything significant. I was afraid for her—afraid for us both. Our only reprieve from the ward was peeling potatoes in the damp basement and scrubbing sheets in the laundry room.

I didn't see Joann often anymore either, but I'd seen Dr. Woburn more in the last few weeks than I had in months. Things in the ward were changing. New therapies I'd never heard of were being tried. Convulsive therapy using injections was now almost entirely replaced with the ever-growing electroconvulsive therapy. Almost every patient had been administered this new treatment.

Mother continued her sessions, but it did not improve her lucidity. It only made her more compliant. I did not believe anything would bring her back to herself. I didn't believe anyone thought there was a therapy that would. But it was clear she'd become an experiment. The shock therapy did seem to make her physically stronger after days of sleeping it off, which made her desire to wander greater. So instead of sitting or lying around for many hours in the day, now she would walk laps in the dayroom in agitation. Like she was trying to find a way out. Like she wanted to climb the walls and seep through the cracks.

In this we were the same.

The rate of sterilizing patients had increased. One of Grace's roommates, Geraldine, cried through her recovery. Her husband had given permission for the surgery, making the twenty-five-year-old woman unable to ever bear children. She was told that the melancholy she'd experienced because of pregnancy and delivery was reason enough to never give birth again. But the forced sterilization had made her little more than a shell of a woman, and her previous melancholy was only a glimpse of what she experienced now. She said she'd never be well again. But no one listened to women like her, and she was forced into shock therapy for the mental wound the hospital itself had inflicted.

I squatted low in my small balcony. The constant rain we'd been receiving had let up, but the cool air around me was still damp. The fresh scent wooed me. With my head back and my eyes closed, I let the call of a cardinal and the high-pitched squeal of a warbler serenade me from a nearby tree. What freedom birds enjoyed.

I held tightly the local paper I'd swiped from Joann's bag earlier and hidden my death certificate inside. Having a newspaper would not get me into trouble. Most of the newspapers around the ward were decades old. A patient from my childhood, Ethel Block, used to read the same several newspapers from 1914 every day because it kept her calm. Was she still alive?

I wasn't.

We had begun to hear of the possibility of war, and we were losing staff at a speed no one anticipated. Aunt Eddie and Nurse Wilma were transferred to other wards. The entire hospital was over capacity—the highest number of patients in the hospital's history with only half the staff. A nurse or aide was charged with the care of over a hundred patients now. Joann was working harder than I'd thought possible. All available camisoles were being used, and some women were restrained for days until a nurse had time to come around again. And while I was busy on the floor helping the staff, I was only allowed to take direction, even if I saw a patient left unattended.

After a distant roll of thunder and a tear of lightning, the rain started again. The bright light reminded me of how with multiple lightning strikes there was sometimes a circle of safety in the center. I'd read once about how a man and his horses were all struck, but the wagon's passenger was not.

Was I that passenger in these moments? Was I being spared?

Louder than the thunder was Rosina's screaming, which squeezed through the cracked open window of the balcony. I ran in from the balcony and rushed toward the yelling. Lorna was pulling Rosina out of her room by her hair. I looked around, and there was no aide or nurse to be seen.

"Grace," I yelled. "I need help."

Then I remembered she was in solitary. I cursed under my breath.

I grabbed Lorna around the back to trap her arms tightly to her body. She wasn't very strong, nor was Rosina, and she let go quickly. Lorna continued to scream and fight, but she wouldn't be able to best me.

"Lorna," I said, "calm down or I'll have to put you in a camisole."

The voice was mine, but the words felt like Joann's or any other nurse's.

"Calm before the storm. Calm before the storm," she repeated a few times and then tried to bite me, but she couldn't get close at her angle.

"Rosina, please, just go to your room and close your door. Push a bed against it. I don't know why she's after you."

"She said I was the devil." Rosina looked confused. "I don't know what happened."

"Speak of the devil. Calm before the storm." Lorna tried to wrench from my grasp and kept repeating the two phrases.

Joann came in and exchanged Lorna for Grace in the solitary room. For the first time in my life I wished for a dozen more solitary rooms. Or maybe just one for me. The dayroom echoed with the groaning of restrained patients. Lorna was still screaming. Rosina's crying could be heard through her door. Grace's dead expression, however, was the loudest in my ears. She stood statue still where Joann had left her. I put her to bed.

Joann and I worked together for the next hour to get everyone else to bed. Then I went with her to the first floor and worked with patients I didn't know. The new night nurse arrived and was more drill sergeant than caregiver. Hours later Joann and I were in the stairwell. We slid down to the floor and leaned against the second-floor stairwell door. The coolness went through my thin gown, and it felt good. Rain cascaded down the outside of a nearby window and gave me a chill. But I was next to Joann, and for a few minutes it felt like old times.

But then I thought about my death certificate. I didn't know who was responsible for it, but because of the conversation I'd heard when I was sixteen about the secrets she had, I guessed she would at least know about it. Why was I considered dead?

"I shouldn't be sitting here. I have well over a hundred patients, and I haven't seen half of them today." She shook her head, and tears began to trace down her cheeks. "Which means that a dozen of them are still in hydrotherapy and have been since yesterday. And my shift ended hours ago. Oh, Brighton, I'm doing nothing more than the custodial care aides provide because there's little time to do anything else."

She wiped the ready tears from her eyes with her sleeve. Sweat lined her hairline. She looked over at me.

"This isn't what I ever wanted for my patients. This isn't what I wanted in being a nurse. The neglect isn't intentional. This neglect—"

She paused and then went on to talk about the war on the horizon. I couldn't follow so much of what she said, but knew the places she mentioned: England, Germany, Poland, Russia. I knew those countries from the globe she had taught me with. What had happened to that globe?

She broke down then, weeping so deeply she had a hard time catching her breath.

I took her hand like I used to when I was a child. It used to make us both feel better. Would it now? The questions about my death certificate sat impatiently on the other side of my tongue. I needed to know more. I opened my mouth.

"Can I tell you something?" Joann said before I could speak. She let go of my hand and put her arm around me and pulled me close to her soft chest.

In a moment I became my ten-year-old self again. She still smelled the same—of some perfume mixed with the sweat of work. It was the scent of the woman who had acted as mother to me.

"Hm?"

"Sid—Dr. Woburn and I—" She paused. "We're married."

I turned in her hold and looked into her eyes. Married? Had I heard her correctly? "Truly?"

She licked her finger and made a cross sign over her heart. "Till death do us part."

She looked down at her left hand and rubbed her fourth finger. She held it up and wiggled her fingers.

"I never wear my wedding band here." She released what I could only interpret as a happy sigh. But her nervousness surfaced when she chewed on her lower lip.

"How long?"

"Last year. A bright, sunny Sunday afternoon—April 14."

"A year now."

She nodded. I knew why she hadn't told me. She knew it would scare me to think she'd quit working. But she was still here.

Silence settled as I wrestled with this confession.

"I'm going to have a baby, Brighton," she said and put a hand on her abdomen. She smiled, and her eyes again filled with tears. These tears looked clear and crystalline instead of like thunderclouds. "I'm going to have a baby."

I didn't know what to think or say. I looked down at her belly. I'd never known anyone who was pregnant. I'd only heard about how babies grew inside a woman's belly and how her stomach got larger every month until the baby was born. I'd seen diagrams in our science books, but I'd never seen it in a real person. I couldn't stop from putting my hand on her abdomen too. It just seemed like a regular belly.

"A baby is really in there?" I asked, feeling something inside myself that I'd never felt before. What was it? In the almost eighteen years I'd lived in the asylum, I'd seen a lot of people die, but I'd never seen anyone born. Would I ever even see this baby?

What this really meant was that I would not see Joann anymore. She would quit at the hospital, ceasing our relationship, or our escape would be successful. Either way, our days together were numbered. For us, it was not like a marriage with the sacred words of *till death do us part*.

She would be leaving me, even though she said she never would. Or maybe I would be leaving her.

I pulled myself from her warm hold, suddenly feeling alone and cold.

She didn't let me get far, though, and put her hand over mine, and our hands were warm for a while. "It's early still. We haven't even told our parents."

I'd never considered Joann having parents. But of course she did.

This child would have grandparents and maybe aunts and uncles. Maybe sisters and brothers or both someday. Joann would be the real mother to this baby, not just a stand-in. I was losing her.

Suddenly I realized this baby was Angel's cousin.

I pulled away from her hold. She didn't seem to notice, and her hands laced on her abdomen.

"What are your parents like?"

Her eyes shone like the springtime dew. She already loved this unborn baby. And she loved the baby more than she loved me, and while I knew that was a good thing, it hurt deeply.

"They're going to be dizzy with excitement that I'm finally giving them a grandchild. It has been a constant argument for years—first to get married and then to have a baby." She inhaled deeply, and her sigh came out in words. "They don't know—well, why it's taken me so long."

She went on to talk about her nieces and nephews and why this baby would be the star of them all. She talked about how she hoped for a girl and liked names like Rebecca or Suzannah but that Dr. Woburn wanted to name a daughter after a famous woman of science like Marie Curie or Elizabeth Blackwell.

But my mind remained on what Joann had said earlier—that her life choices had been an argument with her parents for years. That was because of me. They didn't know why she'd said no to that boyfriend long ago or Dr. Woburn for years, because they didn't know about me. I was her secret—the girl who died on her birthday but was still alive eighteen years later.

"You'll be leaving, then," I interrupted her.

Should I tell her I was leaving too? With Angel and Grace? Of course I wouldn't. I wouldn't let myself wonder if it would ever happen. Joann's mouth froze, open mid-word. She held her breath. A few long moments later she looked at me and pressed her lips together. "Yes."

"When?"

"Soon. Nursing colleges have graduation in May. We are hoping to hire some then."

"That's next month."

Silence like dust floated in the air.

"One more thing," she whispered. "I saw Grace's name on the list."

I looked over at her. Did I even have to ask?

"She's going to be sterilized soon. Her father has already approved it."

Later this conversation rolled and spun in my mind as I lay sleepless in my bed. I thought about how Joann was having a baby and she'd be leaving the hospital. About Grace's fate. And would we ever leave here? The little protection I had would be stripped away, and I might even be subjected to the therapies and treatments that other patients went through. A new nurse would come in, and I would be considered just another patient claiming to be sane. None of the secrets I thought mattered would matter anymore; I would just sound like another lunatic.

Grace was already suffering, and the worst was yet to come. Angel was being worked worse than an employee, because he was just a patient, after all.

An idea had come to me on how to get out. Maybe it was crazy to try, but I believed now that it was crazier not to.

If we couldn't find a way out, this life would be my second death. It was time to at least try.

1941

Lightning

I woke to learning that Grace was in solitary again. So I would have to wait until she was released. I tried to act normal during our sparse meals and hid a slice of bread and a few boiled potatoes—we'd need to take any food we could pull together. I didn't know how or where we'd get food once we were out. Angel wasn't anywhere to be seen, and I had no way of getting a message to him. He slept in the tool shed now, and I believed if Grace and I could get out there, we could quickly find the tools to free us.

When Grace was released the following morning, I said nothing to her about my plans, but I did tell her she had to behave. I was her shadow until bedtime so she wouldn't lose her temper and get thrown back into solitary. With so little supervision now, I was able to hang around the stairwell door. The new aide with his strange shaven upper lip and dark beard framing his jaw was too new to notice me catch the door behind him when he rushed away from the floor. He didn't see me stuff a piece of newspaper into the doorjamb space so that the latch could not catch. Things were changing in the ward and supervision was low. If we could get through this locked door, we had a chance.

I knew I wouldn't be able to sleep in the hours before we'd make our escape. Not just because of the plan with the door, requiring me to be alert—but because these might be the last hours I'd ever have with Mother.

I sat cross-legged a foot from her bed through the night and watched her. I didn't have to memorize her face. I'd already done that every day for as long as I could remember. The spray of lines at the edges of her blue eyes. Her thin, dried lips. The patchy, dusky, gray-blond hair that curtained her ashen skin. This was my mother.

But I knew that someday when someone asked me, "What was your mother like?" I would tell them that my mother had golden-blond hair, and I would describe how it would flow behind her when we ran through our huge flower garden, chasing butterflies. I'd say that she loved hide-and-seek and liked to eat cake more than anything else, even though she wasn't much for kitchen work. Mother's laugh was the sound of silver dewdrops, and she cried in the beautiful way that made other women envious. That was really who Mother was. I knew that was what she would've been like if she'd had the chance.

I believed she loved me. Because I believed this, I knew our escape was what she would want for me. I knew I needed to do this. I needed to leave Mother behind.

It seemed odd to me that in a few hours—the quietest time of the night—I would walk away from this place in the hope that I'd never see it again. I was so ready to leave. Leave the old Brighton, the unknown girl, dead at birth—for the bright unknown.

Mother's camisole lay over her bed rail. After a few days of wearing it, I was glad an aide I'd never seen before had come around frantically removing camisoles and relieving women in the hydrotherapy.

Now her breathing was even, and her arms and legs had lost their stiffness. She seemed peaceful.

Long gone was the safe and secure existence of the hall I'd been raised in. Joann had made my room and hall into some type of counterfeit world—a wonderland in comparison to the way the other patients lived. Isolated just enough but with lawns, friends, and a doting nurse-mother.

Everything was different now. It wasn't surprising to go more than a day without food. Patients were left in wet packs with drying sheets tightening around them or in hydrotherapy baths or restraints for days. I couldn't do this for the rest of my life, and I wouldn't subject Grace to it either. But what did it mean that I would leave these people for the outside world instead of staying and trying to help? Who would hear their cries? Wasn't I bound to remain and help since I knew there would be no rescue?

And how would I survive in the real world? I could sew. I could peel potatoes. I could garden. I could read. Were those ways I could take care of myself? I didn't even know my father's name. Grace knew about the world and had said we could become our own family and maybe make it out to San Francisco and find Jonah. I was sure Angel would want to find his mother, and I felt the same way about my father. These were three different directions—all our needs could separate us more than we already were.

I got out of bed, and before I did anything I checked the hall. It was empty and dark. I ran across and down a little to see if the door was still unlocked. If someone had caught on to my scheme, my entire plan would be foiled. I checked, and the door hadn't latched. This plan never would've worked in the days when we had someone on the ward every hour, so the understaffing was to our benefit. Now I could only hope that the door on the first floor would be abandoned. Thankfully, with the coming war, only a few night guards remained.

I returned to the room I shared with my mother and stripped off my pillowcase to use as a bag. I put the few photographs I had, my death certificate, the bread I'd wrapped in a piece of cloth I'd torn from the corner of my sheet, the camera, and the hidden half-dozen film cartridges inside. I pulled my blanket into a sling around my back and shoulder. It had been rainy and cold this spring, and we might need it.

I wished I had socks or shoes, but what I was wearing would have to do. It didn't take long to gather everything I could take. My breath was held hostage in my lungs when I looked at Mother. It was time to say goodbye. I wanted to touch her. To give her one more hug. I put my hand on her arm—it was the best I could do. It was so thin and bony. Her skin was rough. She seemed entirely hollow, but I knew better—she was trapped inside herself. She wasn't just a shell; she was still somewhere inside.

I'd touched her for too long, making her stir. She turned over with fire in her eyes. The slap she sent across my face was so unexpected I gasped loudly. The second one came even harder. I put a palm to my face, and my eyes stung from the pain that came from every space inside of me. I wasn't prepared to feel such rejection. All the words I'd wanted to say to her would have to be left unspoken. I had meant to tell her how I would miss her humming and that I loved her—but especially that I was going to find someone to help her and the other women on the ward. Someone to be a rescuer and savior.

And then she turned away and faced the wall and curled up with her knees to her chest and quietly hummed. Her sudden calmness after such an outburst was unsettling. Maybe Grace was right and she really didn't know me. But I knew her, didn't I? I knew how to calm her and how to feed her.

I took a step toward the door. I needed to wake Grace. When I looked back at my mother, one last look, her humming turned into groaning.

I should stay. I can't stay.

I exhaled all of my doubt and ran quickly to Grace's room. She woke with confusion and turbulence, but after a minute I calmed her and put her beloved letters in my pillowcase and pulled her blanket into a similar sling and fitted it around my friend. She just watched me do everything without a word. She had four roommates; two were dead asleep and two were away, either in some drawn-out therapy or solitary, I didn't know. The room was crowded but quiet for these precious minutes.

We scurried back down the abandoned hall toward the door I had rigged. I wouldn't say goodbye to Lorna or Rosina or anyone else. I didn't have the dark courage it took to rest my eyes on the incomprehensible misery and still walk away. I knew them in ways I'd never known Mother, and in the morning they'd recognize my absence in a way Mother could never express.

They would understand—of course—but would they feel I'd abandoned them? What would they think about how I'd taken Grace with me but asked none of them to come too? When I lightly shut the stairwell door behind me and led Grace down the stairs, I let my second-floor thoughts go. Let them wander away with the women I'd loved enough to call family. I wanted to rescue them all, but I couldn't begin to do that if I didn't rescue myself first.

I carefully unlatched the back door's internal locking mechanisms, knowing that once we let it latch behind us, we would not be able to return inside. We would be entirely shut out. But as soon as I knew we were safe in the cover of darkness and I saw no security, I let it click shut and then we ran to the groundskeeper's shed where Angel slept in Mason's old space. The old groundskeeper Angel had assisted had passed half a year ago. Angel now did the job of two.

I tried the door, but it was locked. I knocked lightly but heard no rustle inside. After a few slightly louder knocks, Angel opened the door. He stood with bleary eyes, but without explanation he pulled me inside the shed and into his arms. I wrapped my arms around him and recognized how bony and sharp he had become. My own thinness against his magnified our desperate situation and hunger. Grace stood outside the door until we together pulled her in and closed the door behind her. She was only half aware of what was happening and cried off and on and said almost nothing intelligible. I knew I'd waited too long to do this and that she might never regain herself.

Without a word, like he read my mind, Angel understood it was time. And as though he'd been preparing for our escape, he was already wearing a coat and grabbed two more near the entrance.

"I found these two in the trash barrels over the last few weeks. I think they were from incoming patients." He gave one to each of us.

I spoke quietly to Angel about needing something to cut the fence. Something strong. He showed us through to the back of the small shed and into a room filled with tools. They littered shelves, every wall space, and a large portion of the floor.

"Mason wasn't much for cleanliness. I've been weeding through these when I can—but time just . . . Well, we mainly just use grass mowers and shovels, you know." Of course, for the dead. "I did put these aside after we found the fence, thinking they might work. They're hedge clippers."

He produced a tool that looked like a large pair of shears only a giant could use. He looked so tired, and I grew angry at how hard he was worked. Why hadn't I noticed before now how frail he'd become and that he was even more colorless than normal?

"You're dying, Angel." I choked on my words.

His hollow-eyed gaze lingered over my face, and such sadness was sewn into his skin.

"We're all dying," he finally responded. "Come on, help me find an ax."

It took us at least twenty minutes to find an ax, and while Grace turned circles in the corner, I also found a hammer, another pair of hedge clippers, and wire cutters that didn't look like they'd be able to cut through the fence but seemed worth bringing just in case. We'd each found old boots crusted with ancient mud. Almost too stiff to be wearable, but we decided it would be better than going barefoot.

Then it was time to go. Angel moved close, so close, and our eyes locked. He snapped up my coat like he was my protector. His arms held mine longer than they needed to in our hurried state. And before he let go completely, his hand went to my face and his touch was so soft. He looked at me with such despair and care all at once that I never wanted to look away.

"If I can't keep up," he said, cupping my cheek, "because of my sight—"

"I'm not leaving you." I gritted my teeth.

"If I can't keep up," he repeated more sternly, "you have to keep going. I'll find another way, another time."

"I'd rather die here with you." I meant it.

His eyes turned to glass but didn't break open.

"Come on," he whispered.

My entire body began to shake, even with the warmth of the stolen coat. Adrenaline. I'd learned that from Joann. My eyes scanned the edge of the hospital lawn and road. On the other side of the road were the large doctors' houses and the nurses' apartments. Joann was in there somewhere. With her husband. With a baby growing under her heart. She wasn't thinking about me right now, so why was I thinking about her? That part of my life was over.

We carefully stepped out of the shed. Storm clouds had moved in. Only an occasional star could be seen and I imagined the little Crux—that cross constellation. Why did crosses carry the weight of promise and hope? Rosina would have crossed herself if she'd been with us. I nearly did myself, but Angel gently taking my hand brought me back to what we were doing.

We were standing in the darkness outside the circle of the electric light that cascaded from the lamp on the side of the little shed. Our eyes connected. As long as I could be with him, I knew I could leave this place. We were two pieces of a whole, he and I, and we had been ever since we'd met.

"Here we go," he said, and suddenly I was afraid those would be the last words I'd ever hear him speak to me.

I pushed that thought away and nodded my head. We'd already wasted a lot of time. The sky lit up, and a loud crack ran across the sky. A moment later another bolt of lightning ricocheted, and the surge of energy startled the ground around us. The long, outstretched fingers of the trees in the horizon flashed, then disappeared.

Suddenly awakened, Grace began running toward the back fence. Angel's grip tightened on my hand and we followed.

1990

The Memory of
Wind and Birds

*H*ow many years has it been since I was in the town of Milton? Since that fateful day when I escaped? And even then, I hadn't gone through the city or ever knew the town my hospital-home had been in. As I come into town, I don't take time to take it in but drive straight to the old hospital grounds.

When I was a girl I'd heard that the town was twenty minutes away, but the community has grown, so the town is closer now. A lot has changed, and Riverside Home for the Insane became known as Milton State Hospital before its doors closed. Of course we don't say words like *insane* or *mad* in the progressive 1990s. We say *mentally ill. Mad* means something different now too. Words are veils and masks, and there's always something more on the other side of them than we want to believe.

Some tried to rectify the messed-up laws and inhumane treatment of people in those bygone asylums days. Some people think it's just a myth that fathers and husbands put women away for not being happy and content enough. But I know the truth. Why anyone would think something akin to a prison sentence would bring back happiness and sanity, I will never understand. It is strange to think that people felt better turning those deemed flawed invisible. That putting them out of sight was what was important. I'm sure there were those who had good intentions and believed the doctors were only trying to help, with a copy of the Hippocratic oath on the wall in every office. No, many families weren't to blame. Naivety and ignorance aren't sins, after all. But I'm not sure the hurt they caused is entirely forgivable.

From my infancy to now, an irritable sixty-something, much has changed with mental-health treatments. But it didn't change my experience or the lives of all those women. Just because society finally realized some of the wrongs that had been done doesn't mean that our stories have been told. The wrongs can't be righted, but remembering and knowing are important. Without remembrance, there is often repetition.

As I drive out of town, I notice a small subdivision and a strip mall with a gas station, a sandwich shop, and one of those new coffee places where people spend three dollars for a cup of something they can make at home. That's what I find crazy—and I don't use that word lightly.

A ball's throw away stands the main asylum building. My lungs and soul gather together like a straightjacket has been tightened around me. I can't breathe. I pull over and get out of the car. I put my hands on my knees. Lines from an old mantra travel through my mind, but I push them away. It has been well over a decade since my last attack and I'm ashamed of myself. Shouldn't I be strong enough now? I'm not even going inside today, but Kelly Keene has promised she'd make it happen another day.

When I'm breathing normally again, I stare at the administration building. I didn't spend any time inside that place, but it is the iconic face of Riverside. It's Willow Knob's placid facade that was my reality for eighteen years and invaded my nightmares for the rest.

I return to my car and drive the remaining distance. Many of the buildings have been torn down or have collapsed over the years. I wonder if the graveyard is still out there. I hope it is. The gravestones are probably all sunk and swallowed into the earth and planted like seeds. Lonesome seeds made of sand, rock, water, but mostly loss.

I lose my very balance the moment I set eyes on Willow Knob. It takes my breath away, but not the way a new baby or a sunset does. My heartbeat changes to the pulse of courage. Am I really here? On the outside of the walls and fences? I almost turn around and return home.

I haven't seen these buildings since I left when I was just a girl. I park along the side of the road and take my camera from the bag on my passenger seat. It hangs around my neck, and as I walk, it taps against my middle in a rhythm that comforts me. The camera itself has become a veil of detachment for me. Giving me space. I am, after all, Nell Friedrich, photographer. Most of that identity has been as a teacher at a local art center, but I've also had the chance to travel with Doc and I have looked into the souls of many, holding this black box between us so that they can't get a glimpse into mine.

I stand where the main drive used to be. The pavement is broken up, and what's left has grayed in the sun. The iron fences left are imposing and ugly. One side of the front gate is connected at the bottom hinge but is otherwise lying on the ground at an awkward angle. The other I can't see anywhere. Long yellow-green grasses are blowing in the constant June breeze, reminding me of a warm, romantic westerly wind from some pioneer romance film. But this isn't a romance.

I don't walk up yet but glare at the Willow Knob building. It doesn't flinch at my presence. It's close enough to be gawked at from the road, but far away enough for the guts and souls inside to be invisible.

Broken. Busted up. Burned. But there stands the building of my childhood. During my years here I thought about all the places outside the walls. And when I was free, I thought about the one place that was tattooed on my heart. This place was a force. A living being in my memories—and to think that my nightmarish childhood was littered with giggles, friendships, and a settling in of dreams. The modern woman might find these dreams of marriage and family too commonplace. They're wrong. Especially when such dreams require a freedom that is out of reach.

The willow tree is still in the front, swaying in the wind like nothing else matters. I pull my camera up to my eye, and I take a picture from the distance and capture its stance against the sun's glow. The idea of capturing the building that captured me puts a smile on my face.

After a dozen frames I walk hesitantly toward it. Even though I told Ms. Keene I want to go inside, right now I don't even want to go near it. There are so many ghosts calling for my attention. But after a few deep breaths, I greet them—they aren't nightmares; they are memories and people I knew. I take pictures and I remember them. My heart softens, and I get the sense they are welcoming me. They know I want to honor them and not forget them.

What will happen to these forgotten souls when the buildings are gone and in their places are recreational fields and office buildings? Will the pain of all the people who lived and died here be lost? Changing landscape doesn't change memories or pain. That isn't the way human souls work. The passing away of buildings doesn't change the past. Memories are immortal and unchangeable.

My finger is snapping so fast that I run through my first roll of twenty-four in minutes. Every frame is filled with exhumed recollections. I reload and go around the back and find the door that we'd always run in and out of in those early days. Our giggles—Angel's and mine—are spread thick through the air. I hear them. And Joann yelling for us not to run to the graveyard. The very same door we'd snuck out of one stormy night. The night everything changed for us.

My gaze roams to that back corner where the graveyard should be. I almost think I will find my former self there.

But I can't go there today.

I take pictures of the brick exterior and the bars on the windows. The word *haunted* is graffiti-painted on one of the walls alongside a scary face that reminds me of a mask from a tasteless horror flick. I walk around to my second-floor bedroom window and take more photographs. I was born and raised on the other side of those broken panes.

I turn to see the children's ward. Only half remains.

The wind and birds sing in chorus together, their voices welcoming me home. They know me. They recognize me. They remember me. They know why I am here, and there's some comfort in that.

I look back up to my old window. Is someone still there? Is it a ghost or the scrap pieces of the soul of the lost girl I used to be? Everyone who used to be here was lost in one way or another. If they didn't start out lost when they got here, they became lost before they left—alive or dead. I sometimes still feel that way. It takes gumption to live, you know, and all the grit you can muster, though there were times in the earlier days I nearly gave up.

The hush of the wind over the grasses lulls me back to myself. I make a loop around to the front of the home—the building. The asylum. It never should have the word *home* attached to it, but it does.

I walk slowly now, knowing that the Juliet balcony is up to my left. I can only see it in my periphery. Can I look at it? I had avoided looking directly at it when I walked up. Like a shield, I put my viewfinder to my eye and turn toward it, but I can't snap the photo. My soul aches. My chest is tight, and every heartbeat hurts. I can't pull my hands down, and through my lens I see things. Things I don't want to see. I see a girl up there. Sitting. Hiding. Wishing. Hurting. And then other faces—skin around souls—stand behind her. They all look at me.

I need to get out of here.

I have snapped four rolls of film. I am doing all I can. I am facing it, and there is good in that.

But when I finally pull the camera from my eye, I can't catch my breath. My feet work better than my lungs, and I turn and run.

I want to be okay with this. I want to feel that if I never gaze on these buildings again I will be all right. Oh, the lies we tell ourselves.

My car is close. I run, feeling the shapes of many behind me pressing against me. When I climb into the car, I don't even take my camera from around my neck or put on my seat belt. I turn the key, make a

U-turn with a spray of gravel behind me, and leave. I am crying and shaking, and I put as much distance between me and that building as fast as I can.

I don't look back.

Not this time.

1941

Gone

*B*efore we arrived at the tree line, the rain started, making it hard to see what was ahead of us. When I tripped in the blackness over M. Porter's grave and cut my leg, a cussword wrestled itself out of my mouth and I nearly hurt myself worse with the ax I was holding.

Angel caught himself before he fell, then helped me up, and we continued to run. Angel and I were two parts of one whole. He needed my eyes, and I needed his presence. We were no good without the other.

Our running slowed down because of my cut leg, but every time the lightning flashed we could see the way a little better. The more we ran, the more my fear swelled. We hadn't even left the property yet and my courage was already failing.

I stopped running and Angel bumped into me from behind.

"Brighton," he yelled. "What's wrong?"

I looked back and could see lights on in several buildings. I couldn't tell which was which anymore. There were so many now on the nearly one thousand acres. So many more than when I was a little girl. Did that mean there were so many more mad people now? It was rare that anyone left, but people kept coming. They wouldn't miss the three of us, would they? Why would anyone care that we'd left? There would be three fewer mouths to feed, three fewer to care for, three fewer to burden the State.

And what about Mother? I dropped Angel's hand from my own.

Suddenly I was spun around to face away from the buildings. Grace's grip was tight on my arm even through the bulk of the coat. Her face was rain-drenched like mine, her hair soaked and flopping down around her ears and forehead. She had the expression of a wild animal, and her chest heaved up and down as she breathed rapidly.

"Come on," she yelled over the storm. "We have to go now."

"I'm scared," I finally admitted as the pelting drops slowed some and the black sky turned to navy. We were already soaked, but if we escaped now, by midmorning these captured raindrops would have evaporated into the air of freedom. I played that possibility over and over in my head. What would it be like to be on the other side of those fences? To not be a patient. To be free. Could we even survive? How long would my mother survive? Long enough for me to rescue her or find someone who could? Or would she be just another body unclaimed and buried? *H. Friedrich.*

"She'd want you to run—to leave," Grace said like she knew my thoughts.

I looked at her, still catching my breath. My hand went to my chest, and I doubled over, releasing what I didn't know I carried in my stomach, the burden of this decision now on the drenched grass.

Mother would want me to leave. I straightened my back and my breathing slowed and I met the eyes of my two best friends and nodded.

I grabbed Angel's hand and again we ran. It was hard to get through the brush and thornbushes but thankfully we had the oversize boots to keep our feet unscathed and we reached the fence faster than the first time.

"Come on, come on," Grace said, hurrying Angel to get out the tools. Angel tried the hedge clippers first, but the wire wouldn't cut. Grace tried. I tried. But we weren't getting anywhere.

"It's not working," Grace said and threw the broken tool into the grass. She pushed Angel's shoulder. "It's not going to get us through this fence."

"Stop it," I yelled. "It's not his fault."

I grabbed the ax and raised it high to swing. The first wallop I gave the fence vibrated my entire body and stung me through. The ax bounded back toward me, and the wooden handle banged against my shoulder with such force I cried out. I took a few deep breaths then tried again, but nothing we were doing even damaged the fence. The ax hitting metal rattled my bones, and my shoulder ached. Because Angel kept hitting it, so did I. But after minutes of this, we still had not done any damage to the fence.

Grace bent over and leaned her hands against her knees, crying. Her crying was raw and deep. I wanted to cry like that, but instead I felt numb. Maybe from the vibration of the ax; maybe because our escape was failing.

We moved down the fence in both directions to see if there were any breaks, but none could be found. We also tried to dig beneath the fence, but with all the roots it was impossible.

Exhausted from effort and breathing heavily, I leaned against the fence. A faint glow had grown and the neighborhood of madhouses almost looked pretty. The misty air hung like cobwebs around us. The beauty in this spring dawn was an insult.

Spring.

"What's the date?" A new panic rose in me.

It was only a beat before it dawned on Angel where my mind had just landed.

"Your birthday," he said, his voice rough and exhausted.

He grabbed me and we ran, leaving Grace alone. I lost a boot before I got out of the wooded and brushy land. I didn't know if Grace was behind me or not, but I had to go. My mother would be in the middle of her fit, and if I wasn't there, no one knew what to do. Who knew if a nurse would even be around? Joann wouldn't be there yet—unless her memory had served her where mine hadn't.

We ran until we had to stop and catch our breath, but when my eyes caught sight again of Willow Knob, I started again. I let the other shoe fall off and ran faster in my bare feet. The ground was soft and didn't hurt. Angel was still right behind me.

"What time is it?"

"Maybe around five?"

Cars pulled into the parking lot far off on the right with arriving employees while the nurses and aides, who lived on the property, walked toward the buildings. They were going to see us, and then we would be in trouble. I ran faster.

Of course the back door was locked. I couldn't get in.

"Open up," I yelled and pounded my fists on the door. "Open the door."

The door flew open, and Joann stood there looking like a used piece of fabric.

"Where have you been? Do you have any idea the trouble you're in?" Her hair was pinned in curls, and her face was pale and unmade. She was wearing a regular dress and a cardigan sweater. Why was she here? Like that? Her eyes were puffy and red rimmed. "And you, Angel, how could you let this happen?"

"I was— We—" I couldn't tell her that I'd been running away.

"You were running away." Joann grabbed my arm and gave Angel a side glance as she let us both in.

"But what about Grace?" I asked.

"You have other things to worry about." Joann shut the door behind us.

"I won't leave her to take the blame for this. It was my plan."

"Neither will I." Angel's voice broke. Was he upset because our escape hadn't worked or because he knew what it meant that I wasn't with my mother? Had she started her phantom labor pains as she did every birthday? I looked up the stairs waiting to hear her wild screams and shrieks.

Angel gripped my hand, and when I looked up at him we both heard Grace's screams. She was being dragged by a security guard and an aide. Grace's stolen coat was nowhere to be seen and her legs were soiled and bloody. Were mine too? I didn't look to see.

"You both know better." Joann was frantic. "This will change everything."

"Just let me go to my room," I said, trying to push past her. "I need to get to Mother."

She blocked me, but I kept pushing.

"Stop, Brighton," she said and then repeated herself two more times, so firmly that I finally stopped.

"What?"

I watched her as she lowered her eyes and shook her head. "By the time I got here it was too late. It was too late."

"Too late for what?"

"For me to help her." She took the pillowcase bag from me.

I looked at her and then at Angel. His eyes grew wide. Mine mirrored his.

"What are you saying?" Angel spoke what I thought.

"Your mother." She looked at me. "She's gone."

"Gone?"

"A nurse found her at the bottom of the stairs. Somehow she'd gotten into the stairwell. The door wasn't latched and—"

"Gone?" My hand went to my neck.

"I'm so sorry, Brighton." Joann pulled me into a hug.

It had been my fault. I'd rigged the latch to escape all the heartache and pain and melancholy. She'd gotten her own escape now. I was still here.

I had killed my mother.

I pulled away from Joann, and somehow she let me and I ran up the murderous stairs and barreled through the second-floor hall.

"Mother," I called over and over. I ran into our room and stopped at the doorframe.

Joann had followed me. "The aide put her here until the morgue could come."

She was so small lying there. Joann had covered her with a white sheet. So still. She didn't need the camisole that was draped over her bedpost. She didn't need an insulin injection that was always at the ready in every nurse's apron. She didn't need anything anymore. She didn't need me anymore. My mother was dead, and it was all my fault.

1941

Metamorphosis

My breath was held captive in my lungs as I stood in front of my mother, my dead mother, when I heard Grace screaming in the stairwell. Joann went down to calm her. Shouldn't I be the one screaming? Wasn't I the one who had just lost my mother and was responsible for it? Grace began calling my name over and over. I heard her being dragged away somewhere downstairs and toward what I knew to be the shock therapy room. Also my fault now.

A minute later a few men in white uniforms came to my room. They pushed past me without giving me a second glance and one started to wrap the white sheet tightly around my mother. The other placed a stretcher next to her bed.

They were going to carry her to the morgue.

They were going to take Mother away.

Without warning, I flew at them. I yelled at them to stop and pulled their jackets, their hair, scratched them with my jagged, ragged fingernails.

"You can't take her. She's my mother." The grief-filled words were like the scrape of a dayroom chair against the old linoleum, and my throat grew raw.

"Hold her while I get the body." His voice was in a shade of panic I understood. But I didn't stop fighting and kicked him between the legs, and he bent over in pain. Then the other grabbed me and pulled my arms back, leaving me vulnerable to a solid punch in my middle.

"You will unhand her." Joann marched in. The man took his arms off of me. I doubled over and fell to the floor, but from the corner of my eye a flash of white crossed the room and tackled the aide who had hit me. Angel.

The blur of chaos continued until Joann whistled and everyone stopped what they were doing. Except for me. I was still on the floor holding my stomach and coughing. The two aides righted themselves. One had a bloody nose from the tussle and both were staring at Angel with clenched fists. Angel's hair was mussed and his shirt had been yanked out of shape, but he was fine otherwise. His gaze was on me, and it was like nothing else was in the room.

He saw what I saw.

He knew what I was thinking.

He knew it was my fault. His face broke into a thousand pieces.

I was ashamed for him to look at me. So I looked away.

He moved toward me and wrapped his body around mine, like a cocoon, like we used to when we pretended to play butterfly the year we learned about metamorphosis. How I longed to change from my caterpillar state and be a butterfly that could fly away. But every time I left Angel's cocoon, I was still the same Brighton.

Our tears mixed, and we watched as Mother was wrapped in a white sheet. Her rest had begun from this life, and I knew now I would never rest.

Before the men could leave with her body, patients began to come. Our friends. Our family. They all entered with such sacred quietness but for a few *hmms* and sniffs. Then Joyful came in. She was crying big, round tears that trailed down her dark cheeks. Her thick hands rested on my back and head, and they felt like heavy blankets that covered me. Her full voice sang a song about a river and prayer. I loved the comfort in the heavy melody.

Rosina left her room for the first time in weeks and walked in, quietly saying the Lord's Prayer. My mouth moved with hers. She cried between her holy Spanish words.

Patients I'd known my whole life and some who were new came. They walked the path as one. In through the door, up to Mother's bed—some of them lightly touching her sheathed body—then turning toward my bed and walking a circle around Angel and me as we sat in the middle of the floor. They were paying respects. They were mourning and grieving with me. With sad eyes they traced from Mother's body to my face. Some of them said they were sorry and some just looked at me as blankly as Mother used to, their sympathies blocked inside themselves. The sheer number of them and their concern brought me comfort.

And the two aides who were supposed to take my mother just stood staring. They did nothing to stop this funeral march and the sorrowful, moaning dirge. The only one my mother would ever have.

My back grew straighter and Angel's wrap around me loosened, but he remained close.

"Everyone's been dreading this day," Aunt Eddie said to Joann. When had she arrived? "We all knew it would happen eventually. How much longer could that poor woman—and our sweet girl—"

Joann sniffed and nodded.

"What's going to happen to her now?" Aunt Eddie wrapped her arms around her ample frame.

Joann flinched at the question, and her eyes flickered to me and then back to the bed.

"She's in trouble, Eddie. She tried to make a run for it. Angel and Grace too."

"It ain't right and you know it." Aunt Eddie's tears rushed as her voice grew passionate. "That she's here. All three of them."

Joann clenched her jaw, but her eyes remained trained on Mother's body.

"She doesn't belong here. She never did. Poor dear hasn't got a soul to care for her."

"I don't know what to do." Joann spoke with thick, pasty words. "Sid will watch out for her, but—"

"That's all you have to say? The little girl you raised could be sterilized before the year's out, and that's all you have to say—that your husband will watch out for her?" She guffawed. "Maybe I should've been her stand-in mother instead. Criminal or not, her father would take better care of her than you."

"Don't." The word squeezed between gridlocked teeth.

"You don't scare me no more, Jo," Eddie said. "Besides, you have a foot out the door. You ain't my boss neither. I've kept quiet for all these years so I could get the safe jobs and good shifts—for my family's sake—but not no more."

Then she looked down at me, her nostrils flared.

"Attempted escape will guarantee you'll be given treatments. Angel too. Anyone who attempts something that crazy—well, they should expect that." Then she turned back to Joann. "You should've let her father take her."

I stood.

"Take me?" I asked Eddie.

"He was nothing but a convict," Joann snorted. "It wasn't possible."

"I looked in my file and Mother's," I said, accusingly. "I found my death certificate."

"What? How long have—" Joann put her face in her hands. "I never wanted you to know—"

"That was wrong and I didn't agree." Eddie eyed Joann. "Joann has his address in a secret file in the records office."

"Don't even try to find it, Brighton," Joann scolded, raising her head. "You're in enough trouble already."

Eddie took a step toward me with a quivering mouth and eyes drowning in their small pools of tears. "I'm so sorry, dear."

She hugged me, then gave Joann one last stern look before she left the room.

"This wasn't the way things were supposed to go," Joann whimpered.

Then she was gone. Eddie was gone. Mother was gone.

1941

A Long, Dreamless Moment

*W*ithout warning, two more white-coated men I'd never seen before came in. One grabbed Angel with rough hands. He struggled in their grasp, but it was useless.

"Stop," I yelled.

I beat the man on the back until the second man's arms clamped around me. The aide's fingers interlaced together like a concrete statue.

Joann rushed back. "You will be gentle as you put them in solitary."

"But I have a job," Angel growled at Joann. The anger he had toward her was remarkable considering how he'd always been so forgiving.

"This one is going to Orchard Row, not solitary, Nurse," the larger aide said.

"On whose orders?" Joann choked.

"Dr. Wolff, by way of Dr. Woburn."

Joann turned pure white. Whiter than Angel. Whiter than their uniforms. She stepped back, filling the doorway with her small frame.

"Bright—Angel—I'm so sorry. I can't—I don't," she stuttered and shook her head back and forth.

"Don't let them." A feral surge rushed through me.

Joann opened her mouth, but the words inside were never spoken as the aide pushed past her with Angel.

"The girl is scheduled for treatment downstairs before solitary," the aide said.

With an animalistic yell Angel pulled out of the aide's arms and lunged for me. Before he reached me the aide beat his back and he was on the floor in the next moment. Blood poured from his face.

I screamed. Joann was mute. And all we could do was watch as Angel was pulled through the stairwell door without much effort. His blood smeared on his clothes and the floor. I kept yelling for him. I kept struggling. I wouldn't quit.

"Joann, you have to get him out," I urged. I pulled and ratcheted my body to try to break free, but I couldn't get away.

Joann swallowed and then came to herself.

"You will put her in solitary. I'm the managing nurse here so you will listen to me. If a doctor asks you, tell him to come to me."

"Dr. Wolff said that if she gives me any trouble, she goes straight to ECT."

Joann pulled out a shot from her dress pocket and after a sting on my thigh I heard, "There, now she won't give you trouble."

The insulin rushed through me. I could feel it. My legs began to weaken and it was harder and harder to keep my hands fisted.

"Don't fight it, dear girl," Joann whispered closely. "Forgive me."

Then she turned and went down the steps where Mother had just fallen to her death.

My head was so heavy and my mouth felt damp and I couldn't wipe the wetness away. My eyes lost their focus, and even though I could feel my body moving, I could only see blurred images flying in front of me—doors along the hallway and wandering patients. The scent was even more acrid than usual, and I began to vomit.

I couldn't keep up, so I was dragged. Once inside, I was put on the cot and strapped down with all four limbs splayed out. And then everything went dark.

I didn't know how long I'd been out, but it seemed like only a moment. A weighty, dreamless moment. Like several pages of a book were turned at once. It seemed like a new me woke. Like the one who'd fallen asleep wasn't real anymore. Like she had died.

Someone had loosened my restraints, but I'd worn them long

enough to have a steady ache in my wrists and ankles. I looked up to see only blackness pour through the broken window. The room spun and my head was pounding and my whole body felt snapped like a rubber band. Dried vomit covered my gown and the rancid scent filled me.

Someone was humming loudly. Mother?

No.

A wave of reality reminded me that she was gone. Was she buried already as *H. Friedrich*—forgotten before she was known?

The humming was coming from across the hall. It would stop for minutes at a time and then resume. I recognized the tune as one Grace used to sing in the early weeks of her arrival. It was a simple melody with words about dreams coming true, and I remember she said it was sung by someone named Ella. That was all I knew. I squeezed my eyes together, wishing she would share the words. Maybe they'd be of some comfort.

Could anything comfort us right now?

My whole body hurt when I pushed myself up to stand. The wound on my leg from our escape had been dressed. My shoulder ached from the ax. I limped to the door and looked through the square hole. I put my mouth to it and whispered her name. The humming stopped briefly, then began again. I called to her a few more times, a little louder.

She quieted again, and there was a shuffling.

"Hannah, is that you?" she returned.

She thought I was her sister.

"Grace, it's me, Brighton."

Grace rushed to the door and put her mouth against the small square hole.

"Be quiet, Hannah." The whisper came like her throat was filled with gravel and fear. "Jonah is coming soon. I left the back door unlocked for him. Don't tell Daddy." She disappeared from sight, and I heard the rattle of her doorknob.

"Grace, I'm not—"

"Hannah." She was angry now. "Why did you lock the door? Did Daddy put you up to this?"

She rattled and pounded on the door and yelled for Hannah to unlock it.

"Grace, quiet," I whispered loudly. "You're going to get into trouble again. Listen to me."

She couldn't hear me. Through the window I could see her bouncing around in wild, erratic movements. It went on for several minutes, then stopped and she was quiet.

"Grace," I said in a loud whisper.

"Brighton?" She looked through the little window.

"Yes." I was relieved. "It's me, Brighton. You have to stop fighting everyone. I think Eddie might—"

"Brighton, guess what?" she said. "Hannah was just here and Jonah is on his way. I left the back door unlocked so he can get in."

"Grace, no," I said, but she didn't hear me. She went through the cycle again with the confusion of the locked door. And when she couldn't unlock it, she went back to scolding her sister.

Grace was lost.

I put my back against the door and slid down to the floor. I didn't remember falling asleep there, but the next thing I knew the door was creaking and pushing me. The person on the other side grunted and I scurried out of the way. My vision was like looking through gauze, but I could see a soft orange light coming through the window high in the wall. I turned to see the blurry figure and round shape of Aunt Eddie.

"Eddie?"

"Oh, Brighty, you're awake." Eddie leaned forward and with little effort pulled me to my feet and walked me to the cot.

"How long have I been in here?" I sat down.

"About eighteen hours, dear." She sat on the cot next to me. "Joann told me what she done. With the injection."

I looked away. It wasn't that I'd forgotten, but the details were only hanging around in the corners, making it easier to ignore. But now the facts had gained traction in my mind. Our failed escape. Mother's death. Angel taken to Orchard Row. Any reserve hope I'd stored for so many years had vanished.

"She done it because they were going to take you to shock therapy if you didn't calm down."

What was I supposed to say to that?

"She been here for hours with you, when her shift finished," Eddie continued. "She was hoping you'd wake. Dr. Woburn made her go home finally." The older nurse shrugged. "You know, ain't good for the baby."

Yes. The baby. Being here wasn't good for her baby.

"Is Angel—" I started.

"Orchard Row."

Grief struck me and I moaned, my body falling slack, crying. I'd lost everyone.

There Is No Grace

I was alone for the rest of the day. The grief over Mother was like the dust and dirt on the walls. It covered everything. There was no way to get away from it. The realization that the hope of escape was nearly gone was in everything else. It was heaviness in the iron cot frame. The way I couldn't see the moon. The way the cot smelled of urine and vomit that weren't mine.

And then there was Angel. The purest soul I knew. Would I see him again in this life? How much longer could we survive? And what about Grace?

Rosina's prayers came to mind. I repeated some of those words as I sat in the corner. I'd cried all my tears. I was too tired to sleep. And the cliff of hopelessness was so close. But for the light that cascaded in from the broken window, all seemed lost. In that small ribbon of warmth and light there was something I couldn't place. I couldn't see how it might all happen—but in film light banished darkness. Could that happen in life? Was my sliver of hope enough?

Approaching steps caught my attention, and I got up from the floor and peeked through the door window. The backs of men entered my view.

"Hey, what are you doing?" I yelled. They ignored me.

They proceeded to open Grace's door, and as though she'd anticipated it, she flew at them. My square window only gave me flashes of aides battling her barred teeth and claw-like hands. She was so small and so out of her mind it didn't take much to best her. I yelled her name. I didn't know if I should tell her to keep fighting or to stop. Both seemed right. The aide kicked my door and told me to shut up, but I didn't.

"Just you wait," he said to me.

Grace's cries as she was dragged away could have peeled paint from the walls. Her door was left open and the emptiness that stood before me filled my soul.

Where was Joann? She said she'd never leave me. She said she wouldn't forget me. Eddie said she'd been here while I slept, but I hadn't seen her. I'd been given food once, dried bread and water. Whoever dropped it off didn't even show their face but slid in the tray and rushed off. The racket in the ward was louder than I thought was common and I heard talk of a stomach influenza. That always caused deaths. Who would we lose this time? I kept my ears out for Lorna's clichés and Rosina's prayers, but heard neither.

I went between watching out my door window for signs of Grace to looking out the window in the wall. At the close of the second day I was greeted by fog and dampness and eventually fell into a fitful sleep, believing my fate was sealed to spend another night in the smallness of these four walls.

The solitary door opened and slammed against the wall behind it. The same aides from before had come for me. One walked in with his arms out toward me as if bracing for an attack. I jumped up from the floor and backed into a corner and analyzed whether it was possible to get past them. Could I grab the keys that jingled on the waist of the smaller one? At the first grip on my arm something arose out of me that brought such understanding of all the women I'd loved over the years; my resisting was savage and natural.

A desperation to fight for my life took over. My muscles contracted painfully against their greater weight and strength. One finally grabbed me around the back, pinning my arms down, and the other held me around my ankles and lifted me.

I bucked and reared and bloodied the nose of the man at my feet. The dayroom was empty as I passed through in their grasp, and they had to reposition me when we got to the stairwell door. We were so close now to the room of my birth, my childhood, my memories, my mother—my whole life.

"Mother." My neck muscles strained, and all the lumps and sighs and stones of guilt I'd swallowed down for the last eighteen years rose up out of me. I was bathed in tears.

The aides' hold on me was unrelenting, and once we were on the first floor and I recognized which room they were taking me to, I started weeping. Not the gnashing I'd just done in a whirlwind and fit of grief, but the kind of sadness that made me only as strong as the bread dough Joyful let me touch once. I was soft and could be molded and separated into a thousand pieces. I now understood the giving-up so many had done who had gone before me.

1941

I Never Knew You

familiar and once-despised voice told the aides to put me on the table. All I could see was the floor and the feet walking on it.

"She's going to fight," one said. "She's a tough one too."

"Leave her on the table," he demanded.

They did as they were asked, roughly laying me on my stomach on the table before complaining about their pay.

As soon as their hands were off of me, I flipped over and saw the door slam and the back of Dr. Woburn standing near a table with medical instruments on it I'd never seen before. I guessed this was the electroconvulsive therapy room.

He turned around, and the scar across his forehead had never looked so prominent. He held a clipboard in front of him, but his gaze fell upon me only briefly and then went past me. A click sounded from behind me. A door. My sight snapped over, and Joann frantically moved in beside me. Her eyes were round, and her hair was not pulled back behind her nurse's cap but instead fell around her shoulders. I didn't know that it was so long. She wasn't wearing her white uniform, and I could feel her nubby sweater against my arm. She was wiping my face with delicate hands and saying over and again to forgive her. The despair in her voice scared me.

"What's happening?" Was she going to help her husband shock my brain? Was that why she was pleading for forgiveness?

"Joann—time." Dr. Woburn raised an eyebrow.

"Right." She looked at him, then back at me, and forced me up to a sitting position and started to unsnap my gown.

"What's going on?" I asked, looking back and forth between the two while trying to keep my gown on. Was this how electroshock was done?

"Go, Sid." He was gone in a moment, furthering my confusion.

Joann won the battle of my gown, and it was off me. She had a bag on the floor next to her, and she frantically stuffed the gown inside and pulled out a tan-colored blouse and a navy-blue skirt. "I didn't have an extra brassiere, but put this camisole on first and see if that will help."

"Help what?" I said, and in my own fear I became frightened enough to put on what she called a camisole quickly. This one wasn't a straightjacket.

"Your breasts, Brighton. You have them, as small as they are, and it's vulgar not to wear a brassiere." She gestured for me to move quickly, and when I was ready she threw the blouse around my shoulders and pushed my arms through the sleeves. It was a fine shirt. Nicer than anything I'd ever worn, and for a moment I smoothed my hands down from my chest to my waist. "Promise me you'll get one as soon as you're able."

"Get what?"

"Get a brassiere."

I was like a doll in her arms and was pulled to standing. She had me change my underpants, then she put the skirt down by my feet and gestured for me to step in. When I did, she pulled the skirt up to my waist in a blink. I had a waist. It was shocking to see. And it was small.

"What's happening?" I nearly slapped Joann to get her attention.

Her hands stopped buttoning at my waist and moved to my face. Gently she held my cheeks and looked into my eyes. I was her little girl again.

"You are leaving tonight, my love." A tear streaked down her face, and she didn't move to wipe it away, so I did it for her. "I should have done this years ago."

She was helping me escape? Tears I didn't know I had left poured and wetted my cheeks. There was hope in that sliver of light.

"It's not going to be easy, Brighton, but you'll have to trust us." She was so firm that I expected her tears to dry, but instead more came. She took off her sweater and put it around me.

"We'll be fired if they figure it out," she said without looking at me. "But it doesn't matter because we're leaving—Sid and me."

"Leaving?"

She nodded. "Florida. Can you believe it?"

While I shook my head in disbelief, tears streamed down her cheeks. She grabbed her bag and pulled me to the door.

"To start fresh." She peeked into the hallway before leading me out.

"What about Angel—and Grace?" I grabbed roughly at Joann's arm and she winced.

"I'll explain everything once we get out."

"No." The passion to exert that small word made me feel woozy and my knees buckled. She caught me and held me up for a long moment, looking around us. When I nodded I was okay, she kept us moving toward the door—the very same one I'd snuck out of with Grace only a few days ago. "Please, tell me."

"Sid is working on getting Angel." She slowly turned the knob to keep it quiet. I knew the trick too.

"And Grace?"

"We can't help her now."

"What does that mean? I promised her." I pulled away from her. I didn't want to leave the building without Grace.

"Promises are minions of love, aren't they? Grace is in the infirmary. Her father was very upset over hearing about her attempted escape and wanted her treatment accelerated. She might be transferred."

I was the reason for all of this. What would they do to her?

"Take me to her," I begged too loudly.

Joann pushed me against the wall and put her hand over my mouth.

"Quiet, you." She spoke so quietly I barely heard her.

I nodded, and she let go of my mouth. "Listen to me. You cannot help Grace. You're going to leave this place and settle somewhere. Then you can write to Eddie—but use a different name on the envelope. She will get it to Grace. Do you hear me?"

I nodded without a word. This was really happening. My heart began to beat too quickly and my eyes blurred with tears. We were so close now, for the second time, but what if it didn't work again?

"Come on." She pulled me outside and quietly closed the door behind us.

"How long have you planned this?"

"Listen, you need to walk normally. Like we're just off-duty nurses." She handed me her purse and she held the bag with my gown.

I nodded but still looked up toward the second floor. The windows were dark, but I could almost see the forms of the ghosts that reached out their arms to hold me close. I looked away and walked on. It was harder than I'd expected. Harder than I wanted it to be.

"My things." My steps stuttered. "My pillowcase."

Joann shook her head and kept me moving forward. "Sorry, love, it's in the attic."

I looked back, and Joann whipped me around to face forward. My things. I'd never see my things again. I wouldn't fulfill the promise I'd made to show the world what was being done to us. All the care I'd taken to hide the film cartridges, and now they were gone.

"But my mother's photo. My film."

"Forget about them. I have a bag in the car. There are other photos of your mother inside, ones you've never seen. Some of her things. They'll have to do."

As we rushed down the sidewalk, Mother's ghost seemed close, pushing me. Telling me to go.

The purple in the sky silhouetted several buildings, and I knew which one was Orchard Row. Joann directed me to look ahead. We stopped next to a car. Joann opened the door and told me to get in the back. She climbed into the front seat—but not behind the wheel. Would Dr. Woburn and Angel come soon? Would they come at all?

Joann and I didn't speak—maybe we didn't even breathe. Until Joann scooted toward the wheel. She gripped it.

"Sid said to only give him twenty minutes." Her grasp was so strong her knuckles whitened.

"Give them longer." My throat was tight with words. I leaned forward on the edge of the cold seat and pressed my hand against the window.

Then I saw movement from the other end of the parking lot. Two men with white coats. They were moving fast in our direction, but they were not close enough yet for me to see their faces.

"It's them," Joann said and moved away from the wheel. I got out and ran to Angel. Holding him was like holding my own heart, so heavy in my arms. Real and beating. He winced.

"Are you okay?" I checked him over as he moved us both toward the car.

We were back inside, and Dr. Woburn started the engine. Angel and I looked at one another and held each other's hands, but as we pulled out of the parking space I looked back. Was this finally happening?

I exhaled a long breath—had I been holding it for years? That exhale pushed out all the sorrow and disappointment and death that were locked away in those walls. It was rotten and dingy air that I thought I'd never be rid of. Though I didn't know who I was without it.

Angel squeezed my hands, and I searched his steady and strong eyes.

"Grace?" he asked.

I shook my head.

The row of houses that I'd learned long ago were for the staff didn't have even one window lit. The dark and sleepy houses were my first glimpse of real homes. Real families lived in them. There were lamps on long poles along the side of the street, but the lights looked more like ghosts. I couldn't put into words how these moments felt. There was such a mixture of grief and anticipation that I couldn't parse. Angel and I ducked as we passed through the iron gates with a night guard. With a wave of Dr. Woburn's hand, we were permitted to exit.

"Where are we going?" Angel finally asked, sitting up.

"The train station," Joann said after several long moments of silence.

"Are you coming with us?" I asked.

Dr. Woburn shook his head. Joann whispered, "No."

"But we don't know how to live out there—out here." I sat on the edge of the seat. "You're sending us away so quickly?"

"It's the best we can do," Dr. Woburn said.

"It wouldn't be safe, love," she said to me. "Sid purchased tickets. You'll leave in a few hours, so you'll have to stay on the platform until you hear the conductor call your train number."

"That doesn't mean anything to us," Angel shot back. "None of that makes sense. What's a platform, and what do we do if someone speaks to us? What if we're hungry? We might have been the more capable ones in the hospital, but out here we aren't. We'll need help."

Instead of answering, she handed us both sandwiches wrapped in wax paper. We grabbed them quickly. Joann told us to take care to eat only a little because neither of us had eaten much in days. My stomach roiled after half a dozen bites so I stopped. Angel didn't. He ate the whole thing like a wild animal consuming downed prey.

"I know, Angel," Joann finally answered. "And I'm sorry that we won't be able to help more. We'll try to explain everything. I've packed more food in a bag. And there's money in there too. There should be enough."

"Enough for what?" I asked. What did that mean?

Joann began to talk in detail about train stations, platforms, how to use money, and what to expect once we got to a city called Pittsburgh. It sounded like another language to me. All I could focus on was the sound of the tires against the road and the whistle of wind coming from the car somewhere. I closed my eyes to it.

"There's an address in your bag." She bobbed her head toward me. "You'll be going to see a man named Ezra Raab."

"Ezra Raab?" Angel repeated.

There was a full beat of silence before she answered. "Ezra Raab is Brighton's father."

I looked at her with eyes that seemed to stretch my skin.

"But how— You said—"

"I know I should've told you more." She shook her head. "He came once."

"For me? When?"

"Listen, he's a convicted criminal. I was not going to hand a one-year-old over to him."

"I was one? What did you tell him?" I asked, but as soon as I did, I knew. "The death certificate."

"I couldn't—" Joann shook her head and bit her lower lip.

"What did he do?"

"He's not dangerous, but—what would he have done with a baby?"

I opened my mouth to respond, but she spoke before I could. "It doesn't much matter if you're angry about it. I did what I thought was best, and we can't go back."

The rough-hewn silence in the car was like a leather strap that tightened around me.

"He wrote," Joann finally said. "Every few years—asking after your mother."

"And?" I looked from her and Dr. Woburn, who was clenching his jaw, to Angel.

"I wrote him back, telling him of her poor condition." She looked straight ahead. "He wanted to know about her."

"But he thinks I'm dead."

"She did what she could." Dr. Woburn's voice burst forth. "She went around to more than a handful of homes for children—orphans, foundlings—and spent weeks looking for a safe place for you."

"What?" I asked.

"Sid, it doesn't matter now." Joann patted her husband.

"Yes, it does, Jo. I won't have her thinking that you didn't try. That you didn't do everything you could for her." Dr. Woburn went on. "Every place she found was dirty or dangerous. The children were always sickly and malnourished. She knew she could do better than those places. And she also put me off for most of that same time."

I scooted back and took my hand from Angel's and put it in my lap.

"No one wanted to adopt a child from a lunatic mother," he added. "Don't think she didn't try that too."

"That's enough, Sid," Joann scolded. "Brighton, it doesn't matter now. I know you've suffered greatly."

"And why now?" I finally asked. "Why couldn't I have gone to my father years ago?"

"After he was released from jail he worked far away. Somewhere out west. And only recently, in the last few years, moved to Pittsburgh. Everything's in your bag. There may also be an aunt."

The car felt like it was moving so fast now. Like we were heading far too quickly into the future.

"An aunt? My mother had a sister?"

She nodded.

"The picture. The hand on Mother's shoulder?"

She nodded again.

"Why didn't you say anything to me?"

"I didn't know much. Just that your father once mentioned her and said she was very ill. I never heard anything more."

An *ill* aunt. Ill like Mother?

"Can I find my mother?" Angel asked, breaking the silence.

"Your father won't ever allow that," Dr. Woburn said, wringing his grip on the wheel. "Take my word for it—walk away from all of this and start fresh."

"Oh, Angel, please listen to Sid about not contacting your family."

Dr. Woburn eyed Joann and cleared his throat. "You're my nephew, you know. Your mother loved you and it was very hard for her to give you up, but she's a proud woman who would never do anything to soil her reputation, and your albinism would've done that. I'm sorry."

"Have you no compassion?" I asked the doctor.

"It's all right," Angel said almost sternly toward me. "I'm not a child, Brighton. I've known that my whole life. Why would I have been at Riverside if I'd been wanted?"

"Your father's a cruel, unrelenting man, Angel, much crueler than any doctor you've encountered at Riverside. He runs an asylum as well—he and Sid went to medical school together. However, their hospital is more of a eugenics factory than anything else."

"Eugenics?" we both asked.

Joann shook her head. "Nothing you need to worry about now that you're on the other side of the hospital walls. Thank God neither of you were sterilized."

"Couldn't you have done this at any time? Just driven off with us?" I asked. "It seems so easy now."

"I don't think so. With all the new staff, it actually might take time for someone to notice you are missing. It's taken days to notice worse things," she said breathlessly. "I don't know, Brighton. I wish things were different."

The sun began to brighten the navy-blue sky. My first sunrise outside of the walls of my room. The silence that returned was nestled uncomfortably between us, giving me a moment to take in the newness. The speed we were going made my knuckles white. But the bench-like seat was smooth and comfortable. The dials and buttons on a panel in front of me, the way Dr. Woburn's feet pushed at the floor and his hand gripped a long stick—none of this was familiar.

All my thoughts about what was confessed and my questions ceased when I saw the train station ahead of us. I'd never seen a real one before, only motionless images in books. The unfamiliarity of it made my lungs fill with air I couldn't exhale. Then a moment later they were empty and I couldn't take a breath. My hands went to my chest. The coat and the nubby sweater were both open, and my hand touched the fine fabric of the blouse. My fingertips felt the smoothness, and I tried to think about how nice it was to help my breathing calm. It didn't work.

"Brighton. Slow down." Joann turned and put a hand on my knee to soothe me.

All I could think about was how we were enclosed in a small car. The air was musky and my breathing got worse. Dr. Woburn pulled to a stop and turned off the engine.

"I need air," I said between loud, raspy breaths.

Angel pounded on the door on Dr. Woburn's side. "Open it for her."

Angel pulled me out, and I stood with my hands on my knees until my breath steadied. He rubbed my back, and his warm hand was the exact weight to keep my heart in place.

"Are you all right?" I looked up at him. The light from the parking lot illuminated the dark circles beneath his eyes and the thinness around his jawline and neck.

He nodded. "Better now."

I wondered if he'd ever talk to me about it. Tell me what it was like at Orchard Row for those awful few days. My breaths became strong and deep as the reality settled in that Angel and I would not die in the asylum. We would not lose ourselves to the melancholy that took over so many souls. We were getting a chance to live.

Dr. Woburn had walked around to Joann's door, and when it clicked open she fell into a frenzy of sobs. Part of me had the instinct to comfort her and part of me wanted to remind her that so much of this heartache could have been avoided if only she'd found a way to get me out sooner.

But the realization that if she had done that Angel never would have been part of my life was like a straightjacket of truth—unmoving and entirely restrictive. Angel never would have survived. If he didn't die in the children's ward, Orchard Row would've done him in. My childhood as it was, was the better choice because Angel and I were supposed to walk this path together.

I saw, for the first time, Dr. Woburn as a husband and Joann as a wife. He knelt next to her seat and put his hands over her hanky-filled one.

"This is what's right, darling," he said, and his eyes were full of what I knew to be love.

Joann nodded first. "But it's all too much. Too much sadness for me and such a burden for them to learn so much so quickly. I tried to give her an education, but that won't help her understand how to live out here. How to shop at the market or get a job or— What if her father won't help her? What will she do?"

Dr. Woburn looked up and our eyes fixed. I couldn't keep them connected, and I looked away, off into the glare of the electric lights. I realized the conversation I was overhearing was one they'd likely had for years. The contradiction of everything we were in the midst of was alive and growing. Freedom was right. But I didn't know how to be free and I had no one to teach me.

"I won't let anything happen to her, Joann." Angel spoke. He took my hand. "I love her, you know. And I'll never let anyone hurt her."

He loved me? Did he mean like a sister?

"I'll never leave you," he told me. "I do love you. You know that, don't you?"

I took him in. His eyes shone more blue right now than red. I nodded. I guess I'd always known we loved each other. His grip on my hand tightened, and I suddenly felt we were going on some grand adventure that I didn't have to be afraid of as long as we were together.

"Come now." Dr. Woburn's voice drew me away from Angel. He leaned in and whispered to Joann. I wondered if it was about their baby or that he was grateful this whole mess was soon over or about Florida. I didn't know what he said, but she nodded her head and he helped her up and out of the car.

Angel reached back into the car and got out the two bags Joann had packed for us. I took mine from him, then we followed Joann and Dr. Woburn into the train station. It wasn't an overly large building, but it was so unfamiliar. Picture books and newspapers really didn't prepare me. It was a red-orange brick color, and there were electric lights guiding us in. Dr. Woburn pointed at a sign and showed us a map and where we were going. A city called Pittsburgh.

The place where we would start our new life. With a man whose only memory of me was my death certificate.

Dr. Woburn cleared his throat and took charge.

"Your train leaves in the morning at nine twenty-seven. A man will call for you to board for Pittsburgh, and he'll stamp your ticket when you're on the train and—" He paused and continued after a deep breath. "You'll have to watch what the others do around you. That's how many of us learn anyway. Do what they do. Understand?"

Angel nodded. I didn't.

"Suppose Ezra Raab wants nothing to do with me—with us?"

Joann inhaled deeply and eyed her husband before looking back at me. "I believe he will at least be willing to help you," she said. "But whatever you do—don't come back here. Milton isn't a large city— Angel is too recognizable."

"And you'll be gone?" How could it be possible that these were our last minutes together? That we would say goodbye for our whole lives?

"We—" She couldn't finish her thought and broke down. Dr. Woburn took a step forward, but she held a hand out to stop him. She sniffed and wiped her eyes before wrapping her arms around herself. This tightened her blouse, and the smallest of roundness boasted evidence of the baby growing within her.

"Maybe I'll be lucky enough to have a little girl like you," she said when she saw me looking.

Dr. Woburn showed us where to sit and where the toilets were and reminded us to keep to ourselves. We had food and money in Angel's bag. He explained about cars called taxicabs and how one could take us right to Ezra Raab's home if we showed the driver the address. He showed Angel how to count money.

Then Dr. Woburn extended his hand to Angel, and after a few beats Angel offered his in return. It struck me that I'd never seen this gesture offered to Angel—and I knew it was the beginning of our goodbye. After the lengthy handshake Dr. Woburn nodded at me, eyed Joann, then stepped toward the parking lot and waited for his wife.

Standing in the train station, its tall roof above us, on a sidewalk open to the tracks, nothing felt familiar except for the hovering sky. At least that didn't change.

After years of so much noise, the silence around the three of us was jarring. None of us knew what to do. Then Joann took a step toward Angel. He put down his suitcase, and they embraced. Angel was more than a head taller than her now. He was wearing denim pants and a button-up shirt and a coat. He had a gray cap on his head. Nicer than the stocking cap he wore sometimes when it was cold. This one had a bill that buttoned in the front in a wooly fabric.

They released one another but held each other's gaze. Angel wiped a tear away and cleared his throat.

"Goodbye, Joann," he said, and it sounded so final.

"Goodbye, my boy," she said as a tear escaped down her pale cheek. Then she turned to me. Angel instinctively took the bag from my hand and stepped back toward the bench where Dr. Woburn had told us to wait.

"I can't say goodbye to you." Until I said those words, I didn't know what I would say. But the words fell from my mouth like they'd been sitting there for all time. Perhaps the truest words I'd spoken, but a truth I had to let go of.

We were near each other's height now, though she was still a mite taller than me. She closed in the space between us and smoothed my hair and tucked the strands behind my ears. She took a handkerchief from her skirt pocket and wiped my tears. She smiled through her own.

"You were a perfect baby—*my* perfect baby. You looked right into my eyes the morning you were born."

I nodded and untangled the words in my throat. "I'm so sorry I've been so angry with you." All the anger I'd been carrying had fallen away somewhere; I didn't know where or when, but it was gone. I loved her.

"Don't." She put a finger to my lips like a mother would, then smiled as she tapped my nose. "Know that you're my first daughter, and I will tell this baby all about their big sister, Brighton."

Then she released a heavy sigh.

"Remember when you were a little girl and we read *Pollyanna*, and you asked me a question? Do you remember?"

My throat was camisoled, and words were fixed tightly in the small crevices inside. I only nodded, but Joann waited until I could answer.

"I asked if I had an aunt like Polly or a grandmother like in *The Princess and the Goblin*." Was I still that eight-year-old and this was just a dream within a dream?

Joann nodded.

"Maybe you do have an Aunt Polly, Brighton-girl."

My brow wrinkled up and my toes wiggled in my shoes.

"But you said you don't know if she's alive. Or anything about her."

"I don't. But I believe there's an Aunt Polly out there waiting for you. It might be your father or maybe this long-lost sister of your mother. But it might be someone neither of us knows but that God has already put in place for you—and Angel. Look for her. Look for the ones with the kind faces like Pollyanna, Wendy, Sarah, Anne, and so many more."

"But those are just children—just little girls. What could they do to help?"

"Little girls grow up and become women." Joann's eyes glassed over and she gripped my hands. "Find them, Brighton, and they will help you. You still have a chance. All this heartache. All these poor decisions. Blame me for all of it. But don't let any of that anger keep you from living a full life."

Her voice got fierce and ragged and old. "You are strong. The strongest person I know. You need to be brave. You need to want this new life."

We held one another and cried. My throat was swollen with hurt and thankfulness. I'd loved the mother who had given birth to me—I always would—but Joann had mothered me. She'd kept me safe and in many ways thought of my life ahead of her own. She'd made some poor choices, but had also given up so much of her life for me. That was what a mother did. She was my mother in so many ways that mattered.

"Will we really never see one another again?" I asked.

She held me close and my head rested against her chest, so near to her heart.

"I don't think so, love."

"What will you say if they ask you—about me?" I wondered aloud.

"I'll say I never knew you." Her ghostlike words created cobwebs in the corners of the train station. "Besides, you're registered as dead."

I pulled away from her and looked at her deeply in her eyes. We lost ourselves in one another's gazes, and I thought maybe we'd stand like this forever.

"I love you." She held me so tightly my heart slowed down. I felt calmer in her arms.

"I love you, Mother." I'd never called her that before, but nothing had ever felt more right than saying that now. Her gasping cry echoed in my ears. Was she in physical pain like I was? My heart hurt.

Then without warning she pulled back and looked me in the eyes.

"You're free now, my bright girl," were the last words she spoke to me before she turned and walked away. She didn't look back.

Questions Without Answers

I need to wash myself. Wash the dirt and sweat that are clinging to me from that place. The place that has too quickly become familiar again. All the ghosts. The voices. The fear.

I don't want to remember it.

I don't want to do this project with this woman. I don't want to be the person I am. I don't want to be Nell or Brighton or Doc's wife.

I want to be a plain, old regular human walking on planet Earth who doesn't have anything special about me.

The phone is ringing when I rush into my hotel room. Doc and Kelly Keene are the only ones who know where I am. But I can't talk to anyone right now. If it's Doc, I'll call him back later. When I am ready to talk about it. Will I ever be? The ringing phone starts to sound like those birds again—the birds from the asylum property calling me by name. The sound reminds me of who I am and how they heard my first cry, my first giggle, my first fit of anger, all of my firsts. And how I am responsible for Mother's death. Did they hear her falling? Would they answer the questions I'd had my whole life? Did she cry for help? Did she hum her song? Did she say my name?

I press my eyelids tightly together upon my twisted wonderings.

I am cold. I am shivering. I rush to the bathroom and pull off all my clothes, and like my son when he was young I let them fall on the floor. I turn on the shower and sit on the floor of the bath. The water comes out so cold it takes me back, so far back that it feels like yesterday. I reach up and turn the knob. After another ten or fifteen seconds the warmth coats me. I lean against the back wall and let it run over me. The pressured water feels like needles, anesthetizing me. My eyes are still closed, which means I can see everything from those years. If I can only open them I will return to this hotel room—this life, *Nell*, the person I am now—and let go of that other hurting girl I used to be.

Breathe. Breathe. Slowly. Deeply. All things bright.

I do what the voice from deep within me tells me to do. But gasp when I realize the voice isn't my own. It isn't Doc's either. It is Nursey.

When was the last time I'd called her that?

I cry and I sit there for a long time. In short intervals the phone rings again—a dozen rings and then silence. After five or ten minutes it rings again.

I get ahold of myself, but it might've been thirty minutes or two hours. I don't know. I haven't felt this sort of attack in a long time. But it has brought something out of me that couldn't wash down the drain, so it still covers me like an invisible shroud.

I dry myself, get dressed, and comb my soaked hair.

I startle when a series of knocks sounds at my door. Then someone saying "hello" a few times. Impatient people do that sort of thing.

"I'm coming, I'm coming," I say.

I open the door to find a small, dark-haired young woman with busy curls. She has big eyes and a round face, like she hasn't lost her baby fat yet. And maybe she hasn't—she is young—younger than my own children.

"Let me guess—Kelly Keene?" I meant to hide the irritation in my voice, but the day has been long and my reserves are low.

"I called a few times," she says gently with a shrug and a nervous giggle that I can't hate her for. "But no one picked up."

"Yes." I cleared my throat. "I was in the shower."

Then we share an awkward pause, and every coherent word has flown from my mind.

"Do you want to go downstairs to the restaurant to talk, or do you want to stay in here?"

I am glad she broke the silence.

I turn around and look. There's really nowhere to sit, so downstairs it is. But it is the last thing I want to do now that the cloak of exhaustion has settled in. All my contracted muscles and nerves have released now and taken all my energy. But we only have a few days together, so it must be done.

Or I can leave and pretend Kelly Keene doesn't exist.

But I know what it's like not to exist. I wouldn't wish that on anybody.

The girl—she doesn't seem to be much more than that—is polite enough to wait downstairs at a table for me while I dry my hair. It's pin straight and quick to dry. In less than twenty minutes we are sitting in a corner booth at the hotel restaurant. The shadow of my panic attack hovers near me.

"About my film." The practice of formalities never caught on. This always perturbs Doc's colleagues.

Kelly doesn't look surprised and hands me a bag like she's proud to have fulfilled a promise. She will never know that the weight of the bag is heavier than just an old camera and a handful of cartridges. I can't look in the bag now or I fear I will have another attack. There's not a whole lot left inside of myself today. I rub my fingertips against the dirty pillowcase. This had been mine. I can't get used to the idea but keep my hands on it.

"Are you going to look inside?" She sounds hopeful.

"Not now." I force a smile. "How did you find me?" I ask without warning. Another question I'm not going to pretend isn't important.

Kelly finishes her sip of coffee and gives a sheepish smile.

"There were letters along with the film in that pillowcase," she says. "Finding this felt like treasure among all the old files. Our job was to look through every item."

"And you connected Nell Friedrich and Brighton Friedrich?" I knew I should've changed my last name, but it was all I had left of my mother, so Doc, as a psychologist, never pushed me.

There's that cute little shrug again.

"Grace's sister's letters mentioned you. And your letters to Grace after your release were put inside also."

That would've been Aunt Eddie's doing.

"I didn't have to make the connection when it was all there." She pauses, then in double speed she says, "I read the letters."

"You read my letters?" Should I be insulted or grateful?

"I did. All of this was before I really understood what I was dealing with. Not just old dusty files but people—real people." Then she touches my hand. "I could tell you really loved your friend Grace."

I move my hand away.

Grace. After I'd escaped I had written those letters with such hope and hadn't known anywhere to send them but Riverside. But I never heard from her again.

"So when you understood that patients were actually human, you stopped being a snoop?" I wish I could raise an eyebrow, but I've never mastered that—but I do smile a little. I can't help but like the girl.

"Not at all." She smiles in return. "I felt it was my duty to find any owners of these items or who they should go to all these decades later."

She is right about that. And just like that we talk like old friends or maybe a niece and aunt.

"So tell me about all the cataloging," I say.

"Two other graduate students and I were assigned for a summer to catalog everything that was left behind because the community center project was in the works. All the archived files, suitcases, clothing, so many personal items—most of which was unlabeled, so we don't know who to contact. They'll either stay in a labeled storage box or get tossed. But there were a few things—personal things— that I couldn't overlook."

There is an unexpected pause, and I can see there is something she needs to say.

"What's that you've got on the other side of your tongue, Miss Keene?" There I go again, not being graceful. Graceful? I am Grace-less.

"Grace's file." She breathes in deeply.

"Have you found her too?" I lean toward her.

Then her face does that thing people do when they don't want to talk about something. Her lips purse. Her head tilts. Her eyebrows have that wavy, knit-up look to them. It's bad. I know it. She just shakes her head.

I never learned anything more about Grace since my last glimpse of her. There were several possible scenarios. Sterilization. Transfer. Even a lobotomy. Of course, at the time I didn't understand what a lobotomy really was. I didn't know, along with so many, that it ruins the person. Shatters them. Traps them.

"Her file showed a transfer—but the place she was taken to shut down decades ago. I'm not sure how to find out more." Kelly shakes her head. "I'm sorry. I really wish I had more news for you."

"Did you contact her family? I'm sure they'd want some of these photographs." I rush my words. "She had a sister who loved her."

She shakes her head. "I'm trying. Her parents have passed. I looked there first. It wasn't like finding you. You were easy. Between your letters to her with your new name and the newspaper's ways of finding people who don't want to be found, I had everything I needed."

Without knowing it, I'd led her right to me. Things I'd done so many decades ago out of survival were giving me a chance to bring pieces of my friends back to life. But excavating all of this is doing something to me that I haven't prepared for.

My face feels red. Warm. Full of tears. I shake my head. I will have to digest all of this later, not now. I inhale deeply and wipe a hand down my face.

She pulls an old envelope from the bag at her side. She slides it across the table.

I look at it. I know the handwriting.

"It's from your nurse," she says. "This was also inside the bag of film. She wrote that she hoped all of this would make it back to you someday. And the photographs of you—as a baby." She shakes her head as if in disbelief of what she's seen with her own eyes.

My breath is caught in my throat. I never saw Joann again. Not because I hated her—I loved her—but because there were too many memories. Too many hurts.

"Did you read it too?" My tough voice cuts up my anguish for a moment, giving me a chance to breathe.

"Wouldn't you have?" She smiles sweetly.

I nod and swallow hard.

"You loved this nurse—Joann—very much."

"Yes, we were close." I want to say more. I want to use the word *mother*, but that word is buried so deep inside of me. My own children were never allowed to call me that; they called me *mom* or *mama* but never *mother*. I brush my hand against the old paper and begin building the courage I'll need to read it later.

"The old photographs of you as a baby have your name, dates, your age, and sometimes even your weight and height. I was hoping it wasn't true or that I was misunderstanding something. All of it seems so crazy."

I can't contain my laughter over her use of the word *crazy*, and it breaks the stunned nature of our conversation and makes a few people turn to look at us. Kelly puts a hand over her mouth.

"Don't." I wave off her embarrassment. "There was a lot of *crazy* that happened." But even in the laughter, nostalgia takes over. "There was also a lot of not crazy in those walls—sadness, loneliness, and misunderstandings."

The pause we share has an almost holiness to it. It reminds me of the moments before you take communion bread in your mouth and chew—the joining of remembrance and thankfulness.

"I'm kind of surprised you're normal, you know? You hear of

children who weren't given a normal upbringing and how it ruins their chance at a typical adulthood." She rambles and I stifle a chuckle. "I'm a psychology minor."

"Believe me, Kelly, I'm not normal—and neither are you, for that matter. What's really normal, anyhow?"

She tucks her lips, looking embarrassed. "I'm so sorry. I didn't mean—I keep putting my foot in my mouth."

"It's all right." Then I pat her hand, because that does feel entirely *normal*. It's odd how fluidly we all use that word, and it's equally as odd how indefinable it is.

"So, it's true then? You were born there?"

I carefully open the old envelope and slip out the few photographs inside. In the first I'm sitting, smiling, in a washbasin for a bath and the young, thin arms of Joann hold me steady. Her face isn't in the picture, but I know she's on the other side of the yellowed edge. I also know that my mother was probably somewhere in the room. Oh, how I long to move the frame one way or another to see them. To see their faces. I'm taken so far back. But instead of the terror, what I see is love and hope. What is more hopeful than a baby?

"Photographs only capture a small square of a scene and there's so much a photograph can't contain. My mother and I both had dirty-blond hair. She had blue eyes and long, elegant fingers—like she might've played the piano if she'd had a different life. I will never forget those details. A photograph cannot serenade me with the voice of my mother saying 'Brighton' over and over after she delivered me."

I turn over the image to show her, even though I know she's seen it before. I feel my own eyes twinkle. The memory of Nursey telling me this story as a little girl has always brought me joy. I know now that children love to hear the story of their birth.

I speak slow and steady and share myself in a way I never have before. "It's almost like I remember my birth—though I know it's not possible. But there are people who say that babies have a way of remembering things that happen to them. My husband is a doctor and he's told me as much." My eyes linger over the photograph. "I was at Riverside from birth until I was eighteen, and I rarely repeat or revisit the memories from those years."

"Was leaving what you expected? Freedom how you expected it to be?"

Oh, that word. "Expectations can be dangerous things, and freedom isn't easily defined."

"It's like a fairy tale. It doesn't seem real," Kelly says.

I smile at her. "More like a Grimms' fairy tale. I've looked for answers my whole life. Why I was born to a mother the doctors called mad and why most of my friends were what the good old days called feeble-minded or imbeciles." That sentence is peppered with those fancy air quotes and laughter. Laughter hurts less than anger that might otherwise build up. But it doesn't reduce how I feel about all of the lines we draw between one another.

"So you don't think the patients needed treatments? They were misdiagnosed?" she questions sincerely.

"True mental illness should be treated—but the treatments were barbaric and degrading and often unhelpful. Mishandling of the human mind breaks the spirit in anyone."

"Do you still keep searching for understanding?"

"No, I've just been trying to forget."

"What will happen if you decide to remember?" And she pushes the pillowcase bag filled with images of dark and light closer to me.

Stranger, Stranger

When I was about six years old I found a caterpillar outside. It was dark brown with a little orange stripe along its back. When I first picked it up it curled into a fuzzy circle in my hand. I thought it was dead, and since death wasn't foreign to me but something to be understood, I watched it so closely I nearly went cross-eyed. But it wasn't dead; it was just getting used to me. I petted it gently and eventually it woke up and started to crawl around my hand and up my arm.

I named her Sister, and when it was time to go inside I tucked her in my little curled-up palm and didn't tell anyone. Joyful had once given me a jelly jar for my little found treasures—mostly pretty rocks—so I put Sister inside and hid her in the corner of the room under my bed. After two days Joann found Sister and made me put her back outside.

That afternoon during our outside courtyard time I cried when I pulled Sister out of her jar and set her on the edge of the sidewalk—close to where I'd found her so her family might find her again. As soon as Sister touched the concrete she curled into a circle like she had that first day in my hand. Maybe she was nervous again. Maybe she knew that people walked on the sidewalk and she could easily be stepped on. I didn't know.

Sister never unwound. The next day she was still on the sidewalk like a small fuzzy circle. The day after that she was there. I called to her—"Sister, Sister," I said. But she didn't move. The third day she was uncurled like the letter *C*. I picked her up, but Joann slapped her out of my hand, saying it was gross because it was dead. Until then I didn't know that dead was gross or that staying in the same place without moving meant death. Sister was so afraid to crawl across the sidewalk that she died where I left her. And I cried about her dying because I knew I had caused it by holding her captive.

I thought I'd done the right thing by putting Sister back in the world where she belonged, but all of my keeping and touching had ruined her. She'd been gone from her world for too long.

That morning as we boarded the train with a few other people, I felt like Sister being returned to my rightful world. All I wanted to do was curl up on the sidewalk because I was so afraid. But knowing I had a father and maybe an aunt out there—could this strange new world actually have inside of it a Pollyanna life saved just for me? I tried to consider this and reminded myself of my new freedom even when everything was strange.

Angel took my hand, and we walked on board the train with our small bags. His eyes were wide and open, and he didn't seem to notice that the man with the funny hat stared at him. No one stared at him at the hospital because we'd all grown used to him and the way he looked—his bright, white self. Out here, however, was different.

But Angel moved us forward and I kept breathing. When I had to let go of Angel's hand and follow him down a narrow aisle, I grabbed the back of his coat instead. I was afraid he would disappear if I let him out of my sight or let him get out of reach.

"Here?" He turned and pointed at two seats.

I looked around before nodding my head. I sat next to the window, then Angel sat too and we held our bags on our laps. Then we just had to sit and wait. Under Angel's vigilant gaze and with him holding my hand, I finally let myself fall asleep. I dreamed I was playing with Angel at the graveyard. I was young and innocent. My young self stopped in front of the gravestone marked *H. Friedrich* and it startled me awake.

When I opened my eyes, the recurring wave of grief cascaded over me.

"I want to go back," I said to Angel, and my breathing sped up.

"Don't, Brighton." He was firm but not mean.

I shook my head. "No, not to stay there. But I want to see Mother's gravestone."

Angel squeezed my hand and gave me a small, understanding smile. His smile was always filled with hope. I memorized it, fearing that one day he would also be gone like everyone else I loved. But he did say he loved me and promised not to leave me.

Promises are the minions of love. I heard Joann's words in my mind. I shook them away. Angel would not leave me.

When I wasn't asleep I was taking in everything around me.

There weren't many in the train with us. The smiling train man with the funny hat and striped shirt said a cheerful good morning to us when he took our tickets and stamped them. There was a mother with a young son. An older couple a few rows in front of us, both had canes and spoke too loudly. We learned they were visiting their daughter who had just had a baby.

The landscape flashed by us so fast my stomach turned. I'd never gone so fast before. But eventually I got used to the steady, rocking pace. I took in the fields and farms. Would I ever be known in this big world? Grace had told me so much about its wonders . . .

Oh, Grace.

Guilt rose in my throat like vomit. This city—Pittsburgh—might as well be another planet. I would never be of any help to Grace so far away. I would write to her once I got to my father's home. I didn't know how to mail a letter, but maybe my father could show me. And would Grace even get it? I would have to try.

"Cows and horses." I pulled at Angel's arm so that he would look through my window. I'd only ever seen pictures of these animals. They were smaller than I'd imagined. The old red barns were nearby with what looked like goats or sheep—I couldn't tell the difference.

Would I ever learn what I needed to know about this world? Even farm animals were new to me.

A boy rode his bike on some small dirt road that ran alongside the train. He waved and pumped his arm and the train *choo-choo*ed.

The sky was a white-blue behind the trees and fields, above the roofs of houses, and in the great horizon that we moved so quickly toward. For years there was no movement at all, then suddenly everything moved at once.

Chase Yourself

*J*ust as the green landscape and rolling hills of the farmlands calmed me, the rush of buildings and concrete spurred my heart rate to a gallop. The entire world went from green to gray, and it wasn't only because of the weather. The buildings were gray, the sky had turned gray, and the haze in the air was gray. Was this Pittsburgh? Nothing looked as pretty as the willow tree outside my small balcony, especially when it bloomed and the petals fell like raindrops. Nothing looked as bright as the row of tomatoes that could woo anyone to bite into one like an apple. Nothing was as familiar as the tiled floor that I'd learned to walk on and Joann's bright, red-lipped smile.

The rhythm of the train changed, and I sat straighter. We were slowing down. I reached out a hand to touch the window. The chill from the glass spread through my body. My other hand gripped Angel's. I looked out the window and could feel Angel's breath on the side of my neck. He was looking out too. But was he afraid like me? He didn't grip me as I gripped him. But at least we were looking in the same direction—taking the same road.

Before I knew it we had stopped underneath a domed roof in what I could only assume was Pittsburgh. I rolled the name around in my mouth without saying it, trying to make the rough, concrete sounds familiar and real. The few folks around us began to stand and stretch. It was time to get off the train. But I couldn't get up. Suddenly I longed for the weight of the familiar and the security of knowing who cared for me.

Angel let go of my hand when he picked up his bag and stood. But I still sat and kept watching the flow of people through the window. On the sidewalk were a man and woman looking toward the train expectantly. They were both dressed in tailored clothes, looking the very opposite of the billowing asylum gown I was accustomed to wearing. My palms smoothed my waistline as I suddenly remembered that I wore clothes like that now too. The suited man had a firm jaw that clenched and unclenched, and the woman's eyes were filled with anticipation.

Suddenly they both broke out in bright smiles and a young man joined them. He wore what looked like a uniform from head to toe in dull green. He greeted the woman first, and her porcelain face broke in half and tears fell through the cracks as they hugged. The man patted the younger one's back as his own face twitched and stuttered.

The shared hug aged the woman. Or maybe the tears had. Tears had a way of doing that.

"Brighton, it's time." Angel sounded so sure of himself.

I inhaled deeply as I grabbed my bag from the floor. I followed Angel down the narrow aisle and carefully down the steep steps. I was afraid to leave the train and walk on the concrete of this city that didn't know me.

When we stepped off the train, no one noticed us. Didn't we have the story of our escape written on our foreheads? I looked down at myself again and was reminded that I looked more like the woman I'd just seen than Mother. My face twitched at the thought of her. I was fake. I was supposed to be wearing a sack-like hospital gown and look like myself instead of like a lady.

Angel squeezed my hand and brought me back.

I looked up at him. The hat made him look older and so handsome and like he knew how to handle himself. His shirt had a collar—I'd never seen him wear something like that before. It didn't seem to bother Angel that we were walking, talking liars.

But after a few minutes, some people did gawk at Angel. We pretended not to notice and kept walking.

"I'm not going to let anything happen to you." He said it like he'd read my mind. "You told me the first time we met that you'd be my guardian; now it's my turn."

I searched his violet eyes. I knew them better than my own. These were the eyes that had looked at me with such fear that first time in the graveyard, but now there was strength in them. He didn't need me like I needed him, and that scared me. A weak smile crossed over his lips. I nodded my head and together we walked into a building unlike anything I ever could have imagined.

My mouth opened, and both Angel and I said, "Wow." We dropped our hold on each other and took in our surroundings. I looked up and my eyes filled with the sight of a bright dome. It was ornamented with decorative squares and made the most beautiful ceiling I'd ever seen in my life. Sunlight descended through the skylights and lit my face. The lights that hung from chains were so large that I didn't stand underneath them. What would happen if one fell? And there were tree-trunk-size pillars that went floor to ceiling of what I could only figure was marble. And there were benches built in a circle where one could sit and enjoy the beauty for as long as desired.

"This is a train station? It doesn't look like the one in Milton," Angel said.

I shook my head. No, it didn't.

My shoulder got bumped as I turned in place, still looking up. Then I got bumped a second and a third time. The large space was filling up fast. I spun around to find Angel but couldn't see him in the sudden crowd.

"Angel?" I whispered it at first but after only a few seconds I said it louder and then louder yet. A man gave me a dirty look and then a woman too. Then another woman said to me, "Oh, chase yourself."

Because of Grace I knew it meant *get lost*. Well, I was lost. Why a strange woman would tell me that didn't make sense. Grace hadn't really explained that part. But I was chasing myself. I was always chasing after my real self and never catching up.

Before I could panic further a hand took mine and plucked me from the crowd. We sat on a bench catching our breath until the crowd thinned out. Then without a word of warning, Angel pulled me up and began walking toward the large section of doors. I could see that familiar gray through them. I wanted to resist, but this was the only direction we could go. Into the daylight and our new lives. Toward Ezra Raab, my father.

1941

Father

The brightness outside the train station hurt my eyes. I squinted at the dull white, and my nose found the scent of smoke and sewer all at once. I wanted to pinch my nose like I used to do as a child, but my hands were full.

This world was so large. So colorless. So tall with buildings reaching high into the foggy sky. The road ahead of us was filled with vehicles moving too fast, but like magic they didn't run into each other. It was so loud and I couldn't look anywhere without seeing too many people and too many things. I saw all of them but they didn't seem to see each other. They didn't look up from their newspapers. They walked fast around corners without care.

There were yellow cars mixed with the more quiet colors, cream, black, tan, dark green. Joann had mentioned something about the yellow cars, right? Green-uniformed men and women walked around in groups. Their strides were firm and sure, and they looked so smart. So different from me.

It started to drizzle, and the drops dotted everything around me. Black umbrellas popped up everywhere. We scooted beneath the awning of the building.

Angel rummaged through his pocket and pulled out money.

"Dr. Woburn said that we should ask one of the yellow taxis to take us to your father's address."

"How do we do that?"

Neither of us spoke, but we did what Joann told us to do—we watched and learned.

"You'll have to be my eyes, Brighton. The rain is making things a little harder to see."

A woman in a raincoat and heeled shoes ran toward the street, waving a hand over her head and yelling, "Taxi." A few moments later a yellow car with the word *taxi* on it stopped. She opened the door quickly and hopped inside.

Before another few minutes had passed it happened again. This time it was a man, and instead of the word *taxi* he gave a loud whistle.

I led Angel toward the corner where I'd seen the first taxi. I waved and, like a miracle, one slowed to a stop in front of us. Angel turned to me and smiled.

"Wow. That wasn't hard," he said.

I smiled back. We stepped toward the yellow car when a man barreled past us and hopped into the cab ahead of us. This happened once more before we finally were able to get into a taxi. By then we were covered in a fine layer of drizzle. I couldn't control my shivering. At least this chilled-to-the-bone sensation felt natural enough.

Angel scooted in first and then me. The taxi smelled like the hospital basement. Like it had been almost dry for a long time. It was dirty enough that I kept my bag and hands on my lap.

"Where you—" the driver started, with a thick accent, then stopped and stared at Angel. "Something wrong with you? You sick?" He tucked his chin.

"There's nothing wrong—" I began, then Angel patted my knee.

"I'm not sick, I just have light skin." He said it like he'd rehearsed it, though I'd never heard him say anything of the sort.

Angel pulled out my father's address and showed him. "Here? Can you take us here?"

The driver's eyes lingered on Angel for several long moments before he finally took the piece of paper. He looked at it, then handed it back to Angel. "All right, I'll take you. You could've just said to take you to J & L."

We didn't know what that meant.

The ride in this car was nothing like when we were with Joann and Dr. Woburn. We braced ourselves against each other and our arms against the doors. The driver didn't seem to notice how we were being thrown around. A moment later a question surfaced. What would happen if my father didn't live there anymore?

And what if he did but didn't want Angel to stay? That idea was like a needle traveling through my brain.

I didn't stop thinking about those prospects as the driver passed us under a drooping clothesline attached between buildings and swaying power lines. People walking along near the road didn't seem to notice our speed. Weren't they afraid to walk so close to the fast-moving cars? The buildings grew drearier and shorter and became more run-down. They reminded me of a few of the older buildings that sat in the back of the hospital grounds that weren't in use.

Then we stopped. The driver turned.

"J & L factory is just up ahead." He put the flat of his hand out. "Two dollar."

Angel pulled out a bill. He looked at it closely; it had a five in the corner. The cabdriver grabbed the bill from Angel and told us to get out. We did as we were told, and a moment later we were standing on the edge of the road. I looked in the direction the driver pointed and heard the taxi speed off.

There was an odor in the air, different from the hospital stench. It was acrid, metallic, and rotten. Angel's face twitched, and I covered my nose.

"Where are we?" I asked, as if Angel knew.

I turned in a circle and took in my surroundings. The buildings in the distance were shadowed in the light gray sky. We were on a poorly paved road that was worn down and broken along the edges. There was a set of rickety-looking wooden stairs that went down the steep hill, reaching to the ground level of what the driver called a factory and all the surrounding buildings. How many worlds would we cross into? This one was dirty and muddy. At the bottom of the stairs were small, two-story buildings stacked next to each other. On their laundry lines dingy, gray clothing hung. People must live there. Smoke poured out of the long tubes that reached into the sky. What were they called? Images from newspapers, magazines, and books came back to me—smokestacks maybe? There was a *J* on one tall tube, a symbol for *and*, and a third with an *L* on it. A nearby sign said Jones and Laughlin Steel Company. Now I understood the J & L.

"How do we know where he lives?" I asked Angel, as if he would know any more than I would.

He took out the address and looked at it again.

"We're going to need to ask someone." He stuffed the address back in his pocket, then I helped him down the stairs. They were tall and rugged, but we reached the bottom safely. There were people milling around on the sidewalks. Some carried bags or walked with children dirtier than those in the children's ward. As soon as we reached the bottom, several scurried away with strange expressions on their faces.

"Ignore them," I told Angel, knowing they'd run because of him.

We followed the flow of people walking toward the buildings with the laundry lines.

"Let's follow them. Maybe we'll see street signs. Or something," Angel said. "I wish we had a map. Remember the maps we made of the hospital as kids?"

Of course I remembered. Suddenly everything good that had littered our childhood came to mind, making me miss Joann even more.

"You'll have to ask," Angel said. "People are afraid of me. Ask that woman where this address is."

He handed me the paper with my father's address on it. The woman he pointed at was sweeping her small porch. She looked tired, and her apron was a dreary gray, as was the color of her skin, though both had been white at one point. I didn't know what to say. Out here everything felt so hard. Angel gestured for me to take a step toward the woman.

I cleared my throat and she looked at me.

"I said I can't pay today," the woman said. Her accent made her words move up and down like a kite. She started to go for the door.

Angel jabbed me in the back.

"I'm not looking for money. Just a question," I said quickly. "We're looking for this address."

I walked up and showed her the paper. She leaned her head back and eyed me from the bottoms of her lids. Slowly she set her broom against the tired wood siding of the house, leaned over the rail, and put her hand out. I stepped toward her and handed the paper to her. The lines of her calloused hands were black and inky, but her face was young; she was not much older than me. She looked at the paper, then looked toward the other two-story buildings.

"It's just there," she said, pointing off to the left. "On the corner. The number will be above the door."

My eyes went above her head to her doorframe and to the number 278 in faded paint.

"Thank you," Angel said and gestured for me to come.

"He hasn't got any money either," she called after us.

I turned. "What?"

"He hasn't got money—Ez hasn't—if that's what you're seeking."

Ez. My father. Ezra Raab. She knew him. My heart tipped and spilled all over my insides. I paused, and my gaze and the woman's locked. I wanted to ask her so many questions. What was he like? Was he handsome? Did I look like him? Was he married? Did I have any brothers or sisters?

I shook my head. "I don't want his money either," I said. That seemed to be what she was most concerned about. "He's my father."

I shouldn't have said that. The woman's face told me more than I wanted to know. She began laughing.

"Father?" she said, then with a smirk she continued. "Well then, I'll wish you luck. He's apartment B."

As Angel and I walked in the direction that the woman pointed, all I kept repeating was one word. *Father. Father.*

I'm Not Dead

There was so much to take in while I looked for my father's house number. The world down here was strewed with broken windows and dingy porches and doors. There weren't many people about. I assumed most were working. But there were children sitting on the porch next to Ezra's.

They were dirty from head to toe. The oldest of the three couldn't have been more than six. There was darkness under their eyes and in the windows behind them and maybe in their whole world. Had they been left alone? They were sharing a slice of bread—the soft white showing grimy smudges from their fingers. In their faces I saw my own—being left in a world unfairly—but the pain of hunger in that season of life was not part of my history. These children didn't appear to have a Nursey in their lives as I had. My throat went tight.

I looked over at Angel. His forehead was creased and leaden. Could he see that the little one had tears streaked through the dirt on his face? They looked sickly and were covered in a red rash and bug bites. The oldest had one entirely white eye. They blended in with the gray and dismal so much it was almost as if they'd grown out of the cracks in the concrete. What world had we walked into?

"Is this it?" Angel squinted at the door.

I pulled my gaze away and matched the written address with the painted numbers. 743. The lady with the broom said apartment B.

There were three steps up to the front door. There were two

windows on either side of the door and two windows above those on the second floor. A few curtains raggedly hung across a few windows. Several others had broken panes.

"Should we go in?" Angel asked, but I think he really meant *we should go in.*

I took the first step that would usher in the next part of my life.

Inside there was an A door and a B door and steps to the second floor. I knocked on the B door, but no one answered. We slouched down all the way to sitting against the wall next to the door. And we waited.

At some point during our waiting we fell asleep, and when I opened my eyes again the sky through the window was dusky. The next thing I saw was a lanky, dirty man looking at me. He was wearing a newsy cap—that's what the fashion magazines called them. It was filthy and creased. His face was bony and smudged. He smelled like the factory smoke. He looked at me with a furrow cut so deeply into his brow it was like he'd never be able to undo it.

I elbowed Angel. He was startled but stood with me. I knew I must be wrinkled and dirty after having slept for hours on the floor. My neck was kinked and every joint hurt.

"Homeless aren't allowed in here," the man said with an accent I couldn't place. He pushed his hand into his pocket and pulled out a few keys on a ring. He moved toward the door. His hand shook as he tried to find the right one. His other hand was bandaged in what used to be a white cloth. It was covered with traces of blood and grime. Small sweat trails traveled down his temples. The factory must have been hot. He wore overalls, and his shirt underneath looked so thin, I could almost see through it. "I said run off, beggars."

"What's wrong with him?" The man gestured at Angel, as if suddenly noticing him. "Some kind of disease? Get him out of here. You too."

"Ezra? Ezra Raab?" I asked. My voice barely sounded familiar.

"I don't have any money," he said and cursed when the keys

dropped from his hand. He picked them up and tried again. If he got inside and closed the door, I'd never get the chance to speak to him. I needed to hurry.

"I'm not here for money. My name is Brighton Friedrich." Then I shook my head. "I mean, my mother was Helen Friedrich."

The jingling keys paused, then he found the right key and the door popped open. He was about to go inside.

"I'm your daughter," I said.

"That's not possible." He didn't look at me. "My daughter's dead."

So this really was Ezra Raab. This was my father. It had to be.

"I know that's what you were told, but it wasn't true. It's not true. I'm not dead."

Ezra continued to stare straight ahead, like a statue.

"Can we come inside?" I asked.

Ezra sighed. "I don't have much food."

"We don't need much. And we brought some." I gestured toward Angel's pack.

He opened the door farther and walked in, leaving it open for us. I wasn't sure what I expected to see inside, but what I did see was far worse than any possible expectations. This dismal place was painted in various shades of gray. If there had once been color, it had not survived. If I stayed here, would I turn into some shade of gray and grime too?

"You can have a seat," Ezra said and gestured to the couch. It was worse than the one that had been in the dayroom at the hospital. The one I'd sat on so many times with Grace. The one I would never sit on again. My heart went flat with that memory yet inflated with hope in the shape of Ezra Raab.

Ezra left Angel and me in what seemed to be a living room. He went into a small bathroom. In the same area there was a few feet of counter space in the corner that had a sink and two burners. There was a miniature, smudged refrigerator against the wall. The window had droopy curtains, and there was a bed in one corner and a small table and two chairs in another. Angel sat on the couch and I followed.

"I can't live here. We can't live here. It's worse than the hospital. Well, it's dirtier anyway," I said, knowing my quick judgment was unfair.

"Let's talk to him first." He patted my knee.

Ten minutes later an unrecognizable man returned. His hair was nearly blond, like mine—only shaded with gray. His skin was bland and his whiskers freshly removed. His blue shirt and denim pants were a few sizes too big and reminded me of oversize hospital gowns.

"I can make coffee." He paused. "Do you drink coffee?"

Angel and I nodded. He did everything in silence before he handed us both mugs. He brought over a chair from the small table. He sat and looked at his hands for a while before he spoke. I sipped the hot drink, finding that it tasted nothing like the hospital's coffee. After a few more tastes I decided I preferred the darker and earthier taste of my father's coffee.

"Your mother, she is—" he asked.

"Gone." The reluctant words clung to my tongue before I let them out. "She died—recently."

The days had blurred together. Had it only been less than a week ago?

He bounced his head up and down and leaned forward with his elbows on his knees. There was silence again for a few minutes.

"How was she?"

"Do you mean, the psychosis?" I hovered strangely between neutralizing everything with a more medical view or falling into my father's arms in a fit of tears.

"Is that what it was called?" His *th* sounded like a *z* and every *w* like a *v*. "I have always worried about Helene."

"She wasn't well. She never was."

His eyes grew glassy and, like a mirror, mine did the same.

"I'm sorry to hear that. She was a good woman. A very good woman."

"Did you know her well?" Had he loved her or only used her? Why hadn't they married?

"We are from the same village in Germany. We were children together. She was a happy girl, and we fell in love when we were younger than both of you." He stopped and looked out the window. "Her mother—she had a hard time and she was very unwell. She—"

"How did she die?" The unplanned words fumbled out.

He looked at his hands. "She didn't always know what she was doing. Didn't understand it would kill her."

She'd killed herself. I didn't know if I wanted to know more so I moved on.

"How did my mother come to America?"

"After Nell's death, Otto, your grandfather, brought Helene and Margareta to America." He spoke in a halting and disruptive way, requiring patience on my part. "To start again."

He stood and walked to a cabinet and after a few moments returned and handed me a photograph. I looked at Angel and then back at the photo. It was the same photo Joann had given me, only mine had been cut. The hand belonged to a sister, I knew now. My grandmother sat stiffly in a larger chair with her hands gripping its arms. A stout man with a strong jaw stood behind her with his hands on her shoulders. And my aunt looked so much like my mother, only quite younger. Really, she was only a girl. The girl would now be an adult.

"This is your mother when she was a little younger than you. That is her mother and father, your grandparents, and her sister."

"I have seen this photograph," I told him but still took in the photo like the first time. "You came with them to America?"

"Otto didn't want Helene and me to get married—he said she was going to be like her mother and that he was sure she could get help in America. But Helene and I loved one another very much, so

I followed her here." His voice broke, and I could see the loss was still fresh.

He shook his head. "You must know that she was a very kind and loving woman and I would never hurt her—I loved her. I still believe I could've kept her from that depth of madness that you say she succumbed to—my poor Helene. Otto did not believe this, though."

I looked again at the photo, at my grandmother's eyes that were like my mother's. Blank and lost. Her wrists were tied to the chair arms with black strips to blend in with her dress. Restraints. Why hadn't I noticed that before now?

On the back was written *Otto and Nell Friedrich* and beneath was *Helene and Margareta*.

"There's so much I don't understand." I stood and walked to the window and stared out into the dirty dusk. "When she found herself pregnant, why didn't you marry her?"

There was a long pause.

"I am not proud to tell you, but I was in jail when she was taken to the hospital." He cleared his throat. "We, her father and I, didn't know she was expecting. Helene may not have known herself. By the time I got out, Otto had died. After questioning neighbors, the police, and the local hospital, I found where she was taken. By then she'd been in there for nearly five months and was not herself. She did not know me. She was near her time, but I had no right to her. I was not her husband."

He straightened his back in his chair, and I could see he was uncomfortable with all of this. The lines on his forehead wrote the story of those years, but it was muddled up and I couldn't read it.

"I visited to ask after you. A nurse told me you had died."

"But I'm not dead."

"I see that now." His voice was quiet, like a dandelion puff in the wind.

"But you would have taken me if you had been able to?" I asked.

He nodded. "It would've been difficult. But it could've worked."

No one spoke for several minutes. My worlds were colliding. My father had wanted me.

"She used to hum a song," I said.

"A song?"

"Just a little tune." I hummed a short part of the melody and was met with his tenor voice joining in, but he was using real words— German words.

"*Shlaf, Kindlein, shlaf.*" He sang several lines, then eventually faded into humming as if he'd forgotten the rest.

"What does it mean?" I asked.

"Sleep, baby, sleep. Your father tends the sheep. Your mother shakes the little trees, there falls down one little dream. Sleep, baby, sleep," he recited softly and looked right at me when he spoke.

He stopped and cleared his throat.

"Where have you been all these years? How did you find me?" My ears heard his questions, but I was sure my face responded in confusion.

"Where have I been?" My breath choked in my throat. Angel took my hand. "Where else? I've been there. At Riverside until yesterday. My nurse—Joann—the nurse who raised me—us—helped us escape and gave me your address." Every word fumbled out of my mouth.

"You were there? At that hospital all of these years?" His voice broke, along with his face.

I nodded.

"You were raised with *those* people?"

I nodded. "Those people were my friends—my family. I saw the good in them the way you did in my mother."

"Of course. I understand."

I believed him because he loved Mother when she wasn't perfect.

"Can you tell me anything about my aunt?" I asked.

"Margareta?"

"Is she alive?"

"Yes. And she is well now after many years of sickness." Then, like he knew I needed to know what sort of illness, he spoke again. "Polio."

Angel and I looked at each other and smiled. This was good news.

"Wait, now, what did you say your name was?" he asked.

"Brighton." I sat up straighter. "My mother said it over and over again to the nurses when I was born. Does it mean something?"

His head bounced up and down, and he pulled in his lips. After a minute he leaned forward on his elbows again.

"That's not your name," he said.

"What do you mean? Of course it is." I wanted to laugh but instead felt panicked and my hand found Angel's.

"I knew your name sounded familiar." He stood and pulled an envelope out from his desk and handed it to me. "Look at the return address. Brighton is the name of the town where your aunt lives. She wasn't choosing your name; she was telling your nurses where to send you. To Brighton, Michigan, to Margareta—your aunt."

I looked in the corner of the envelope and saw for myself that the city was Brighton. He was right, Brighton was not my name. It was the name of a town.

I had no name. I was registered as dead and I was nameless.

Love, Nursey

I am not sure how prepared I am to hear from Joann. It's been decades since I hugged her goodbye. Called her Mother. And watched her walk away. I am back in my hotel room with the letter in my hands. One letter after all these years.

I know that if she were alive, she would be eighty-five. Our years have grown closer; we wouldn't be like child and mother anymore.

The front of the envelope has two Return to Sender stamps from a postman years ago. One is scribbled out. My father's Philadelphia address was written in Joann's curled script. I turn the envelope over in my hands and read what has been written on the outside flap.

My darling Brighton, I don't know when or if you'll ever get this letter. I sent it to your dear Aunt Eddie to put with your precious belongings in the hopes that maybe someday it will all be returned to you.

I lift the flap and remove the photographs again. I don't look at them this time, not wanting to travel that journey twice in one night. But this diverging road I am on will be much harder to bear. When I inhale, the pungent stench of the dayroom and the feel of a razor running along my scalp return to me. My hand grazes my bobbed hair—still there. Just a memory, I remind myself.

September 15, 1941

My dearest Brighton,

You've been gone for four months now, and there have been days where I've stayed in bed missing you. If it wasn't for Sid and for our baby, perhaps I would still be there. The realization of all that I did that hurt you is overwhelming. I must ask your forgiveness again. Though that grace may be a deeper scar yet.

I have walked the halls of our ward in my mind looking for your smile, but I know I won't find you there. And that is as it should be. The guilt and regret I carry is also as it should be. But they play tricks on my mind, and I have fought to hold on to reality.

I never returned to Riverside after your escape. And while there was some investigating, everyone covered for us. In the end, your escape just became more skeletons in the closet. I do know that Angel's father was furious after learning of his disappearance.

I need to tell you something. In one of your father's letters when you were around ten, he mentioned an aunt. He said she was recovering from polio in Brighton, Michigan, and asked if Helen would ever be able to live with her when she was well. Of course Helen was too ill to do that, but this was when I realized that your poor mother meant for you to be sent to your aunt in Brighton— not to name you. But, my darling girl, you are still Brighton. You've never been anyone else in the world but Brighton. Please don't question who you are.

I regret I never learned anything more about your aunt. But since you'd been documented as deceased for so many years, Sid and I both would've lost our licenses to undo the mess I'd made— and I would've lost you, which I wasn't prepared to do at the time. I don't suppose I'll ever really forgive myself for all of this.

I wish I could tell you that I did everything out of my love for you. But there was more to it. All around me were women who were hurting and unable to bear the burden of their pain. That was and still is my greatest fear for myself. My fear that I would become one of them if I lost you, since losing you would be like losing a part of me.

I don't suspect we will meet again in this life, but I pray you can forgive me, though undeserved. So I ask God to give me peace. Know I love you and always will.

Love,
Nursey

P.S. I have a baby son. His name is Jason, because it means "healer."

Have I forgiven Joann? Yes. Every day. That's how often I take it back and then spit the venom of bitterness from my mouth. Perhaps I will go to the grave still learning how to forgive the woman who both loved and hurt me most.

Unbright

It would not have mattered if Lorna had walked into the apartment yelling one of her clichés. Or if Carmen was complaining loudly from the other side of the room that there hadn't been enough food on her plate to feed a mosquito. I would not have heard anything. My ears were filled with cotton. Filled with water. Filled with lies and the bitterness of truth.

I looked at Angel. My eyes must have covered most of my face and my mouth was open, but nothing was coming out. I looked then at Ezra. My father. His mouth was moving, but I still couldn't hear anything. He looked sad and worried. What was he saying?

I was shaking, but it seemed like it wasn't me. Angel was shaking me. Trying to wake me up from being awoken.

"Brighton, Brighton," I finally heard.

"That's not my name," I whispered back. My ears were ringing.

"But it is. It became your name, regardless of what your mother intended. My name was never really Angel. I don't know what my name is." His voice was like the peeled wallpaper from my asylum room—brittle and broken.

I squeezed my eyes closed until they almost sank inside my head. I needed to get away from this new pain. I needed for it not to fill my mind and taunt me. Surely Joann knew what my father had just explained to me. The anger I'd let go of last night came back to me like the years I'd spent at Riverside were stacked upon my heart, pressing down.

The burden of truth had exhausted me. My eyes were heavy. My arms were like rods of iron. My very heart seemed to question if it had the strength to beat once more—and once more.

And what would happen next? Would my father ask me to stay? The tenderness we had shared in those moments speaking of Mother had to mean something. But he had said nothing of helping or of us staying or of how we could start a life together.

Did he wish I'd stayed dead?

My father's face was pained and waning, but he didn't look away from me.

"I'm sorry," I said, not knowing what to say.

"For what?"

For coming. For intruding. For not being dead.

"For"—I wasn't sure which one to say—"coming."

His eyes burst with blueness, and I could see where there were fragments of a handsome face.

"Do you see this way that I live?" He gestured around the room, his gaze landing out the window briefly before returning to me.

Was I supposed to nod? Then he went on.

"This isn't the life I wanted to live. Helene and I wanted so much more. We talked about children and family."

Why had he never married another?

"I made many promises to your mother and couldn't keep any of them. Your grandfather was a harsh man, but he did his best—life was hard."

"Because of my grandmother?"

He nodded. "When he saw Helene fighting the same demons, he thought America the beautiful would hold all the answers." He paused. "Do not be sorry, for I am not sorry that you came. You are like a star in the night sky. Now I know Helene will live on."

"But?" I asked.

"But you cannot stay. This is no place for you."

"I could get a job. I wouldn't be any bother to you. And Angel is a hard worker too."

"It will not work, *meine schatzi*."

Hearing him call me *meine schatzi* was like a gentle restraint around my heart. Was I really his dear one? Was he avoiding the use of the name that wasn't mine as a kindness or manipulating me with a false endearment, or did he really see me as dear? Pretty words were soft like cotton. But when a patient was wrapped in cotton for therapy, when dampened and allowed to dry, it squeezed the breath from their lungs, forcing some to faint from lack of oxygen. That's what his words did to my soul. "There's no room here for three."

"But we have nowhere to go."

"I have family." Angel spoke like the rush of a breeze coming through the enclosed room. He looked at me. "I went through my bag when you slept on the train. I found part of an address."

"But Joann—" I started until I saw Angel pull out a folded paper. Lines of black marker crossed out large sections. Angel showed Ezra the address.

"These are admission papers and an address is here. I think they just missed crossing it out," he said.

"This address is not so far," Ezra said. "It's on the outskirts of the city." Then he paused. "And this is your family?"

"Joann said not to go to them," I inserted and had to fight the urge to grab the paper from his hand and tear it up.

"I have to try." Angel looked at Ezra. "Maybe you could help me find this address?"

While this exchange had lasted only a few minutes, Ezra's rejection would linger with me much longer. He didn't want me.

In slow and unhampered movements he pulled out a map from his cabinet. With quiet steadiness he showed Angel the area the address was in. I didn't look at the map but heard soft words about a cab drive and asking if we had enough money.

Ezra didn't want me, but he had wanted my mother—even with her fits. And soon we would leave and I would probably never see him again.

I got up. I needed air. I needed the expanse of the inky sky. I needed out.

"Where are you going?" Angel asked.

"I need—I'm just going to take a walk."

My step out of the house did not lift the weight I bore. The stench in the air was insulting and severe. I'd withstood horrible smells my whole life, but the outside air had always been a salvation and rescue from that. But here, I was trapped.

My toes wiggled in my shoes as I stood on a burdened sidewalk that had known more lives than I could wonder over. Across from where I stood was another row of wearied, dull houses and farther in the distance were the initialed stacks that poured putrid smoke into the night air. My eyes traveled up. The sky was a mere charcoal canvas. No blue night, no splash of stars, no tiny Crux to be seen.

"In Germany the sky bursts with stars over castles and forests." My father's voice came from behind me. I hadn't heard him come outside.

"It does at the hospital too," I offered.

Ezra stepped up to stand at my side.

"The factory and city lights have stolen away all that beauty from us." He said it so dearly and affectionately I turned to look at him.

"You deserve better, *meine schatzi*." He'd said *dear one* again. He squared his shoulders to look at me. Was he going to hug me? His arms went up a little, then he lowered them. "I have nothing to give you. But your aunt and I write sometimes," he said with a shrug. "I have her address. It is different from the one you have."

"Why didn't she come and get my mother out?" I asked. "Even if she thought I was dead?"

"She was very ill for a time—polio—and had to care for herself. She has had a hard life. When she was well enough, she asked me about Helene, but the asylum doctors had already told me that your poor mother was too unwell to be released to anyone." He tilted his head as he looked at me. "You remind me a little of Helene's mother."

But hadn't she been mad and hadn't she committed herself to eternity?

"Don't worry—not the way you are thinking. You do not have their eyes, where the madness shows. You have mine. But your build and porcelain skin, the way you are. Mannerisms, I think they are called, are your grandmother's before she was afflicted." He smiled and stepped forward, touched my shoulder-length hair. "I knew her before her mind deceived her. You would've liked her. A woman of light and—well, nervous energy, Otto used to say."

He dropped his hand.

"Please, let me stay."

"Brighton, go to your aunt. Maybe someday you will let me know that you are settled. I will write back. After everything you've been through, you deserve a real home. I cannot give that to you here." His eyes lingered over mine for only brief moments. I knew what shame looked like because of my own reflection. His shame would force him to give me up a second time. The first time because I was dead and the second time because I was alive. Then he cleared his throat and looked back off into the night.

"There's a war coming, you know."

I shook my head. We'd heard very little about it in the hospital.

"I will tell you that Germans are not loved here in America because of this war." He niggled the sidewalk pieces with his toe. "They will let me go from this job soon, I know this."

"Because you're German? But you're not in a war." This was all very confusing.

He didn't answer right away.

"We are always in some war." His gaze returned to me. "When you make it to your aunt's home, let me know—perhaps if I am let go from this job, as I suspect, I will travel to you. Come now. You and

Angel stay for the night. Everything will look better in the morning."

But it didn't. The next morning I said goodbye to a man I'd only just said hello to. I agreed to write him, and he promised to write back. This was all I could hold on to.

Ezra hugged me gently when we parted and gave me some photographs and my aunt's address. He was going to work, and we were setting off into another unknown.

1941

Welcome Home

When we walked out of the apartment, the same three little children were on their steps again. I went over and gave them the rest of our bread. I was sure they needed it more than we did. The oldest took it fast and distributed a slice to each.

"Thank you, lady," the oldest said, and the others followed after a few elbow jabs.

I stood there and watched them. What did their future look like?

Angel came up from behind me and wrapped an arm around me. His other held his bag. This way of holding me was new. There had been so many new things.

"I don't know if I can leave." I was glad I didn't have to look at him when I spoke. My tears were at the ready, and I didn't want them to spill over.

"Your father said he'd write back." Angel turned me around, put down his bag, then wrapped both of his arms around me. I nodded but didn't trust my voice. The way he looked at me made me think about what he'd told Joann in the train station parking lot. That he loved me. "We will find our place, Brighton."

"Don't." I looked away and closed my eyes. "Not that name anymore."

He leaned into me and whispered, "Brighton."

Then he did something I wasn't expecting. He lowered his lips and pressed them gently against mine. For several long, perfect moments my worries were gone and my heart glowed like his skin. This was a kiss. I'd only ever seen Dr. Woburn do this to Joann but never imagined I'd ever get the chance to be kissed myself. What else I hadn't expected was how our lips touching would bring to the surface every bit of love I'd ever felt for Angel. His hold on me tightened and my arms mimicked his and brought an added headiness to the kiss.

When he pulled away I looked at him in confusion. Why now, and why did he stop?

"You can call yourself whatever you want. But you'll always be Brighton to me, and you will always be the person I love most in the world."

I sank into his chest and loved him back with all my warmth and my hold, even though I had no words to put to it except for one question.

"Why now?"

As he held me he rubbed my back through the thin satin of my shirt, sending warm sensations from my abdomen to my head. I didn't know what that feeling meant or what it was, but I'd never felt so whole. It gave me such hope and expectation. He pulled me away and looked into my eyes.

"I've wanted to do that for a long time. But now we get to start a real life together." His voice was husky and serious. He kissed me again with a surge of passion I didn't know existed in him. I didn't want him to stop.

"For the first time in our lives, we get to make choices for ourselves. And I choose you."

I caressed his face and couldn't believe how long I'd loved him this way without knowing it. "And I choose you."

Then we picked up our bags and, with fingers entwined, I led him back up the steps we'd traveled the day before.

When we reached the top, we began walking toward the city. There was a strange feeling where my heart, mind, and stomach were three tangled strands because the skyline ahead of us bore a familiar engraving in my memory. How quickly memories could master the soul and make natural things that were unnatural only a short time ago.

This alien familiarity happened again when out of a reflex I didn't know I had, I raised my hand and called out, "Taxi." The driver waved an arm out his window that he'd heard me. I turned and grabbed Angel's arm and pulled him with me. The instinctual moment made me smile. I had learned something in such a short time in my new world.

This cabdriver was not like the last one. He had black hair that waved over his forehead. He had tan skin and friendly, dark eyes.

He winked at me when I got in, but Angel's entry put the driver in a different mood quickly.

"Whoa, there, fella." He looked over at me. "This weirdo with you, sweetheart?"

My face twitched. I didn't like that he called Angel a *weirdo* and me *sweetheart*.

"We'd like to go here." Angel ignored the driver's words and handed him his parents' address. The driver cautiously took the paper. But before he looked at it, he glanced over at me again.

"You're too beautiful to be with this jack."

I opened my mouth to speak but said nothing. Joann was the only person to ever call me beautiful.

"Aren't albinos witches or something?"

Why wouldn't he stop talking and drive?

"He's my friend," I finally said. He eyed us both and mumbled something as he turned around. He looked at the address once more, then threw the paper back at us and started driving.

This time as we drove everything became more green; the yards grew longer and wider. The houses became more ornate and oversize. Families lived there. The word *family* was such a strange and fickle word.

"Here you go," the cabdriver said and put his hand out. "That's a two-fifty, pay up."

Angel quietly counted out the money and handed the change to the driver.

This neighborhood was different from Ezra's, but we didn't belong here either. A woman pushed a baby carriage down the sidewalk— something I'd only ever seen in picture books. When the baby cried she stopped and patted it and the baby stopped crying. Another child ran in circles around her. Like she could feel me watching her, she looked up and our eyes met. She moved quickly away from us, yanking the little boy by the arm to stay close to her.

"This is it. This is my family's house." Angel nodded his head toward a huge house as he stuffed his hands in his pockets. "I can't believe it."

Joann had used the word *dangerous*. She'd warned us of his father. But I understood the primitive and innate need to know where you come from. My mother was mad and a German immigrant and my father was a convict, but it was my history, so therefore it was important. The imprint Ezra made on me had changed me—I'd lost my very name—and yet, he wanted to write me. The paradox of what it had cost me to gain a sliver of a father, I would never understand. Would these people change Angel? I would defy anyone who would want to change him.

Angel didn't wait for me as he opened a white gate and walked down a long, straight sidewalk with a flower garden on both sides toward a large brick home. It boasted white pillars in the front, and a woman was sweeping the patio. As we got closer we could hear her humming a tune. She had dark skin like Joyful. She was wearing a black dress and a white apron. She didn't look much older than me.

"Hello?" Angel's voice broke through the girl's tune.

She was startled and jumped and pushed her back against the house. The broom dropped, slapping loudly. She spoke some words that sounded like a different language and then she switched to English.

"You are money," she said with slow pronunciation and slid toward the front door. "You should run."

"What?" I asked Angel.

Angel kept looking at the uniformed woman. "I need to speak with Cynthia Sherwood."

Angel didn't seem bothered by how afraid of him the woman seemed to be. Or that she called him *money*. What did she mean? He stepped closer to the front porch. The girl carefully walked toward us and looked so hard at Angel it was as if she wasn't sure he was there. She raised her hand up and touched his face and checked her fingertips. I stood with them but felt invisible.

"Be careful," she whispered.

"Careful?" he asked.

"Where I come from, you are money." Her English was broken and her accent unlike anything I'd ever heard. People sold albinos for money? She looked over at me and then back at Angel. "Why are you here?"

"I'm here to see Cynthia Sherwood."

"What's going on out here?" A woman's soft, lilting voice came from the front door. "Reni, who's here? What have I said about talking to—"

"This stranger come to see you, Mrs. Sherwood," she interrupted.

The woman's eyes followed the girl. Reni kept her head down and picked up her dropped broom. The woman's eyes were sharp and lips tight as she waited for an answer.

"They be turning bewitch. Be careful of the light one, ma'am." The whites of Reni's eyes shone brightly.

"I've told you not to use those island phrases anymore. Dr. Sherwood doesn't . . . ," the woman started but then turned toward us and her voice faded away, as did her natural rosy complexion.

The woman's gaze only grazed over me but stopped on Angel. It didn't take long for her eyes to go from confusion to something like recognition.

I wondered at how much they looked alike. The shape of their eyes and mouths. His mother was a beautiful woman with light-blond hair, though nothing like Angel's. Her skin was creamy, but she was turning paler by the moment.

Suddenly she ran down the steps and threw her arms around Angel. And he hugged her back, like they'd done this before. Like he remembered her. Maybe he did but never told me. How opposite it was to my father's reaction when we met.

She wasn't as tall as Angel, and she pressed her head against his chest and he bowed his head into the crevice of her neck and shoulder. She began to cry, and I'd never seen Angel cry the way he did now. He'd cried once when he'd broken his leg and another time when Joann had to give him stitches on his arm. There were other times, but never tears like this.

Why couldn't Ezra have greeted me this way? But he did what he could. I knew that much.

His mother pulled away and looked at him in his eyes. Her gaze roamed his entire face. She took off his hat and handed it to me without a glance. She ran her hand through his hair, almost rustling it like a mother would a small boy, and then her palm cupped his cheek. They both giggled in the way you do when you share a memory.

"Is it really you, Luke?" Her tears were like a row of diamonds that trailed her face. She looked even more beautiful when she cried.

"Is that my name? Luke?" he asked. He looked at me, smiling. "My name is Luke."

I raised my eyebrows and smiled back. Angel had just been given his name; mine had been taken away.

"You didn't know your name?" she asked, her voice hiccupping in her throat. "Then what were you called all these years? How are you here?"

"Angel," he said and then pointed toward me. "She named me Angel, so everyone called me that."

"Angel," his mother said in a whisper, like she was contemplating the name. "Well, now you'll be Luke."

"I like Luke," Angel said. *Luke* said. Which one was he now?

The two looked at one another for several long moments. Then her countenance shifted, and she peered around the sidewalks like she was wondering if anyone was watching. Her expression went from shock and joy to concern.

"Let's put your hat back on, Luke," she said and put her hand out toward me. I handed the hat to her and she returned it to his head. "Come inside with me." She took his hand and began leading him inside, then she stopped and took me in. I had not moved from my spot. Was I to go with them? "Are you two—married?"

Angel turned to look at me and took a deep breath before he spoke. "No, we're not married. This is my best friend, Br—"

"Nell," I interrupted. "I'm Nell."

"Nell." Angel's flossy voice felt approving even though I knew what he preferred.

"Nell." The polished beautiful woman nodded as she said it. "Please, come inside with us and we'll get acquainted."

I followed behind the two. My father said I resembled my grandmother, but I still wondered why I had chosen her name to use as my own. She had died unhappy and not in her right mind. She'd been like my mother. Had I just sealed my fate? But I wouldn't take it back, because as soon as I'd spoken the name, I knew it was what I would use for the rest of my life. It was small, simple, and almost invisible.

Once we got inside, the woman dropped Angel's hand and went to the girl, Reni, who had snuck in behind us. She spoke quietly to her as I looked at our surroundings.

"Can you believe this?" Angel's smile was bursting from his face.

I shook my head but didn't look at him. If I had, I would've cried. Because his mother loved him. Because his real name was Luke. Because he had a name. Because his family didn't live in a gray world but in one full of color. I wasn't sure how to be happy for Angel—Luke—in my sadness. I had lost so much, and I was afraid of losing him.

This morning we'd stood in my father's one-room home with decades-old furniture, scampering mice, the scent of sewage and something rotten in the air, and everything had a fresh layer of coal soot. And now here we were, in a redbrick home that stood statuesque against the expansive yard framed by a bright blue sky—no smokestacks in sight.

I had no idea people lived in such luxury. Of course, I'd never been inside a real house, a real home, for a real family. My father's place wasn't really a home; even he said so.

A curious-eyed girl walked down from the curved staircase to my right. She was beautiful. She was also fair, like her mother, but not like Angel. Her blond hair and pink shiny blouse both beamed in the sunlight that flooded the staircase window. She stopped halfway down and looked at Angel, her gaze passing over me unconsciously.

Maybe I was dreaming all this.

Angel was looking back at the girl on the stairs. Neither said anything for the length of about twenty or more ticks from a large clock in the corner. The ticking was so loud I couldn't help but count it. It calmed me and gave weight to my legs so I wouldn't float away.

Finally she spoke. "I found a photo of you about two years ago." She came down a few more steps. "You were a year old and you were smiling."

I looked at Angel and he swallowed hard but remained silent.

"I was only thirteen, and I wasn't sure why Mother would have a faded photo of a boy I could see was—different. I knew it wasn't Howard Junior." She walked the rest of the way down the stairs and stood a few feet away from Angel, looking at him so intently. The way she clasped her hands and tilted her head—it was like she was part water, her movements were so fluid. "I asked Mother about it and she told me. I couldn't believe she'd kept you a secret for so long, but she said she couldn't do it anymore. Daddy was angry and threatened to take away my trust fund and cut Mother's allowance if we told anyone. But here you are. What would Daddy say now?" She shook her head, and her wood-thrush laugh filled my ears.

What was a trust fund?

"My school library had a book about albinos. Besides the obvious facts, there was folklore and myths about magic and sorcery. I didn't believe it, though. I was sure that you weren't much different from me."

Angel nodded and chuckled. He was smiling now. She stepped closer.

"Hi, Luke. I'm your sister, Bonnie," she said and put her hand out. "We resemble one another, don't we?"

He awkwardly shook her hand.

"Bonnie, there you are." Angel's mother returned from wherever she'd been. She inhaled deeply and shook her head. "Oh my, to see the two of you together."

Her eyes were glassy, and the newly introduced sister and brother looked at each other and smiled. This was a family.

Angel—Luke—was home.

From Dark to Light

That girl Kelly had the dark room at the local high school secured for us by morning. A fact that causes so many contradictory emotions inside myself. I feel pulled in two. The night before, Kelly and I talked until the restaurant closed. I was surprised how talking about my stories and life at Riverside to a perfect stranger loosened the straightjacket I'd worn around my soul for so long. And brought the kind of healing I'd never given myself over to. Talking things over with my husband and throwing occasional prayers up to the Big Guy were the extent of my raw openness. Nobody needed to walk all over the brittle fallen leaves of my life.

But I am thinking a bit differently about it now.

"What happened to your arms, Ms. Friedrich? How did you get so scratched?" Kelly gently touches my skin. I bristle and pull back. "Does it hurt?"

Yes. It hurts. That is the truth of it. But the scratches are not what I mean. The reason why they are there is what hurts. It happens sometimes. Often enough that I don't always notice in the mornings.

I shrug. "I'll be fine. And please, call me Nell. Ms. Friedrich feels so formal."

"Why didn't you take your husband's last name?"

The question surprises me.

"It's just so modern and unexpected."

I smile. "My husband understood it was important to me." I clear my throat, not expecting the emotions it brings up. "To feel closer to Mother."

She smiles and doesn't ask again about the scratches.

She also is trying to convince me to attend the town hall event promoting a positive vote for the demolition of the old asylum so a community center can be built. I started considering going when she told me that the town council was planning to name it Wolff Community Center after a hospital administrator who was documented as handling the overcrowding and understaffing during wartime and was considered a hero. A man they didn't know. But I did. I hadn't thought of Dr. Wolff by name in years. I didn't have many dealings with him, but I could picture his face. I knew him to be a heartless and cruel human being. The idea that he might be honored for the torture he put Mother, my friends, and me through brought back the reason I took the pictures to start with—so that someday I could expose what was happening inside the walls.

Once we get to the dark room my mind shifts gears. I force myself to wear the hat of professional photographer and teacher instead of former asylum patient. I thread two filmstrips at a time, one for each of us. I teach Kelly along the way—this is what I do. Once we develop the five cartridges, I start exposing the negatives. I use the enlarger, and after I teach Kelly how to rock the developer trays, she handles that part.

There are many duds—my amateur photography skills are obvious—but when the photographs begin to appear correctly, I have to fight the urge to run away. The faces of my past appear, and with them the sounds and smells that photos should never be able to convey so distinctly. But these do.

These photos—memories—had been captive inside these small cartridges for almost fifty years, and I was afraid bringing them freedom would make me captive a second time. But as each photo comes into focus, I am also freer. I am recognizing that my version of moving on looked a lot like hiding. These pictures will finally be seen and the truth revealed and my friends from long ago will be heard. Will this mean telling the world all of my secrets? I'm not sure I can do that.

My eyes glance over the images, but I fight allowing my soul to take them in. I only view the images with the eyes of a technician and nothing else. Not yet.

"How could you have—" Kelly searches for the right word, her eyes surveying the many photographs. "Survived all of this?"

"Someone told me a long time ago that 'all the darkness in the world cannot extinguish the light of a single candle.'" This wisdom of Saint Francis is like a long exhale. "As long as I kept my eyes open there was always a sliver of light to follow."

The five empty canisters line up like valiant soldiers having done their jobs. Within those slim pieces of plastic so much has lived. I release a long-held breath and finally let myself walk around and look at the images hanging on the wire. The faces are everywhere. They are all around me, and it doesn't feel bad. I smile at them until my eyes settle on Grace.

My Grace. I remember the day I took the picture. It is from those early days with her on the ward. Her hair had been shorn, like mine. Her beauty was still profound and brightness beamed from her eyes. She didn't think the stay would be longer than a few weeks—a month at the most. She thought it was just one more ploy by her parents to control her.

"She's bald." Kelly stands next to me. "She'd seem like a revolutionary now for doing that."

"Not her decision." I smile. "It was lice."

I take the photo from its place on the wire and press it to my chest.

I'd never even told my husband that I always look for her—for Grace. I don't just mean in every building I go in or every sidewalk I travel on—though that is true. But it is bigger than that. When there had been a choice to move to dull, factory-filled Pittsburgh or warm and faraway Texas, I still picked Pittsburgh. I had a feeling Grace wouldn't have gone that far. She might be somewhere in Pittsburgh.

A few times I made phone calls to people I found with the name Grace Douglass or Hannah Douglass, hoping I'd recognize the voice or be able to probe enough to know if I'd found the right person. Once, when the kids were in school and Doc was out of town, I drove all the way to the address I'd found for Grace's parents. It was a two-hour drive. I was in my midthirties by then, and I was sure I'd used up a lifetime of shocks and surprises. That was not true. The opulence and luxury of the home Grace had come from was startling. She'd told me they were wealthy and influential, but the iron gate with the name *Douglass* scrolled at the top was far more than my imaginings. I never got closer than fifty yards from the front door and was still on the other side of the grand gate. I never caught a glimpse of anyone but the gardener. That day I learned that the Douglass family owned the newspaper and the banks in town. Had donated wings of hospitals, libraries, and schools.

Just last week I heard someone say the name Grace at the grocery store, and when my head snapped over I found a toddler, not my dear friend. I'm not sure I'll ever stop looking for her.

I place her picture on top of the stack. I need Grace to see what I am trying to do for her—for all of us.

1941

Rose-Colored Glasses

With angelic movement Angel's mother gestured for us to follow her. "Come. Let's sit down together. Reni poured some iced tea and set out some cake."

Angel turned around and looked at me. His expression was shock, awe, and fear all mixed together. Where disbelief and guilt had veiled my father, I saw joy and confidence in Cynthia Sherwood. But shouldn't she have some guilt too? Ezra had been told I was dead, but he had had good intentions. From what I knew, Mrs. Sherwood had given up Angel. I didn't trust her.

I touched Angel's arm and pulled him a few steps away. "Don't you think we should—"

"She can come too," his mother said, interrupting me.

"Come on." Angel walked away from my hold and nodded for me to come with him. I followed behind him, and his mother linked her arm through his with a fluidity that tightened my rib cage and squeezed my heart. His sister led the way for all of us and opened doors that led to the outside patio; she even pulled a chair out for him. Her smile reminded me of Joann's when I was a little girl. Cheerful and happy and loving—and like there was something to cover up.

Angel was between his mother and sister, and I sat opposite him. All of us were looking at him while he sipped his tea from a sparkling, rose-colored glass. Angel's chair scraped against the patio floor as he moved to keep his eyes in the shade of the awning. It was bright today, and nothing like the gray day from yesterday.

"It's too bright for you, isn't it? I read about this. Mother, maybe we should go inside. His eyes are very sensitive. Do you want to go inside?" Bonnie was already protective of him. I'd watched over him my whole life, and suddenly she had taken my place. My jaw tightened.

"It's okay." He waved off her words. "As long as I'm in the shade and . . ."

His voice faded away. Explaining his vision issues, why his eyes looked the way they did, why his skin was so light—clearly made him uncomfortable. He inhaled deeply, and through the glass patio table I could see his knee nervously bouncing.

His stuttering and the sweat beads at his temples made me sit up straighter, considering how I might need to come to his defense.

"So, Luke—" his mother started.

"That sounds so strange to me." He chuckled and rubbed the tops of his legs.

"Well, it's your name, Son." Cynthia reached and patted his forearm then rested her hand on his.

He nodded with that innocent smile I knew so well and sipped his tea, his eyes diverted away from all of us.

No one spoke. This was wrong. Even though my father hadn't welcomed me with open arms. Even though he hadn't been able to give me a life then or now. Even though he had pulled the veil of my identity away—he still gave me answers.

Images of Angel at the graveyard all those years ago flashed through my mind. With no name. No mother.

This perfect woman with her perfect daughter couldn't get away with all of this without answers—I wouldn't let that happen.

"Why did you leave Angel—Luke—at the asylum? Do you know the life that he lived?" I hoped my nerves weren't as transparent as my hopes had been with Ezra.

"Bri—I mean, Nell—I mean," Angel stammered, then looked at his mother. "I—um—"

His mother cleared her throat, and his sister raised an eyebrow high off of her forehead.

"It was because of your father." The words rattled out of Angel's mother like she'd been shaken. Her eyes buzzed around. "And my parents. They forced me to give you up. They told me you couldn't learn and that you were better off in the asylum, where people could take care of you."

He pulled his hand free of her touch—gently, but intentionally.

"But you didn't visit?" Angel's voice cracked when he spoke. "I didn't even know my name."

Angel paused and rocked back and forth a bit—his hands back on his legs, rubbing up and down. I tilted my head, watching him. He'd never done this before. The rocking was something the patients did when they were agitated.

"Your father said you weren't normal." Her voice was firm and her breathing was fast and erratic. "They all convinced me. Howard told me it would be better if you were with other people like you. Mother agreed. They said you would get a suitable education for a boy like you and that you would never even remember me because of your condition." Her words came so fast it was hard to keep up. Her elegant perfection had fallen away, and she was nothing more than a ragged woman with poor excuses. Ezra had been more prepared to handle my questions.

"I understand. It's okay," Angel said quietly. So quietly his words could've been missed. His eyes rested on the cake in front of him.

"No, it's not." I blurted out my words before I could arrest them. "Have you ever visited Riverside?"

"Riverside?"

"The hospital where Angel and I lived."

"Yes, Riverside. That's the place." She turned away from me. "After you were born I moved to Pittsburgh and Mother hired round-the-clock care for you for almost three years, until that nurse couldn't be trusted any longer. Mother said Howard had found a special school for children like you. She wouldn't let me see you anymore. It was 1923 when they took you. I had no rights to anything. If I left Howard for you, I would have lost everything. My husband, my parents, Howard Junior, who was a baby then, everything. I would've had to give up everything."

"But what about me?" Angel whispered.

"Riverside doesn't have a school," I prodded.

Everyone was as silent as snow.

"But Howard said— I didn't think you'd know any better, Luke. You can't blame me for that."

Angel just stared at his hands gripping his iced tea in the prettiest glass I'd ever seen.

"I was told my brother would watch out for you." She plastered a smile on her face.

"Watch out for him? Did you know that when Angel broke his leg if I hadn't found him he might've died waiting for help? And that for years of his life he was bathed with a cold water hose?" I paused briefly, looking between his mother and sister, who were both stoic and motionless. "They made sure to do it on the side of the building so that no one else would see what was happening. Did you know he was in a crib until he was ten and had terribly achy joints because of it? He ate like an animal and didn't even know how to use a spoon. He didn't even know what *mother* meant when I met him."

"Stop," Cynthia said. "Why are you telling me this?"

"You don't get to not know anymore. It was nothing like you could ever imagine in your worst nightmares. That's the *school* you sent him to."

"Luke, you don't blame me, do you? Mother visited, and she never told me any of this. It couldn't have been as bad as what your friend says."

"No, it wasn't as bad as she says." His voice was a low rumble, and he looked directly at his mother. "It was worse, Mother. If it wasn't for Brighton, I wouldn't have survived. But I still don't know why. Why didn't you—"

"I couldn't raise you as our son." She twitched and gasped between each word. Then suddenly she gathered her composure. "It would've been so hard for you, Luke, so different from everyone else. We didn't want that for you. There you could at least be with others like you."

"I've never met anyone *like me*." He remained sober and contained. "I was the only one."

"That can't be true."

I hated her. I hated her so much that I couldn't even bear to look at her. I stood, and the scrape of the chair vibrated my brain. I didn't want to leave Angel, but I couldn't stay.

"Wait," Angel said to me and took my hand. Then returned his gaze to his mother. "I think we should go."

My surprise at this couldn't be measured. The shock of the other two was just as palpable.

"You'll be back, won't you? Do you live nearby?"

"Live nearby?" Angel almost laughed aloud. "Your brother, Dr. Woburn, helped us escape the hospital only two days ago. We don't have any place to stay. We've lived our lives in the halls of an asylum, and we need help." He was passionate now. "That's why we're here."

"Oh?" She blinked and put a hand to her chest. "You thought you could stay here?"

"Did you think this was just a casual social visit?" I yelled.

Angel twitched and stood so quickly his chair fell backward.

"Oh, Luke— Well, your father, he'd never—" Her eyes bounced everywhere except at Angel. "How could we— There would be so much to explain." She shook her head. "I could make some arrangements—maybe?"

Angel and I looked at one another.

"Arrangements?" Angel asked.

Cynthia Sherwood bit her lip, but a moment later her polished demeanor returned. "Your father would never allow you to stay here—and we could never tell him. It would be very confusing for our friends, not to mention Howard Junior. I'd have to find a way to pay for it, but as long as your father never finds out, I might be able to help you."

"We could use my trust. Daddy never checks how it's spent," Bonnie piped up.

"You mean you might be able to help *us*?" Angel said, nodding his head to me.

His mother turned toward me. "Nell, right?"

I nodded. Angel's hand gripped tighter.

"Surely you have family—or someone—to go to who could be responsible for you. You wouldn't want to hold Angel back, would you?"

My panic heightened, but I couldn't find the heart to recite my mantra. There was nothing bright or beautiful about this. She was asking me to leave Angel. And Angel wanted his family so much. Enough to stay by himself? My breathing was more shallow with each passing moment.

"What's happening to her? Is she having some type of fit?" Mrs. Sherwood said.

"Brighton." Angel gripped my shoulders. "Breathe."

Then he pulled me close and whispered to me, "I'm not going to let her separate us. We're staying together. I won't leave you. I love you."

"Didn't you say her name was Nell? Who are you, really?"

Her voice was like a crystal bell in my ears, even though I felt like I was breathing underwater. But Angel was here, his warmth and presence and words reminding me that we were doing this together. He was bright and beautiful. My breathing started to even out— quicker than usual. But even though my breath was returning, the lingering sense of dread didn't go away.

"She needs doctors and help," Angel's mother said. "She never should have left the hospital if she has fits like that. She needs to be with others like her, not in civilized society."

"I'll never let her go back," Angel growled. The strength in his voice that had seemingly been lost all day was back. "We won't be separated."

"She'll hold you back, Son. We could get her the help she needs—we know doctors. Think about what I could give you. There might be some medicine now that could fix your complexion."

"Fix him?" I said between breaths.

"I would have to be kept hidden?"

"Father will have you readmitted if he catches wind of you," Bonnie blurted out.

"Never." Angel held my hand tightly, tethering me to him.

His eyes, caught by the sun's rays, reddened. He squinted, then moved his free hand to block the glare. "We won't be separated, and we're *not* going back there."

"Not your hospital. He would take you to his." Bonnie started crying. "You won't survive, Luke. Neither of you will. Mother, you won't let that happen, will you?"

"Bonnie, get ahold of yourself."

"Why do you live with such a man?" Angel looked at his mother, yelling now.

"You really don't know anything about the world, do you? What choice do I have?" His mother's voice filled the space around us. She stood and turned away, weeping. "I'd be ruined. Everything would be ruined. The children would have no future. I'd be cast out. I'd lose everything."

She'd chosen to send her son away to salvage a reputation, which made her a prisoner worse than Angel and I had been.

"Go, Luke," Bonnie breathed quickly. "She will call if she feels threatened."

"Bonnie," she yelled. "You will—"

"Call who?" Angel asked.

"Father—or his hospital. Go, now."

His welcome had been so deceiving—her joy mixed with deception. There was such heartbreak in rejection, and if my heart wasn't already shattered it would have broken for him.

"We have to go, Brighton," he said in a deep, guttural voice. "We just need to go."

He took my hand and we walked back inside, through the opulent rooms, and into the large entry where our small tattered bags still sat on the shiny floors. When we turned around, Bonnie rushed up behind us. She was crying.

Bonnie threw her arms around Angel, and when they finally let go of one another, we left through the large, heavy wooden door. We turned before it closed, and once again his mother was nowhere to be seen.

Not an Angel

$\mathcal{I}$ was certain we would never see Cynthia Sherwood again. Not her light-blond hair. Not her bright blue eyes. Not her perfect house or her daughter, who had tried to save us.

When we left the house, the afternoon sun was bright and Angel put his hat back on low, down to his eyebrows. He stood his coat collar up and tucked his chin down. Going unnoticed was the best plan. Though we had no idea where we were going.

As we walked we didn't speak. We didn't look at each other. Leaving the Sherwood home felt like a second escape, but I knew for Angel it was like losing his mother a second time.

After walking for a few hours I found a bench and sat down. I didn't want to go one step farther. I didn't know where we were or where we were going. I didn't know anything. All I wanted was to be somewhere safe and to sleep so I could get away from all the hurt and confusion. How I wished Grace was with us. She knew the world. She would know how to get around in it. I wondered if we should go back to Ezra and ask him for help—but I didn't want to walk away from my father again.

Angel plopped down on the bench next to me but didn't say a word. He sat next to the armrest on the other side. He rarely did that. He was the one who would sit so closely that we breathed each other's air. But since we had run out of his mother's home, he hadn't touched me or spoken a word. His grieving was in the aging day and all around in the balmy May air. It reached me like the long fingers of the ghosts we'd left behind, making me nervous.

His chest looked empty. Her tarnished and broken response to him wasn't what I'd expected—but I couldn't help but remember the warning. I wondered if Mrs. Sherwood would tell Angel's father about our visit or if she'd keep that a secret.

"I'm sorry, Angel," I whispered. He turned his face away from me. He'd never hidden his tears from me. This hurt wasn't something he had made room for—he hadn't expected her response. What had been before him for years was behind him within an hour. I kept thinking that Joann would know what to say. She would have some words that would help that I didn't know.

We sat on the bench as people came and went, through the lunch time. He didn't say anything. Maybe he couldn't. Maybe if he did try to speak, everything inside of him would come out and leave him as a shell of skin. As my death certificate and the death of my mother had done to me. By the time Ezra Raab stripped me of my name, I was completely numb and nameless. Now we were both like husks without seeds. How would we survive this world?

The bench was near a park, and like the asylum dayroom we'd sat all day. The sunset was in full bloom, and most people were indoors. We were alone. But in our aloneness I was burdened with the noise. Everywhere. Car engines. Car horns. Sirens. Sometimes yelling. The noise at the hospital had always been steady, but this was so different.

I scooted close to him and rested my head against his shoulder. He didn't stiffen at my touch, but he didn't warm either. I wasn't sure when I fell asleep. When I woke his arm was around me and we took up the whole bench now. At some point I'd pulled my legs up and Angel also slept.

There was a layer of dark clouds overhead, and the world around us was quiet. The tree branches around the park bobbed up and down, throwing leaves into the breeze. I sat up and hugged my arms around myself. It had cooled considerably.

"You're not supposed to sleep here." An abrasive voice barreled through the cool, calm night air. A man was coming toward us. He was wearing dark clothes and rode a horse. The animal was much larger up close than in the fields or a storybook. I leaned back. I shook Angel's arm to wake him. Then the horse made a terrible sound, and I hid my face in Angel's shoulder and a shrill scream escaped my lips. This woke Angel. He sat up, and the man spoke to us again. "I'll be back around in about an hour. You'll need to move on by then."

He made a clicking sound with his mouth and his body began to jostle forward. The horse's hooves sounded sharp against the pavement. I squeezed my eyes shut until the sound grew quieter.

Angel was groggy and rubbed his face and stretched.

"Who was that? He said we had to move on." My voice shook. I was cold. I was scared. I was confused. I couldn't stop shaking.

"I think he was some type of police officer."

"Police?"

"I've seen them before bringing criminals into Riverside." Angel stood, and I felt colder on the side where he'd been sitting. I shook harder. "We have to go."

I stood. My teeth chattered. "Where?" I never imagined how empty such a small question could sound.

He turned and put his bag on the bench and began rummaging through it.

"What are you looking for?"

"A map." He said it so quietly I wasn't sure he'd spoken.

We stood under the lamp and shared the glow with a swarm of bugs. On the top of the map was printed the words *State of Pennsylvania*. Angel put his finger near Pittsburgh. He moved it left until it went off the page. He put his face as close as he could. We were in the circle of light together, but I felt disconnected from him. His weight of grief was heavier than he had experienced in his life. I wanted him back.

"We'll go west, to your aunt." The emptiness in his voice hollowed my heart.

There was such finality in his words. He didn't look at me when he spoke them either. He was lost somewhere inside of himself, and I couldn't blame him. At least we were together in our grief. A loss like this was like veins of sadness flowing through your entire body. "Ezra showed me how to read a map."

"Can we take a train?"

He shook his head. "We don't have enough money."

"What about a—"

"It's way too far for a taxi. That's for short distances." His tone was irritated, and when he abruptly folded the map, he turned away from me.

"Ezra did say she was nice," I added and put a shivering hand on his arm. I didn't know how to give to Angel the comfort I also needed. I knew my words were thin and shapeless. "Ezra thinks she'll take us."

"Sure." He nodded. I'd have to be okay with the pieces of Angel that were left. What else could I do? He was the reason I hadn't curled up somewhere and died alone.

"We'll do this together, Angel. Me and you." The kiss and his profession of love always hovered over us. I wondered if he regretted it.

He swallowed hard—I could see it in his throat. But he didn't look at me.

"Would you have stayed with me and my family if—" He finally looked at me, and his stare wandered around my face for a moment before finding my eyes. "Would you have given up on your aunt?"

While there was a slight edge to his tone, his voice was like a single thread that could snap in two at any moment.

I opened my mouth to speak but stopped. I hadn't belonged there as much as he hadn't belonged to Ezra. I only would have stayed for Angel's sake. His mother's embrace had made him happy for those precious few minutes. The happiest I'd ever seen him in all of our years together. Happier than I'd ever been. Happier than when he'd kissed me? I didn't know. Maybe. This evolution of our hearts was painful and left many unanswered questions.

"What matters now is that we'll figure this out together, right?" I didn't answer his question, and my soul winced at my cowardice. He looked away and walked around me. "Angel?"

"I think I'd like to be Luke." He stopped and looked just above my head—as if he could see all the way back to that big brick house where his dreams had died.

"But your mother. The things she said. I don't—"

"You don't understand," he yelled suddenly. He'd never yelled at me before. "I wanted to be that Luke. I wanted to be the kind of son she would love. I wanted that life. Not this one."

The words themselves made me step back and out of the lit sidewalk and into the soft grass. He didn't want me was what I heard.

"Your father at least wants you to write him."

That was what he saw? What I saw was a shocked man who only offered to write because he felt beholden. I saw a man who had stripped me of my name but not given me another. Angel and I were not so different, I thought. But from the beginning his expectations were too high for truth to match them. If only we'd heeded Joann's warning.

"Please—Nell." My new name sounded strange in the tenor of his voice, and I nearly regretted my request. I searched his face. His eyes were bloodshot and his skin ashen. And he was so thin. Getting him well was what mattered.

I nodded in agreement, that I would call him Luke. Then we walked into the unknown darkness of the night. Toward Margareta. Toward Brighton.

1941

Behold the Crux

We walked in the dark, cool evening for hours. We were alone, and I didn't know how Angel knew where we were going. Did he sense west?

The few cars on the road slowed as they passed by but didn't stop. I looked the other way so they wouldn't see me. Angel did the same. My stomach growled in my hollow insides—except for my mind. It was full. We had nothing left to eat. We'd gone hungry so often; maybe it had been preparing us for this.

With every hour we walked the houses grew farther apart. The starry sky took me back to the little Juliet balcony and to the conversation I'd had with my father. After a long stretch of road there was a subtle glow that marked the navy sky.

"I can't see what that is, can you?" Angel called back to me and I ran up ahead to him. I was glad to hear his voice. He hadn't spoken in hours. The only voice I'd been hearing was the one in my head.

The small bloom of light came from some type of building.

"I don't know. Some small building, only one story. I can see cars and trucks in front of it. There're a lot of windows. The sign says 'Diner,' but I don't know what that means."

When we got into the parking lot, we could see people inside. It was some type of dining hall. Everyone was eating or drinking at tables. Only a few cars were parked in front, and there was a truck with a large white rectangular box on the back. It sat up high and intimidating.

I'd longed for the cake that had been set before me at the Sherwood house—I hadn't even taken a bite. I could almost feel the spongy texture in my mouth. Why hadn't I eaten it before I opened my mouth to defend Angel? Watching the people eat now only made me hungrier. Hungrier than I'd been at the hospital. I fought feeling weak from hunger and fear.

Angel sighed, and his shoulders sagged under the parking lot light. He looked through the windows and then at me and then back again. He had to be as hungry as I was, and he hadn't eaten that lovely cake either. He was close enough to the window that I could see his faint reflection in the glass. The person on the other side of the diner window was startled by Angel standing so close. Angel didn't notice, but the man's brow furrowed and he slid away. I pulled at Angel's sleeve and brought him closer.

"I'm so hungry," he finally said.

"Me too." But would food fill us?

"We'll watch what other people do, like Joann said." He sighed. "Maybe it won't be hard."

As nervous as I was about going to this place called Diner, I wanted to eat. I took Angel's hand and he clung to mine.

When we walked inside, everyone turned toward us. Their gazes lingered for several beats of my held breath, then they turned away. A few people looked over their shoulders at us a second time. Whispers floated around and brushed against my ears, but I was glad I couldn't make out the exact words. The only other sounds came from behind a large opening in the wall where a man in a white apron worked in the kitchen. He must have been the one making the food. I didn't know that men cooked in kitchens. Only women cooked at the hospital.

The sizzling and slapping of kitchen implements came in bursts. There was a haze of smoke and bright lights, making me squint. Angel pulled his hat down even farther. His eyes squinted painfully, having gotten used to the dark. The scent of food surrounded us and my emptiness craved even the unfamiliar smells.

"Just the two of you?" The tired voice of a woman came from my right. Her head was down, and she was counting paper money in front of some type of gray machine with a drawer. Her yellow dress and white apron went to her knees, and her little hat reminded me of a nurse's cap. Her brightly made-up face didn't keep her from looking tired and bored. She pushed a pad of paper and pencil into her apron pocket, then her eyes raised to meet us—to meet Angel.

"Another albino? Good Lord, I thought you freaks had left already." She looked at Angel and then at me as if we'd already squandered all of her patience, even though we'd just arrived. "What're you, doll, some kind of handler? You're not beefy enough to be his bodyguard."

A handler? I couldn't fathom what she meant.

"It ain't natural, with those red eyes and all. That lady albino was the first I'd seen, ya know, just about scared me solid."

"A lady albino?" Angel stepped toward her. "Here?"

She scoffed. "Don't pretend you don't know about that side show that's been moving through here." She raised an eyebrow.

"Side show?"

"You know, the strong man, dwarves, bearded ladies." She made a gesture like she was pulling something down from her chin. "The lady albino with the see-through skin like you. You ain't part of the troupe?"

Angel and I shook our heads.

"Well, it don't matter to me as long as you don't give me no trouble." She walked down the aisle of tables and gestured for us to follow her. "The name's Sandy. I'll be taking care of you tonight."

Taking care of us. With little understanding of what that meant, I walked with Angel to the table where Sandy pointed for us to sit. We slid into the bench-like seats facing one another. They were cushioned and not uncomfortable, considering we'd slept on a park bench not so many hours earlier.

The lady put two papers down in front of us and turned to leave.

"What is this?" Angel asked me but loud enough that Sandy turned back toward us.

"Your menu." Her expression was loaded with confusion.

"A menu?" When Angel spoke I wanted to hide under the table. Why was he so open about his ignorance?

"Just lay off the act, rube," the woman said. "I've got my eye on you two. Don't yous leave without paying neither."

Rube?

Paying for the food hadn't even crossed my mind. What else would we have to pay for that we were used to being given?

"You ask too many questions," I whispered harshly at Angel. "We don't need more attention."

"How are we going to learn if we don't?" He glared. "At least we know what this is called now." He tapped the menu.

The menu had rows of what I knew were foods, but I'd never heard of some of them. Omelets, eggs Benedict, French toast. I didn't know what any of those things were. Angel was looking at his menu wearing an expression that mirrored my thoughts: confusion.

"We get to choose one?" Angel said finally.

"There are dollar signs next to each meal. Do we have enough money?" The writing was quite small. I leaned forward and whispered, "Can you read it well enough?"

Angel looked a little closer at the menu. His eyes were only a few inches away.

"Let's share something just in case."

I nodded.

"The foods sound so strange. Listen to this—" I turned my menu and pointed at the word *omelet* again. It didn't make sense to me. I read, "'Plain omelet with ham or bacon.' What is an omelet?"

"Anything we get will taste good."

Angel actually smiled, then he squinted and moved closer to the menu. A moment later he reminded me of the pancake Joyful had brought us a short time ago. We'd split it, only getting a few bites.

We'd also eaten eggs before. So we ordered what they called the Classic Breakfast. Just one, though. We each got a pancake, a fried egg, and a slice of bacon. It was my first time eating the salty, crunchy meat, and I savored it from the moment it touched my tongue. It was also my first taste of syrup. It all tasted so good, but the food was gone before my stomach was half full.

Half full was better than nearly starving. At the hospital we'd been starved for food, love, and a family. Would finding Margareta Friedrich change that reality? Would it be days or weeks or more until we found my aunt, and would she even want to be an aunt to me? I'd seen maps as a child and generally knew the geography of our country. Michigan was so far away. And what seemed further away was the idea that a family member cared enough. What if she'd also grown to be more like my grandmother and Mother? What if she wasn't able to help? Then what?

It seemed like years since my mother died, but it had only been about a week. It seemed like years since Joann put us on the train, but it had only been days. It felt like an eternity since Grace knew herself and we'd made plans.

When Sandy kept the three dollars that Angel handed her and said, "Thanks for the tip," I was reminded that I had so much more to learn. Who would I ask?

"You been looking at that map an awful long time." Sandy looked over Angel's shoulder. "You trying to get somewhere?"

"Brighton, Michigan."

"You got a way to get there? I didn't see no car with yous."

Angel shook his head.

"Herb," Sandy called over her shoulder. "You want some company again?"

When It Rains

*O*nce we got outside, I looked up. My little Crux constellation—full of hope—was long gone, having passed through our northern sky only briefly. But the rest of the sky was still unlike anything I'd seen before. I wasn't looking through a dirty, broken, barred window. This was like sitting in the center of the universe and I could look up and see it all happening at once. The dark part of the sky directly above me had small pinholes of light, and then as my eyes cascaded down toward the horizon, the colors went from pink to yellow to a deep blood-orange.

I let myself get lost in the painting of light and hope when a voice called and reminded me that we'd just accepted a ride with a stranger driving a big truck with a white rectangular box on the back.

"So you ready to go, cowboy?" The man, Herb, wore a wide-brimmed hat, baggy denim jeans, and a shirt that was well-fitted around his belly. He had a smile on his rough-red face. He clapped Angel on the back, hard, and it pushed him forward a step.

Cowboy?

"We're ready." Angel righted himself and looked nervously between Herb and me.

"Well, aren't you as cute as a button, little lady," he said, looking at me as he opened the door that was several steps up.

I nodded and walked toward the open truck door.

"So an albino and a mute—got it," he said and nodded a little and then kept talking.

Angel and I got settled in the truck, and it was different being so high up. It reminded me a little of riding in the train. But when we got on the road it didn't have the smooth, rocking rhythm of the train; instead, the buzz from the engine was loud but strangely relaxing.

"Gets awful lonesome driving as much as I do. Nice to have the company for a few hours here."

"We don't have any money." Angel tossed his words toward the man.

The man sighed. "Sandy said that was probably the case. But that's okay. I get paid to drive anyway."

After having walked for hours and eaten a meal, sleep was all I could think of. In my sleep I could see familiar faces and step away from my fear for a time.

"I can get you into Ohio, but once I unload there, I'll be going back to Pittsburgh," Herb said. "Maybe you can find another trucker who can take you a little farther."

Herb paused for a few long moments.

"But be careful, not everyone is as nice as I am." He winked, and when we didn't have anything to say, he began fiddling with a knob that turned on music.

That was the last thing I heard before I fell asleep. It was a calm, dreamless sleep. I wished it had lasted longer than a few hours. My body must have sensed when the truck stopped and I opened my eyes. It was gray, and I knew what that meant. We would have a day of rain.

The driver door opened, and Herb's wide smile and loud voice infiltrated the small space.

"Good morning, travelers," he said. "You were terrible company, I have to say."

I didn't know how to respond. I jabbed Angel, and he roused. "What?"

"We're stopped," I said.

"Oh, you ain't a mute after all." He laughed a little.

Herb helped me out of the tall truck and shook Angel's hand.

He pulled Angel aside, and they looked on a map and talked some things over for a spell. Angel nodded more than he spoke. Then Herb pointed us to a diner across the street. Another one?

The diner looked so much like the one we'd been at only a few hours ago, except it was bigger and looked older. There were large windows in the front, like the other one, but these windows had curtains on the inside that could be pulled. This time Sandy was named Bobbi Jean, and she was wearing blue instead of yellow. She looked at Angel with wide eyes but didn't say anything about another albino. We didn't have to ask what a menu was. Even though I'd never seen or eaten an omelet, the word was familiar now, and it felt strange that it was. We split the same meal but ordered an extra pancake for us both. We also ordered a few muffins for the road.

Not much later we were on the road. But this time our legs were all we had. For the next several hours there was a constant drizzle. I was soaked. My feet ached. My shoes weren't meant for this much walking. Angel looked as miserable as I did, but we didn't talk much.

Angel had started a cough the day we fled, but it was much worse today and his lips were almost the same color as his skin. His eyes drooped. Was it melancholia or was it the influenza that had been going around the wards when we left? But he kept walking. When one of us stopped we'd eat some of the food we'd purchased at the diner that morning.

The long stretches of road and stretches of sunset were ahead of us now. I was up in front, but when I looked back I could only see the shadowed figure of Angel. He was so far behind and coughing more. I started looking for shelter. A few flashes of lightning peeled open the sky and forced the drizzle into a steady rain. When the rain began piercing through us like liquid needles, I went back and began pulling Angel. He was shivering uncontrollably, and his teeth chattered loudly.

"There," I yelled and pointed. The rain was so loud my voice drowned in the roar. "I think it's a barn."

I had never been inside a barn. I'd only seen pictures of them in books and encyclopedias. The prospect of encountering animals made me hesitate, but I had to get us out of the cold rain. It took me a few minutes to figure out how to open the door—it slid. Why didn't it open like a normal door?

I stepped inside to find that it was mostly empty, and this relieved me. It was also cleaner than I had anticipated. The dirt floors even appeared swept. Was that common? There were stacks of hay or straw—I didn't know the difference—up the side wall. I pulled Angel through the doorframe in the midst of another coughing fit, and his hacking filled up the high rooftop space. The only thing louder than Angel was a large animal in the corner. Once I drew closer I recognized it as a horse. It was the only animal in the barn, and it was disturbed by our racket, neighing and stomping. On the other side of the barn was some type of black carriage.

"Come on," I said and pulled off Angel's coat. "I need to warm you up."

"So cold," he said through chattering teeth.

I pushed him down to sit on one of the bales and scurried around the barn looking for something to keep us warm. I focused hard on Angel's needs through the creaking of the barn in the wind, the horse's occasional racket, and a constant skittering from something unknown. I grabbed a large, thick pad that I put in the empty area on the other side of the horse's space—a pen or something? The horse was starting to quiet, so it was okay to be near it, I supposed. Then I went to the carriage.

"Blankets," I yelled, excited. Then I clapped my hand over my mouth. A house sat only a stone's throw away, and I hoped no one had heard me. It was dark, but we couldn't risk getting caught.

I pulled out the blankets and took them back to the pen where the pad was. I used a rake and gathered some loose hay into a pile and put the blankets over it. I helped Angel over in the dark. My eyes had adjusted well enough, but he stumbled the whole way and I wasn't sure if it was his eyesight or sickness. I stripped him down to his undershirt and long underwear. I took my soaking coat off too but didn't feel right about taking off more. Though Angel and I had been best friends since we were children and Joann had on more than one occasion stripped us down to give us a quick washing together after an outdoor escapade, this was different. Things had changed between the two of us, and I knew enough to try to maintain some modesties. I used a wet handkerchief in his suit coat on his forehead, but it was hot in minutes.

The night fell, and we only had one diner muffin left. I broke it in half, but Angel waved off eating and fell into a restless sleep. I ate my share, hoping he would eat a little in the morning. Between Angel's coughing, his rattled breathing, and the heavy rainfall, I wasn't sure I could sleep. My eyes roamed around the room until they landed on our shoes. Worn and falling apart. But they were walking us to freedom. I wrapped the last blanket around me and held him as tightly as I could until he stopped shivering. Then I relaxed my own body and followed him into a deep sleep.

I didn't wake until I felt that strange awareness that someone was watching me. Angel's breathing was even; he was still asleep. I was afraid to open my eyes, but the stare was too heavy. I opened my eyes and saw a child watching us. A little boy. Maybe five or six. He was wearing a black wide-brimmed hat and a black suit. He had hair cut straight across his brow, and his brown eyes were big and round.

"Hi." I pulled my bag near me. I quietly shook Angel awake and whispered for him to sit up. He didn't move much, and I jabbed him again. I wished I'd kept his clothes closer. Angel roused. He was still feverish but had cooled some. When Angel noticed the little boy, he tried to get up, but fell into a coughing fit instead.

The little boy just stared. He spoke a few words, but I didn't understand him. I carefully stepped away, and the boy watched every move I made as I grabbed the stiff, dry clothes off the wheels.

The little boy's face was clean and looked freshly pink and washed.

He had round and full cheeks, and his mostly black clothes didn't fit him perfectly but looked to be clean and crisp. I'd never seen a well-cared-for child, but I knew he was one. The only children I'd seen were ward children—though mostly at a distance. Joann refused to let me go over there, afraid they would keep me. The children at the factory houses looked about as bad off as asylum children. But this boy, I enjoyed looking at him. Looking at his wholesomeness and the appearance of being cared for.

"Don't you worry about us," I said in a sweet voice like Joann used to speak to me. "We'll be gone in a few minutes and you don't need to tell anyone we're here."

"Freemie?" A woman's high voice cut through the quiet in the barn. "Freemie?"

He took a few steps toward the voice and spoke, then pointed at us. I rushed to help Angel put his clothes on, then grabbed his bag.

"We have to go," I said and yanked him toward the barn door.

There stood a plump and strangely dressed woman. Even I knew she was strangely dressed, in a black dress and white bonnet. Her face was clean and plain looking—it wasn't made up like I usually saw. I knew there was a tradition in the real world to wear black when someone died. Or was this the way she always dressed?

"Hello. Are you in need?" She spoke simply and stepped back as if afraid, even though her face didn't reflect that. I felt bad. We knew what it meant to be afraid, and I hated for anyone to feel that about us.

"We're leaving. We were caught in the storm," I said. Angel was hunched over with one of the blankets balled up in his arms. I held both bags and my damp coat. "Can we keep a blanket?"

She nodded. "You can take whatever you need."

I looked at Angel, then back at the woman. She had a nice face. "We're awfully hungry. Do you have any food?"

The woman nodded with an unalarmed expression and walked toward the house. She said a few words to the boy, and he ran inside ahead of her. What was the strange language they spoke?

I helped Angel tuck the blanket around himself tighter. Where we stood waiting I could see the woman moving around in the house. She moved with a steady grace and not the rush fear brought. She seemed undeterred by our presence.

After ten or fifteen minutes she came back and handed me a bag—it was a rough weave with threading loosened on top. It was full and heavy.

"May God be with you," she said plainly and with such softness in her eyes and face.

I reached for it and said thank you. She turned to leave and I asked for her name.

"Lydia," she said. "And this is my son, Freeman Junior."

Freeman. Free man. I liked that and nodded to her.

Then we were off again. I looked back twice, and the two kindly strangers stood at the end of their driveway and watched us.

The day was damp but more like the leftover rain than fresh. But Angel continued to cough. I had to find somewhere for him to lie down. We started to enter a town, but I veered us off in another direction. Too many people. Eventually we were on a gravel road that was lined with woods on both sides. There were a few smaller barns, like our previous shelter.

It was late afternoon, and the gray and dampness were heavy. The road we traveled ran through a dense forest. It would give us good cover and get us out of the drizzle.

"Over here," I said and took Angel's sleeve. We walked deeper into the wooded area, and I was sure I could find a space for us to at least rest.

I made sure the ground was dry before I helped Angel down, then tucked the blanket around his curled-up body. I took off my coat and put it under his head. He was asleep in minutes. I leaned against a tree trunk and tucked next to Angel to keep myself warm. I ate a little of the bread and cheese Lydia in the black dress had put in the bag, but Angel didn't want to wake to eat.

I looked up through the clearing above the treetops. A collection of gray clouds raced over us. Somewhere in the midst of the whistle of a wood thrush and the skittering of a small animal, I fell asleep and woke to the night when the stars outweighed the dark.

Night sounds choired alongside the rattle in Angel's chest. His head was hotter than ever. I tried to wake him up to give him some of the water out of a jar Lydia had put in the sack. But he wouldn't rouse. I rocked him back and forth, but he didn't even so much as groan. I tried to be like Joann and take his pulse, but I was shaking too much. I started shoving him hard and yelling for him to wake up. What was I supposed to do? I yelled for Joann. I stood in the forest yelling over and over for help. But who would come? We were alone.

1941

Fancies and Fears

$\mathcal{I}$ yelled for Angel. I yelled for Joann. I yelled for my mother. I yelled for anyone to help me. My gaze landed on every part of my surroundings until I finally saw lights. I frantically ran while still yelling for help. Running toward the lights between the gaps of tree trunks.

I ended up at the road. There was a long line of vehicles. Trucks and some that reminded me of a train car and others looked like a small house on wheels. I couldn't see how many there were, but it reminded me of a train without rails. Could I trust strangers? They were all I had, and all I could think of was Angel. Losing him would be a wound that would never heal. Life without Angel would be the kind of alone that might make me want to die or, worse, return to the hospital and be forgotten and forget myself. No, I couldn't do that. I could never let that happen.

I turned to look back to where I'd run from. Angel was out there, out of sight. Feverish and sweaty on the ground in a dark forest. So I kept following the voices and the light because Angel needed me. I started yelling again and stepped so close to the road I nearly got run over. I heard horns blaring and shouting to stop. They'd heard me— seen me. I stopped my yelling and running. I watched as the vehicles pulled over. In the starlight and beams I saw some faces looking out through the windows. Mostly women. My head told me this was a bad idea, but my legs betrayed me and wouldn't run away.

After another minute no one had approached me.

"My friend needs help," I yelled. "I need help." My voice was so ragged it could've scared the bark off the trees.

A door opened in a truck from the back, then I heard fast footsteps against the road coming toward me. I held my breath.

A few moments later, someone stood in front of me—the tallest, largest person I'd ever seen. Broad shoulders. A thick neck. I took a step back. Then my fear pushed me a few more steps back.

"What's going on?" This voice came from the shadows. A man with dark hair and ready eyes. I caught his gaze instantly and his face softened. "Hello. I'm Conrad. Who are you?"

When I didn't answer Conrad spoke again. "Are you in need of help?"

He took several strides toward me and I turned toward him and my hands posed like claws—like an afraid asylum patient. Conrad raised his hands in surrender, but before he could speak I was squeezed from behind. It was the giant, and the hold was tighter than a straightjacket. My lungs constricted and I couldn't breathe. All I could think of was Angel. He would die without help, I was certain. It would be my fault. Another death. But no amount of struggling freed me.

"Let go, let go, let go," Conrad repeated rapidly to the giant. I saw concern in his eyes. "It's all right. She's just afraid."

The grip around me loosened, and the giant stepped away. People were everywhere now, one of them a masked man, and I regretted my decision to come this way.

"It's okay. We aren't going to hurt you." Conrad reached out toward me, and just as I realized my balance was failing, he steadied me. A heavy wooziness hung over me, and I began to see things that didn't seem real. Three identical women. The giant holding a woman who was as small as a doll. A woman who was as white as light. Like Angel. Was I hallucinating? They were all standing around the vehicles, some in blaring headlights, some in the shadows. Who were these people?

It didn't matter. I needed to help Angel, and they said they wouldn't hurt us. I pulled my arm free and pointed toward the trees.

"Do you need help?" Conrad repeated and our gazes connected, and I was sure he knew everything I was thinking.

"Is there someone with you? Out there?" He pointed over his shoulder toward the woods.

I nodded. "My friend. He's sick. He needs help."

He looked past me and nodded, and several rough-looking men and the giant ran off to where I'd come from. I wanted to go with them, but when I tried to follow light-headedness overtook me. A gentle arm came around me and kept me upright.

"We found him," I heard voices saying from the woods. Then a few minutes later one of the men ran back with a furrowed expression. He whispered to Conrad.

"An albino?" Conrad said breathlessly, dropping his arm from me.

"Yes, but that's not what's wrong with him. He's sick. But please don't take him to a hospital."

Would they think he was feebleminded like his mother had believed? I couldn't—wouldn't—let them hurt him.

"Get Gabrielle," Conrad said. Then he turned to look at me. "We won't hurt your friend. How long have you been out here?"

I was afraid to say too much. "We've been walking for a few days."

"Just the two of you? Alone?" His voice was soft and kind. He had a shadow of whiskers that matched the dark hair that fell naturally over his forehead and eyes. He swiped it away every so often.

"Just us."

The giant with arms as round as tree trunks came out of the woods carrying Angel. I tried to walk toward him, but Conrad regained a grip on my arm. I was feeling so physically weak all I could do was watch. Hadn't I left the hospital to avoid this overt control over our lives? But I also needed help.

Then a woman appeared. But not just any woman. It was the woman of pure white light that I thought was an illusion. She was beautiful and glowed like Angel. She wore a long pale dress that wrapped and tied at her small waist. She was tall, and with elegant steps she moved toward Angel. Even in my fear, the serenity in her movements brought some measure of peace. The giant stood there on the side of the road holding Angel steady for her.

"Oh, my sweet boy," she said, touching his face and mothering him like she knew him. She looked around until she found me, her eyes doing what Angel's always did. When she found me she came close; her gaze pierced through me. "What is his name?"

"Angel, I call him Angel." I winced, wishing I'd called him Luke.

"Angel." The way she said it sounded like a magic spell, then she returned to Angel.

"I need to go too." I pulled my arm roughly away from Conrad, a surge of strength returning. Flashes of my history with Angel burst into my mind—playing, crying, dreaming. He was all I had, and I wouldn't lose him.

"We will not hurt him or take him away from you. We have a doctor who will give him attention." Conrad's voice was a braiding together of sincerity and mystery. But Angel. I stepped toward Angel when my eyes caught sight of three men walking out of the woods with our things. Each nodded a hello to me as they passed me. One man came and wrapped my blanket around me, and it was heavy and warm and weighted with care and relief. I didn't know that I was shivering.

Angel was carried away from me with the bright woman at his side. I decided to trust—for now—the kindness of strangers. Yet there was something odd about the group that made me question why they were so willing to help us. Especially when there was sickness involved. Conrad held the heavy blanket around my shoulders and kept an arm around me.

"We are friends," he said and walked me in the same direction as Angel.

Angel was taken to a truck with a room built on the back. A door was opened and a yellow, inviting glow poured out. Angel was placed inside, and Gabrielle slinked in after him. Then the door was shut.

"I need to go inside with him."

"It's okay. Your Angel will get some medicine, and you both need to rest. We'll talk in the morning. You won't be apart from him for long."

"But where are you traveling to?"

"West. Toward Chicago. But we will be setting up camp in the morning here in Ohio."

I thought for a moment and pictured where Chicago was on a map, thankful for being taught geography. We would at least be heading in the right direction.

"Come." He nudged me forward, but I resisted. I looked him in the face and tightened my jaw, hoping he wouldn't see my fear.

"First, who are you?"

He paused and seemed to consider my question. "Well, you know my name. What's yours?" He stepped back and smiled, waiting.

I began forming the sound of a *B*. But then I stopped.

"Nell," I said.

"Nell. All right." He smiled and nodded. There was something so honest in the way he looked at me that it made me hope I could trust him. "Come. We must be off."

He led me to another truck, similar to the one Angel was in. He opened the door and gestured grandly for me to enter.

Inside were several women, and it looked as comfortable as I'd ever seen a bedroom look. I turned back to Conrad.

"You haven't answered my question." I gestured to the line of vehicles. "Who are you?"

"Who are we? We are the Fancies and Fears, my dear." He bowed and rose with a flourish. "The show that will thrill your dreams and confirm your nightmares."

He looked at me as if he was waiting for some response. But I stood there ignorant of what he was talking about. I'd already had enough nightmares in my life. He must have understood something in my expression.

"We're a troupe of performers," he explained further.

"Performers?" I repeated.

He squinted at me like he saw something in me that shouted my stupidity. "Where are you from?"

I would never tell him the truth.

"Pennsylvania." Then without warning I lost all my breath in that single word. My chest tightened.

Conrad put his hand on my blanketed shoulder, and I looked up at him. His mouth was moving, but I could not hear him. His eyebrows and forehead wrinkled up in concern. My hand went to my chest, the blanket fell, and I was heaving for air. Why now? My eyes remained on Conrad. He helped me stumble, step over step, into the truck room. I fumbled my way through the doorway, half resisting, half relenting.

A woman spoke. I could hear her words but didn't understand them. I looked at her, but everything was moving in slow motion as I tried to catch my breath. The woman had dark hair, tanned skin, and Rosina's smile. Oh, I missed Rosina. Her hair was slicked in a knot at the back of her neck, but Rosina's was often short because of the lice. But the slack jaw was also the same.

The woman who was not Rosina sat me down next to her on a soft mattress and rubbed my back and spoke in a soft, unknown tongue that soothed me. Her words were laced with a thick accent I didn't recognize, and even though she wasn't singing, it reminded me of a lilting tune. After another few minutes my breathing began to slow down. But every part of me was afraid, and I wished I'd never found these people who had just managed to separate Angel and me.

"You okay now, my dear?" were the woman's first words in English. It was a voice of age and weight and wisdom all folded together as one.

I shook my head. I wasn't okay. I was scared. And then the pressure in my chest came again and I gasped for air.

"Now, now," she said and patted my back. "What you afraid of, *kotik*?"

Even though I didn't know what that last word meant, the affection and tenderness in her voice weren't lost on me. She shushed me, and her hand against my back was the kind of touch I needed.

Across from me were three identical girls who appeared around my age. The three tilted their heads to the left exactly the same way and smiled.

They sat so closely to each other, like they were one. They were beautiful. Dark eyes, dark hair, dark skin. Their faces were all eyes and smiles. Their straight black hair hung like thick curtains down the sides of their faces. I was mesmerized.

"We cannot pronounce their real Hindi names, so we call them Persephone, Penelope, and Thalia. They are the Sirens. Say hello, *kotiks*." One year I'd read a little of the *Odyssey* and knew Sirens could lure the hardest of hearts.

"Hello," they said together.

"I am Alima, *kotik*."

"What does that mean?" My question was breathless and quiet.

"Mean?" Her accent separated her from my memory of my asylum friend. She was different.

"It's not English," I said, still gathering my breath.

"*Kotik*?" Her eyebrows lifted into her hairline. "Oy, it means 'little kitten.'"

She'd called me kitten. I liked it.

There was silence for a few long moments, and then I had to ask another question. "They won't take Angel away from me, will they?" *Breathe*, I told myself. *Breathe*.

"Your friend? The sick one?" Alima's thick voice rested in my ears.

I nodded my head.

"He will be okay," she said and patted my knee. "Doctor will take good care of the albino boy."

His name is Angel, I wanted to yell. *He isn't just an albino boy.*

"So it's true?" one of the Sirens asked. I didn't know which one had spoken, even though I was looking right at them.

"True?" My breath was still thin, and I had to concentrate so it wouldn't thin further.

"An albino came with you?" one of them asked.

"*Tishe*, quiet about that," Alima admonished. She smoothed my hair from my face, then returned her attention to the three across from us. "Sing for her. Soothe our new friend."

And without consulting one another in any way that I could see, they began. And everything in my body was heavy and tired and moved slowly. A small thread of smoke from a corner began dancing as the truck moved and rocked me to sleep. It was warm, and suddenly I couldn't keep my eyes open.

The Sirens sang me to sleep.

Evolution

*K*elly wants an explanation of every photograph, but when we get to Angel I pause. She wants to know, but I've always held him tightly to me and can't tell her. She doesn't push.

The photo of Angel, however, makes me laugh a little. His trademark innocent smile is so wide, like it had always been. But I can see now, as an experienced photographer, that I'd gotten the exposure entirely wrong. It made for a decent photo for our purposes, but I wish that I'd done better. The photo is washed out and brighter even than his albinism. The boy I knew. The boy who had saved my life so many times and in so many ways. He'd also broken my heart more than maybe anyone else ever had, but that was well after this picture had been taken.

When we get to Rosina and Carmen, I tell Kelly about the prayers and the food and how much they loved each other. And Lorna. The room full of women in tightened camisoles. I will never be able to remember every name. Then the picture of hydrotherapy surfaces.

"I can't believe I got it right," I whisper, that day returning to me.

"What?" Kelly asks.

"See the light in that window?" I point. "The beam didn't take over the photo but made the steam more visible, and for a photo older than the hills—it's good. We broke the rules taking this shot, and I've wondered since I was sixteen if I got it right."

Then there is me.

A river of hot tears washes my face. Oh, the girl I was. The girl in the photograph didn't know what life she was about to live and all she would have to endure for the freedom she needed. I grieve for her. How lost I was without Brighton. That girl believed she would never see anything but the four walls around her, even though she had hopes and dreams. But being forgotten in the asylum was her truth at the time of this photo. I know better now.

The next set of photos brings such dark clouds. My hair had grown, but Grace's had begun to fall out. She was so thin. Her skin, even in the black-and-white photos, looked ashen and aged. The twinkle in her eyes couldn't be caught in a photo any longer. Her smile had been lost long before.

"Tell me about her?" Kelly asks quietly.

I nearly forget she's with me.

"This is what the asylum did to her—what it did to most patients." I tap the photo and hold it up so she can really see. "I was spared some of this—*evolution*—because I'd been, well, as Dickens would've put it, I was raised by hand there. I'd been cared for and loved and, for a time, kept away from so much. I was played with and educated. It was all I knew. But Grace had lived in the real world with a real life. Then she had to give it all up." I pause and look. "I wish I could've saved her."

1941

A Family

When I woke, I was alone. I was curled up among heaps of blankets with remnants of the earthy scent from the night before still circling in the air. Light came through the thinly curtained windows. Voices snuck in from outside, though indiscernible and so mixed together that it reminded me of the asylum dayroom. But I wasn't there. I was somewhere in Ohio in some type of house truck with people who called themselves the Fancies and Fears. Performers, the man had said.

I sat up with a gasping inhale.

Angel.

Where was he? It took me several nerve-wracking moments to remember everything from the previous night. He'd been carried off under the watchful eye of an elegant albino woman. She made me feel far away from Angel. Like he would never see me the same way again.

I had to find him. My bare feet chilled on the truck floor. Where were my shoes? I pictured Alima taking them off and tucking me in like I imagined a grandmother would do. But she didn't seem real anymore. Had there really been a woman who had spoken sweet, oddly comforting words to me? Had I really seen three identical girls? The visions from the night before were blurry.

I found my shoes and slipped them on, breaking the shoelace of the left one. I cussed and then slapped my hand over my mouth. Joann would have threatened to wash my mouth out with soap if she'd heard me. But she was far away. I closed my eyes and breathed in and out, in and out. I rubbed my hands over my face and smoothed my hair into a small ponytail, then opened the door.

I welcomed the cool breeze that caressed my cheeks. We had moved from the road to an expansive field, and all the vehicles were parked along the edges. Numerous trucks with those rooms on the back and some larger vehicles that looked like something between a bus and a train car. I'd never seen anything like it. Some had curtained windows and a porch on the back, like a caboose on a train. A few tents had been built, and the smell of food found my nose.

Farther ahead a small platform and walls were being constructed. A dozen people carrying crates passed me without even noticing me. Children helped with smaller items and their wiggly bodies zoomed around with spills of laughter every few moments.

Beyond the movement of workers and the vehicles I saw a small town. With a lineup of storefronts. Another diner. A building with a cross on the top of a white point—a church? My eyes lingered on the cross, and I could see Rosina making the sign of the cross over her body. I almost did the gesture myself. Beyond the town and all around us there were houses and other buildings and a large lake off into the horizon. The scent of a farm was in the air.

But where was I? And more important, where was Angel?

I looked back at the truck where I'd slept and noted that the door was yellow, chipped and crooked too. I didn't want to forget where my bag was. I would leave it for now. I needed to find Angel. Besides my apprehension about this unusual group of people, my main concern was helping Angel get well and finding out if we could trust the doctor.

I went to the truck house next to me and nervously stood in front of the door and knocked. The door opened and the smallest woman I'd ever laid eyes on opened it. I could've held her on my hip like a child. I stepped back. Was this the woman I'd seen in the arms of the giant last night? She was dressed in a multicolored red and purple skirt threaded with gold. Her hair was wrapped in a scarf. Her shy smile revealed gaps between her few teeth.

"Oh, it's you," she said in a hundred-year-old voice. An untucked strand of silver hair contrasted with her dark skin.

My brow knit up. None of this made sense to me. The vision of the giant from last night and then this tiny woman in front of me. The other albino. Conrad had called them Fancies and Fears and said they were performers. What did they perform?

In shock I shut the door in the woman's face and ran to the next truck, but before I knocked I would try to see through the window. This one had no curtains. The words from the first diner lady, Sandy, came to mind. Something about a troupe and an albino woman, and she'd used the word *freaks*. Were these the freaks she was talking about?

Then through a hazy side window of the truck, I saw him. I saw my friend. My only friend. The one who said he loved me. He was sitting up and looked better than the night before. What sort of doctor had been able to do that? No doctor at Riverside could have. When patients were as sick as Angel, they often died. He had that healthy subtle pink in his lips again. He was wearing different clothes. A white shirt that was cut low in the chest, cuffs unbuttoned. His pants were white also. There was no harsh crease down the middle, and both the shirt and pants were loose on his body. The clothes reminded me of his hospital uniform and were nothing like what Dr. Woburn had given him.

And she was there too.

Gabrielle. Hadn't that been the name Conrad had called her?

I could see that she was older than him. Nearly his mother's age, I guessed. Her white hair trailed down to her waist, and her white lacey dress was also cut deeply down her chest. She was holding his hands. Was he holding hers back? Every now and again she would take one of her white, graceful fingers and stroke his face or smooth his hair. He tilted his head and looked so intently at her. Like he was studying her face.

Had he ever looked at me like that? Then she put her arm around him, and he nestled against her chest like a small child would with his mother. His real mother had held him also—but then rejected him. He closed his eyes and seemed to be more relaxed and content than I'd ever seen him. The kind of contentment his mother had never offered.

Then Gabrielle turned and looked right at me. It startled me, and I turned away from the window, only to find that Conrad had come up behind me. He stood so close that his smoky and musky scent encircled me. He was handsomer than I'd remembered. He wore denim pants and a loose shirt that was similar to Angel's. A blue bandanna was tied around his thick neck. Under other circumstances I would have said that his dark hair and light eyes were memorable, but in the presence of this group with such unusual appearances, he was entirely commonplace. The giant, the tiny woman, the three Sirens, Gabrielle, and even something about Alima seemed almost mystical—though I couldn't reason it out. But Conrad wasn't like any of them. He was like me. Ordinary.

"You have questions?" He lifted his eyebrows.

I nodded.

"Where are we?" I needed this simple question answered first.

"We're somewhere in Ohio still. A few hours from where we found you—or you found us. Come, let me show you around."

"What about Angel?" I didn't want to leave him again.

"You can see he's made a remarkable recovery—our doctor is gifted—and is in good hands with Gabrielle." He gestured toward the truck.

"If he's well, then we need to be on our way. We—"

"All in good time, Nell." He offered his hand. "Come."

I studied his confident expression. It reminded me of Dr. Woburn's arrogance—but diffused with such charisma it warmed instead of cooled me. So I took his hand.

I'd never held any man's hand but Angel's. It didn't feel the same. Angel's had always been soft next to my own, warm and familiar and protective. But Conrad's hand was thicker, and his skin was tough.

He held my hand a little tighter, but not protectively; it felt controlling. My guard was up, but I wasn't frightened.

He led me back toward the trucks. He waved at some people, and they all looked from him to me and then back to him with different expressions. Some winked. Some raised an eyebrow. Conrad's arm stretched back holding on to my hand, and I had to work hard to keep up because of my broken-laced shoe, and my insecurities.

"Who are all these people?" There really were so many more than I'd realized the night before and so many of them were ordinary like Conrad and me, confusing me further.

"The common ones are our workers and builders, and the gifted ones are our performers. You might use the words *normal* and, well, *abnormal*." He turned around and smirked.

The way he said *normal* was something I understood—the inflection, the insinuation. I knew what he was trying to say, and it made me feel itchy as if I wanted to slip out of my skin. It took me too far back to where I didn't want to go. But I couldn't resist the memory of Joann calling me normal, saying that I wasn't like a real asylum patient. I wasn't what they called feebleminded or mad. I wasn't mentally disturbed and had never starved myself like Grace—though I had been starved. I didn't hear voices or see people who weren't there—though now I often heard the voices of my patient friends in my head and recognized them everywhere in the people I was meeting. And here I was being called normal again, because I wasn't too tall or too small or too light.

On the other side of the erected tent, there was a wooden fence. It separated our field of tents and trucks from the sidewalk and town. Boys ran over from the neighborhood and stood on the bottom rail.

"Freak show, freak show, freak show," they chanted over and over, reminding me again of Sandy's words.

A small group of children on our side of the fence who were playing with marbles stopped and looked over, listening. The largest two boys stood. Their fists balled and their mouths grew straight and solid.

Conrad called to them and nodded a stern *no*. Discontent dripped from their faces, but they retreated back to their game playing. The taunting, however, did not cease.

Unflinching, Conrad kept our conversation moving. "These men here build the stage and the walls and the corridors for patrons to come and look."

"Look?"

"At their fancies." He let go of my hand and turned to walk backward to face me and gestured with grandeur. "And fears." His eyes sparkled.

I was starting to understand, though what they performed was still a mystery to me. I just looked at my surroundings, taking in as much as I could. Conrad lowered his arms and stopped walking. His gaze locked on me.

"You have a question."

"What do the gifted perform?"

He smiled and put his hand out to me again. "You'll see tonight." I took it and he comfortably tucked my arm close to his side and led me on. "But now you must meet someone very important."

Conrad walked me toward the colorful tent behind the stage. The only thing I could think about was a picture I'd seen once of a circus. It was from a brightly illustrated children's book Joann had read to me when I was a child. Was that what this was? A circus? But didn't circuses have animals? Lions, horses, tigers, monkeys. Was there such a thing as a circus without animals?

When we got to the curtains, I wasn't sure how Conrad could find his way through, but he held open the curtain for me, revealing a dimly lit hall. I hesitated and looked back at the truck that held Angel and Gabrielle.

"He'll be okay," Conrad said with a convincing smile. "Don't worry about him."

I let him lead me through several curtained hallways. I didn't see anyone else but I could hear voices. I recognized Alima's voice and the Sirens singing quietly, but Conrad kept me moving and led me to a curtained wall, then stopped.

"Lazarus?" he called loudly.

"Yes?" the voice said.

"I brought the girl," Conrad responded.

It was strange to be referred to as *the girl*. It was like nothing had changed except the people around me. I was still just *the girl* who didn't belong.

"Come on in," the curtained voice said.

With Conrad's hold still firm on my arm, together we ducked through the lighter-curtained doorway and entered a fabric-lined room. The room inside was darker than even the hallway. There was a table, dark wood and heavy looking. A man stood behind it with his back to us. He wore a soft-looking jacket that I wanted to touch. It was a shade of deep red like almost everything else around me. The man was fitting something over his head, and we stood there for a few stretched seconds before he turned.

I gasped. It was the masked man from the night before.

He was just average height. His red jacket was longer in the back than the front, and it made his belly protrude. What made him remarkable was that his face was half covered with a black mask. There was an almond-shaped hole where his left eye could see out. It traced around his nose and across his cheek, near his mouth, with straps that tightened like a belt around the back of his head. Everything else about him was of no significance.

"Lazarus Hale, at your service." He put his hand out to me. Conrad let go of me, and I slowly reached out and took the man's meaty hand. "Don't be afraid of me. Or of this." He pointed to his mask. "It's just a piece of leather to cover up some ugly scars from the war. Mustard gas and— Well, you understand."

No, I didn't. I didn't understand at all. I didn't know what mustard gas was, even though I knew what leather was and it always made me think of restraints. But that leather had caused wounds, not hidden them.

"Your name is—" He looked at Conrad.

"Nell," Conrad reminded him.

"Ah, yes, Nell," Lazarus Hale said. "Such an unusual name. Where does it come from?"

"My grandmother," I answered too quickly.

He nodded and kept his eyes trained on me. "And you came with the albino. Angel." He widened his arms out like he had wings. He cast his face to the ceiling as if catching some glow from heaven that wasn't there. My skin tingled in a funny way. I didn't like this man.

After a moment he lowered his arms and his eyes connected with mine—despite the mask. "It's perfect—really, quite perfect."

"Perfect?" I asked.

"The albino boy with that name." Lazarus chuckled a little. "That's perfect. That's all I mean. Where did you find him? How are you—together?" Lazarus sat and leaned back in his chair. "Are you married?"

I would never tell him the whole truth, but I did say, "We grew up together. We're not married."

"And why are you two alone on the road?" This man was asking too many questions. What was he after?

He leaned forward and laced his fingers together, and his thumbs twirled around themselves. I thought for a long moment about how I should answer this. But when I didn't he spoke again. "Did Conrad here tell you who we are?"

I cleared my throat, hoping to make my voice strong and full. "Fancies and Fears, right?"

"You know what else we are?" His uncovered eyebrow rose.

I shook my head.

"We're a family. And I'm the father." He pushed the chair back and stood. "And I don't trust outsiders."

His words hung out around us and became like the tent poles, holding up the heavy curtains.

"He wants to make sure you're not running from the law or something," Conrad leaned in and clarified.

I shook my head. We weren't running from the law. We were running from the men in the white coats, though.

"No. We're traveling to see my aunt," I said without a stutter, taking on the strength and boldness I'd witnessed in Grace. I made eye contact with both men. "She lives in Michigan. A town called Brighton." I paused again. They didn't say anything. "We don't have any money so we're walking. We got a ride with a truck driver a few days ago."

"I see." Lazarus nodded with several bobs of his head. "Well then, you can stay—for now. But everyone pulls their weight around here."

I hadn't asked to stay, but I kept my face stoic and sure. Angel needed help, but the moment he was well enough, we would leave. I had never asked to stay at Riverside either, and I was there for eighteen years. I wouldn't let that happen again.

"Can you sing?"

I shook my head.

"Acrobat?"

"No."

"Can you talk to the dead?"

"What?" I said louder. I didn't know anyone could and I was sure my face displayed my ignorance.

He sighed. He looked at Conrad, then at me. He came from around the desk toward me, lifted my chin, extended my arm out straight, and looked my body up and down.

"Conrad will figure out what you're good for. Alima will help." He walked toward the curtain opening.

Then with a wink he walked out.

"What does he mean? What will Alima help with?" I asked, having too many words in my mouth at once. "We aren't staying. We're going to my aunt's as soon as Angel is strong enough." I hesitated for a moment. "We don't belong here."

Conrad turned and looked me right in the eyes.

"Where do you belong, *Nell*?" And the way he said my name gave me gooseflesh. What had Angel told these strangers?

1941

The Sirens' Call

I wasn't taken to Angel; I was told that he was still weak and needed to rest. But I had been fed, and since I'd slept through breakfast I was ravenous. But serving me a meal didn't eradicate my distrustful suspicions.

Conrad left me with the cook since he had things to do for tonight. Before he left, he reminded me that everyone had to do their part—including me. I was certain I was being kept away from Angel intentionally and that it had something to do with their show. But I also was sure he was safe, so I was going to bide my time and maybe slip away during the night.

Until then, I peeled and cut potatoes—just like I'd helped Joyful. After hours of it, my hands ached. And the sun was setting. A few electric lights on long wooden poles were turned on and the half a dozen colorful tents illuminated.

"Hmm, maybe I did find what you're good at." Conrad jogged up and pointed at the potatoes and flashed a smile at me.

"It's just peeling," I said. "I'd like to see Angel now."

"Soon. I have something for you and then you can see your Angel." He put a hand out to me—this was becoming a habit. I was glad to put down the peeling knife and take his hand.

He led me past the truck house where I'd seen Angel earlier. I tried to look through the window as we walked by, but it appeared empty. He took me to a tent on the fringes of their circled area. He bowed in a grand gesture, directing me inside.

283

Alima was there, with a smile on her face and a makeshift bath and shower next to her. She looked different from the previous night. Her face was made up, and her lips and cheeks were bright. She was draped with beautiful scarves and jewelry.

"Come inside, *Nell*." She said my name the same way Conrad had.

I looked back at Conrad, who encouraged me with a smile to go ahead.

"I don't understand."

"Since you are not planning to stay, we want you to look your best tonight and show you a good time."

I inhaled and looked back at the shower and bath. How nice it would feel. One night here. Just one.

"A shower would be nice," I admitted. "And then I can see Angel?"

With a nod Conrad left me with Alima.

Over the next hour several little girls came in with pitchers of hot steaming bathwater. When I was finished, Alima dressed me in the most beautiful dress I'd ever seen—pale pink, nearly the color of my skin. She styled my disarrayed hair that was just past my chin and put makeup on my face for the first time in my life. It felt strange sliding across my skin and lips.

"*Krasavitsa*," Alima said. "Such a beauty."

"I'm not," I said, feeling shy at her compliment. I knew what I'd seen in the mirror my entire life was nothing but a girl with ashen skin and stringy, dirty-blond hair. Joann was beautiful, with porcelain skin and bright lips and shiny blond hair. I had always been plain.

"Oh, you know this, huh?" Alima's eyebrows lifted high. "Let's go to mirror."

She walked me out of the tent bathroom and my dress whisked around my ankles in the breeze.

"Shoes and mirror—come," Alima said and flicked her hand for me to follow.

She took me into another tent, and inside was a woman in a pink dress. It was like the one I was wearing, only she was elegant and her face sparkled.

"You like?" Alima pointed.

"What?"

"That's you, *kotik*."

That wasn't another woman; it was *me*. I walked toward the mirror, within inches of the glass. I'd never seen myself like this before. The dress was sheer across my shoulders and heart-shaped over my chest, and there was a wide, shiny belt at the waist. The sheer skirt went down to my ankles, and the underskirt slipped softly against my bare legs. I was mesmerized by my reflection. I gently touched my hair that was rolled in beautiful waves similar to Joann's. My face was smooth and creamy like a doll. And my eyes looked wide and large.

Alima placed a pair of shoes in front of me and told me to fit them onto my feet. They were a little tight, but it didn't matter. It was one night. But the fact I'd never had so much personal attention since my childhood wasn't lost on me—and by strangers, no less. And they were helping Angel get well. Maybe my distrust of Lazarus was unfounded.

"Why?" I asked Alima.

"He wants you to be beautiful tonight." She winked at me.

"Conrad?" I felt heat come to my face and under my arms.

"No." She leaned in toward me. "The Mentalist."

"The Mentalist?"

"Father Lazarus, of course. Our keeper, our deliverer."

Why would that man want me to be beautiful tonight? My spine prickled. Was Angel feeling the same concern and suspicions that I was? I took in my appearance again. This wasn't me, and I wanted to get my other clothes back on. But I had the feeling I had to play a part right now in order to get to Angel. Lazarus might want me to look beautiful, but what he really wanted was Angel. I could see it clearly now. Why did it take me so long to see that?

"Why does Lazarus want me to be dolled up for his circus tonight?" I tried not to sound suspicious.

"Circus? *Nyet, nyet.*" Alima made a face. "Don't let Laz ever hear you say that word. We are not circus. We are performers. The circus is for simpleminded beasts."

Alima took me outside and told me to wait for Conrad. The scent of roasted chicken danced in the air, and my stomach growled loudly. Beyond the tent was a line of people, like the entire town was here to see these performers. The Fancies and Fears.

There was a booth and an archway where a line formed and a few men were taking money from the townspeople. The people began making their way toward the seating area and followed signs directing them into another tent with a sign that said *Oddities Inside.* People exited with hands over their mouths, wide eyes, tears. I even heard a few screams from inside.

"You are beautiful, Nell." Conrad was suddenly at my side, though I hadn't seen him walk up. "Alima did well."

I didn't know what to say. He wore a suit, and his black hair was greased back. When he smiled at me, I felt my heart drip like wax into my stomach. That was also new to me. He took my arm and curled it around his own.

"Do I get to see Angel?" I was hopeful but feared he had other plans.

"Of course. But first I want you to meet a few others." His voice was as smooth as cream, and his smile lit our way toward the oddities tent.

When we stood in front of the first curtained door, my heart began to pound harder.

"Don't be afraid," he whispered closely into my ear and caressed my arm. I had tightened my hold on him without realizing it. "I won't leave you."

I didn't like to hear him say that. Joann had said that. Angel had said that.

When we stepped into the first room of the tent, a gasp escaped my mouth. The room was lit enough for me to see a small boy. He couldn't have been much older than ten. He stood there with only pants on and made muscles and did poses. But what was I seeing? He had two extra arms. They hung limply at his sides. They did not move with the rest of his body. There was a sign near him that said "Rollie, the Four-Armed Boy."

"Good job, Rollie," Conrad said and squeezed one of his muscled arms and feigned being impressed.

"Four arms?" I asked when we turned around.

"He was born that way. Nobody wanted him—so Laz took him in and is his father now."

In the next room the tiny woman from earlier sat on a small chair on top of a table. She was smaller than a two-year-old child. She nodded and smiled, and her eyes glinted with tenderness. Next to her was the sign saying that her name was Bitsie and that she was the smallest adult in the world and that she came from South America.

I stared at the display in the next room for several long moments until Conrad explained that it was the remains of a mermaid. Laz had acquired her from some Romanian gypsy. The skeleton was exceptionally small and inside a glass case.

"Mermaids don't live long outside of the sea." Conrad spoke gently and closely. "They don't belong here, but imagine how beautiful she would've been if she'd never left the ocean."

In the next room was a caged man covered in scales. His hands were webbed, and the skin between his shoulders and his ears had a webbed appearance. He didn't frighten me, though he seemed to try. I let go of Conrad's arm and drew closer. I put my hands on the bars that kept this man contained. When he hissed at me, I didn't falter. I was used to this sort of behavior, but my throat thickened. Conrad warmed me from behind.

"The cage," I stuttered. The sight brought memories of the cries and banging of many patients inside solitary. "Get him out." I hit the cage, and the man stopped hissing. His gaze softened.

"He's okay," Conrad whispered, his breath filling my ears and senses. "This is just his job."

I looked from the caged man to Conrad.

"This isn't right." I banged on the cage again.

"Get her outta here," the webbed man said, baring his teeth.

Conrad escorted me quickly past the next rooms of more cages and people ready to shock their onlookers. I didn't like this.

"No." I pushed Conrad's touch away. "This isn't right. They are people, not—"

"Not what?"

I didn't know what.

"They are making a living, Nell," Conrad explained.

"But why?" I yelled loud enough to cause others to look over. Conrad pulled me farther away. "Why put them on display like this?"

"What else can people like this do but shock people? And look at this crowd. Everyone loves oddities. Like your Angel." His hands held my waist and he pressed his body close to mine. My hands rested on his forearms.

My entire body heated at both his words and his touch.

"How do people really see him?" he asked. "As an angel?"

Several words came to mind, none of them nice. I shook my head.

"Feebleminded. Incurable." My voice was all breath and realized fear and almost no sound. "Like he should be ashamed of himself."

"Right. But here he's different. He's worshipped and adored and is perfect, the way God made him."

When he said *God* it didn't have the sacred ring to it like it did when Rosina said it.

Then he leaned in to my ear. "What's odd about you, Nell?" Then he kissed my cheek and without a response from me he led me through the crowd toward the rows of chairs in front of the stage.

We passed by a tent with a sign of a large hand with circles drawn on the palm. I could see Alima inside with a woman opposite her. Her hooped earrings and bracelets jingled as she reached for the woman's hand. We walked around men on stilts, juggling knives and fire, and another man swallowing the length of a sword in front of a small gasping and impressed crowd.

Conrad took me to a seat, but I wasn't sure I could sit. My nerves had tightened like a noose. I never should have let them take Angel anywhere the previous night, but he had been so ill.

"I'll be back shortly. Just wait here and enjoy the show until I return." He said all of this while stroking the outside of my arm, sending a tingle up my back. Then, with a smirk, he was off.

"Ladies and Gentlemen," a man announced, and a crowd of townspeople flooded into the chairs, making it impossible for me to do anything but sit.

Then the lights and the music began. Voices like magic started to sing. Voices I recognized from the night before.

Then a beaming light shone on the stage—and the red curtains slowly opened. The three Sirens, Persephone, Penelope, and Thalia, floated to the middle of the stage, their feet not visible beneath the one large skirt they wore together. They moved like one person. And they sang. Oh, their voices. I'd never heard anything like it. The sign on the stage said that the Sirens were conjoined triplets. I'd heard of this before from medical books I'd read of Joann's. As shocked as I knew I should be seeing all of these oddities, all I could think about was that there was still something I was missing. And it had something to do with Lazarus, and maybe Conrad also.

Everyone around me was spellbound by the Sirens' voices, and by the time their song was done, there was not a sound to be heard.

Not even a whisper.

The Mentalist's Call

As the Sirens retreated back behind the curtain, Lazarus bounded up onstage. The cane in his hand had a golden handle, and he raised it high as he welcomed the crowd from the town of Springville, Ohio. He introduced Octavia, the armless woman, and a curtain opened off to the right. She was sitting on a table, and between her toes she had paintbrushes. On the floor in front of her was a canvas. Lazarus announced that she would be painting the most beautiful woman in the crowd. Ladies began batting their eyes, and I heard a few men telling the woman at their side that surely it would be her. A few scoffed at the possibility of an armless woman painting at all.

"We are the Fancies and Fears—the show that will thrill your dreams and confirm your nightmares. And now—" With a grand flourish Lazarus regained the crowd's attention, and there was a loud rolling, booming sound offstage that stopped when he called out, "Golithia, the strongest woman in the world."

The giant who had carried Angel away the night before was a woman and not a man, as I had assumed. She walked onstage and performed feats of strength. There were aahs and oohs from the crowd. But I could only see the face of a sad woman. I'd seen that face so many times in the hospital and recognized it well.

After Golithia's act she marched her sweaty body offstage and Lazarus returned. The spotlight narrowed so that only Lazarus was lit. Out beyond the stage the sky was black, and the moon was covered by inky clouds, leaving only a small patch of gray in the sky. The poor moon was held as captive behind the haze as I was in the confusion of this new world around me. Another world I didn't belong in or understand.

"For those of you who have never seen one of our shows, you may not know my story." Lazarus walked the stage, and the tap of his cane on the wooden stage echoed in the quiet of the crowd. "You might know Lazarus from the Bible, though."

He stopped walking back and forth and turned to face us. He didn't say anything for several long moments. Not a breath could be heard around me.

Rosina had told me some Bible stories, and the name Lazarus was vaguely familiar.

"The Bible says that Lazarus was one of the most beloved friends of our Savior, Jesus Christ." He looked up into the sky with a dramatic pause. "So loved, in fact, that Jesus brought him back from the grave."

Lazarus continued, "As some of you know, I died in the Battle of the Lys. I was nineteen years old and was blown off of my feet." The crowd murmured. He held his hand out to the crowd. "You don't have to believe me. It's all right. Not everyone believed that the Lazarus of the Bible walked out of his tomb either or even that Jesus himself did the same after three days dead."

The crowd silenced.

"I lay on the battlefield for three days, so I'm told. My company and my commander had already listed me as dead. Until I wasn't—anymore. I wasn't without wounds and scars across my face, but I had been returned to the living."

The crowd whispered loudly this time, and a few men called out that he was a liar and a fraud.

"Oh, it's all there in the war records." He lifted his chin and resumed his pacing. "My own return to life after death opened a door of sorts. I became a mentalist. And can now speak to them—those lost souls beyond the grave where I once was. And tonight I'll prove it to you all."

The murmuring crowd became louder, and a family near me

left. A few others went as well. The buzz of voices heightened until Lazarus put his hand in the air. Everyone went silent.

With that raised hand he removed his hat and tossed it offstage, then put his hand on his head. He closed his eyes. The crowd was completely still. Lazarus hummed. For almost a whole minute we watched Lazarus hum and sway.

"I see a woman," he said. "A mother. She's sick and frail and is mostly kept to bed. A small room. There's a window—a broken window—in the room. When she was alive she would scratch at the walls, like she was trying to get out."

I inhaled and pressed my back against my chair.

"Woman, what is your name?" he asked out into the air, and I was certain that all of us held our breaths as we waited for an answer. Would we hear it along with him? "She's not telling me her name yet, but she says she knows one of you."

He opened his eyes finally and pointed at the crowd, and my heart thrummed deeply in my chest.

"She says that one of you here knew her in her life and that one of you was her daughter."

There was more than hushed conversation now.

"Is it my mother?" A woman on the other side of the aisle stood. Her voice quivered. "Her name was Alice. She died last week. She was sick with pneumonia."

Lazarus held a hand out to her as if to have her wait and after a few moments answered. "She says her name is not Alice."

The woman sat down in a fit of tears, and the man next to her began to comfort her. My gaze snapped back to Lazarus.

"I see something bright. But it isn't the sun. It's a person. She was also in the room. She was the daughter. But she is not dead. She is here"—he paused—"in the audience. Today. This bright daughter is one of you. Woman, what is your name?"

My eyes began to burn. But I didn't want anyone to notice me so I didn't leave. I was like a rock buried in sand with a current of water rushing over me, sinking me deeper. My body was heavy and stiff and unmovable. Was he speaking to my mother? How much of this could I believe?

"She wants to say something to her daughter. She says that the world is a scary place. That she must find a family to *protect* her. She is reminding her that there was a nurse who protected her when she was a child—and other women, Mickey, Rosina, Grace—and she still needs protection from the world. To walk alone out in the world will be her destruction—like a mermaid out of the sea."

I fought the urge to buy into this, knowing he could've learned all this from Angel, but the way he was describing my life strangled my senses, making it hard to parse out what was real and what wasn't. I pinched my mouth shut, hoping to hold back my racing heartbeat and shallow breathing.

"There's another bright one in the room. A bright soul who is alive. She says that he will not be enough to protect her daughter— this daughter who sits among you now."

"Who is it?" a man yelled from the audience.

A woman in the front stood up and turned to face everyone. "Yes, stand up, woman, and show us who you are."

"Brighton," Lazarus yelled. "Your mother is speaking to you."

I gasped for air I couldn't find and ran down the center aisle toward the back. I needed to find Angel. We needed to leave. These were not our people. There was something wrong with a man who would choose to do this to someone else.

Lazarus was calling out for me to return. "Brighton. Brighton," he shouted several times.

Before I got far, Conrad grabbed me from behind. He shushed in my ear that it was okay, that he understood how hard this was. He began walking me back up the aisle, and no matter how I fought him, I couldn't break free from his grasp. I craned my neck to look at him and he didn't look the same. His jaw was tight. His eyes had sharpened and even seemed to have grown darker.

"Brighton," Lazarus, the Mentalist, called out, "is that you?"

I looked at the man onstage. His face was red with heat and passion. I could see a forehead vein pulsing.

He pointed at me. "Are you Brighton?"

"Tell him the truth," Conrad hissed in my ear as he held his arms around me. To others it might've looked like he was comforting me, but in reality he was my straightjacket. "Then all of this will be over."

The shroud between my past and present was so thin that for a long moment I wondered if Lazarus really was speaking with Mother, who was locked away in eternity.

"Answer him." Conrad broke me from my doubt.

"My name is Nell." I didn't yell, but I was loud enough to be heard by a few rows around me.

"Just play along," Conrad said in my ear. "Let this be your gifting."

"No, I will not." I didn't yell, but I did break free from his hold.

Then I ran. I saw the truck where Angel had been and ran to it as fast as I could, throwing off my heeled shoes, but when I yanked open the door to the truck I was sure was his, remembering it had a long scrape along one side, he was not inside. I went to the next one with a red door and it was not his either. I ran farther and opened another with a green door. Angel was not there, but there was a girl about my age in the bed. A small man sat next to the bed. He was not as small as Bitsie; he was a different kind of small. A dwarf, I remembered. We'd had one as a patient long ago. A woman sat on the other side of the bed. She was beautiful with glowing red hair.

I was out of breath and just stood there not knowing what to do. The younger girl's arms, neck, and shoulders were covered in black drawings. I knew they were called tattoos from magazines and books, but I'd never seen one, let alone the many this girl had. The red-haired woman looked at me, and her eyes were filled with pain and maybe an entire sea of sparkling water.

"You're the new girl?"

I nodded, still breathing heavily.

"Find your angel and run away as fast as you can." Her voice warbled. "Get away from Lazarus."

I looked back at the girl in bed who was perfectly still and then back at the woman.

"Hurry," she said. "He's probably backstage."

I slammed the door and ran toward the tent. I could hear Lazarus talking again of another spirit that he was conjuring with his powers. The audience was silent again.

I raced into the tent, and the dark hallways closed in on me. I followed the corridors farther, deeper, until I got to the center opening of the tent. From where I stood I could see the back of the stage. The light seeped through the edges and center of the red curtain. On a wooden platform was a young boy ready to pull the curtains open at the appointed time.

I took a step closer, and then I saw him. And her.

Angel and Gabrielle were inside a large cage.

They were wearing white and faced each other with their palms pressed together. And on their backs were the largest, most beautiful feathered wings I ever could have imagined.

Gabrielle's winged back was to me. I moved closer, and Angel's eyes found me. I was just far enough away that I could see he didn't know who I was. I had forgotten how Alima had dressed me like a doll and made up my face. I walked closer. I was angry with him for telling Lazarus about us, even though I would do whatever it took to free him. He was caged in a new way now.

As I drew nearer I could see recognition dawn over his eyes. And as I walked closer still, he shook his head ever so slightly, prompting Gabrielle to turn and see me. Her eyes were on fire, red and passionate.

"Leave us," she rasped, then turned back to Angel.

From the other side of the curtain came Lazarus's voice. "Not even Mr. Barnum has anything close to my next and last act. My grand finale. He might have the tattooed man and a grand menagerie, but he doesn't have what you're about to witness with your very own eyes." He paused. "Are you ready?" he yelled, and the crowd went wild.

"I give you . . . the Fallen Angels."

The Sirens began humming a wordless, haunting tune as the curtains opened and Angel and Gabrielle's cage was rolled onto the stage. The audience gasped in wonder.

1990

Shifting Light

The keys are cold in my hands and shouldn't feel so heavy. It is late afternoon, and the town hall meeting is the next day. Yesterday, when we developed the film, I told Kelly I wouldn't attend unless I could get inside my building. She'd handed me a set of keys within hours.

"And what did the mayor say?" I asked, pretending to hold the keys casually even though they burned the palms of my hands.

"Well, he really wants to create some excitement about the fundraising and wants the bill to pass for the new community center, and he thinks your—" She cleared her throat with a smile. "*Stories* will help donators, supporters, and voters to really turn out for the meeting."

"He's agreed to my entry and me sharing the photos?" My heart skipped a beat.

She nodded. "He'll introduce you and then you have the floor." She bit her lip and paused. I wondered what she was about to add. "He doesn't know you're going into the building—but because I've been in there recently, I know it's safe."

Safe. It's not safe. It's never been safe.

This conversation rolls over in my mind as I park my car near the old iron gates. My camera is heavy against my soft chest, and my heart hammers beneath it, though it feels tinny and empty.

Seeing the photographs yesterday heightened the bidding from the building. I couldn't quell it, even in my sleep, seeing visions of everyone I once knew walking the halls. A younger and older Joann bustled around me. And Grace with hair and without. All of them with cloud-like bodies. And I kept wandering the halls, trying to find Angel, saying I wouldn't leave without him. Even Doc was there, walking the halls. He told me I shouldn't be there and reminded me to walk right on out.

As I walk around to the back now, I imagine the grad students cataloging the left items. The spirits of women who had been pulled apart and broken here can never be cataloged. But I can do something for them.

I stand and stare at the door for so long I almost grow roots. This is the door I escaped out of almost fifty years earlier. Impossible, surely. How can it be that long ago? How am I that old? All of these moments feel so fresh. Time is such a thin and frail thing, I know.

I pick one of the keys to try, but then I drop the ring. The dull *clink* on the rough concrete slab spins my nerves. Careful not to let my camera swing out, I pick up the keys and try the first key my hands touch. It doesn't work. The fourth key on the ring is the one that slips in, and before I turn it I look around, making sure I am alone, even though I know better, before I open the door.

The knob takes some convincing to turn. But finally it does, and I pull hard to open it.

I instinctively reach for the light switch and know right where it is—but of course it doesn't work. Before I completely return to the familiar darkness, I pull out the flashlight from my back pocket and click it on. As strange as it is, I am not afraid. Nothing I will encounter today could compare to what I have already endured in this same space in my past.

But when I stand there, I hesitate and consider leaving. Not just the building, but leaving Milton completely. But Kelly has all of my negatives, and I will not lose those again.

I need to do this; there's no other choice. I need to see my room.

My mother's room. Where she'd lived and where she'd died is all so close now. I push into place a rock big enough to keep the door ajar, then I go inside.

The light from my flashlight catches the metal rails of several stretchers strewn about in the hall. A few are intact; others are not. One even has a sheet lying on it. But for the dirt and dust, it's almost as if someone had been on it only moments ago.

A breeze pushes at the door, throwing slivers of light into the space. I exhale, then bear up my courage and walk past the stretchers and toward the stairs that are to my right. My breathing heightens, and by the time I force myself up a few steps, I am reciting Rosina's prayer that over the decades has also become mine.

When I get to the top, the quiet and gloom creep through the broken windows and cracked walls. And the deeper I get, the more unnerved I am to be there alone. I wish I'd agreed to let Kelly come along. But I told her I needed to do this by myself.

The door at the top of the stairwell is off its hinges and lies sideways. There are marks up and down the inside of the door. Deep, like something metal had been used.

I step over the door and walk off to the left down a hall, toward the double doors. One is ajar and hangs crookedly, and the other one is closed. I gently pull one open, and the squeal sounds like a greeting. Like it has been waiting for me. I go through the doorway and I am standing in the dining hall.

Only a handful of tables and chairs remain. Everything is in disarray. I'd eaten so many meals in this room. I don't go in far or touch anything—afraid memories will swallow me up. But I stand at the edge of the room and close my eyes and I can see it all as it had been and hear the mumbling of voices that stirred through every meal. I can hear the scrape of spoons and the shuffling of cups and plates. And I am reminded of how hungry we were.

"Are you going to finish that?" I can almost hear Carmen ask.

"No. You can have it," I almost answer aloud.

I didn't expect to feel any sense of warmth inside this decrepit building, but here I am smiling in the dining hall. Smiling. Because there really had been such love woven through the despair and fear.

I walk back to the hallway. Words in graffiti about rejection and loss and needing help litter the walls.

I'm facing the little Juliet balcony that had been my favorite place in the entire building. I walk up to it, and when I try to open the window, the glass rattles and the hinges creak. When my hand rests against the glass window that is covered in a thick film of dirt, I see that I'm trembling.

I step back from it and watch as the window moves in the thread of wind that courses through the opening, cooling me in the warm stickiness of these walls. I follow the rest of the hall and dodge a stretcher, mattress springs, and a rolling doctor's chair—all rodent-chewed. I don't touch anything but walk past the ruins like I might any historical sacred space.

Straps of memories begin to wrap around me, and I am eight again.

Aunt Eddie brought in roller skates that tied to your feet or shoes. All day I skated—back and forth—and then she took them home. They were her son's. Strangely, I still remember that his name was Wayne. Did he know that for one whole day an asylum patient had used his beloved roller skates? I giggle at the thought, and the sound that echoes weakens the rafters and framework of this house of horrors.

The small bathroom and some closets are off to my left. To my right is the hall leading to the dormitory rooms. My heart is heavy and light all at once. Like it doesn't know if it will drop through the floor or float high above me. Maybe I shouldn't be here at all. Maybe Doc is right—that this gateway of remembering is too much. These stirred-up ghosts, camisoled to the very air inside, might never leave me now that I've awoken them. Considering the intensity of my panic attack only a few days ago, I should've listened to him. But I didn't, and instead I keep moving in deeper.

The dormitory door on this end of the hall is shut. Fear wraps around my courage like a leather restraint. What if after all of this I won't get inside my room? I decide that if the door is locked and no key on the ring unlocks it, it's a sign I should leave.

My hand shakes when I reach for the metal knob. It's locked. And I tremble as I try all seven keys. None of them work. The disappointment is greater than I expect. I lean my forehead against the door and breathe in this old familiar air. What I've seen so far is enough, right? Maybe this is all the closure I need. Maybe this is all I can handle.

I don't waste time but walk back the way I came. Now I'm on the other side of the dormitory. The side with the smaller infirmary. I peer inside the infirmary window. There's a stretcher inside and a corner metal medication cabinet lies facedown, the glass shattered around it.

But there are no memories for me to exhume here, so I force myself to move on. I come to the solitary rooms. I won't look at them, having spent some of the worst hours of my life inside. I don't need to revisit those rooms—where I last saw Grace. Was she still inside?

I turn away and toward the second dormitory door at this end of the hall. It's open.

I am supposed to go inside, I conclude.

I am supposed to see the room where I'd been born and where my mother had lain in her death. The room that had for a short time looked like a real bedroom because Joann had tried so hard to make a home for me. Books lining the walls. Curtains on the windows. Even wallpaper when I was very young. A cozy rug on the floor. But Dr. Wolff didn't allow that for long, so then the books were pushed under beds and in closets. The curtains and the rug were taken away, and eventually the wallpaper peeled off.

"You're going to learn if it's the last thing I do," I can hear Nursey say. Her voice echoes against these ancient walls, and instead of strangling me as they would have a few days ago, they warm me. The dorm rooms line both sides of the hall. Every room welcomes me to peek inside and promises to show me what they remember. I only sneak a glance at most of them, afraid their memories will take me captive. I'd walked too many corridors and peeked through too many doorways in my life and seen things no one wanted to see—but those things will remain in my memory, unstirred. What I need to see is my room.

I step slowly past the rooms and their broken-down doors. Bed frames leaning against the walls. Broken windows. Several medical books, some equipment, and even a stethoscope are tossed about. Then I get to it. I turn toward my room and stand in the doorway.

It is nearing sunset now, and light is streaming through the broken and busted window. The tumbling of light comes through like a small rainbow against the floor. There is only one bed frame in the room. The paint is entirely chipped and one of the legs is broken, putting it at an awkward angle.

All I can think to do is sit and be here. I lean my back against one side of the wall that faces the window and slide down to the dirty floor. I sit cross-legged and watch as the light shifts across the room and just let time pass. The orange glow eventually falls toward the bedroom door. I stare at the side of the room where Mother had been and remember that last day when she'd died while we tried to cut through the fence. The desperation is painful to remember, and I choke on my breath and tears.

The series of events plays out—the realization of my birthday, the race back with Angel at my side. The way Joann met me at the door and told me that while I was busy running away Mother had fallen to her death. Angel cocooning me to let me grieve. Oh, the pair that Angel and I had been in those clashing years and how things had changed so much after that day. In the days to follow and in the weeks as we journeyed. That sacred path that bonded us so tightly to the other also divided us.

1941

Stay

What was I supposed to do? Angel was caged like a prisoner. How would we leave? And worse yet, would he want to leave now that he had Gabrielle? Considering this and considering what Lazarus had done onstage, how he knew so much about me, I knew we needed to leave before Angel was too deeply entangled in this life.

We did not belong here. But it wasn't because of the oddities of the members of this troupe. It was Lazarus's malicious strength over them that frightened me. It was more like he owned them than fathered them. It reminded me of the power the doctors had over the patients at the hospital.

I would not stay. But I could not leave without Angel.

Would I have to convince him to leave with me? I swallowed down the force of panic that wanted to fill me up.

A breeze pulled through me and the sheer dress I wore, and I shivered. My arms wrapped around myself, and all I could think of was the time I'd been restrained and my hair had been shaved. My fingertips moved to touch the ends of my short hair and my wrists ached remembering. Standing in the open air, with no walls and with no restraints, the invisible boundaries tightened.

"Why did you run off?" Conrad's voice sounded from behind, and his presence gave me a greater chill than the evening breeze. My mind carried a mixture of fear, anger, and curiosity toward him. A man treating me like a beautiful thing was new—but he knew what Lazarus was going to do onstage and had forced me to endure it. "We wanted you to see how welcome you are. How much we want you here. How much good you could bring to our show. Everyone needs a job. Remember?"

His breath smelled like something strong and ripe—I couldn't place it. Part of me enjoyed his presence—I had to admit it. But I despised myself for it. His betrayal toward me didn't keep my body from responding to his closeness as he drew nearer. And while he had angered me with how he had held me in place as we stood before the stage, there was also something about him that stirred me.

He ran the back of a finger down my arm a few times. His eyes drilled into me in a way that no man's ever had. I opened my mouth to tell him I didn't need a job, because we were leaving, but he interrupted me.

"I know you don't want to cause problems—especially for Angel."

"What?" I questioned.

"We owe the audience a good show." His hand continued to graze my forearm, shooting a sensation through my stomach. The expression on his face wasn't alarming or frightening, but it was soft and reminded me of how Dr. Woburn looked at Joann when they were alone. "You lied to us about who you are and now you owe us, right? We didn't call that wretched place, and we have kept you safe from being sent back."

"Owe you?" Was he threatening me? I swallowed in sudden nervousness. He was so close, and it made it hard for me to think clearly. The air stirred around us and tightened and tightened as he got closer and closer.

"Don't worry, we won't call that asylum." He rubbed his hands down my arms. "Listen, we healed your Angel, fed you both, gave you shelter. Those things aren't free. He told us everything because he trusts us. You should too."

His finger grazed my jawline.

"I'm not the girl you think I am." Could he see through my lie? "Why do you think I belong here?"

"Because you're like all of us. None of us belong anywhere. I wanted you to see tonight how much we want you to stay." Then Conrad leaned in and whispered in my ear, "With me."

My body warmed and I felt embarrassed. Had anyone heard the desire in Conrad's voice as I had? I held my breath.

Then Conrad pulled me toward the painting the armless woman had created using her feet. I saw at once that it was a painting of me standing among the crowd of people. Everyone else was a shadow but me—I was the bright spot in the painting, with my pink dress and glowing face.

Conrad squeezed my arm and left me to stand alone. He walked toward a long table that had been set up where the troupe and workers were eating, the show now over. The townspeople had returned to their homes.

The boy with extra arms walked around with a chicken leg in his hand and the sauce all over his face. He was smiling, and even though he wore a coat that covered his extra arms, I knew they were there. The giant woman, whose name was not really Golithia but Norma, carried Bitsie around and they ate off the same plate. All of the people who had been in those dimly lit curtained rooms were suddenly around me. They didn't seem strange or unusual, just like people who could be my friends—maybe even my family. But I thought of my aunt. That was where I wanted to go.

"Why do you let him touch you like that?" Angel asked, moving close to me.

"You saw?" was all I could say as he turned me toward him, putting his hands gently on my shoulders.

I wanted to ask him why he did it. Why did he tell them about us and why did he agree to go in that cage? But all I wanted in that moment was to be in his arms and to feel safe and to be away from here. Like he knew, he pulled me close and nestled his head in the crux of my neck.

"I've missed you, Brighton," he said, and I could feel him breathing me in.

It felt good to hear his voice say my name, and I wanted to cocoon inside his arms and stay there.

"I've been looking for you all day." We parted to look at each other. "How did you get well so quickly?"

"Their doctor had Gabrielle give me a tonic over and over through the night, and it didn't take long before I started feeling better." He was smiling and the worry lines across his forehead were gone. "I still feel a bit weak, so Gabrielle said I still need a lot of rest."

He moved closer to me and whispered, "Isn't she incredible?"

I didn't answer his question. "Why did you do it, Angel—the cage and wings?"

"After all their help, I couldn't say no. And it felt nice not to hide myself."

I could only imagine the relief he had in that, especially after what happened with his mother. But still, I couldn't shake the feeling of betrayal.

"Why did you tell them everything about us? Did you see what they did to me? That man, Lazarus, pretended to talk to Mother's spirit."

"I didn't know Lazarus would do that. I was just so glad to be feeling better, and they kept asking me questions and I got caught up in my excitement over Gabrielle." Angel tucked my hair behind my ear, then rested his hand back on my shoulder. "I'm sorry."

I would forgive him, of course.

"They really do want to help us. They aren't bad people." Then he smiled and drew a little closer. "I hardly recognized you at first."

"Don't say that. I'm just a made-up doll."

"You're beautiful, Brighton." His eyes roamed my face in a new way, and when I opened my mouth to tell him we needed to make a plan to leave, he caressed the curve of my jawline. His touch against my skin radiated through my whole body. "We *could* stay, you know. Start a life together with them. It really does seem like a family. They don't care that I'm albino. And they don't care where we come from."

I looked around, then pulled him farther from the crowd. I told him about the girl in a bed and how the woman said we needed to leave. "She said we should get away from Lazarus right away. They've lied to us and to the audience. We don't belong here. And what about my aunt?"

Angel scoffed and shook his head, then stepped back.

"But I'm free for the first time. I can be albino without hiding. Out there—" He pointed toward the town. "That's not free. That's me hiding and pretending to fit into a world that will never see past my skin."

"So we give up on my aunt and a life out there?" I said a little too loudly.

"Think about it. I can be myself here. Out there is where I'm caged." He paused for a moment. "Give it a chance—for me. Gabrielle is like a mother to me."

"Hey, Nell." Conrad strode up. "Is he upsetting you?" He put his hand on my arm, and before I could pull away Angel grabbed Conrad by the coat and threw him to the ground, away from me.

"Keep your hands off of her." Rage burned from his tightened muscles and bared teeth. The last time he'd done this he was defending me from asylum aides.

Conrad didn't appear rumpled over his fall. He smiled up at Angel.

"Sure, pal," he said and got up and walked right back to me. "Remember what I said." Then he walked away.

"What does he mean?" Angel said, breathing hard.

"He wants me to stay too." I looked up at Angel. "To be with him."

"What?" Angel scoffed, his jaw and fists still tightened. "But you barely know him."

"No less than you know Gabrielle." I hated that we were arguing in the few minutes we had together. I wanted to take his hand and run as fast as we could, not caring if we left everything behind. I wanted to leave with him and not look back. Conrad meant nothing to me in the ways that mattered, in the way Angel did.

"Angel." A woman's stern voice spoke. It was Gabrielle. "Come."

At first he didn't move. He swallowed hard and moved toward me and put his hand on the back of my neck and gently pulled me close. He lowered his gaze and our eyes met. "Please, Brighton, don't let him—"

"Angel." Gabrielle's voice cut through.

"I have to go," he whispered in my ear before delivering a quick and unseen kiss to my cheek.

Then he jogged over to Gabrielle and she linked her arm through his and led him away from me.

1941

Invisible Cages

The troupe was on the road again by morning. I felt trapped. I didn't want to be there, but I didn't know what to do about Angel. Part of me understood how he felt. In our short time outside of the hospital he'd been stared at, called a freak, and rejected by his mother. Then last night he was considered beautiful.

But this wasn't just about him being accepted. It was about being under the thumb of the deceitful man and what he expected of the people he seemed to have a strange power over.

I was comforted that at least we were still going toward Michigan. The second night I was put in the same house truck as before, with the Sirens and Alima. The next morning, however, I was determined to find the girl with the tattoos. I wanted to know why the other woman had warned me. And who was the girl in the bed?

Were we actually in danger?

We were in a new town in Ohio before noon the next day. And as we settled into an open space, everything was built again like it was before. Conrad was directing the assembly. He caught my eye briefly and winked.

"You look a little different," he said when he approached me.

I looked down at my clothes. My pink dress had been taken away from me sometime during the night and a pair of slacks, a shirt, and shoes had been left in its place. Men's clothes. Alima said the clothes I came in weren't suitable or practical for me since I needed to work. These new clothes were for workers.

I was consigned to more kitchen duty, but as soon as I wasn't being watched, I went to see if I could find the tattooed girl.

When I found the truck with the green door, I put my ear to it. I couldn't hear anything, so I knocked quietly. The door cracked open. It was the small doctor. His face and large nose protruded from the door.

"What do you want?" he asked in an abrasive whisper.

I stepped back for a moment and asked myself the same question. What was I after?

"I have questions for the woman in there," I said with a strange sense that I was breathing for the first time in my life—making the next move on my terms.

The doctor's eyes darted around.

"Quick, before anyone sees you." He widened the door.

I scurried inside.

The scene looked the same as it had the day before. The sleeping girl and the red-haired woman sitting by her side with tired eyes. She didn't even look at me when I entered.

"Why did you tell me to run?" I said, knowing I was asking too much for her to focus on anything but the girl.

She waited so long to look at me I wondered if she'd heard me.

"This is my daughter." She offered a weak smile as she gently moved a strand of hair off her daughter's forehead. "Lazarus's daughter. I am his wife."

"And she's unwell?"

"Why do you think she's lying there like that?" the small man said, rolling his eyes. He looked at the woman. "I'll be back in a little while to check on her." And then he left.

"I'm sorry to bother you," I said when we were alone. "I am trying to find a way to make my friend leave with me."

"The angel?"

I nodded.

"What's your name?"

This was a hard question for me, but I knew how I needed to answer it.

"Nell. What's yours—and hers?"

"I'm Cara. This is Becky."

"What happened to her?" I asked quietly and sat next to Cara.

"One of Barnum's biggest crowd-pleasers is his tattooed man—George Costentenus. Laz said that he was going to outdo him and have a tattooed woman. He picked Becky—his own daughter—to fill that role. It became an obsession. To be the best at any cost."

She paused and I decided to wait until she was ready to speak again.

"The doctor says she has a blood infection from the tattoos. He's never seen that happen before."

Cara uncovered Becky's arm from under the sheet. The underside was a bright red, swollen tattoo surrounded by cracked skin.

"This is just one of the infections." She retucked the girl's arm before speaking again.

"She didn't want to do this, but I convinced her. She wanted to leave and have a normal life. She's never been a greedy girl—she just wanted the life she saw the townsfolk living, not what we have here." She brushed her daughter's hair away from her face. "He knew if she was tattooed, she would almost certainly have to stay. And I didn't want her to leave me, so I didn't stop him."

She choked on tears before speaking again. "She hasn't woken up in over two days."

We watched Becky's chest rise and fall in the sacred stillness of the small space.

"You're next." Cara broke the quiet.

"Next?"

"He has a plan for you—to be his tattooed woman."

"But I can tell him no."

Cara shook her head. "He won't accept that. You owe him because he's fed you and cared for your Angel. Leave while you can. Even if you have to leave Angel behind, you need to go," Cara said, her eyes darting from the window to the door behind me. She kept her voice no greater than a whisper.

"I won't leave Angel."

Her gaze lingered over me and then went back to her daughter, who was so still it was like she was already dead. Then she looked back at me.

"Becky wouldn't leave without me either, and now she's going to die because of it. I would rather be here alone and have her out there somewhere alive, even if it meant I'd never see her again, than this. Leave, Nell. Before he owns you like he does everyone else."

"Owns?"

"He adopts the children. And tricks the adults into servitude. It doesn't matter. He makes sure they can never leave without great risk or consequence."

"But they seem so happy. Like a family."

"What other choice do they have? Where will they go after what they've become here? After what he's forced them to become." She paused. "They're good people, with a taskmaster who will use them until they're in the grave."

The more I watched this mother sit vigil at the bedside, the more I felt like a caged beast. With quick words I told Cara how sorry I was and thanked her. She never even looked up from Becky when I left.

"What are you doing?" Conrad came up behind me as I slipped from Becky's truck.

"I-I—" I didn't know what to say. "I thought this was my truck. They all look the same." I tried to giggle my lie away.

He was studying my face. He knew I was lying.

"Careful—my sister's sick. It might be catchy." It sounded more like a threat than concern.

His sister?

So Lazarus was his father. How trapped was he?

"Is she going to get better?" I said, pretending not to know the truth.

"The doctor, well—" He didn't finish, then looked away.

"Have you always wanted to live this life?" I asked before I could pull the words back.

"What do you mean?"

"All of this. Is this what you want for the rest of your life?"

"I was born into this." He lit a cigarette and took a long drag as he looked far off into the distance and then back at me. "It's all I've known."

"But—why this life? Why not live out there?"

He shrugged. The cigarette smoke masked the air between us.

"I need to go to my aunt," I said slowly and quietly. "Angel and I can't stay. My aunt is my only family."

He came so close I could smell soap underneath the scent of the cigarette. "I don't think your Angel wants to leave."

I inhaled deeply, taking in a lungful of his smoke. How did he know that about Angel? I exhaled the smoky air, not letting him see my worry.

He leaned back and handed me the cigarette. I'd never smoked before, but the scent alone dulled my senses and I took it. I put it to my lips and inhaled just a little. Then turned my face away from his and blew out the smoke.

"Ah, you're a natural," he said, and his smile congratulated me. He let me have the rest of it, and I smoked it until there was nothing to hold on to.

1941

Unmasked

The rest of the night was almost the same as the night before. Except I didn't wear the pretty pink dress. Conrad pretended not to care. But I knew he did. And it meant Octavia had to paint someone else and the Mentalist had to dig for someone else's secrets.

When Angel came out in his cage, the gasps were even louder. I'd lost Angel a little more with this show. Gabrielle was winning him over.

And then Becky died.

It happened near the end of the show when Lazarus—the Mentalist—was doing one more mind trick on the crowd. I hung out on the fringes. I was still in men's working clothes, and I'd pilfered a hat. I wore it tightly on my head and tucked my hair inside it. I was so thin I looked like a young boy.

As the audience sat in awe, Cara came running into the tent screaming. Her arms flailing. Her face streaked with tears.

"It's all your fault," she yelled, pointing at Lazarus. "She's dead because of you."

The portion of Lazarus's face that was unmasked lost all color. He stepped back, like he'd been pushed by the unseen force of her grief. I wondered if he had been. Maybe there was some power in Cara's sorrow that could do that. If there was, I understood it.

"Conrad," Lazarus called, his chest heaving and his voice like a sail without wind. "Get her."

Conrad seemed to materialize, and he had his mother by the back of the arms. He was coaxing her gently, but she pulled away from his grip. She turned around and looked at Conrad. She took his face in her hands and spoke so gently but loud enough for all to hear.

"Oh, Son. She's dead. Your baby sister is dead." Ragged words fell like heaps of rubbish, mounding between mother and son.

She sounded like the ladies at Riverside. Grief-stricken to the point of losing herself. Her eyes buzzed and her breathing was erratic. *My own eyes filled for her loss and for the life that had been taken.*

"Mother," Conrad said, sweetly and almost reverently, "come with me."

Hearing his voice break broke another piece of my own heart.

Her wailing quaked into a growl. I sensed what was coming next, but Conrad wasn't prepared. She pulled away roughly, then slapped him across his face. Then she flew onto the stage with a leap and clawed at Lazarus. He tried to get away, but anguish was a strong monster and she took him down and ripped off his mask. There was yelling and crying. Some of the audience stood and leaned in to see better, and some covered the eyes of their children.

Lazarus stood, clutching his face. My gaze instantly went to find his distinctive scars from the Great War, but instead I saw that there was nothing wrong with his face. The crowd saw it too and gasped. It was unblemished and without a single mark. His story had all been a ruse. He was a liar. What else was he lying about? Everything?

"He's not scarred," a woman said from the front row. Words like *fraud* and *liar* came next, and a few men stormed the stage as Lazarus ran through the back curtains.

As Conrad pulled his mother from the stage floor, our gazes locked. For several long moments it was just the two of us—like no one else was there, and he knew that I knew all of this was a farce.

And that Lazarus wasn't the only liar. He was a liar too.

Many of the townsfolk streamed out faster than they'd come in, leaving behind overturned chairs and tent walls pulled down. The few who stayed were either angry or nosy. The building crew ran them off quickly. Then Conrad finally had his fainted mother in his arms, like a child, and moved toward the trucks.

"Quick. Follow me," he said, and without questioning, I did.

He opened up the truck where I had been sleeping and put his mother inside on my bed, and when he caught sight of the small doctor, he waved him over. He closed the door behind them both, then he grabbed my arm and pulled me behind the truck.

"Let's go," he said.

"Go?"

"You and me," he said, his eyes wide. "Let's get out of here and start a life somewhere and forget all of this."

"I—" I stepped away from him when he pulled me close, and before I could consider what was happening, he was kissing me.

Not the way Angel had kissed me. The hard edges of Conrad were gone and he was soft against my body and his lips were soft against mine, but he was kissing me with an urgency I couldn't keep up with. Panic took over. I tried to push him away, but he was so strong and his hand held my head in place.

I began struggling and hitting him, trying to make him stop. This wasn't what I wanted.

"What's wrong?" He stopped kissing me but kept his hold on me. "Don't you feel it between us?"

"Feel what?" I wanted to hate him, but I couldn't. "Your sister is dead and you're kissing me?"

He didn't say anything. He just looked at me.

"Conrad. Son." Lazarus's voice was unhinged and riotous, so much like the voices I'd been raised with. Nothing like the controlled and cunning way he'd been since my arrival.

Conrad let go of me and walked to his father. Lazarus looked entirely different. He was still in his performance suit, but his mask was stuffed into his pocket and his whole, unscarred face was white with grief, shock—reality. He suddenly appeared entirely common and small.

"Where is she? Where's my little girl?" His movements were twitchy and erratic. He was crying through his words. "Where's my Becky-girl?"

"Pop, over here." Conrad put an arm around his father and guided him away. "Come."

Lazarus continued to speak, but his words didn't make sense. The powerful man I'd met only a few days ago was reduced to a raving man grieving over something he himself had caused. I couldn't divert my eyes from them. Conrad loved his father, despite the deceit. Lazarus was as responsible for Becky's death as I was my mother's. I was no better than this man.

Conrad stopped for a moment and turned to me. He mouthed the word *wait*. He wanted me to wait for him? And run off together?

He was in front of me a moment later, digging through his pockets, then handed me money. My hands were full of bills, and several coins slipped through my fingers. Next to Conrad, Lazarus collapsed on the ground like a puddle.

"If you walk through these woods, you're going north. There's a town on the other side of it. This little town here doesn't have a bus or train station. Find one in the next town and get as far away as you can with the money." He spoke fast and rushed. "If you don't have enough, wash dishes at a diner or find a boardinghouse where you can work until you make enough. Be tough. Be smart. Now go."

"I'm not leaving without Angel." I shoved the money into my pants pocket before he could take it back.

"Listen, once my father comes to his senses, he'll be worse than ever. He'll find a way to own you, Nell—Brighton—whoever you are, whatever your name is. I don't want that to happen. Do you know how hard it is to come across a girl like you? No ties to the world. No one to come looking for you. He'll send out his men to find you if you don't go now. These people aren't free. He owns them. And he plans to own you too." His arm gestured to all the people who stood nearby. Some of them looked at me, and the sorrow in their eyes was more than just because of Becky.

Then I watched as the rest of the troupe walked toward Becky's truck. The Sirens were weeping, each in her own skirt, walking on her own legs. Alima gathered them close. The child with the extra arms had his working arms around the woman without any. The reptile-looking man and the acrobatic man stood there, eyes cast down. The crew who built the tents stood with hats in hand, chins quivering. Their weeping filled the night air.

Gabrielle stood in the very back with Angel. Holding his hand.

The few townspeople who were left were taking photographs, but no one seemed to care.

This was our chance.

While Conrad pulled his father from the ground and led him away, I ran to Angel.

"Angel?"

Gabrielle let go of his hand and didn't look at us when I pulled Angel away from the crowd. He was still wearing his white costume, except for the wings, and every part of him glowed.

"Conrad said we need to go," I told him. "He gave me money and told me what to do."

Gabrielle twitched. She was listening.

"We have to." I told him about Conrad's warning.

Angel's stoic expression from yesterday softened. His hands found my arms and his touch reminded me that we were doing this together. He turned and looked at Gabrielle, then back at me. I knew this was hard for him.

"Okay," he whispered.

"Will she stop you?" I asked. "I think she heard me."

He shook his head. "No, she wouldn't do that. She's a good person."

We made a plan to meet after he changed his clothes and grabbed his bag while the crew dismantled the tents. There would be so many people around it wouldn't be hard for us to slip away.

Then the Sirens sang their melancholy tune as desperate as the song of mythological Orpheus. And like his song, theirs could bring no one back from the grave. It was a song of farewell.

It was time to go.

1941

Disturbed Places

The Sirens' song ended and slowly everyone retreated to their trucks in small groups. Including Angel. The tents went down in record time, and none of the townsfolk lingered further. I tried not to look suspicious. I hadn't seen Lazarus since he'd melted like butter before Conrad took him away. And I'd only seen Conrad at a distance. He'd caught my eye once and nodded his head for me to leave. I looked away, not wanting him to see the secret behind my eyes that I was waiting for Angel.

Another hour passed, and the performers were all tucked into their trucks. Where was Angel? Conrad had taken his mother back to her own truck, but Alima and the Sirens were asleep with sorrow-dampened faces. But I sat and waited until a quiet knock came to the door.

"Nell." The whisper pushed through the cracks. Angel would've said Brighton. This had to be Conrad. "Nell."

I peeked around to see if the whisper had disturbed anyone else in the truck, but it hadn't. I leaned over and opened the door.

It was Conrad. I tiptoed outside and into the cold air. "What are you doing?"

"Why didn't you leave when I told you to?"

"Angel went to get his things but hasn't come back yet. As soon as he comes we're leaving."

The work crew began calling out instructions and the men headed to their designated trucks. Headlights and motors were turning on,

320

covering the song of the crickets. I looked around, sure Angel would appear soon.

"Do you have the money I gave you?" Conrad asked.

"In my bag," I said and pointed to the truck.

He stepped toward the truck, opened the door, and in a moment tossed my bag at me.

"What?"

"You're not coming with us." Conrad started to walk backward, away from me. "Remember what I said about how to get to your aunt's."

"Conrad? I'm not leaving without Angel. He'll be here any minute." I craned my neck to see if I could catch sight of him. I started walking toward his truck.

In a few big steps Conrad rushed toward me and had his hands tightly around my forearms. His face was so close to mine I could almost feel his whiskers against my skin. His breath smelled like cigarettes. He pushed me away from the line of trucks. When I fell backward the wind was knocked out of me. But I rushed to stand, sputtering to breathe.

"You aren't hearing me, Nell. Lazarus knows you're trying to take Angel and that you know everything about Becky. You have to go. Now." His eyes were wilder than they usually were.

A few of the trucks started moving slowly through the field toward the dirt road we'd come through. I frantically looked around for Angel's shadow coming toward me.

"Where is he? Gabrielle's behind this, isn't she?" I yelled, making my throat raw.

"She doesn't have that kind of power. Lazarus already owns him. He has to pay us back for all our help. It's too late for him."

He looked me up and down. "Things could've been so different." He shielded his eyes from the glare of headlights and moved closer to me. "I would've taken care of you, you know." Then, without warning, he ran over and jumped into his truck and was gone.

I started running alongside the moving trucks, yelling for Angel.

Lights inside the truck houses started turning on, and I kept yelling. I knew his was the one with the long scrape on the side. It was rolling forward, but not quickly.

"Angel," I called after him without pausing.

"Brighton," he yelled back over and over.

His truck was moving faster, and I couldn't keep up. I heard him calling my name, but I couldn't see his face. I might never see his face again. I kept running, but then the last truck in line was passing me.

"It's over, Nell. Just go," Conrad yelled from the passenger side of a passing truck.

The caravan was completely out of sight before I finally stopped running. My lungs had never burned so much. My broken heart was scattered around me on the edge of the empty field. The crickets were my Sirens, singing my funeral dirge. I turned and looked at the empty field. It was dark. The only visible signs of the troupe were the deep ruts from the trailers and a few tent pegs that had been left behind. Like me. But otherwise it was like no one had been there.

The Fancies and Fears were gone.

Angel was gone.

And I was lost.

My grieving cast an iron-strong echo into the night. I had no cocoon to mourn within. I had no restraints to hold me down. I only had my skin to keep everything inside from exploding into a thousand pieces.

I wasn't sure if I fainted or if I'd actually fallen asleep crying, but at some point the brightness of the dawn assaulted me. I was lying in the tall dried grass on the edge of the field where the caravan had been, my bag on top of me.

I ached. My body felt too solid for the emptiness inside. Through swollen eyes, my blurred vision fell upon the cascading sunrise. I didn't want to see the beauty. I didn't want a new day to start. But maybe it was a sign that the east held my future. East was the direction of Riverside. East toward Joann. East toward an expected life instead of unpredictability and loss. East.

My tears fell onto the fragile, brittle grass and wetted the ground. As the grass continued to grow, would I still be here? Even if my body moved on, some part of me would be left behind. The shape of me. The sprawling and curl of my body like an imprint of the wrong that had been done.

I didn't move for hours. I hummed Mother's tune. I wrapped long handfuls of long and dry blades of grass around my wrists. My skin became raw and chafed in the nature-made restraints. By the time night came, I had grown to be part of the husks around me. Empty and done—growing dead. Dead in the ways that mattered. I still lay there when evening fell, and when the first star shot across the sky, I heard it.

I heard Joann's voice in my head. *You are strong. You need to be brave. You need to want a new life.*

Hot tears burned as my mind told me to listen to her voice while my heart ached at the idea of moving on.

I pushed up, then stood. The shape I'd made in the bed of crinkled-up grass didn't look like a girl had stayed there for a whole day. It didn't look like anything but a disturbed place on the ground. And that's what I was becoming. Disturbed. And invisible.

It took all my energy and grit to grab my bag and begin walking.

I winced when I flung my bag around my shoulder. There were scratch marks up and down my arms. When had I done that to myself? I started walking. My feet shuffled against the dead earthen field, then scraped against the paved sidewalk. Away from the empty field. Away from the broken-up pieces of myself, knowing I'd never have them back. Away from the lake in the east, where the sun would rise. Away from the kind woman in black and her little son. Away from Riverside, where the fragments of my soul could float away into memories.

I heard Rosina's voice in the wind. *Our Father, who art in heaven.* All the disturbed places in my mind rose to the surface, filling in the spaces and gaps inside. *Hallowed be thy name.*

I stopped walking. In a world where only the sky and stars were familiar, hearing these words reminded me of home. Was it a sign pulling and wooing me back to a home that had almost killed me? But then I realized the words were not coming from my mind.

"Thy kingdom come."

The voices were nearby.

"Thy will be done."

I followed the words. It wasn't Rosina's voice but many voices—speaking together. I came back to myself, and the voices took me up the steps of a tall white-steepled church.

"On earth as it is in heaven."

I stood in the open and ready door.

"Give us this day our daily bread."

These voices spoke in unison and my breath escaped my lips in a whisper as I recited with them.

"And forgive us our trespasses, as we forgive those who trespass against us."

How could I forgive what had been done to me? Hot tears rushed my eyes.

"And lead us not into temptation—" I spoke and faces turned toward me.

"But deliver us from evil," I yelled and I yelled. So loud my ears rang. Over and over again until finally I couldn't speak another word.

All the other voices had stopped. Every head had turned toward me. Every eye saw my rough, dirty clothing and the marks on my arms.

But my eyes drew past them and to the Crux in front of me. But this time it wasn't a star in the sky, sparkling at a distance, only to disappear shortly after, but a wooden one, hung high in front of me, with a man on it. He had restraints in the shape of nails, and his face was so sad.

I couldn't help him from his captivity, but I wondered if he could help me from mine.

Then I fell. The wooden floor was softer than my heart, and all my pieces filled in the spaces between the nailed boards. I couldn't hold myself together anymore.

1941

Pieces of Myself

*B*ut there were hands and voices that held me together, and the image of that man wouldn't leave me. I was picked up, or maybe I was floating. Being helped to live or allowed to die, I wasn't sure.

I could do nothing but dream. I dreamt of Conrad and Gabrielle and Becky and everything that had happened the last few days. But mostly I dreamed of Angel. How was it possible that days felt like years? I'd only been away from the hospital for a week, though it felt like months.

I heard words like *poor dear* and *where did she come from?* and *was she part of that carnival troupe?* There were also many whispered prayers.

The darkness behind my eyes fought against these gentle, velvety words. Evil was inside the dark, and I could find no delivery from it. So I let my mind roam into all the safe places and maybe I could find my way home. Maybe I could wake again.

But before I did, I walked back—far back in my dreams—and found her. And the others who had loved me so well. Grace's shadow was far away, though. How I wanted to see these dear ones, to hear them talk, to feel their nearness.

"Where have you been, young lady?" Joann said, pushing a cart of medications down the hall.

"I got lost," I said and picked up behind her. "I couldn't find my way."

I had to walk fast to keep up with her and passed by so many open doors.

"You're a fish out of water," Lorna parroted and ran across the hall into Rosina and Carmen's room. They called out my name and waved.

But when I tried to wave back, my arms wouldn't move. They were wrapped in dried grass and strips of leather. I could hear Mother hum softly. She was close. I walked into my old bedroom. The restraints were gone and Mother was sitting there with a nursing baby nestled in her arms. Her hair was a golden brown, softly cascading down her shoulders. Her face was rosy and full, and her smile was so real.

She looked up and found my eyes. She found my eyes.

"Come, look at my baby. I call her—"

"Brighton," a voice called to me, and I turned. Grace. She had her hair back and her rich olive coloring had returned. She smiled and without any effort pulled the restraints away from her arms, and suddenly her hands were outstretched and our film canisters dripped through her fingers.

"Don't forget. Don't forget," she said.

"Where's Angel?" she asked as I tried to catch the falling canisters, missing every one of them, then she faded away.

"I lost him," was all I could say.

Then everyone vanished, and the image of my aunt was all that was left in my mind.

1990

Safe and Free from Violence

*K*elly Keene is right. More people are at the meeting than I'd expected. There are several hundred in the high school gymnasium, and the palms of my hands get sweatier by the moment. When I walk in I'm sure I'll faint from heat and nerves. My stomach roils, and I have to find a bathroom before I can even think of talking to Kelly.

When I've calmed myself, I see her. She's talking to an oversize man with huge eyes, red cheeks, and a smile a little too big for his face. I have a feeling this is the mayor.

She walks him over to me and I put on a calm, confident face—which almost breaks it in half.

"I'm Mayor Vince Keene and you must be Nell Friedrich. Kelly has told me so much about you." Hm, Vince Keene? I smell a rat. I eye Kelly *Keene*.

I shake his offered hand.

"Is that right? What have you heard?" I probe. I want to make this young woman feel a little on the nervous side for not having told me that she's related to the mayor.

"Well, Kelly here tells me you have some pictures to share and some stories that will help my constituents see the need to remove those run-down buildings. I'm counting on you to help."

"And how do you think I'll be helpful with a few pictures and stories?"

He leans forward then and becomes the world's best close-talker.

"Any attention that this proposal can get is good attention. Those buildings are an eyesore for a pretty town like ours, and something's got to be done. Doesn't really matter what you're going to say, as long as you're not planning to lobby against me." He looks at Kelly with a raised eyebrow. "She's not, is she?"

Kelly shakes her head and smiles. "No, she's not lobbying against you."

He winks at me, then moves on to the next person waiting to greet him.

"So, you're related?" I ask Kelly, looking at her from the corner of my eye.

She tilts her head in that sweet way she does.

"Yes, he's my father," she says. "But my motives are pure, I promise. When he asked me to be part of the cataloging for a summer job, I had no idea what I'd find. The attention helps his cause, but regardless of all that, it's time people know what you and those women went through. I think your story brings hope."

"Hope." While I have gone through a lot in the last week in reliving and reconsidering my life as a patient at Riverside and my escape, I don't know how that will affect anyone else. I'm not even certain what I'll really share tonight—how deep I'll go. They need to see that there were people mistreated in that building, that my fellow patients along with those before and after deserve to be remembered. That people are people—regardless of diagnoses. They need to see so that it will never happen again. I move in close to Kelly, whom I've grown to care about in the past few days. "I'm so nervous. I'm not sure what to say now."

"After everything you've shared with me about your friends, they'd be so proud of you. Just be yourself, *Brighton*," Kelly says quietly before skipping away. She turns around and calls back to me. "Everything is set up. Just tell me when to change the slides. Oh, and your reserved seat is up in the front row."

I nod. But my mind is stuck on hearing her call me Brighton.

The crowds are congregated in rows of chairs on the floor and in the stands. A local TV crew is set up. Not all of the crew look excited to be there, but they all have their cameras aimed at the microphone and the reporter standing in front of it is speaking.

Why are so many people and a TV station here for a simple town hall meeting? Milton is a well-known tourist town with a downtown that boasts of the best food in Central Pennsylvania. Sure, the hospital is old and ugly and doesn't fit in here, but even with all of that, it doesn't seem newsworthy enough for such a crowd.

I walk up toward the right side and find my reserved seat on the far end of a row. Then I wait. A woman wearing a red pantsuit taps at the mic on stage, startling us. She gives a sheepish grin and scans her eyes from left to right, taking in the crowd. She clears her throat, and the mic picks it up; it sounds like thunder across the domed ceiling. People around me chuckle, but my nerves just tighten.

"I'd like to bring this town hall meeting to order," she says with an official-sounding voice.

The mayor takes a moment to greet everyone. They go through some of the administrative items. A few people shuffle on and offstage, and then he gets started on a few small community issues. Waste management. A library reading program for the summer season. And then a little excitement over high school football. Of course.

"The main reason we're all here today is because of Milton State Hospital. The hospital has not been used since 1965, and I don't have to tell anyone what an eyesore it is now twenty-five years later." He goes on to explain that for the last ten years there have been efforts to tear down the buildings, but the proposals were always voted down. He explains that the proposal this time comes with more than just a teardown, but a building-up as well.

Maybe this is why so many people are here. They don't want their taxes to rise because of this project.

Then red-pantsuit woman, who is the community director for

Milton, is introduced as Mari Silva. She flips through slides that show animated images of the current buildings disappearing and new ones being erected, bright and shining. She mentions that the main building is projected to be called the Wolff Community Center to commemorate a well-known hospital administrator and town council-man. She reminds everyone that he donated an unseemly amount of money to the town. When she finishes everyone claps. I do not.

Mayor Keene shakes Mari Silva's hand with gumption.

"Now I have a special guest for you all," he says with a smile. "As many of you know, these buildings were used as a hospital from 1845 to 1965. That's a long time. As many of you also know, last summer we had a team of graduate students go through the buildings to catalog everything that was left behind. Listen, we don't want these buildings around no more, but we still want to be respectful of what was left inside over all these years. My daughter, Kelly, was one of those graduate students, and as you saw in the paper, this special guest has some interesting things to share with you about this hospital that will give you some insights on how the buildings were used. Everyone likes *vintage* everything these days, so I expect it'll be quite a treat to see these exclusive, never-before-seen vintage photographs."

I'd been mentioned in the paper? Kelly hadn't said anything about that.

A rumble moves across the audience like a physical wave. Whis-pers and smiles and people sitting a little taller. I hear someone saying they are hoping for pictures of crazy people and for the photos to prove that the buildings are haunted. Another woman cranes her neck to see the projection screen better, as if she's ready to watch a movie.

"Show us the freaks," a loud voice shouts from the back of the stands, and there's laughter throughout the gym. A few others hoot and holler in agreement.

Is this why so many people came to this meeting? Because Kelly said something about me putting on some type of freak show? My mind returns to my days with the Fancies and Fears. Is that all I'd turned out to be, a freak onstage for everyone to gawk at?

I get up and walk through the aisles. I won't do it. I won't be that person. Not again.

"I'd like to invite my new friend Nell Friedrich up to the stage," I hear Kelly say.

I turn to see her behind the mic, searching the audience for me where I'd been sitting. Even at my distance I can see her eyebrows knit together. The crowd murmurs, and I imagine Kelly sharing my photos without me or not at all. It will be as if my photos are still stuck inside those black canisters. Our stories still hidden away.

And what will the point have been for me to have taken the pictures if after all these years I continue to hide them? My mind goes back inside that building, inside the room I'd shared with my mother. Inside the halls where I'd wandered for so many years. Inside the solitary room where I'd been so isolated. *Cat got your tongue?* I can hear Lorna's voice in my mind like she's standing right next to me.

"No, it doesn't," I respond to her in a whisper, and it gives me the courage to walk up the center aisle.

Kelly smiles nervously at me, and I hope my knees won't give out. When I stand in front of the microphone, I look out, and the crowd of faces looks so eager.

"Thank you, Kelly, and hello, everyone," I say first and get used to how I sound in a microphone. There is utter silence. In my nerves I clear my throat, take a breath, and then begin. "Milton State Hospital wasn't always the name of these buildings. It used to be Riverside Home for the Insane. Some people call these hospitals names like *loony-bin* or a *lunatic asylum*." A few laugh, and that same boy from the back screeches the word *freaks* again. I ignore him. "*Asylum* comes from the Latin word *asylos*, and it means 'safe' and 'free from violence.'"

I look at Kelly, and the lights dim and the first image is projected. A collective gasp sounds as they view a picture of Lorna. She's standing tightly camisoled. Her mouth is wide in a scream and naked patients stand around her but aren't paying her any mind. I can hear her scream in my mind still.

"This is Lorna and this picture was taken in 1939. She was elderly by this point and diagnosed as schizophrenic. In her later years she only spoke in clichés. She was admitted to the hospital in 1900 when her husband decided she didn't seem happy enough. This was a typical scene during the day in the Willow Knob building for non-dangerous female patients. To get put in a straightjacket like that she might've attacked a nurse or simply been a nuisance or yelled about being hungry."

I gesture for Kelly to click to the next picture.

I go on to show images of Carmen in bed restraints, Rosina's arm reaching out of the solitary door window, and many patients in hydrotherapy. I explain hydrotherapy and how it could last for days, even though it was never meant to. The crowd is captivated; I see open mouths, wide eyes, all completely still and silent.

"Riverside also had a children's ward. Being bathed with the spray of a cold-water hose outside the building was normal for these youngsters. Generally, many of them were diagnosed with Down's syndrome, mental retardation, basic erratic behavior, blindness, deafness, and a number of the children were simply unwanted or were orphans. There was even an albino there for almost twenty years—though he is not in this picture. We know now that albinism is not a mental illness, just as blindness and deafness aren't, but there were many years when people believed otherwise."

I go through more. A dayroom full of naked patients. A plate of the food the patients were served that we wouldn't give our dogs. A memory of getting this image in the kitchen with Joyful runs through my mind.

Then someone finally stands. "How do we know these awful images are real?"

"It's creepy," someone yells loudly.

"Humor me for a few minutes and I will explain more," I say.

The woman is exasperated but sits back in her seat.

The slide advances. I swallow hard.

"This is Brighton. This picture was taken after she was in solitary confinement, where her basic needs were barely met. Most of the patients' heads were shorn because lice were pervasive in the dormitories. But she didn't have lice. She was dragged to a chair and strapped in leather restraints. Her head was held still by her nurse while another nurse shaved her head. She was angry and sad, and when the nurse put her hand over her mouth, she didn't think she would ever tell her story to anyone." Warm tears are running down my face, and my fingernails dig into my soft palms.

"You didn't answer my question," the same woman demands.

"To answer your question, how do I know if these images are real and why do I know these stories?"

The woman's shoulders slump as if in response.

"Because I am Brighton. I am that girl in the picture. My friend Grace and I took all of the photographs that I'm sharing with you today."

The crowd isn't simply murmuring now. They are all talking at once, and when I think I need to run off the stage, I find that my spine and heart have strengthened and my throat is open and my voice is strong. I raise my hand to quell the voices, and the simple gesture works.

"I was born at Riverside. This is my mother, Helen Friedrich." Kelly moves to the next slide. "She was emaciated and sick. But even weeks before her death she would hum to me. She knew me and she loved me, and she deserved a better life and a better death. She gave birth to me in that room, and that's where we lived together for eighteen years. She was a German immigrant and was put into the asylum when she was found alone in an apartment unable to care for herself."

Kelly goes to the next shot.

"When Grace was admitted into Riverside she brought her camera, not knowing where her parents were leaving her. We had a nurse who looked out for us—" I pause, my throat turning to knots. I clear it because I need to tell this story. "She tried, anyway. We blackmailed her into allowing us to take pictures. She agreed because she knew we'd never get the chance to develop the film. In the time we had the camera, we took these photographs, but they've been sitting in a pillowcase in the attic since 1941, when I escaped with my friend Angel—an albino boy I met when I was five. I got the film back last week." I pause and nod to Kelly. "This is Grace when she arrived at age eighteen. She was vivacious and full of life. She was unlike anyone I'd ever met. She taught me a lot about the world—your world—the one I'd never lived in. She was institutionalized because, according to her parents, she loved the wrong man."

Kelly moved on.

"This slide shows Grace after she was hospitalized for about a year. You can see that she's just a skeleton. Her hair was falling out by then. She couldn't eat much without vomiting. Her skin was dusky and flaky because of dehydration." I have to pause as I look back and stare at the large image of her on the screen. I loved her so much. "And I escaped without her." I choke, and everyone gives me a moment. "I still don't know what happened to her. But she was my friend, and I loved her. I believe many of you would've also, and I hope she found a way out. And she's why I'm here today. We made a promise to one another, and today I'm able to fulfill it by sharing with you how we lived and how so many died. We knew if someone didn't speak up, our stories would be lost and our voices muted. I wish she could be up here with me today."

I have to catch my breath with a long, shuddering inhale. I don't know if I can keep talking. But Kelly continues with the slides. It is hard for me to speak when I see the next image. He was so beautiful and lovely. He was so bright. He was my Angel. Can I even speak about him?

"I met this boy in the graveyard in the back acreage of the hospital property. He didn't know his name. He didn't know what a mother was or what a bath was or what a book was. He didn't know anything. I taught him to eat properly. A kindhearted nurse taught us both to read—though he required a magnifying glass. He was given up by an affluent Pennsylvanian family when he was a toddler because they were ashamed of him being albino. He was at Riverside until he was twenty-one. He was an intellectual young man and my best friend. I called him Angel."

My entire face is now wet with tears as I relive these friendships that meant so much to me. The friends I lost so many years ago. Who would they have become if they'd been given a chance?

I turn back to the crowd, and everyone is in stunned silence.

"These patients weren't just patients to me. They were my friends. My family." Kelly continues to click through the other photos. "This is one of my friends, Rosina. She taught me the Lord's Prayer in Spanish and some basic Bible stories. B.J. read me her favorite story no less than half a dozen times, so if any of you high schoolers need help with Robin Hood and his Merry Men, I can help." I smile as I see some of the good and humorous in all of this hurt. "There were aides taking care of us, and fewer nurses and even fewer doctors. The nurse who raised me, Joann Derry, at one point had over a hundred and fifty patients to take care of with the help of only one attendant. We were at almost double capacity when I finally escaped just before we entered the Second World War. This was a trend nationwide in asylums, not just at Riverside."

I look at all these faces. What do I want them to know? They'll have these images with them forever, I know that. But what do I want them to think about when the images come back to their minds? Because they will.

"Build your new buildings, if that's what you want. Build them and make them a great place to connect as a community and to enjoy each other. But don't forget the sacred ground that they will be built upon. Don't forget that thousands of souls lived and died there and were ostracized by society. Many are buried in the back corner because no one claimed their bodies. Don't forget the history of what has happened at Riverside and other facilities like it, and don't let history repeat itself. And when you meet someone who might struggle with mental illness, see the person behind the frightened eyes. Not just the diagnosis."

I pause, reluctant to say what I feel I must. It was not my agenda to besmirch a person's reputation, but I can't turn away from this. "The hospital administrator, Dr. Wolff, did not keep his Hippocratic oath, and if I had a vote, I wouldn't want anything named after a doctor like him. Name it for your community and let it be a place where hope exists instead of the darkness I and so many others experienced."

The place is more silent than it has been throughout the entire talk. I pause and know that I am done, but I'm not sure how to finish. So I say something I haven't said in decades. "My name is Brighton Friedrich. Thank you for hearing my story."

It's hard to leave the gymnasium. People are trying to talk to me and even surrounding me. They want to know more. They want more pictures, more stories, more of everything. All I want is to leave and clear my mind.

Kelly helps me, and finally I'm in the gym parking lot with her. My body feels fuller than it has in a long time. The stories I told today I am now ready to tell the important people in my life.

"You were amazing in there," Kelly finally says when we are at my car and she's helping load all the photos and slides into my trunk. "You held them captive."

I smile, and it doesn't feel fake. Her choice of word makes us laugh together.

"What's all this about a newspaper ad?" I ask. "And did you call the TV station?"

"I wanted as many people as possible to hear your story." Her voice carries a sigh in it. "I may have called the station and the newspaper saying that a special guest would be sharing stories that would 'thrill your dreams and confirm your nightmares.'"

I purse my lips and raise my eyebrows at her.

"You mentioned them in your letter to Grace."

Then I exhale and smile at her. "I can't believe I'm saying this, but thank you, Kelly. For all of this. I didn't know that this was what I needed for so long."

When we hug, she hugs me back like a daughter would, and I like that.

"I don't think you're finished, though." Her excitement is bubbling over and she can barely keep up with herself.

"What do you mean?"

She throws a thumb over her shoulder. "The local TV station is sending your talk to the national networks. They want your story to be heard by more than just our audience."

"I don't know what to say." My hand goes to my chest, holding my heart in place.

"I also heard my father say something about changing a part of the proposal."

"Really? What change?"

"The name." She pauses. "He said that Grace Place has a nice ring to it."

I nod in agreement. It does, and Grace would be so pleased.

"And I have this for you." Kelly hands me several envelopes. I put on my reading glasses. I file through them, not recognizing any of the names. I stop at one that lists *Hannah James* as the sender.

"I don't know who this is. Or any of them."

"These are the families of the asylum patients I've been contacting about belongings. I told them about you and they have written you."

She pauses and puts her hand over mine.

"That top one is Grace's sister," Kelly says, and like a healing balm she adds, "I found her."

I gasp and don't hold back fresh yet long-held tears.

"Just tell me—" I pull off my glasses and wipe my eyes. "Is she alive?"

Kelly inhales deeply. "No, she's not, but she did not die at Riverside. Hannah fought for her and got her out, but not, unfortunately, before she was sterilized and lobotomized."

"No," I gasp and wonder why she is ruining this special day with such awful news. My hand shakes as it covers my mouth.

"But Hannah says that she lived a happy life despite her terrible years in the asylum. She only passed a few years ago because of health complications. Hannah called her the best, most fun-loving aunt her children could've had because she was so childlike. There were challenges, but she was happy and they were together. It's all in the letter."

I press the letter to my chest. How I long to have one more conversation with my Grace.

"I didn't want to give this to you before the meeting." She shrugs. "I didn't think that would be fair."

I nod. My words are stuck in my throat. I hug and thank her again. I can't ever repay her for how she's helped me. For all she's done for my Riverside friends.

But I have one more stop to make.

1941

Something Pretty like Hope

The first week under the care of the church in a town I didn't know was a quiet one. A woman named Natty, who had a round belly and was expecting her first child, took care of me in the softest bed I'd ever been in. The blankets were warm and feathery. I sank into the mattress that felt like a large pillow. No one made me talk, and they hadn't even pushed to know my name; they cared so well for me. I'd slept and dreamed most of those hours.

"Where are you from?" Natty finally did ask a few days after my arrival. She brought me a mug of hot chicken broth.

I sipped it carefully, and the salt in the broth made my tongue come alive. I took another two sips before I answered her. I didn't want to stop drinking in the broth, and I had to think about what I would tell her. Where was I from?

"Milton," I said quietly. That was true. I couldn't possibly tell her that I was from an asylum.

"Milton?"

"In Pennsylvania." I sipped again. I tried not to look too hard at her rounded belly that was carrying a baby. I'd never seen someone so pregnant, or a baby for that matter. It made me think of Joann.

Her brows pulled together, and her lined forehead looked like stairsteps up to her brown hairline. She just kept bringing me food; she put salve and bandages on my arms for days. The sun threw its light and warmth through the lacy curtain, and next to the window

339

was a cross on the wall—only this one was plain wood without the man on it. Like he'd been rescued. Like the restraints had been taken from his hands. I believed that.

"Where are you going?" Natty asked on the fourth day when she brought me a hot drink that afternoon. I'd never tasted anything like what she gave me. She called it hot cocoa.

"To my aunt," I said before I could swallow back the words. "She lives in Brighton, Michigan."

"Would you like me to write her? To tell her you're safe?"

"No," I said too quickly and without explanation.

"Why didn't you just take a train or a bus there from Milton?"

I was afraid to answer questions, especially because of what happened with the Fancies and Fears. But I knew she deserved some answers, given all that she was doing for me. I looked at the cross, and I could almost feel the smooth wood on my fingertips.

"I don't have much money," I said.

"We found money."

The chocolaty drink burned my tongue and I didn't mind. My tongue needed to be restrained or I would let everything inside of me out.

"Someone gave me the money to buy a train or bus ticket, but I don't know where a station is."

Someone. Conrad. The one who stole Angel.

I was given everything I needed and left alone as much as I wanted for the first two weeks I was with them. I just kept staring at the small wooden cross on the wall opposite. Natty was always so kind and quiet and loving. She looked tired some days, and her belly grew larger than I thought possible.

I slept so much during the day that at night I felt wide awake and I would look out the window for my bright little Crux. I'd look for Angel. But found neither. I did discover that Joann had packed in my bag all my birthday photographs. I'd stare at the one with Angel, willing him to come back. Then I'd return to sleep.

On the second Sunday in this little Ohio town, I didn't stay in bed. I sat in Natty's parlor when her church friends came over, and I listened to them talk. They talked about a local woman who had been awarded with a Teacher of the Year designation and a diner owner who was doing a pancake breakfast to raise funds for the high school. They ate cake and drank tea and spoke so kindly to one another. And they just let me listen.

I started to sit at Natty's kitchen table for meals. She served me food but never made me feel bad for being quiet. Her husband, she said, was in the army and not home right now. She told me all about him and he sounded like a nice man. She said I could stay as long as I needed to and that she liked my company.

One night I got out of bed quietly. The wood floor was warm under my naked feet, and a thin breeze rustled my hair and the night-gown I'd been given. I stepped through the bedroom door, down the steps, out to the front porch, then stood on the sidewalk. My toes curled from the touch of the rough concrete.

I looked up. It was an entirely dark night. A black canvas hovered above me and felt heavy on my heart, pushing me to sit on the bottom step.

"The Ladies Aid raised enough money for you to take the train all the way to Brighton." Natty's voice pulled me from my melancholy. "We want to help you get to your aunt."

I turned and watched as another angel in my life sat next to me on the porch step. She leaned back and sighed. She smelled of sweet things that I didn't know well enough to place. Her hair was rolled and covered with some type of net. She wore a robe even though it was warm.

We sat in silence, and I looked off into the field across the road and down the hill. Where so much had happened. Where I'd lost the last person I had loved. It was empty, and the tracks from the trucks weren't visible anymore. It was as if they'd never been there.

"I don't know what to say," I finally said. I'd spoken so little, it was odd to hear my voice. It was so different from the voice I spoke in my head telling me how to feel, what to do, and where to go. That one sounded like the sixteen-year-old girl yelling at Joann.

Then she put her hand on mine, and for a moment I thought it would feel as if she were holding me down, keeping me there, confining me. But it didn't and she wasn't. She was lifting me up. She was letting me go. Then she jumped and laughed.

"This baby is busy tonight."

"What?" I asked, sitting up straighter.

"The baby is kicking." She put her hand on her swollen abdomen.

"You mean you can feel it moving?" I turned toward her, shocked. She nodded. "You don't know these sorts of things, do you?"

"I've never—" I didn't know how to finish my sentence. I've never seen such a pregnant woman. I've never felt a baby move. I've never seen a baby except in a storybook.

Natty took my hand and pressed it against a bulging spot on the right side of her belly. A few breathless moments later I felt it. This little person inside Natty had just kicked my hand.

"Wow," I said, and a surge of something I couldn't name surfaced. "Is it a boy or a girl?" I asked, keeping my hand in place.

"You're silly—I don't know yet—not till it's born." She sighed and looked up. "Look, the first star."

She pointed and I looked up. The pinprick of light was brighter than any star I'd ever seen.

"'All the darkness in the world cannot extinguish the light of a single candle.'"

If I could've weighed the truth of that statement, this one would've toppled the entire earth.

"Is that in the Bible?" I asked.

"No, but close," Natty said with a giggle. "Saint Francis said it."

"It's true, though, isn't it? Even though it's not in the Bible," I asked, hopeful.

"It is."

We watched in silence as the little star was met by one more, then another, and then hundreds burst out of hiding.

"I want a girl." Natty patted her belly.

"What will you name her?" I asked almost thoughtlessly, but as soon as I'd spoken the words I wished to take them away. Names were too important to throw around on porch steps.

"Something pretty, like Hope." She looked at me.

"Hope." I repeated the name, and for the first time I realized that sometimes the very best things in our lives are those things that take time to unfold.

Then I told Natty everything, and she cared for me anyway.

One Bright Window

*F*ive days later Natty delivered her baby. And just like she wished—it was a little girl, and she named her Hope. She was pink-skinned with a burst of red hair and rosebud lips. Her cry sounded like a song, and her eyes shined like a mirror into the future.

"Here." Natty put her in my arms before I could say no. I was so afraid of hurting her.

And there she was, innocence wrapped in the softest skin I'd ever touched. For the first few minutes she was awake, her glassy blue eyes looked right at my face. But as her eyes drooped in slumber, she gripped my pinky finger in her whole hand and I was sure I could never give her back to Natty. But of course I did when she bawled to be fed. Natty took her, gently rocking and nursing her.

"It's time for me to go," I said as we sat together.

It was finally time for me to make my way to my aunt and into the unknown that was hidden with expanding and growing hopes. In the weeks since I'd lost Angel, I began to realize that my next steps would be alone. Hope and sorrow braided together into one path. But standing still was not an option.

But oh, how I missed him. Where was he?

When I'd been with Natty for nearly two months and Hope was a few weeks old, I accepted the money from the church ladies. They gave me new clothes to wear and many hugs and prayers and requested a visit back someday. And they told me that if it didn't work out with my aunt, I had a permanent home there, with them.

I arrived at the Brighton Depot with a shadowy black sky over-head. My fingernails were nubs. My jaw ached. My mind raced. My ears rang. More so than when I left Riverside and when I was about to meet Ezra. Maybe it was because this was my last hope, or maybe it was because an aunt was the closest thing to my own mother I would ever get. And maybe she would know how to find Angel.

But what if she didn't want me? What if she didn't even live there, even though Ezra said she did? What if she was dead? What if by tonight I was still alone? Natty said I could come back. That she would take me in as long as I needed.

But I had to take this chance. I'd given up everything for this— even chasing after Angel for now. My breath caught in my throat when my loss surfaced in my soul, and I swallowed to push it back into place. He was always on my mind. Every thought I had was hemmed in with wondering about him. Every sleepless night was filled with memories and tears like the scattered stars. Was he trying to escape? Or had he just accepted his new life? When I knocked on Margareta's door and knew if she'd accept me in or not, maybe then I would know if it had all been worth it.

I went to the ticket clerk and slid my aunt's address to him.

"Is this nearby?"

He picked it up and looked through his small round glasses that sat at the end of his nose. He nodded.

"Ithaca Drive. Well, it's a bit of a walk, maybe ten blocks away." He pointed past the depot. "For a nickel I'll give you a map."

I pulled out a few coins and ran through my mind which one was the nickel. I found one—proud of the lessons I'd learned with Natty. He took it and slid a town map toward me. In a few minutes I found the depot on the map and then under the light of the train platform my finger traced the line of streets until my aunt's road was at my fingertip. Ten blocks was nothing compared to how far I'd come. I wasn't going to stop now.

So I started walking. As I walked through the neighborhoods

I could see shadows and outlines of people behind curtains of a few dimly lit windows. When I finally turned onto Ithaca Drive, I stopped and caught my breath. I was in what appeared to be a simple and quaint neighborhood. The tall ash trees hung over the road like a magical pathway.

I inhaled and caught the scent of rich, damp soil, evidence of an earlier rain. Then I took a step off of the curb and crossed the street toward the house number Ezra had given me. A yellow light cascaded out onto the front yard. This house stood out from the rest of the gray shadowy houses.

I didn't have to look at the envelope with Margareta's address because I knew the house number was 102 and the lit window was the place I had walked this long journey to find.

In the dim light of the moon, with old wispy clouds passing over, I just stood there. I closed my eyes and imagined that when I opened them I'd find Angel ambling along and that he'd tell me that he had only been a step behind all along. A naïve dream, I knew. When I opened my eyes, I was still alone and my eyes burned brightly with tears that I blinked away.

My eager toes wiggled in the shoes Natty had found in something called a missionary barrel. I was clean and looked unlike myself in the white blouse with lace at the cuffs and a blue skirt. I even wore stockings. Natty had cut my hair into a real style, and I had been taught how to fix it. I'd learned what Nell looked like. Perhaps I should've journeyed wearing the hospital gown with my hair hanging around my face—maybe that was the way my long-ago aunt should have met me because that was the me I knew. But I wasn't that girl anymore. She was gone now. Lost and far away.

I looked back at the house. The bright window. Then up to the moon, my only companion but for the little cross that was shining up there somewhere, reminding me to endure.

Halfway up the sidewalk path, leading to the front door, I still didn't know what I would say. How would I tell her who I was and where I'd come from? How would I even know that it was, in fact, my aunt? As I got closer, the strains of a piano came through the golden window. A ragged voice sang, and I waited at the front door until the song was done. It seemed rude to interrupt, and I liked hearing her sing. Then I took my chance to knock.

At first I was afraid it was too quiet. But then I heard movement, shuffling, a creaky floor, something inside that had stirred at the sound of my knuckles against the door.

When the rattle on the other side of the door sounded, I inhaled and almost ran away. The porch light turned on, then the door opened and there she was—a small woman, shorter than me, leaning on two canes. She had white hair that was cut to her chin and round, soft features. She didn't look like my mother at all except in the shape of her eyes, but hers were brimming with life.

"Hello," she said musically and with a smile.

My mouth was open, but nothing came out for a few beats.

"Are you Margareta Friedrich?" I finally said softly.

"I am." She twinkled and smiled.

"I'm—" I stopped. Who was I? "I'm Helen Friedrich's daughter."

Her hand shook and went to her mouth with a gasp, and one of her canes hit the floor with a slap. She fell against the doorframe. Her other cane also fell. Her face twitched. And her tears were like stars as she opened her arms to me, and I bent close to her and rested there with my head on her shoulder. She was soft and warm, and she was my home.

Then there was a shadow of a man behind her. I straightened and looked more closely.

When he stepped out of the dim light, everything became bright.

"I got away. I told you I'd never let you go."

He'd found his way back to me.

Angel and I were finally home.

1990

All Because of Grace

I'm not afraid to make my final stop anymore. The sun is half set by the time I get there, and the broken old buildings don't scare me this time. I don't need to creep around, but instead I walk freely onto the property that used to hold my soul. That used to hold me captive. But doesn't any longer. Not me or anyone. The long grass brushes against my legs, and I enjoy the gentleness of it and I don't rush the walk back to my haunts, back to the graveyard.

From a distance I can see that many of the gravestones have fallen and it is in great disrepair. But as I get closer I realize that it isn't the same place it used to be for another reason.

Where once only dried grass and death had persisted now a meadow grows, bursting with color, not unlike the sunset that washes over me. Wildflowers now grow where nothing else could. The old ground has found a renewed purpose. The breeze rushes over the tips of the tall flowers and grasses, and they dance for me. There is new life. Uncultivated and rogue and unfettered. Free.

Then I see him.

He's walking around to the front of the angel statue that he is repositioning back on the pedestal. The angel figure looks so small now—it is so much bigger in my memory. With his hands he brushes away old dust and dirt. He has a smile on his face.

His ever-pure white hair moves in the breath of the evening air. He's as handsome as he ever was.

Angel.

"You're here?" I walk up to my husband, and he takes my hands in his. "But how?"

"From the Pittsburgh airport I took a train and two cabs to get here." He can't drive because of his vision, so he's always finagling ways to get around. Nothing slows him down. "I knew you'd come here."

He takes in everything around us. I'm not the only one who needs to heal from those hard days.

"You were amazing up there." He looks back at me. "I'm so proud of you."

"How could I have missed you?"

"There were a lot of people and I've learned ways of going unnoticed." He winks, and it's almost too innocent for a man of his age but so believable. "This was *your* promise to keep, not mine. I didn't want to be a distraction."

He gestures with his head for me to follow. The dried-up grass against our feet is so familiar that I wonder if the blades remember us. The sun is setting off to our right, casting bright rays upward across the sky.

"I found your mother," Angel says, and we stop in front of a marker. "H. Friedrich."

We both bend over. In my mind the stone should be brand new because I've never seen it before, but it's decades old, sun worn and chipped. I trace her name with my finger.

"H. Friedrich," I repeat, thinking of our old game. "Dirty blonde. Hums. And loves her daughter."

We sit together and I rest my head against his shoulder.

"I'd like to move her. She should be buried next to Dad, Aunt Marg, and Rebekah Joy." Angel and I had so many years with my aunt and my dad once he moved to Michigan. The four of us made quite a family before our own children came along.

"Do you sometimes wish you'd kept in touch with Joann?"

I don't need time to think about this because this choice has been part of me for so long. "Knowing she was okay through Bonnie's news was enough for me. I'm sad that she's gone, though."

Cancer took her five years ago.

The silence bears aged voices that say my name in that abiding and surviving way that reminds me that souls are eternal and our stories don't cease to exist after death.

"Kelly found Grace." I tell him everything I learned about our friend as I gather a handful of wildflowers around me and put them by Mother's grave.

His sigh is so heavy it makes a hole in the ground. "She had joy." He pulls me closer. "I'm so glad Kelly found her sister. Though I'm mortified that she had to experience those barbaric surgeries."

"I know." We're quiet for a while. "We've had such a good life, haven't we? Mostly as Dr. Angel Sherwood and Nell Friedrich." We both laugh a little, having had such angst about our names and making independent choices that worked the best for us.

"We had to fight for everything," he adds. "There was so much pain then, but there was always a light on our path to keep us from giving up."

I nestle closer to him, knowing all about slivers of light and the courage hope gives. But the losses have been great.

"Oh, what a life Grace could've had if she'd never been admitted in the first place," I say.

"But if it wasn't for Grace," Angel suggests.

"I never would've had all those photos and no one would've ever known them. Known you. Known me."

"If it wasn't for Joann putting you in solitary, you might never have forged the relationship with Grace that you did." He kisses the side of my head. "A lot of bad had to happen for us to have all the good in our lives. For the truth to be told. For people to know."

I nod. "Yeah." My little word is featherlight in the air and travels around the graves, greeting them. My throat is filled with knots and tears and a bittersweet joy I can't explain. For several long minutes we sit there. We don't speak but let the voices from our past rise up to meet us, to welcome us, and to be grateful that we've shared so much life and love.

Angel stands, but I don't know if I'm ready. We could sit together on the dry earth and reminisce forever. I know we won't be back. I know when I leave I'm done here.

"Come on, Nell." He puts his hand out to me and helps me up.

I inhale and shake my head and speak the words I've longed to say since I was eighteen.

"It's okay now, Angel. You can call me Brighton."

Acknowledgments

With the completion of each book I'm always at a loss for how to really thank and acknowledge all the people who made it come together. It's never a solo effort. Without so many this book would never have come to be. And more than with any other book I've written, I needed every bit of the light these people shared.

To God, the Father of lights: Every reference to light in these pages is a reference to You and Your goodness.

To my grandma-in-love, Joann: It was the true story you shared with me at my kitchen table that was the seed of this story. I honor you with this book.

To my husband, Davis: You are my Angel, and you are the brightest person I know.

To my daughters, Felicity and Mercy: You are both hope wrapped in skin, and the future is in your eyes.

To my family: Your constant encouragement and persistent belief have been a buoy to me.

To my agent, Natasha: You are Natty, delivering wisdom and love with great conviction.

To my friend Kelly: You know what this book has meant to us. The path is bright and filled with grace.

To my editor, Jocelyn: Your faith and confidence in this book carried me when I lacked the faith and confidence in it myself.

To marketing and sales and Kristen for her cover design: You've all put so much of your wisdom, knowledge, and understanding into this book. I am humbled and grateful.

To Julie Breihan: I am in awe of your editing ninja skills. Know that you were a bright spot in this book journey. Thank you so much for your hard work.

To my friends: So many have gone out of your way to pray for me, encourage me, and help me spread the word: Alicia Vaca, Pam Weber, Carolyn Baddorf, Carla Laureano, Jennifer Naylor, Susie Finkbeiner, Carrie Fancett Pagels, Becky Cherry-Hrivnack, Jolina Petersheim, Rachel Linden, Amanda Dykes, and Cathy West and my launch team. Even if you didn't realize it at the time, your kind words or simple messages have meant a lot to me.

To the Community Evangelical Free Church Book Club, for your sweet encouragement and support. It was so unexpected, and I'm so grateful to call you my home church.

And finally, to my readers. May each of you find the brightness and hope you need in your life. May it come from the Father of lights, and may you find peace within the lines of this story. Thank you, thank you, thank you for reading.

Discussion Questions

1. *The Bright Unknown* begins with an epigraph from Emily Dickinson: "I am out with lanterns, looking for myself." How does this quotation foreshadow the story?

2. Describe the relationship between Brighton and Nursey as compared to Brighton and her mother. How do both women fulfill the role of mother for Brighton?

3. Why is Brighton reluctant to escape? What holds her back, and what is she afraid of confronting and leaving behind?

4. When Brighton and Angel meet, they form a unique friendship. How would you describe the type of bond they have? Why is it different from her friendship with Grace and Nursey?

5. Grace comes from an affluent family and is punished because she doesn't want to keep their family secrets. How have you seen secrets dividing people and families?

6. At one point in the novel Brighton wants to give up. She believes that letting her mind roam will be less painful than engaging with her reality. How do you understand Brighton in these moments? Where do you see yourself gaining strength when in the midst of sorrow and pain?

7. Angel talks about feeling free among the Fancies and Fears because his differences are celebrated instead of demeaned. How does this ring true? If it is true, why would staying with the troupe have been dangerous for Angel and Brighton?

8. Nell challenges the definition of *normal*. In what ways do you see society defining what's normal or abnormal? Do these views help or hurt individuals?

9. Mental illness and its treatment play an important role in *The Bright Unknown*. In what ways have views changed since the 1930s and 1940s? What stigmas exist that still need to be overcome?

10. Do you believe that the novel ends with hope? Why or why not? What do you think happens next in the story?

The Solace of Water offers a glimpse into the turbulent 1950s and reminds us that friendship rises above religion, race, and custom–and has the power to transform a broken heart.

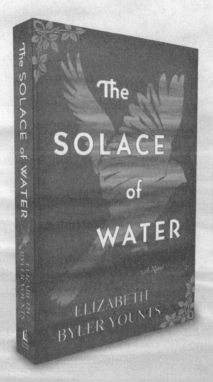

"Younts's powerful novel reverberates with love that crosses religious and racial boundaries to find the humanity that connects us all. Highly recommended."

—*Library Journal*, starred review

AVAILABLE IN PRINT, E-BOOK, AND AUDIO

THOMAS NELSON
Since 1798

About the Author

Author Photo by VPPhotography

Elizabeth Byler Younts gained a worldwide audience through her first book, *Seasons: A Real Story of an Amish Girl*. She is also the author of the critically acclaimed novel *The Solace of Water* and the Promise of Sunrise series. Elizabeth lives in central Pennsylvania with her husband, two daughters, and a small menagerie of well-loved pets.

Visit her online at ElizabethBylerYounts.com
Twitter: @ElizabethYounts
Facebook: AuthorElizabethBylerYounts
Instagram: @ElizabethBylerYounts